INTRODUCTION TO LITERARY CONTEXT

American Post-Modernist Novels

INTRODUCTION TO LITERARY CONTEXT

American Post-Modernist Novels

SALEM PRESS

A Division of EBSCO Information Services, Inc.

Ipswich, Massachusetts

GREY HOUSE PUBLISHING

Publisher's Cataloging-In-Publication Data
(Prepared by The Donohue Group, Inc.)

Introduction to literary context. American post-modernist novels /
  [edited by Salem Press].—[1st ed.].

   p. : ill. ; cm.

  Includes bibliographical references and index.
  ISBN: 978-1-61925-210-3

1. Postmodernism (Literature)—United States. 2. American fiction—20th century—History and criticism. I. Salem Press (Salem, Mass.) II. Title: American post-modernist novels

PS374.P64 I58 2013
813/.509113

First Printing

CONTENTS

PUBLISHER'S NOTE

With this volume, Salem Press launches a new series—*Introduction to Literary Context*. This series is designed to introduce students to the world's greatest works of literature—including novels, short fictions, novellas, and poems – not only placing them in the historical, societal, scientific and religious context of their time, but illuminating key concepts and vocabulary that students are likely to encounter. A great starting point from which to embark on further research, *Introduction to Literary Context* is a perfect foundation for *Critical Insights*, Salem's acclaimed series of critical analysis written to deepen the basic understanding of literature via close reading and original criticism. Both series – *Introduction to Literary Context* and *Critical Insights* – cover authors, works and themes that are addressed in core reading lists at the undergraduate level.

Introduction to Literary Context: Post-Modernist American Novels is the first in the series. Other volumes will cover American Short Fiction, Poetry, British Fiction and World Fiction.

Scope and Coverage

Post-Modernist American Novels covers 37 novels written by American and Canadian authors, and published between 1960 and 2000. The list of authors is diverse – including male, female, African Americans, Latin Americans and Native Americans – and their stories are based on real life experiences and struggles, as individuals, as groups, and as countrymen. Not many happy endings here. But who better than the likes of John Updike, Kurt Vonnegut, Toni Morrison, Barbara Kingslover, Margaret Atwood, Don DeLillo, and Anita Diamant to tell stories of vulnerable characters in non-traditional roles, living lives that are difficult and challenging? This volume is postmodern literature at its best.

Organization and Format

The essays in *Post-Modernist American Novels* appear alphabetical by title of the work. Each is 6–8 pages in length and includes the following sections:

- Content Synopsis – summarizes the plot of the novel, describing the main points and prominent characters in concise language.
- Historical Context – describes the relevance to the story of the moods, attitudes and conditions that existed during the time period that the novel took place.
- Societal Context – describes the role that society played within the novel, from the acceptance of traditional gender roles to cell phone etiquette.
- Religious Context – explains how religion—of the author specifically, or a group generally, influenced the novel.
- Scientific & Technological Context – analyzes to what extent scientific and/or technological progress has affected the story.
- Biographical Context – offers biographical details of the author's life, which often helps students to make sense of the story.
- Discussion Questions – a list of 8–10 thoughtful questions that are designed to develop stimulating and productive classroom discussions.
- Essay Ideas – a valuable list of ideas that will encourage students to explore themes, writing techniques, and character traits.
- Works Cited
- For Further Study

Introduction to Literary Context: American Post-Modernist Novels ends with a general Bibliography and subject Index.

ABOUT THIS VOLUME

The Post-Modernist movement in literature gripped America as solidly as it did Europe following the conclusion of World War II. That event influenced writers and artists in a similar manner as the generation before them was altered emotionally by the experience of World War I. To acquire a more exact understanding of the Post-Modernists, readers must first look at the writers and artists who laid the groundwork for that movement. The earlier generation—the Moderns—was weaned on the art of their fathers and grandfathers who were steeped in the trappings of the 19th century. World War I proved the great game changer. Both the direct combatants, like notable authors including Ernest Hemingway in America and Erich Maria Remarque in Europe, and those with second-hand exposure understood that the world that sired them was a casualty of the trenches and that a darker, more cynical society was emerging. This mood was reflected directly in their art. Unlike 19th-century works such as Stephen Crane's *The Red Badge of Courage*, the soldiers in Hemingway's *A Farewell to Arms* and Remarque's *All Quiet on the Western Front* rejected the concept of war as a glorious introduction to manhood and saw it as a carnival of death and destruction. These Modernists protagonists don't flee the battlefield in fear, they abandon it in rejection of the politics and antiquated ideals that fueled it. These characters realize that war isn't jeweled swords, plumed helmets, and brass-band parades; it's severed limbs, rivers of blood, hunger, and dysentery.

Post-modernists came of age with this history embedded in their collective psyche only to have these ideas reinforced fully through their own experiences in World War II, culminating in the finality of the atomic devastation unleashed on Japan. While a hallmark of the art produced following World War I was a rejection of the graying concepts of straight lines and happy endings, the Post-Modernist artists advanced to the next level where stories didn't necessarily have an ending at all. The writers whose works are represented in this collection provide prime examples of the overriding sense of delusion, rejection and empty spiritualism that permeated American novels beginning in the 1950s.

This collection sports essays on 37 of the notable Post-Modernist novels published since roughly 1960 by many of the most important male and female American writers of the latter 20th century. Each essay provides a detailed plot synopsis of the work and identifies the main characters and their roles in the story. The essays additionally evaluate each novel in the context of what the assorted elements the author presents mean to the story and the world at large. These include:

- Symbols & Motifs: What symbols does the author employing to define the characters' true selves and the lives they lead? In order to truly fathom the author's intent, readers must be aware of what's happening beyond the mere action of the plot.
- Historical Context: How does the action of the novel reflect the time in which it was written and the time in which it takes place? How do members of the generations included in the story compare and contrast to those of other generations? Also, how does an author use flashbacks to compare one time period with another or to show character development?
- Societal Context: An integral feature of Post-Modernism is the deterioration of societal norms, particularly marriage and family. Other standard community conventions that buttressed previous generations also are lacking in these works.

- Religious Context: Along with marriage and family, religion takes a pummeling in Post-Modern fiction. Each essay discusses the role of religion in the story.
- Scientific and Technological Context: The works covered in these essays were written when technology was changing everyday life on a previously unprecedented level. Everything from kitchen gadgets and hair gel to television is evaluated.
- Biographical Context: Each essay includes a biographical section on the author's life and work.
- Discussion Questions/Essay Ideas: Each essay is capped with a series of thoughtful questions designed to generate discussion and deepen a reader's understanding of the book, as well as presents subjects for possible essays concerning the work that would benefit students.

John Updike was one of the early progenitors of the Post-Modernist American novel. Born in Reading, PA, in 1932, Updike is one of only three American authors awarded the Pulitzer Prize multiple times (he received a total of three). Updike displayed writing talent at a young age (his mother was an unsuccessful novelist) and received a full scholarship to Harvard University where he edited the *Harvard Lampoon*. Although he is considered one of the finest literary writers of the latter half of the 20th-century, humor is a hallmark of his writing. Following Harvard, Updike worked at *The New Yorker* where he produced numerous short stories while garnering national attention with 1960's *Rabbit, Run*, the novel that introduced readers to Harry "Rabbit" Angstrom, who, ultimately, appeared in four books. Rabbit is the epitome of the all-American small-town boy: a former high school basketball star who is married; the father of one child and with another on the way; a young man with a budding career. On the surface, Rabbit may seem the personification of the 1950s

American dream, but, in truth, his life is a roiling cauldron of turmoil. He married only because he impregnated Janice, his equally unhappy wife who is free-falling into alcoholism in her 20s. He despises being squeezed into a small apartment with Janice and their son, and his job as a kitchen-gadget salesman is a dead end. The book opens with Rabbit intently watching boys play basketball, the game that brought him glory in his youth before he was shackled to the responsibilities of marriage and parenthood. If given the choice, it seems clear that Rabbit undoubtedly would return to that time and shuck the yoke of his adult life for the irresponsibility and freedom of childhood. Ultimately, he does exactly that: he abandons his pregnant wife and son but returns to his family when Janice gives birth to a baby girl. Their reconciliation, however, is a failure, and Rabbit continues to implode while Janice becomes so lost in a haze of alcohol that she allows their infant daughter to drown in the bathtub.

Updike and J. D. Salinger, another Post-modernist covered in this collection, are among a number of writers presenting characters who suffer from a type of Peter Pan syndrome that renders them incapable of functioning as adults. Unlike the war-ravaged protagonists of Moderns Hemingway and Remarque, Angstrom and many of Salinger's characters aren't tortured by their experiences in combat. For them, adulthood is the battlefield upon which they are destined to lose an emotional limb for which there is no prosthetics. Rabbit embraces the standard adult responsibilities: marriage, parenthood, a career, but, ultimately, is unable to fulfill those duties. The members of Salinger's Glass family featured in the novel *Franny & Zooey* included in this collection and in the short story volume *Nine Stories* are of a similar ilk. None of the Glass siblings seem capable of functioning as adults. Seymour Glass, the eldest brother, takes his own life, and readers easily can imagine suicide in the future obituary of Holden Caulfield, the teenage protagonist of Salinger's most popular novel, *The Catcher in the Rye*. Indeed, scholars have interpreted Caulfield's actions of sitting in the rain in Central Park while his little sister rides the merry-go-round as a suicide attempt. Caulfield also personifies what we see in Rabbit: after he's dismissed from yet another school, Caulfield, like Rabbit, goes through the machinations of being an adult by consuming alcohol in bars, smoking, and soliciting a prostitute for sex while hiding out in New York City. However, Caulfield, who is described as very tall and already sporting some gray hair (physically like an adult), is emotionally unequipped to accept the responsibilities of adulthood, or responsibility period—the book opens with him leaving his school's fencing equipment on the subway following a match.

The themes presented by Updike and Salinger are further advanced in Don DeLillo's 1985 novel *White Noise* included in this collection. Protagonist Jack Gladney is a college professor and Chair of the Department of Hitler Studies, a ludicrous discipline he created himself. Although he is the study's progenitor, Gladney feels inadequate and threatened by others in the field because he doesn't speak German. Appearing decades after *Rabbit, Run* and *Franny & Zooey*, DeLillo's novel presents a deeper analysis of the role of television and the media as an enslaving and destructive force in society. The Glass siblings all are former child radio stars and Rabbit loathes TV and dubs his wife dumb for enjoying it. DeLillo pairs Gladney with fellow professor Murray Jay Siskind, who lectures on pop culture epitomized by Elvis Presley, and the two present a joint lecture on their respective pet subjects. DeLillo seemingly is proposing that TV and the media has so anesthetized the public's ability to think for themselves that they no longer can differentiate between a man responsible for millions of deaths and a pop singer—they're both simply media events. Television is presenting a false front to a public that is too stupid and too

desensitized to realize it. Worse is that academia also has been brainwashed by TV. The disintegration of marriage and the family previously seen in Salinger and Updike also is in full vigor in DeLillo: Gladney is on his fifth marriage and his ex-wives and their assorted mix-and-match children have further burst the concept of family and its place as a cornerstone of society.

These concepts are not strictly the perspectives of male authors. Much can be inferred from the title of Anne Tyler's Pulitzer Prize-winning 1988 novel, *Breathing Lessons* included in this collection. On the surface, *Breathing Lessons* refers to the exercises learned by pregnant women to ease the pain of the delivery process when giving birth. In a metaphorical sense, breathing lessons are what the characters populating the story need to survive the pain of their daily lives. Utilizing the traditional literary motif of the road trip, Tyler presents married couple Ira and Maggie Moran, who are driving to the funeral of the husband of Maggie's childhood friend Serena. The journey unfurls both in the present and via a series of flashbacks revealing their pasts. As the plot proceeds, readers learn that both Maggie and Ira had grand plans for their lives that neither pursued and brought to fruition. When they arrive at their destination, Ira enters the church where the funeral service will be held and immediately begins playing solitaire, which he does throughout the novel. Tyler uses this solitary activity as a symbol of Ira's loneliness and isolation. Ira's married life is a game of solitaire.

Serena asks Ira, Maggie, and other attendees to sing the same songs they performed at her wedding to her deceased husband and shows their wedding video while he lies in his coffin. The characters are trying to relive their past while Tyler seems to be equating marriage as a type of death. As we've seen in Updike and DeLillo, marriage has ceased being the positive anchor in life that it was for previous generations: Rabbit leaves his wife, Jack Gladney is on his fifth spouse after a series of disposable marriages, Ira and Maggie's son Jesse is separated from this wife Fiona, and in flashbacks Maggie recalls other men she wishes she'd married instead of Ira. Updike's Rabbit, as we have seen, marries Janice not out of love but because it's what the social standards demand after he impregnates her.

The concept of marriage as a union of love and a lifelong bond has been replaced by wedlock as temporary security—in another flashback, Serena reveals that she only married because she grew weary of dating. Maggie also believes she hears her daughter-in-law on a radio show declaring that she is getting remarried, although this time purely for security rather than love. For Maggie, this concept is amplified in a scene set in a restaurant in which she is shown to be capable of holding a more in-depth, honest, and open conversation with their waitress—a complete stranger—than with her husband. Fiona's daughter Leroy is a virtual stranger to grandparents Maggie and Ira, who she doesn't even recognize when they visit her. Perhaps Rabbit, the Glass family, Jack, and other Post-Modernist protagonists are all playing solitaire.

Michael Rogers

Alias Grace

by Margaret Atwood

Content Synopsis

In this fictionalization of a notorious 1843 Toronto murder case, a budding psychiatrist visits Grace Marks who, at sixteen, was convicted for the murder of her employer and his housekeeper. Dr. Simon Jordan's purported interest in Grace is to obtain information that will help him in setting up a private asylum for the mentally ill. As Grace tells her story, however, he finds himself entranced and intrigued by her; at one point in the novel he almost falls asleep to the sound of her lulling voice.

From the very beginning, Grace resists easy judgment; while at first Dr. Jordan imagines he sees a hysteric, he is then caught off guard by her intelligence and beauty. Much of the book explores the interchanges between Marks and Jordan, which are more than just mere conversation; they are complex texts in themselves to be examined as much for what they don't reveal about each of their motives and judgments as for what they reveal about Grace's life and Dr. Jordan's interest in her. Surrounding these talks are the different judgments of those around them—the Reverend Verringer and the governor's wife and her daughters, who believe Grace is innocent, and the current and former heads of the prison and asylum, who are convinced she is not, one of whom calls Grace "an accomplished actress and a most practiced liar" (71).

Grace narrates her history as the daughter of emigrants from Ireland. Her mother dies on the ship, and when they arrive in Toronto, Grace and her siblings find themselves at the mercy of their alcoholic, abusive father, with no other friends or family around. Grace begins work as a domestic servant at the age of thirteen at the Parkinsons'. It is here she meets Mary Whitney, another servant who becomes her friend and acts as something of an older sister to her, giving her advice and enlarging her view of the world. Within a year, Mary Whitney has gotten pregnant by the son of their employer, who refuses to do anything to help or even acknowledge her. After getting an abortion, Whitney dies in the bed next to Grace. The death has a big impact on Grace. That day, while Mary's body lies in the bed, Grace believes she hears Mary's voice speaking to her. She thinks that she wants to be let out of the room, due to the superstitious belief that one should open a window to let a dead person's spirit get out. Not long after this incident, Grace falls unconscious for ten hours. When she wakes up, she speaks of "Grace" as another person and acts delusional. After falling asleep again, she wakes up normal, though "the happiest time" of her life "was over and gone" (180).

Grace moves on to other jobs. It is at her sixth job that she meets Nancy Montgomery, the housekeeper for Thomas Kinnear in Richmond Hill, a suburb of Toronto. Grace decides to take a job at Kinnear's as a servant, largely because Nancy reminds her of Mary. She finds her relationship with Nancy complicated, since one day she will be treated as a servant, and the next she will be treated more as a friend and confidant. In a short time, Grace pieces all the clues together and understands that Nancy is Kinnear's lover. After this discovery, she loses much of her respect for Nancy and has frequent arguments with her. The hired man, James McDermott, stays to work out the month after being fired by Kinnear for being insolent to Nancy. As a result, McDermott resents Nancy more day by day.

During her short time at Kinnear's, Grace has two friends: Jamie Walsh, a young boy about her age who does odd jobs for Kinnear and a peddler named Jeremiah, whom she only sees occasionally. Walsh, whom Grace regards more as a younger brother, tells her he wants to marry her when they're older.

One night, Grace overhears Nancy telling Mr. Kinnear that she is thinking of firing her. This is on the same day Grace realizes that Nancy is pregnant and thinks that if Nancy were to marry Kinnear, it would be unfair compared to what had happened to Mary Whitney: "Why should this one be rewarded and the other punished, for the same sin?" (276). Grace dreams that she gets out of bed and walks out to the yard. In her dream, a man comes up from behind her and begins to kiss her. She is not able to tell who it is; at turns she thinks it is Jeremiah, McDermott, Kinnear and someone else from her childhood, who, given the earlier accounts of his abuse of her, we might take to be her father. When she awakes, she finds the hem of her nightdress wet and footprints in the earth outside, and concludes she's had an episode similar to the one she'd experienced after Whitney's death.

McDermott tells Grace he plans on killing both Nancy and Kinnear. Not sure whether she should believe him, she gives him reasons to delay the murders. When the murders occur, Grace blacks out and cannot remember later all the details of what happened. After the murders, Grace

convinces McDermott to flee, all the while fending off an impending rape. She puts on Nancy's clothes, because, being a practical-minded girl, she thinks that Nancy would no longer need them, something that will later be held against her. When she is looking for her kerchief, McDermott tells her it's on Nancy's neck, as she herself had strangled her with it. She does not deny it, thinking him a madman.

En route to Buffalo, she manages to keep McDermott from having sex with her by telling him they must marry first. The next morning, they are both arrested. During the trial, Jamie Walsh, who had previously professed his love for Grace, testifies against her. Grace is sentenced to death, but the sentence is commuted because of her youth. She goes to prison for twenty-nine years. During her imprisonment, she is sent to an asylum for a short time for having shrieking fits. By the time Dr. Jordan meets her she is a "model" prisoner who is allowed out to perform domestic work at the Governor's house.

Interspersed throughout the novel is also a narrative about Dr. Jordan. He finds himself seduced by his landlady, Rachel, whose husband has left her destitute. He also becomes acquainted with various persons, including a Jerome DuPont, a "mesmer" or hypnotist, a kind of pseudo-psychiatrist-entertainer of the kind that emerged at that time. When Grace meets DuPont, because her supporters hope that he will hypnotize her in order to tease out her secrets, Grace realizes he is the peddler Jeremiah. Grace submits to hypnosis while her supporters—Reverend Verringer, the governor's wife and her daughters—watch. Mrs. Quenelle, a spiritualist who leads séances, also present. After Grace is put under hypnosis, a series of knocks is interpreted as a ghost trying to communicate, which lends to the reading of Grace's "double-consciousness" as actually a ghost-possession. Reverend Verringer suggests this possibility; Dr. Jordan meanwhile insists it must be something neurological. Since it is Dr. DuPont who actually seems to know about earlier cases of "double-consciousness," readers might question whether Dr. Jordan has simply been an unwitting audience to a show. After all, DuPont/Jeremiah has a prior relationship that nobody else present is aware of. Dr. Jordan even questions whether Grace has been "play-acting" and that he may "have been shown an illusion" (407).

When Dr. Jordan returns to his boarding-house, Rachel informs him that her husband will return. She insinuates that Dr. Jordan should kill him so they can be together. He concocts a ruse to get her out of the house, and he packs up and leaves. He decides to be more practical about his plans for an asylum; instead of continuing to study the insane, he will focus on raising money and setting up an institution that will please the families of the inmates—in other words, the ones who pay the bills.

Grace is finally freed in 1872, after almost twenty-nine years in prison. She writes in a letter to Dr. Jordan that upon her release she went to New York State through the agency of an anonymous benefactor, who turns out to be Jamie Walsh. He has been plagued with guilt for his part at Grace's trial, and they end up getting married and living together on his farm in central New York. Grace is happy and comfortable in her marriage, though she confesses she is a bit uncomfortable by Jamie's insistence that she tell her story of the murders over and over again. They seem to work as a prelude to sex for him. She also confides that, at forty-six, she is pregnant.

Readers of "Alias Grace" might enjoy following the hints and clues Grace drops about the truth of her guilt or innocence. In the end, however, since we only have Grace's words to determine it, the truth remains elusive. Even she, near the crucial part of her story, wonders what she should tell Dr. Jordan. Atwood almost seems to be speaking directly through Dr. Jordan when he says to Grace "'It is not the question of your guilt or innocence

that concerns me…. I simply wish to know what you yourself can actually remember'" (307). Grace replies that nobody has believed what she's had to say before; when Dr. Jordan replies that he will believe her, her realizes that it is "a fairly large undertaking" (307). In a woman of Grace's position as a poor servant girl, an immigrant, and having been accused of murder at the age of barely sixteen, her authority to speak, even about her own involvement, is questioned by society. Since Grace's own account consists of blackouts of memory, Grace is also one of the truth-seekers. She tells Dr. Jordan: "'It would be a great relief to me, to know the whole truth at last'" (320).

At one point in her narrative, Grace ponders on what she would "pick out" from the "rag bag" of her mind to tell Dr. Jordan (353). Grace's refusal to fill in gaps in her story could be read as sign of her believability. Later, when she meets with her lawyer, she is told that she needs to tell a story "in a coherent way" and that "the right thing was, not to tell the story as I truly remembered it, which nobody could be expected to make any sense of; but to tell a story that would hang together, and that had some chance of being believed" (357). Perhaps this was not bad advice on the lawyer's part, as claims to having blacked out might certainly play weak as a defense in a court of law, especially in the middle of the nineteenth century, before the dawn of modern psychiatry. Grace, after all, escapes McDermott's fate of hanging and instead is imprisoned.

The patchwork sensibility of Grace's story is reinforced by the quilt motif. This motif appears frequently throughout the novel as an organizing tool as chapter headings and as references in Grace's story. History can be seen here as a quilt of sorts, rather than a coherent story with a definite beginning, middle, and end.

Historical Context

A look at the acknowledgements page indicates extensive historical research for the background of the book. The Author's Afterword, as well as her lecture, "In Search of 'Alias Grace,'" elaborates on some of the historical context, and on the difficulty of determining the true facts of the case. Simply, what we do know is this: in Toronto in 1843, a sixteen-year-old servant girl, Grace Marks, was tried and convicted for the murder of her employer and his housekeeper. Another servant, James McDermott, was also tried and convicted. He was executed by hanging. Partly because of her youth, Grace Marks was sentenced to prison. A visit with Grace Marks was recorded and published in the book "Life in the Clearings" by Susanna Moodie in 1853. It is this record of her that drew Margaret Atwood's attention initially in the 1970s, when she wrote "The Journals of Susanna Moodie" and a television script based on the murders. In the 1990s, she took up the story again, doing more research and questioning Moodie's account of Marks.

Atwood draws on newspaper clippings and other historical documents, many excerpts of which appear as epigraphs throughout the book. Much was written about Marks, yet, as Atwood notes, they perhaps reveal as much, if not more, about attitudes about women as about Grace Marks herself. Some saw her as a temptress who seduced McDermott and directed the murders; yet others saw her as an unwitting accomplice. Even Marks's own reports and confessions are contradictory. Therefore, much of Grace Marks's story, and the character of Dr. Simon Jordan, is fabrication.

Background historical research also helped Atwood fill in some of the gaps. She explains Grace's frequent change in employment as common for the time, as Toronto was short of household help because of the exodus of a large percentage of poorer people after the 1837 Rebellion. Mary Whitney's abortion is, according the book's author, based on a real case described in "Langstaff: A Nineteenth Century Medical Life" (Duffin). She also describes spiritualism and mesmerism, which were popular interests of the time. Mesmerism,

an early form of hypnotism, according to Atwood in the Afterword, "was discredited as a reputable scientific procedure early in the century, but was widely practiced by questionable showmen in the 1840s" (464). James Braid introduced a newer version, "Neuro-hypnotism," and ushered in a new respectability for hypnosis, though it was not to achieve "wide acceptance as a psychiatric technique" until the end of the century (464). Atwood further reports that at this time, there was "intense curiosity and excitement about phenomena such as memory and amnesia, somnambulism, 'hysteria,' trance states, 'nervous diseases,' and the import of dreams, among scientists and writers alike" (464). Dr. Jordan's interest in Grace is therefore not remarkable for the times. (For more discussion of spiritualism, see Religious Context.)

Societal Context

An analysis of gender and class in the book can produce a richer, more complex reading. Unlike the men who overlook the "trifles" of women's lives in their search for evidence to indict the wife of a murdered man in the famous play "Trifles" by Susan Glaspell, Dr. Jordan is aware that "the small details of life often hide a great significance" (162). Still, he is ignorant of what they are, revealing the limitations of his upper-class male perspective. His curiosity about the foreign world of female servants had begun in childhood, with his memories of sneaking into the servants' quarters. In an upper-class household, the line between master and servant was tenuous and his own trespass, as well as that of the unseen Parkinson son with Mary Whitney, suggests that boundary-crossing was not only often sexually charged, but also quite common. Grace tells us: "He really does not know. Men such as him do not have to clean up the messes they make, but we have to clean up our own messes and theirs into the bargain" (214). Most obviously this statement speaks to the situation of Mary Whitney in which the man in question refuses to have anything to do with her when he learns she's pregnant.

Grace learns further about the double bind of being a female servant in the patriarchal society of nineteenth-century Toronto when she goes to the Kinnear household. Nancy, in response to Grace's wonderment of Kinnear's never being married, says he can have anything he wants if he pays for it "If they want a thing, all they have to do is pay for it. It's all one to them" (221).

Grace learns about the limitations of her role as a female servant, but she also learns about hidden sources of power and subversion. Mary is her principal educator here; it is she who arranges for male stable-hands to help keep Grace's abusive father at bay when he comes for her money. Mary acts as a consciousness-raising tool for Grace: she rails at the economic disparities in the society in which she lives; she even claims she is part "Red Indian." When Grace made a mistake, Mary would tell her that she should remember that they "were not slaves, and being a servant was not a thing we were born to, nor would we be forced to continue at it forever; it was just a job of work" (156). Like many servants, Mary hopes to marry and have her own house some day. Of her employers, Mary notes that there "were few secrets they could keep from the servants" (158). Grace summarizes Mary's attitude as having "very democratic ideas" (159). Grace is obviously less spirited and rebellious than Mary; it is unsurprising, then, that her "alter-ego" would be named after her. According to some critics, the alter-ego is actually a part of Grace that is "possessed" by Mary's ghost.

While most of the men in the novel seem to see Grace in terms of either martyr or whore, Jeremiah is a notable exception. He seems to offer Grace a glimpse at another alternative from domestic servitude in the form of servant or wife: she fantasizes about becoming his wife and traveling with him. Jeremiah "is one of the few truly heroic men" in any of Atwood's "Gothic" novels, according to Colette Tennant (80).

Religious Context

Grace is a Protestant from Northern Ireland. Certainly she professes a belief in God, and seems to draw on this faith in order to comfort herself as well as to explain the events of her life. As many Christians before her, Grace tries to explain her fate in terms of spiritual lessons. When describing the ship voyage to Canada, she observes that the voyage and prison might both be seen as "a reminder to us that we are all flesh, and that all flesh is grass, and all flesh is weak." Yet she herself calls this belief into question with the very line that follows: "Or so I choose to believe" (117).

An important event that occurs on this voyage is the death of her mother from a mysterious illness. It is after her death that a woman on the ship, Mrs. Phelan, who is probably Catholic, tells her something that will come back to haunt her—perhaps literally—later in the book. Mrs. Phelan laments that they are unable to open a window "to let out the soul, as was the custom" (120). Later, when Mary Whitney dies, Grace believes she hears Mary calling, and opens the window to let her out.

When Grace accompanies Nancy to church in Richmond Hill, she hears the minister sermonize that Divine Grace is a mystery, "and the recipients of it were known to God alone" and that good works and prayer does not automatically guarantee a soul's redemption in Heaven. Grace's interpretation of this sermon is that "you might as well forget about the whole matter, and go about your own business, because whether you would be damned or saved was no concern of yours" (254).

Throughout the book Grace insists on "spirituality" that sees God in everything and everywhere, not just in churches. She observes the people of Richmond Hill and thinks "[t]hey are hypocrites, they think the church is a cage to keep God in, so he will stay locked up there and not go wandering about the earth during the week, poking his nose into their business, and looking into the depths and darkness and doubleness of their hearts… and they believe they need only be bothered about him on Sundays when they have their best clothes on…. But God is everywhere, and cannot be caged in, as men can" (254). Speaking from the standpoint of a prisoner, Grace obviously takes comfort in the idea that God "cannot be caged in." Even though she is imprisoned bodily, she resists the identification of herself as something less than a person—she insists that she has a soul and it is she alone that must answer for her deeds.

Grace's unique spiritual sense is revisited in her account of a night before the murder. Here, perhaps, she has added a dramatic flourish for the benefit of Dr. Jordan, since she includes in her story details of the laundry having been left out and looking like angels in the trees, "and it was as if our own clothing was sitting in judgment upon us" and that she could not "shake the feeling that there was doom on the house, and that some within were fated to die" (281). Not only does this add a dramatic foreshadowing of the kind in gothic novels, it also takes away some sense of agency on Grace's part, in that the murders that then occur were somehow an act of God.

More broadly, the novel, of course, deals with the questions of sin and redemption in a Christian society. It also gently pokes fun at one of the popular activities, especially among upper-class women, of the time: spiritualism. Spiritualism, the belief that one can communicate with the dead through a medium, grew in popularity at this time and was "the one-quasi-religious activity of the times in which women were allowed a position of power—albeit a dubious one, as they themselves were assumed to be mere conduits of the spirit will" (Afterword, 464). Additionally, we see here the rising convergence and divergence between religion and medicine in the tense relationship between Reverend Verringer and Simon Jordan.

Scientific & Technological Context

Grace is suspicious of doctors; she correctly connects them with their powerful ability to determine the limits of her freedom. This attitude is displayed at the very beginning of her narrative, when she observes that the Governor's wife likes "liberal-minded" people, whom she associates with science, which was "making such progress." To Grace, though, a doctor is "a bad sign" since she associates them with death (27). Her own experience has taught her that doctors and medical institutions are instruments of power. She relates her time in the asylum, noting that many women were put there not because of genuine mental illness, but because of alcoholism, domestic abuse, and homelessness. Her distrust of doctors comes to a head when she believes she sees knives in the doctor's bag and begins to scream. She is a bit unsure how to react to Dr. Jordan, who seems to want nothing more for her than to talk. It takes her a while to learn to trust him.

The letters that appear in the novel add another discursive dimension. Many of these letters are either to or from Dr. Jordan and some are from other professionals interested in or acquainted with Grace Marks. The language in these letters operate as a lens with which Simon looks at Grace—as an object of scientific study.

Biographical Context

Influential and prolific, Margaret Atwood is known worldwide and has the distinction of being one of the few literary writers who can command a wide audience. An author of poetry, prose, nonfiction, criticism, screenplays, and children's books, Atwood has been publishing work since her poetry collection "The Circle Game" appeared in 1966. (An earlier collection, "Double Persephone," was self-published while she was in college in 1961). Her first novel, "The Edible Woman," was published in 1969. Her most recent book is "The

Penelopiad," a retelling of the story of Penelope, the wife of Odysseus.

Born in 1939 in Ottawa, Canada, Atwood was the daughter of unconventional parents. Her father was a field entomologist and her mother was something of an adventurer, preferring life in the bush. The family spent winters in the city of Ottawa and the rest of the year primarily in the remote areas of northwestern Quebec. According to her own account, Atwood did not spend a full year in school until she was in the eighth grade and her family moved to Toronto. She has an older brother and a younger sister.

Atwood attended Victoria College at the University of Toronto and, after graduating in 1961 with a BA in English literature, she went on to Radcliff College at Harvard University to study for her MA and PhD. She received her MA, and then took a teaching job in Vancouver. She returned to Harvard in 1965. Since her focus was on Victorian literature, she chose several Victorian Gothic writers to focus on for her dissertation, which she never finished.

Undoubtedly Atwood's graduate work in Victorian Gothic literature had an effect on her writing of her own Gothic novel, "Alias Grace." Atwood published a portion of her thesis in James Reaney's "Alphabet," in which she examines female characters in the Victorian Gothic's and concludes that the "'true enemy of the hero's salvation and spiritual fulfillment proves to be The Angel in the House; the only good woman is a dead woman, preferably swathed in the grave-clothes of mystery'"; "[o]rdinary women were boring, shacked in domestic virtue… . Only the supernatural females were allowed to be sexy. And they were deadly" (Sutton 176–177). It is no wonder Atwood would later become fascinated with the historical figure of Grace Marks, who, according to Holly Blackford, can be read as symbolizing the "dangerous" female threatening domestic arrangements for her own domestic desires.

Atwood has received numerous awards and recognitions, including the Booker Prize for "The Blind Assassin" (2000), the Governor's General Award, Canada's highest recognition, and the Commonwealth Literature Award, for "The Handmaid's Tale" (1985). She was named "Woman of the Year" by *Ms. Magazine* in 1986. She co-founded (with Graeme Gibson) the Writers' Union of Canada in 1973 and the English-Canadian Centre of PEN, the international organization advocating freedom of expression for silenced writers. Atwood currently lives in Toronto with writer Graeme Gibson. They have a daughter named Jess.

Alyssa Colton

Works Cited

Atwood, Margaret. *Alias Grace*. 1996. New York: Anchor Books, 1997

_____. "Author's Afterword." *Alias Grace*. 461–65

_____. "In Search of Alias Grace: On Writing Canadian Historical Fiction." Bronfman Lecture Series. Ottawa. November 1996. *Rpt. in Writing with Intent: Essays, Reviews, Personal Prose, 1983-2005*. New York: Carroll & Graf, 2005

Blackford, Holly. "Haunted Housekeeping: Fatal Attractions of Servant and Mistress in Twentieth-Century Female Gothic Literature." *Lit: Literature Interpretation Theory* 16. 2 (Apr–June 2005): 233–61

Duffin, Jacalyn. "Margaret Atwood: Alias Grace." *Literature, Arts, and Medicine Database*. 17 November 2003. New York University. 23 November 2005

Lannon, Mary. "Margaret Atwood." *Writers Online* 3.1 (fall 1998). Albany: New York State Writers' Institute. 23 November 2005

Sutton, Rosemary. *The Red Shoes: Margaret Atwood Starting Out*. Toronto: HarperCollins, 1998

Tennant, Colette. *Reading the Gothic in Margaret Atwood's Novels*. Lewiston, New York: 2003

For Further Study

Knelman, Judith. "Can We Believe What the Newspapers Tell Us? Missing Links in Alias Grace." *University of Toronto Quarterly* 68.2 (1999): 677–687

Margaret Atwood Reference Site http://www. owtoad.com

Margaret Atwood Society Homepage http://www. mscd.edu/~atwoodso/

Michael, Magali Cornier. "Rethinking History as Patchwork: The Case of Atwood's Alias Grace." *MFS: Modern Fiction Studies* 47.2 (summer 2001): 421–47

Miller, Ryan. "The Gospel According to Grace: Gnostic Heresy as Narrative Strategy in Margaret Atwood's Alias Grace." *Literature and Theology* 16.2 (June 2002): 172–87

Siddall, Gillian. "'This Is What I Told Dr. Jordan…': Public Constructions and Private Disruptions in Margaret Atwood's Alias Grace." *Essays on Canadian Writing* 81 (winter 2004): 84–102

Wilson, Sharon Rose, ed. *Margaret Atwood's Textual Assassinations: Recent Poetry and Fiction.* Columbus: Ohio State University Press, 2003

Discussion Questions

1. Do you think that Grace Marks is guilty of murder? What in the text points you to this conclusion?
2. Do you find Dr. Jordan a sympathetic character? Why or why not?
3. How much accountability does a novelist have in writing about historical events? What in the text can you verify as historically accurate, and what is the effect of this?
4. How does Dr. Jordan's narrative enrich Grace's story? In what ways does it give the reader more insight into Grace's life and times?
5. Is Grace a reliable narrator? Why or why not?
6. What assumptions about women do men reveal in the novel, and how do these assumptions create tensions in the story for female characters?
7. Define "gothic" and discuss the ways Atwood draws on the gothic form in this novel.
8. Discuss the motives of the various characters in the novel and why they may or may not want to see Grace pardoned or exonerated.
9. Discuss how Grace's gender, age, and class affect the choices she makes and her treatment by others.
10. What does the quilt motif say about the nature of this story, and about storytelling in general?

Essay Ideas

1. Examine the roles of gender and class in the text.
2. Analyze the understandings of truth, both implicitly and explicitly, in the text.
3. Analyze the use of the quilt motif and explain how it reinforces the themes of the novel.
4. Analyze the role of historical excerpts in the novel itself. What purpose do they serve? How do they aid in telling the story?
5. If Simon Jordan was to be seen as having a "fatal" flaw, one that causes his failure in his ultimate quest, what would it be?

Above, Harry Houdini, who was the inspiration for The Escapist in *The Amazing Adventures of Kavalier & Clay*, gets ready for his escape stunt in the New York Harbor. Photo: Library of Congress, Prints & Photographs Division, Carl Dietz, LC-DIG-ppmsca-23992

The Amazing Adventures of
Kavalier & Clay

by Michael Chabon

Content Synopsis

"The Amazing Adventures of Kavalier & Clay" opens in October 1939 with the meeting of Czech-born Josef Kavalier and his American cousin Sammy Klayman at the latter's Brooklyn apartment. Kavalier has recently arrived from San Francisco, via Japan, as part of an effort to smuggle himself and the legendary Golem of Prague, a giant-sized clay homunculus believed to come to life in moments of crisis to defend the city's Jewish Ghetto, from under the noses of the Nazis who were occupying Czechoslovakia. The two young men collaborate to create the Escapist, a comic book character meant to rival the new and commercially very lucrative Superman, appearing for the last two years in National Periodical's "Action Comics." The Escapist is Tom Mayflower, a Houdini-esque theatrical escape artist by day, but when night falls he fights alongside the League of the Golden Key, "coming to the aid of those who languish in tyranny's chains" (121) and against the evil organization of slavers, the Iron Chain. The Escapist makes his debut in "Amazing Midget Radio Comics" under a Kavalier-painted cover of the Escapist punching Hitler in the jaw; this new character is a great success.

Sammy, under the pseudonym "Sam Clay," writes "The Escapist" as the fulfillment of a wish to be able-bodied, since he is nearly lame following a childhood bout with polio. But he also harbors the desire to be blonde and Protestant (Mayflower as a surname is a transparent marker of waspishness). For Joe Kavalier, the Escapist not only makes heroic his own short-lived career as an escape artist in Prague, but also feeds his desire to take action against the Nazi army who euphemistically "superintend" his Jewish family in Prague. Through the comic, he is able to fight Hitler. Joe puts the money he makes drawing the Escapist into a fund to free his family, going so far as to substantially bankroll a ship, the "Ark of Miriam," whose mission is to take Eastern European Jewish children (including his younger brother Thomas) from a Catholic orphanage in Lisbon to the United States. In 1940, Joe briefly considers joining the Royal Armed Forces to join the fight against the Nazis more directly, but Clay is able to talk him out of it.

The Escapist makes the two cousins stars. Invited to a surrealist Greenwich Village garden party where Salvador Dali is the guest of honor, Joe meets Rosa Luxembourg Saks, the daughter of the host, and she becomes his lover and the inspiration for Judy Dark, a. k. a. Luna Moth, the first female superhero and the anchor of an anthology title of female characters called "All Doll Comics." Sammy discovers homosexual longings he never before acknowledged, and is seduced by tall, broad, and blonde Tracy Bacon, the voice of the Escapist on the radio serial adapted from the comic book. Kavalier and Clay don't own the copyright to character of the Escapist, having signed over all rights for a flat fee when they first brought the character to Empire Comics partners Sheldon Anapol and Jack Ashkenazy. Sammy and Joe are both making very good money, and Joe is able to sponsor a dozen other children on the "Ark of Miriam" beside his brother Thomas, but this is nowhere near the amount of money Empire Comics is making. This situation is grounded in a reality of the history of comics; Joe Shuster and Jerry Siegel, who created Superman, were bilked of their share of the profits, as would be Jack Kirby and many other significant comics creators.

In exchange for a 5% stake in future radio, moving picture, and merchandising revenues, Sammy perjures himself in a deposition that he did not create the Escapist as a rival to Superman, a preemptive legal maneuver Empire Comics is forced to make because National Comics, Superman's copyright holder, is trying to push all their comic book rivals out of business by claiming all costumed superheroes infringe on their copyright. Joe goes along to earn more money, to be able to save yet more Jewish children, but three days before the Japanese attack Pearl Harbor, a German U-Boat sinks the "Ark of Miriam," with Thomas Kavalier aboard. For days, Joe is consumed by grief, but when, after Pearl Harbor, the United States enters the war, Joe enlists in the Navy, finally able to fight and ready to kill.

Simultaneous to the sinking of the "Ark of Miriam," Sammy has accompanied Tracy Bacon to a weekend retreat with other, prominent homosexual couples. When the retreat is raided by the police, Sammy fellates a police officer to keep his identity out of the police reports and press, and decides that his secret is too damning to risk revealing. He decides to stay behind instead of accompanying

Tracy to California, who has made the leap from being simply vocal talent to landing the role of the Escapist in the motion picture serials contracted by Parnassus Films. After starring in two "Escapist" motion picture serials, Tracy joins the Air Force and is shot down and killed over Europe.

The novel, up till this point a nearly day-by-day record of life for the two men in the two years after the 1939 genesis of the Escapist, skips ahead two years to 1943 to find Joe at the Kelvinator Station, a Navy listening post in Antarctica. An accident asphyxiates everyone at the station but Joe, a Navy pilot named Shannenhouse, and a dog, Oyster. Alone, and forced to wait months before a September thaw will allow for the possibility of rescue, both men begin to go insane. Pushed beyond the limits of boredom, Joe reads through a sheaf of letters sent to him, over the last two years, by Rosa, letters that until then he had never read but put away unopened. In the letters, Rosa explains that after he left, she married Sammy and was having his child, a boy they named Tommy in honor of Joe's late brother. Later letters include photographs, more details of the birth and little Tommy's development. Read at the time they were sent, it would be easy to swallow Rosa's story. But read back to back and with nothing else to occupy his mind, Joe notices the chronological and developmental inconsistencies in the story of little Tommy, and arrives at the correct conclusion that Tommy is his son.

Still trying to complete his listening post mission, Joe intercepts transmissions from a German geologist, named Klaus Mecklenburg, the sole survivor of an incident at a German station on the other side of the frozen continent. Joe convinces Shannenhouse to fly the two of them there so that Joe can kill this German in retaliation for his brother's death. Between chapters and strangely unnarrated, the plane crashes and Shannenhouse is killed; fueled by hatred and the need for revenge, Joe manages to get the plane in the air again, but when he finally stands facing the German scientist, his anger evaporates, but not before he accidentally kills the man. Joe wanders to an abandoned German camp at the shore of the Weddell Sea, fueled by morphine to dull the pain of his injuries and to counteract the cold, and is rescued.

The novel skips another ten years between chapters, this time taking us to Bloomtown, NY in 1953. Sammy and Rosa live in the model Long Island suburb; their son Tommy is twelve and up to something; he is caught twice playing hooky, and on occasion glimpsed wearing an eye patch despite his relative ocular health. It transpires that Tommy has been visiting with Joe Kavalier, whom he has been told is his uncle, but who hasn't been seen by the rest of his family since 1941 (Joe went underground after recovering from the Antarctic experience). Joe has illegally taken up residence in an office in the Empire State Building, and it becomes clear he is trapped, unable to reconnect with his old life. Tommy concocts a scheme to flush Joe out of hiding that snowballs till Sammy is called to the Empire State Building to watch Joe, dressed in Tracy Bacon's old Escapist costume, preparing to jump from the building's observation deck, with only rubber bands tied around his waist to stop his fall. The stunt fails, but Joe only falls a few stories; he is injured, not killed. Reunited with his cousin at last, Joe is evicted from the office in which he'd been living, and agrees to live with the Clays in Bloomtown till he decides what to do next. He has all his things, mainly 102 boxes of comics, shipped from his office to the suburban address. Another crate finds him there as well; shipped by an unknown agent, the Golem of Prague finally arrives at the end of its globe-spanning peregrinations, now disincorporated and reduced to a pile of river mud.

After their reunion, Joe shows Sammy what he has been working on for the last decade, a forty-nine chapter comic epic centered on the Golem of Jewish folklore. Nearly wordless, it is thousands of pages long, and, as Sammy confirms when he skims the pages, a masterpiece. Sheldon Anapol explains to the two creators that National Comics copyright-infringement suit is finally coming due after winding through the courts for a decade. He has decided to settle, and to give the copyright to the character of the Escapist to National Comics. He is looking to sell Empire Comics, and Sammy is tempted to buy it, even though the sale would not include the rights to the character he and Kavalier made famous. He and Joe make plans to buy the company: maybe they will publish the Golem comic Joe has drawn. There is, however, a historical interruption that will stand in the way of the creative reunion of the two friends.

Sammy's predisposition to create kid sidekicks for the costumed heroes he writes makes him a target of psychologist Frederic Wertham's book "Seduction of the Innocent," a study that seeks to link juvenile delinquency, immorality, and homosexuality to reading comic books. Congress holds investigative sessions to determine the truth of these charges, and Sammy is subpoenaed to talk about his writing. Testifying in televised hearings held in New York, Sammy is outed as a homosexual by Senators Kefauver, Hennings, and Hendrickson. This reveals to everyone the sham-conventionality of his marriage to Rosa, which Joe at least thought was a genuine heterosexual union. Sammy is at first shattered by this unmasking, but then comes to see this as his chance to escape the life he has made for himself and go to California as he should have done with Tracy Bacon back in 1941. He explains this desire to Rosa and Joe, who has usurped Sammy's place in the marital bed while Sammy has taken Joe's place on the couch. And then, while the two reunited lovers sleep, Sammy departs for the West Coast.

Historical Context

The turbulent social history of the middle decades of the 20th Century plays a determinate role at several key moments in Chabon's novel.

The novel's opening suite detailing Josef's escape from Prague is informed by the German occupation of Czechoslovakia, and when in New York City, Chabon regularly updates his reader with what information would have been available to Joe about the ongoing "superintendence" of the Jewish community in Prague. Similarly, the creation of the Escapist follows the 1937 publication of Superman's first adventures, in "Action Comics," at a time of explosive growth in the number of superhero titles and characters to take advantage of the interest in the Last Son of Krypton.

In other instances, Chabon's history is less exact; as he explains in his "Author's Note" at the end of the novel, "I have tried to respect history and geography wherever doing so served my purposes as a novelist, but wherever it did not I have, cheerfully or with regret, ignored them" (637). There was no actual "Ark of Miriam" whose sinking motivates Joe to join the Army, though German U-Boats were known to harass the Atlantic shipping lanes. Likewise, Bloomtown, Sammy and Rosa's model suburban community on Long Island is clearly patterned on Levittown, but it is not that first, famous planned suburb, only one of its innumerable imitators.

In other cases, the historical record impinges on the novel in more significant ways: the court case "National Periodical Publications, Inc. v. Empire Comics, Inc." whose settlement signals the end of the publication of the Escapist's adventures, is patterned closely on another suit which when settled did end the publication of the Captain Marvel character because of real and imagined similarities to Superman (similarities that, cosmetically at least, are much easier to see than those between the Escapist and Superman). And Frederic Wertham's book "Seduction of the Innocent" did lead to Senate inquiries into whether comic books encourage delinquency, homosexuality, and moral decline. As Chabon implies (623), though, there was no second day of New York testimony, and

obviously, no historical testimony offered by Sammy Clay.

Those characters Chabon created in his novel regularly rub elbows with historical persons; Salvador Dali and Orson Welles, obviously, were real people, though Rosa Saks father and host of the surrealist garden party where Joe meets Rosa, Longman Harkoo, is not. The kaffe klatch that meets at the Excelsior Café (likely named after Stan Lee's famous 1960s sign-off in his Marvel Comics editorials) is a mixture of real and invented characters. The real Gil Kane sits beside the imaginary Julie Glovitz. Likewise, the lists of comics titles and characters Chabon periodically gives the reader are a mix of real imaginary characters and imagined imaginary ones; if one didn't already know, it would be hard to tell the two apart, since they are all equally ludicrous.

Chabon notes that this novel, and all his work, is indebted to the work of Jack Kirby (639), one half of a series of partnerships that created some of the most enduring characters in comics history (The Hulk, The X-Men, The Fantastic Four, etc). History is unclear how much of these characters are his, and how much of them rightly belongs to his collaborators, a situation parallel to that which Joe faces; like Kavalier and Clay, Kirby never saw a fraction of the revenue generated by his creations, and at the time of his death was still struggling to have his original art returned to him from Marvel Comics. This story, sadly, is repeated throughout the history of comics.

Other figures, less clearly acknowledged, but still instrumental to the story, include Will Eisner, whose pioneering page layouts in "The Spirit" reappear in the splash pages of Kavalier's "The Golem." Likewise, Luna Moth and her psychedelic adventures owe a debt to Steve Ditko's 1960s work, through the character design and basic character of Nightshade, and the other-dimensional adventures of Dr. Strange. To make Kavalier's influence on the world of comics more profound, Chabon regularly collapses the actual timeline of comics' development. So, in 1954, Kavalier has finished what is essentially the first graphic novel, about two decades before the actual publication of those texts who vie for the title now (Joe Sternanko's "Chandler: Red Tide," Will Eisner's "A Contract with God, and Other Tenement Stories," or Gil Kane's "His Name is…. Savage"). The character of the Escapist bears more than a passing resemblance to Mister Miracle, a super-escape artist created by Jack Kirby for DC Comics in the 1970s. And the stylistic revolutions and evolutions of Kavalier's pencil and ink work prefigure the best work of fifty years of dozens of actual cartoonists.

Societal Context

The historical time period Chabon mines for his novel allows him to explore the intersections of three marginal communities: Jewish, homosexual, and comic book artists.

It makes for a potent stew in the novel: nearly all the comic artists in the novel are Jewish, and Chabon suggests more than once that the Jewish need to be at once part of and separate from mainstream American culture informs the ways in which superhero characters, with their alter egos and masked identities, their double lives, develop. Chabon is not the first to notice the uniquely Jewish nature of Superman's character, and the story of Joe's escape from Prague, the last son of a community that is essentially wiped out, and his settling on welcoming but foreign shores, is not only the stereotypical immigrant story, but also a real world analogue of Superman's origin.

Likewise, Sammy Clay's nascent homosexuality implies another way to read the double lives of comic characters. His desire, first for the character he creates, then for the living embodiment of that character, Tracy Bacon, suggests a perfected narcissism: the desire for a better positioned, more culturally privileged version of the self. This same desire, perhaps, inspires Clay to create kid

sidekicks, since in his relationship with the tall and blonde Tracy Bacon, he sees himself as the sidekick. Chabon himself is deliberately ambiguous when he talks about the importance of homosexual desire in Clay's creation of these sidekicks; Clay notes that sales jump 22% when a sidekick is introduced, and it's unclear if the reason for this is some sort of latent homosexual identification or simply a broader desire for younger readers to locate a character with whom they can identify in their escapist fantasies. Chabon is a lot less ambiguous about the corrosive effects of Clay's secrecy regarding his sexual orientation, and it is clear in the book's final chapters that it is only by "escaping" conventional standards of appropriate desire that Clay can be happy.

None of the main characters make a big deal out of practicing Judaism, but nearly all of them operate in a Jewish demimonde that provides a social backdrop for the novel: a key moment in Clay's relationship with Bacon is taking the actor to his mother's Shabbat meal. And Joe Kavalier has an emotionally rewarding sideline business as a stage magician at the bar mitzvah's of boys who are the natural fans of the Escapist. Judaism, in this way, introduces to the novel a series of cultural benchmarks that have a lot to do with daily life and little to do with the explicitly supernatural elements of religious practice. Except, of course, for the Golem, who in the novel is evidence of the supernatural, and in other ways is the divine spark that sets Kavalier and Clay going.

Religious Context

As noted above, most characters in the novel are raised as part of a Jewish milieu that connects them to a common experience, whether they are American like Sammy or European like Joe. This background functions, mostly, as more of a social than a religious touchstone, but the influence of Jewish mysticism and myth is relevant, especially when it concerns the Golem and Kabala.

The Golem, both Rabbi Loew's Golem of Prague that Joe helps to liberate from its city of origin, and "The Golem," Joe's long, nearly wordless graphic novel, exist as fantastic commentaries on the creative process. Mythically, the Golem is made of clay, and life is "breathed" into him by carving letters from the Hebrew alphabet into his forehead. In this way, "breath" becomes "speech," a communicative act that summons the Golem into being. In Jewish tradition, there is talk of a line of Golems who have, at different times, protected and served the Jewish people, including even a clay goat, talked into life and then killed for its meat so that its creators would not starve.

When Joe first tries to draw what Sammy describes as a superhero, he draws a Golem, which then evolves, after a weekend of cigarettes, coffee, and hours of talk, into the Escapist. Later, he plots and draws the epic graphic novel he calls "The Golem" that explores the history of the Golem in relation to the history of the Jews. This work also features appearances by the archangels of Kabala, the mystical and numerological arm of Judaism.

From what we are told, "The Golem," as a work, seems a history of sorts. The motivating idea, though, seems to be the way language, and speech, lend animation to a man (Joe Kavalier) and a people (the Jews) via the intercession of a divine spark, breath shaped into words. As Ken Kalfus noted in his review of the novel for the *New York Times*, "Chabon… always returns to the incantatory power of the word."

John Podhoretz, writing about Kavalier and Clay in the magazine *Commentary* sees the pile of dirt the Golem of Prague becomes, when it has finished its travels and finds Joe in the garage of the Bloomtown house as Chabon's recognition of what became of the Jews in ghettos in Prague, Krakow, and Lviv. It is true that Rosa mistakes the Moldau Rover mud as ashes, and recoils in horror at the implication when the crate is first opened. But this reading feels to me a little overstated, given the relative calm with which Joe confronts the evidence. Instead, Joe speculates that the Golem has degraded to dirt because the soul has gone out of it, and it's easiest to believe that's what Chabon means by having it lose its animation in America.

Scientific & Technological Context

The physical facts of early comic book publishing played a strong role transforming Josef Kavalier, late of the Prague School of Fine Arts, into Joe Kavalier, penciller and inker of the Escapist, the Luna Moth, the Four Freedoms, and Mr. Machine Gun. Printed on the same rolling presses as newspapers, and onto crude wood pulp, the cheapest grade of paper available, the fine feathering of Josef's early work would not reproduce on the inside pages of the comic (the covers, printed with different stock, are where Joe does his most artistic work, like his famous cover of the Escapist punching Hitler). Joe's art evolves to be at once bolder and more simple, because this is the extent of what the poor quality reproductions will allow. The path followed by Chester Gould, artist of the blocky and thick-lined Dick Tracy newspaper comic, is parallel to that Chabon assigned to Kavalier; as Dennis Drabelle notes in *Civilization*, "Gould overcame… the pulpy pages… by drawing shapes so strong that you hardly notice their flatness." Writing for *American History*, Richard Marshall explains that "factors of technology and commerce played important roles in the birth of the comic strip," and the limited technology, and the limits of what men like Sheldon Anapol were willing to spend on as uncertain a venture as costumed superheroes meant that the work was kept basic and primal. It was working in this vein, however, that Joe became a legend, an inspiration via his line to both the surrealists and the pop artists after them.

Biographical Context

"The Amazing Adventures of Kavalier & Clay" marks a transitional period in Michael Chabon's writing. It's the fifth book in a career marked by what critics note as strong early promise in his first novel, "The Mysteries of Pittsburgh," and a well-received movie adaptation of his second novel, "Wonder Boys," starring Michael Douglas and Tobey Maguire. Two short story collections also predate the writer's third novel.

The differences between this novel and his earlier works is worth remarking upon. In the first place, "Kavalier & Clay" is a closely observed and research intensive work of historical fiction. Its setting is also striking: in his previous novels, Chabon had carved out a niche for himself by setting his novels in the also-ran cities of the Eastern seaboard, Pittsburgh where he was born and Baltimore. But in this novel, Chabon trades that distinctive quality to immerse himself, and his narrative, in New York City. That said, he tackles the project with gusto, indulging internecine borough squabbles like a native.

Likewise, Sammy Clay's questions about his sexuality echo the casual bisexuality of Art Bechstein, the protagonist of "The Mysteries of Pittsburgh." In this new novel, though, the theme of struggle over finding oneself is developed in a more closely observed context: Clay struggles with his attraction to men, unlike Bechstein who is blasé and a bit omnivorous in his sexual conquests. All of this, of course, emanates from the imagination of a writer who is happily married with children.

As much as this aspect of the novel looks back to Chabon's earlier work, the sustained interest in "Kavalier & Clay" in genre writing charts a progression that, so far, has dominated his subsequent work: the first book Chabon published after this one was "Summerland," a novel for children that some have described as an American entree into the Harry Potter marketplace. This was followed by "The Final Solution," a detective novel, and not, as a reader of "Kavalier & Clay" might imagine, an exploration of Hitler's policies toward the Jews.

As a child, Chabon was given comics to read by his father, and he cites this early exposure to the brightly colored adventures as the secret origin of his interest in superhero comics (Tobias). He has shown an sustained engagement with genre writing beyond these books he's written: speaking at the 2004 Eisner Awards Ceremony, an industry event where comics professionals honor their own, Chabon scolded publishers for chasing an adult audience at the expense of their character's appeal to children, and he proposed several ideas that would, he says, bring kids back to comics. In that Eisner keynote speech, he develops the importance of escapism in a way that is consonant with the novel, but in this new formulation, the only ones who get to escape are young people. This is in direct contrast to how Lee Behlman, in "SHOFAR," sees "Kavalier & Clay" as "remarkable for the intimate ways it shows how much pleasure and value may be found in producing and reading fantasy," especially for American audiences and artists wrestling with the disparities between "the unbridgeable historical divide between a relatively comfortable American Jewish present and the dark European Jewish past." It is difficult, at times, to reconcile what Chabon seems to be after in his novel (the way pulp and genre literature managed the tensions of its adult writers) and what he proposes now for how pulp and genre writing is, or ought to be, consumed by its audience. He has also written a number of short essays under the name Malachi B. Cohen; in this guise, he has extended the publishing history of the Escapist beyond the embargo leveled against the character in 1954. Under the masthead of a prodigiously profligate series of small publishing houses, Cohen tells of the further published adventures of the Escapist and the Luna Moth, adventures that reflect contemporary trends in comics, such as the socially relevant comics of the 1970s, and the grim-n-gritty style of the 1990s. One of these essays was published in "The Amazing Adventures of the Escapist," an anthology of comics creators creating Escapist stories to flesh out these publication histories; for the first time in February 2004, the Escapist saw print in a superhero comic, making the belated transformation into real imaginary superhero.

Chabon's novel played a role in the rehabilitation of comics as a site for legitimate literary work. He has also taken up arms alongside Dave Eggers and his McSweeney's Press to promote a return to genre prose writing by established authors, and has edited a collection of pulp writing for the press. It's possible to read the theme of escapism that runs through the novel in contradictory ways, but Chabon's comments are less ambiguous about simultaneously enjoying pulp writing and denying its potential as worthy of "serious" attention.

Matthew Dube

Works Cited

Behlman, Lee. "The Escapist: Fantasy, Folklore, and the Pleasures of the Comic Book in Recent Jewish American Holocaust Fiction." *SHOFAR* 22.3 (Spr 2004): 56–71.

Chabon, Michael. *The Amazing Adventures of Kavalier & Clay*. New York: Picador USA, 2000.

_____. "Interview with Scott Tobias." *AV Club*. The Onion. 22 November 2000.

Drabelle, Dennis. "Weird Fantasies and Amazing Adventures." *Civilization* 4:6(1997/1998). Academic Search Premier. Grand Valley State University Zumberge Lib. 9 Jan. 2005.

Kalfus, Ken. "The Golem Knows." *New York Times* 24 Sept 2000.

Marshall, Richard. "100 Years of the Funnies." *American History* 30:4 (1995). Academic Search Premier. Grand Valley State University Zumberge Lib. 9 Jan. 2005.

Podhoretz, John. "Escapists." *Commentary* June 2001.

Discussion Questions

1. Is the Golem of Prague a superhero? Why or why not?

2. What secret identities do characters in this novel adopt? What do they conceal? What do they reveal?

3. Who or what inspires the creation of the Escapist? Does he remain true to these inspirations?

4. Is Joe Kavalier an artist? Is Sammy Clay?

5. Why does Joe return to practicing magic? Is it for the same reasons he started to learn magic?

6. Whose story is more interesting to you, Joe or Sammy? Could one be told without telling the other?

7. Are you as a reader prepared for the "death" of the Escapist? What about the congressional testimony?

8. Is Sammy Clay gay? Why does he say he writes kid sidekicks for his heroes? Do you believe him?

9. What do you think happened to the Golem since it was sent from Prague in 1939? Who do you think mailed it to Joe at the address in Bloomtown?

10. What does it mean in this novel to be Jewish? Is Judaism a religion, a culture, or both? Does it matter that almost all the characters in this novel are Jewish, or would it be the same if they were goyische?

Essay Ideas

1. Joe Kavalier thinks a lot about what a golem is in the process of creating his graphic novel "The Golem," especially on page 582. Based on what he says there, is the Escapist a Golem? Is "The Amazing Adventures of Kavalier & Clay" a Golem?

2. Chabon explained in his Keynote Address at the 2004 Eisner Awards that comics should be, first and foremost, written for and enjoyed by kids, and that attempts to use comics to explore more adult themes and situations is a perversion of what comics should be. Is this a surprising position for him to take in the context of "Kavalier & Clay?" Why or why not?

3. Develop the similarities and differences between Harry Houdini and the costumed superheroes. Is he the father of the Escapist, Superman, et al? Or is he more like a cousin?

4. The most artistically successful works in the novel (the Escapist, the Luna Moth, the Kiss) are the product of collaborations between writer and artist. Develop how that collaboration works in at least one of these instances, and compare it to the "making" of a more individualistic work of art (Picasso's "Guernica," DaVinci's "Mona Lisa," etc). Alternately, consider if there is another form of art that you think is similarly collaborative. What are its major works?

5. Chabon's novel is pieced together from a variety of different writing styles, sometimes personal, sometimes factual or critical, especially when it uses footnotes, and on occasion lyrically poetic, as when describing the origin of the Escapist or that first comic after Sammy and Joe watch "Citizen Kane." Pick a particular chapter or scene where this meeting of styles is striking. Consider the way these different voices interact: is the novel itself a "collaboration" of these different voices, or one where the voices contradict each other? Is "The Amazing Adventures of Kavalier & Clay" one unified thing, or instead a collection of conflicting accounts of a time and a group of characters?

Are You There, God? It's Me, Margaret

by Judy Blume

Content Synopsis

Pre-teen Margaret Simon is the lead character in Judy Blume's "Are You There, God? It's Me, Margaret"—a text that has become canonized. In this novel, the youngster discovers puberty, boys, and herself, while exploring larger issues of faith.

The novel opens with one of the direct addresses to God that recur throughout the book. As Margaret starts or ends her day, she will often reflect on it. This reflection easily translates into talks with God. The convenience for the reader is that the summative nature of her talks with God allows for easy exposition, and so segues right from an update for God to an update for the reader; an update that provides necessary background information.

The book begins with Margaret explaining how her family moved to Farbrook, NJ from New York City for a host of reasons, but primarily to put some distance between herself and Grandma Sylvia, a sixty-year-old who has a lot of energy to lavish on Margaret. Since Sylvia does not drive nor like busses and trains, the whole family is surprised when she makes her way out to Farbrook for an unannounced visit.

Meanwhile, Margaret is getting to know the other kids and beginning to fit in. Although neighbor and new friend Nancy Wheeler had expected Margaret to be more cosmopolitan and developed,

she befriends her. At their first meeting, she checks out Margaret's breast size, brags her own will be as large as those in a "Playboy" magazine, and illustrates how she practices kissing with a pillow. Nancy informs her that boys are all lascivious, and instructs Margaret not to wear socks at school the first day.

On the first day of school, Margaret is sorry she didn't wear socks. She meets her teacher, Miles J. Benedict, Jr., who is new to the teaching profession. Margaret's mom worries that he won't be that good, but she is not allowed any further discussion on the topic since Margaret curtails the first-day, end-of-school chat to attend a club meeting with Nancy and her friends. Her mother and father will also be shut out of discussions regarding Sylvia, as much as Margaret can manage. Both she and Sylvia sense that her parents resent their close bond, and so the two agree to coordinate nightly phone calls without parental knowledge.

On the brink of teenage-hood, Margaret is not too keen on much of what she sees and hears. Her mother mentions with disparagement, "when you're a teenager," as if she will be substantially more difficult, encountering incredible acne, body odor, and the like. Sylvia likewise seems to be rushing her development, as she constantly asks if Margaret has a boyfriend, and if he's Jewish.

Margaret herself is not sure what she is, having been raised without religion. Thus, it is odd that God figures so largely in her life, and she spends much of the book working on a research project. She says, "My mother says God is a nice idea. He belongs to everybody" (14). Margaret is on a quest to find the church that houses her God.

Margaret makes some new friends. Nancy draws the foursome together, often dictating and criticizing the others. Gretchen Potter is Jewish and her father is the doctor who fixed Margaret's Dad's hand after a lawnmower accident. Janie Loomis is Protestant, and short like Margaret. Together, the girls form a club, the Four PTSs, which stands for the Pre-Teen Sensations. In this club they are given new, more exotic names, which become confusing and are jettisoned early on. They each need to contribute a rule as well. Nancy decides they all should wear bras, which means Janie and Margaret have to run out and get some. Gretchen decides the first to get her period needs to tell the group the details, especially what it feels like; they all know the facts, but lack the experience or information about the experience. Janie decides they must keep Boy Books, listing out which boys they like and in what order. Margaret goes last, stalling for a bit, and finally making her rule be they have to meet weekly on a set day. That leads to the discussion about religious obligations and the girls find out that Margaret is no religion in particular because her parents come from two different faiths. Margaret's mother was raised as a Christian, and her parents forbade her to marry Margaret's Jewish father. When the two eloped, her parents cut them out of their lives. The girls are fascinated with this story, as well as the notion that Margaret should choose her religion when she is older, but Margaret is uncomfortable with the attention given to her. Not belonging to one of the two primary religions has its social drawbacks as well, as Janie posits the question about whether they will join the Y or the Jewish Community Center. When Margaret responds they might not join either, Janie informs her that everyone belongs to one or the other.

At school, there is one girl who is taller and better developed than the others in the class, and she is Laura Danker. Laura has been wearing a bra since fourth grade. Laura is ostracized from the first day and Nancy tells Margaret that Laura is loose and goes behind the A&P with Moose and Evan (Nancy's older brother). Although Margaret's initial impression of Laura is that she is pretty, she becomes increasingly critical of her, due to Nancy's stories. When they are learning to square dance, Mr. Benedict uses Laura as his partner, claiming she is closest to his height. Since she towers over her male classmates, and since males and females alike ostracize her, this gives her a chance to be included, but Nancy presumes it is a sign of Laura's immorality and Mr. Benedict's lecherousness. She claims his eyes are often fixed on Laura, and yet she is the one who seems to think it natural that developed women would want to appear in "Playboy."

On the first day of school, Mr. Benedict gave them a short survey. One of the questions was about what they hate. One of the things Margaret listed was "religious holidays." He later called her to his desk to inquire about that, and she explained her situation. At this point, Margaret reflects on how she managed to live eleven years in New York City with hardly one discussion on religion and how now it seemed ever-present.

Moose is a boy who is friends with Evan, Nancy's brother. Margaret met them the first day she was in town. They overheard part of their first club meeting, and mocked them afterwards. Moose is hired to tend to the Simons' yard. Although Mr. Simon had originally claimed that tending to his yard was part of the new suburban life experience, a run-in with a lawnmower blade both allowed the family to meet Dr. Potter and to decide to hire Moose to tend to the yard. This means that Margaret gets to watch him work, while feigning that she is reading a book. Margaret would have listed him as first in her Boy Book, but she was embarrassed to do that, fearing Nancy's mocking and criticism, so instead Margaret listed Philip, who was first on all their lists. Margaret says he is the most attractive, but that she doesn't really like him as a person. The only other boy Margaret does know is listed as her second choice, and Nancy gives her flak about that until Margaret gives her the evil eyebrow raise to tell her to back off. As she grows to know Philip more, she realizes he's not such a likeable person, and she wonders if they all really liked Philip, or were they all insecure nonconformists? (69).

Meanwhile, in the classroom, the students give Mr. Benedict a hard time. At one point the whole class makes peep noises, something even Margaret does when she is pressured by Nancy, and on one test they all omit their names. Mr. Benedict takes it good-naturedly and triumphs by figuring out whose tests belonged to whom without the names. He also responds with assigned seats, putting Margaret between "Lobster" Freddy Barnett and Laura.

When Margaret decides to attend temple with her grandmother, her mother says," I just think it's foolish for a girl of your age to bother herself with religion" (86). Her grandmother is pleased, and says, "I knew you were a Jewish girl at heart!" (55). Although she attends synagogue, Margaret does not feel anything and finds she cannot understand much of it. Margaret and her father grow closer as they laugh over counting hats in synagogue. Margaret accompanies Janie to church once, and for Christmas service, Margaret joins Nancy, but she doesn't feel anything special there, either. Only alone in her personal prayers does Margaret connect with God. "Why do I only feel you when I'm alone?" (120).

One aspect of these religious services which Margaret does like, no matter what religion, is the music, and yet when Mr. Benedict volunteers his class to serve as the chorus for the holiday concert, two students complain about singing the Hanukkah or Christmas songs. Mr. Benedict tries

to explain that songs are for everyone, but the two are not convinced and opt to remain silent for the songs that are not of their faith.

Norman Fishbein has a supper party for his birthday, and the entire class is invited to a sophisticated evening. The boys quickly remove their ties, and eventually shoot mustard at the ceiling through straws. Freddy taunts Nancy and her pocket is ripped off her dress. Mrs. Fishbein is appalled but continues to leave them unsupervised. They play spin the bottle and Margaret has two minutes in the closet with Philip.

Gretchen is the first to begin menstruating, and Nancy expresses surprise that it was not her, since she is more developed. Gretchen then is stuck with the repercussions of her own rule about telling all, with Nancy pressing for more and more details. Shortly after, Nancy sends postcards from her vacation, announcing that she "GOT IT" (101). Later, when Nancy actually begins menstruating, Margaret is with her and is surprised to find she's been lied to.

When Margaret and Laura are assigned to a group project, Laura points out to a distracted Margaret that she can't copy word-for-word. Margaret's temper flares, and she attacks Laura for her illicit liaisons with boys. Laura lets Margaret know that the assumptions and allegations are off-base, and rude. Laura then storms off to her next obligation, confession. Margaret trails her and slips into the confessional afterward, and when the priest addresses her, at first she thinks it is God. Then she bolts. Ultimately, Margaret realizes that she behaved too much like Nancy and that the stories might also be false.

Margaret's grandmother, Sylvia, moves to Florida, and takes up with Mr. Binamin. They plan for Margaret to come visit, but her maternal grandparents, the Hutchins, in response to a holiday card sent by Margaret's mother, decide to visit. This puts the kibosh on her trip, and causes her parents much stress. Although the Hutchins say "maybe we were wrong" (122–23), it is clear that they feel no remorse for their actions. Now that they realize that their son will not give them grandchildren, they are hoping to redeem Margaret. Traditionally, mothers' faiths determine the religion of the children, they argue. When the Hutchins discover that they cannot convert Margaret, they leave again.

Margaret concludes that she will raise her own children with a religion because picking one is too difficult, and she is not ready to do it yet. Although there is a period when she is mad about canceling her trip to Florida and there are times throughout the novel when she refuses to speak to God, it is clear that Margaret has a personal reaction to God and he is her closest confidant.

Margaret confronts Moose about Nancy's stories of him and Laura, and Moose is surprised that Margaret believed them. Margaret then discovers she has begun menstruating and is relieved to find that she is normal after all and not developmentally delayed.

Historical Context

Gender representations are interesting in this text. Published in 1970, "Are You There God? It's Me, Margaret" presents women's issues from a dated perspective. Nancy Wheeler's character is very active, socially adept and attuned to the upper middle class, suburban lifestyle. She knows what teacher has run off over the summer, the details of the dance, and how to interact with Mrs. Fishbein due to her mother, who is a stay-at-home, PTA-joining, dance-chaperoning, bridge-playing housewife. Given that Betty Friedan's "Feminine Mystique" was published in 1963, the Wheeler representation is neither that unusual for the early 1970s, nor is it fully endorsed by Blume's characterization. By 1966, the National Organization for Women (NOW) had formed and was working towards "bring[ing] women into full participation in the mainstream of American society now, exercising all privileges and responsibilities thereof in truly equal partnership with men" (NOW). Nancy presents herself as someone who

is knowledgeable and confident, ready to lead and organize. She arranges the club, coordinates their plans, and even chides them regarding their choices of boys that are listed in their boy books. She also expected to lead them to maturity and is disappointed when Gretchen begins menstruating before her. Yet Nancy is also sexually confused, and presents an image of sexual confusion that is not deconstructed or analyzed, partly because it is so much an example of the times. Historians such as David Allyn have noted that the key to the "sexual revolution" of the sixties was not so much experimentation and sexual acts, but instead an increase in the discussion and openness of these behaviors, including pornography. Thus, Nancy is typical of the times.

Nancy is obsessed with breast size and projects this onto men. Moose and Evan, according to her, are constantly thinking about and looking at breasts. The exposure Moose is granted in the novel is primarily limited to his yard work business—soliciting Margaret's family as a client, performing the work, etc. The one exception is when Moose and Evan come upon the first meeting of the PTSs, the meeting during which the girls conclude with an exercise that Nancy alleges will increase their chests, involving arm exercises while chanting, "we must, we must, we must increase our bust…". As they leave their first meeting, the boys mock them, repeating this line. Nancy projects desire and lust onto Mr. Benedict, who may actually ask Laura to be his partner because she is tall, or because she seems so friendless, as well as onto Moose and the other fourteen-year-old boys.

Nancy mentions "Playboy" very often, and knows its layout. At one meeting, Gretchen brings a medical book with male anatomy displayed. Nancy makes Margaret locate her father's "Playboy," which has moved from a more public location to his bedside table drawer as Margaret has aged. The text describes how Margaret is trying to recall where it is, "I didn't want to ask my mother. Not that it was so wrong to show it to my friends. I mean, if it was so wrong my father shouldn't get it at all, right? Although lately I think he's been hiding it…" (71). This shows the acceptance of sexuality which was common after the free-wheeling sixties and how the sexual revolution worked its way into the lives of young suburbanites. Nancy is familiar enough to open to the centerfold, and yet her mother presents the image of propriety and decorum. Accepting male sexuality, and the notion that women should want to be physically appealing to attract males, Nancy leads the other girls to an understanding of maturity which is not that affirming of the liberated woman of today. "Playboy" was at its pinnacle of success at this point, as the tamer of top-selling pornography (as opposed to the newer and more graphic "Penthouse"). While "Playboy" is still a top selling magazine, since 1988, when Hugh Hefner's daughter Christie took over as CEO, the increase in competition (such as "Maxim," "GQ," and "Esquire") has cut the magazine's circulation somewhat ("Playboy").

With research by Alfred C. Kinsey, and William Masters and Virginia Johnson, the issues of sexuality became more often discussed. At the same time, women in the workforce and better forms of birth control led to liberalization on financial and economic counts. The Supreme Court's ruling on Fanny Hill in 1966 set such high standards for obscenity that it virtually eliminated bans. All of these things collectively led to an increase in discussion about sexuality and an acceptance of these topics as valid. For example, Masters and Johnson's faces adorn the front cover of the May 25, 1970 issue of TIME magazine, proclaiming "Sex Education for Adults."

Societal Context

The nuclear families and communities that offer continuity are waning as more families move to a suburban sprawl, and Blume traces the beginning of this phenomenon in her work. Also played out is the concept of young couples who need a "space"

of their own to form their own family units, independent of other generations. The shift of a population from urban sites to bedroom communities is recorded and typical, particularly since the 1960s.

Divorce is an accepted part of the culture. Janie's aunt, who visited the nudist colony, is divorced, which somehow indicated she was destined for such behaviors. Aside from this peripheral character (who is only discussed and never actually portrayed in the novel), the novel is silent on many social aspects which might have been relevant at the time across the United States at the time it was written. The 1960s were a time of civil rights, intense political action, drug use, ecological conservatism, and Marxism, and yet none of these filter into the suburban lifestyle that is mirrored in this text.

Religious Context

Religion is a primary concern in this text. When Margaret is mad at God, she begins her usual address, but does not complete it. Instead of "Are you there, God? It's me, Margaret," all she gets out is, "Are you there, God?" and then she trails off, remembering she's not speaking to him (135). Although some could see this as Margaret questioning his existence, she then wonders if he will strike her down for her attitude. This indicates she invests as much faith in her denial of him as in her own personal worship.

Interesting also is that the other children in the novel, although receiving training, education, and regular attendance at their services, seem to value religion only insofar as it determines their social memberships, at the Y or the JCC. Margaret's view of religion is constantly more personal. She neither wants to discuss it with the world, nor does she really share with others how much she talks with God. She indicates that if people knew how much she talked with God, they might think she was crazy. Her narrative includes, "My parents don't know I actually talk to God. I mean, if I told them they'd think I was some kind of religious fanatic or something. So I keep it very private" (14). Although her parents acknowledge that God "belongs to everyone" (14), they do not transmit the message that would encourage Margaret to create such a relationship with God. In pursuing God, she is actually violating the precept of honoring one's mother and father. Margaret's faith and observation of faith is nonetheless strong and consistent. Even in her rejection of God, she acknowledges his power.

Her version of God coincides with the overlapping precepts of Christianity and Judaism and is inclusive and tolerant. Interestingly, this leaves out the huge discrepancy between the faiths, that of Jesus Christ and his role. Without addressing this aspect, Margaret's exploration of the various religious choices seems to rely solely on congregations, services, and secular views. Margaret does explore the Catholic confessional, but not the concept of Confession. She writes in her report that she has consulted various religious texts, but nowhere in the book does she discuss them or reflect consideration of the dogma, doctrines, or principals of faith.

The concept of a personal relationship with God, rather than a church-based one seems to reflect the younger generation's need for faith in conjunction with their parents' cynicism and rejection of the grandparents' version of religion as divisive and exclusionary. After moving through rejection or apathy, one can arrive at a personal level of faith which requires no service, no ornate or incomprehensible service, no tedious sermons, and no silly hats. Music ministry is the one aspect of faith that consistently appeals to Margaret, and as such, the music does not need to celebrate any specific religion's holiday, but rather a universal appeal of music and belief in God.

Scientific & Technological Context

Science and technology are not significant elements in this text, aside from the issues of transportation. When the family moves to the suburbs, transportation to the city becomes relevant. Also, Sylvia's move to Florida and her cruise indicate a migratory pattern to the elderly which is prevalent in contemporary society. The modern ability to uproot and relocate in alternative climates with ease is notable and the by-product of a transportation technology which makes such movement possible without losing the societal connections from the previous residency.

Also relevant for keeping in touch is the telephone, which figures into the Margaret-Sylvia relationship. Interestingly, when they supplement with letters, they find that they cover more material with greater depth, indicating the phone's limitations as a communication device. Written before the advent of e-mail, this text hints at the shift away from depth which comes with the faster modes of communication. Nonetheless, with such transportation and communication technology, it is possible for families who are living in far-flung corners of the world to keep in touch and maintain contact.

Biographical Context

Judy Blume has written many children's and adult novels over her thirty-year career, and made a name for herself that is part of the canon of children's literature. Confronting serious issues such as sibling rivalry, peer pressure, divorce, sexuality, and maturation, Blume attracts both a sizable audience and critics.

Blume said to John Neary, "I think I write about sexuality because it was uppermost in my mind when I was a kid: the need to know, and not knowing how to find out. My father delivered these little lectures to me, the last one when I was ten, on how babies are made. But questions about what I was feeling, and how my body could feel, I never asked my parents"("Judy (Sussman) Blume"). While this has attracted readers, it has also been a difficulty, as some resent the idea that fiction can provide the kind of authoritative or conclusive information a young adult might need. Further, the topics and language are frank. "As a result, Blume's works have frequently been the targets of censorship, and Blume herself has become an active crusader for freedom of expression" ("Judy (Sussman) Blume"). Blume counters that it is important to bring these topics out and foster discussion.

In addition to works of fiction, Blume collected letters that had been written to her, "Letters to Judy: What Your Kids Wish They Could Tell You," along with her commentary. She used the royalties to fund various projects, including the KIDS Fund, which contributes to nonprofits focused on improving child-parent communication ("Judy (Sussman) Blume"). Blume invests her efforts in such a manner that reflects her values and her commitment to candid communication.

Blume cites her love of reading as a child as a strong influence, and lists some of her favorite authors at the time as being Louise Fitzhugh, E.L. Konigsburg, and Beverly Cleary ("Transcript"). Regardless of the target audience and topic, Blume brings an empathetic voice, with a "humorous and easy to read" style of writing ("Judy (Sussman) Blume").

Anne K. Erickson

Works Cited

Allen, David. *Make Love, Not War: The Sexual Revolution: An Unfettered History.* New York: Little, Brown, 2000.

Blume, Judy. *Are You There, God? It's Me, Margaret.* New York: Yearling, 1986.

"Judy (Sussman) Blume." *Dictionary of Literary Biography.* Gale. Atlantic Cape Community College, NJ. 22 Dec. 2005.

NOW. "Frequently Asked Questions." 6 Sep. 2006.

Playboy. "Frequently Asked Questions." 8 Aug. 2006. 6 Sep. 2006.

"Transcript of *Judy Blume's* Online Chat for the New York Public Library." 19 Nov. 2002. 31 Aug. 2006.

Discussion Questions

1. Margaret has a lot of questions that she asks her friends and God, but she does not ask her parents. Why do you think she doesn't? What do you think would happen if she did?
2. There were attempts to ban this book. Why do you think people wanted to ban it? Do you agree or disagree with those arguments?
3. Margaret worries about being "normal." What defines whether a person is normal?
4. Is Margaret right that religion should be taught to young children or are her parents right in saying children shouldn't worry about religion?
5. Does Margaret's voice sound believable? Why or why not?
6. What qualities shape who we are? Why does religion seem so much more important in Farbrook than it was in New York City?
7. How does Mr. Benedict handle the students? Margaret says she thinks it is important to have a little fear of your teachers. Do you agree or disagree? How does Mr. Benedict manage his class?
8. Judy Blume is very interested in parents and children communicating. How well does Margaret communicate with her parents? In what ways does their communication break down?
9. In what ways was this book, published in 1970, dated? In what ways is it still relevant?
10. How does our society inform our ideas about how bodies should be shaped, used, and perceived? What do you think about that influence?

Essay Ideas

1. Write an essay comparing the ways various adults in this text feel about religion.
2. Research customs for deciding the religion of a child from a mixed union. Write a paper presenting your findings.
3. Write a paper to parents, explaining how to keep the lines of communication open.
4. Write a paper to young adults which encourages them to share information with their parents.
5. Write an essay about an important rite of passage and what you learned. It may be useful to consider the contrast between what you expected and what really occurred.

The Bean Trees

by Barbara Kingsolver

Content Synopsis

"The Bean Trees" follows the journey of a young woman from a small Kentucky town to Tucson, Arizona. Marietta Greer is determined to be different, to not become pregnant and wind up stuck in a dead-end marriage like many of the girls around her. Her mother, who supports herself and her daughter working as a domestic, believes in her daughter and believes she can do just about anything she sets her mind to. After five and a half years of working in a lab at the hospital, Marietta buys a used car and announces she's leaving.

When Marietta drives out of her small hometown of Pittman, Kentucky, she vows that she will change her name and that she will drive west until her car stops running. Her first promise is fulfilled, and she changes her name to Taylor after the name of the town where she runs out of gas. The second promise she breaks, because it turns out to be in the "great emptiness" of the Cherokee reservation in Oklahoma (13). She reflects on the irony of finding herself stranded there, since her family has Cherokee roots. It is while she's at a bar next door to the repair shop that she encounters a woman with a young child, who then leaves the child in Taylor's car. Not knowing what else to do, Taylor drives to a motel, and, having no money for a room, she talks the owners into letting her stay there in exchange for doing housekeeping. She ends up befriending the owners and staying with them for several weeks. In January, she takes off again, with the little girl, whom she's named Turtle. Turtle has quickly attached herself to Taylor, literally clutching onto her tightly and reminding Taylor of turtles from back home. While Taylor guesses the little girl is about two, when she takes her to a doctor at a later point in the novel, they discover she is at least a year older, and that there is evidence of sustained abuse. The doctor calls the stunting in her growth and development "failure to thrive."

Taylor stops in Tucson after her tires go flat. Here she meets Mattie, the owner of Jesus Is Lord Used Tires. Since she can't afford new tires, Taylor decides to stay. She eventually gets a job working at Mattie's shop. In her search for a place to live, she finds Lou Ann Ruiz, also a transplanted Kentuckian, whose husband has left her and her infant. Lou Ann becomes a friend, and by the end of the book Taylor considers Lou Ann and her son Dwayne Ray her family. Mattie, who shelters refugees from Guatemala, also becomes another important person in her life. Taylor learns about the political repercussions of American involvement in Central America first-hand when she meets Estevan and Esperanza, who have escaped persecution for their involvement with a teacher's union in Guatemala. Esperanza is grieving for their lost daughter and is drawn to Turtle. Taylor falls in love with Estevan, but knows she can't pursue a relationship with him. The two spend a night together on the couch, becoming intimate but not sexual, while Esperanza is in the hospital for attempting to kill herself.

One day while Turtle is in a nearby park with a blind neighbor, a man approaches them, possibly to assault or abduct Turtle. Turtle escapes him, but the attempt undoes all the progress she has made in her development, as she reverts back to silence and inactivity. When the police and social services take the report, the circumstances of her "adoption" become problematic. After a crisis of conscience in which she feels unfit to be Turtle's mother and believes Turtle would perhaps be better off in a foster home, Taylor decides to try to legally adopt her.

Taylor subsequently volunteers to drive Estevan and Esperanza to Oklahoma, where they will be able to pass as Cherokees. The trip will also give her the opportunity to find out what she can about Turtle's family. When she returns to the bar where she had first seen Turtle, however, the bar has turned into a diner and there is no sign of anyone she'd seen before. Taylor realizes then that there "had never been the remotest possibility of finding any relative of Turtle's" but that she had made this trip for a reason unknown to her: "I must have wanted something, and wanted it badly" (203). She decides to go to Lake o' the Cherokees, a scenic area on the reservation, without really knowing why. While they are there, Taylor connects Turtle's love of burying with her cries of "Mama" when she sees a cemetery. She asks Turtle if she'd seen her mother get buried, and Turtle affirms her suspicion. It is at that point that it is clear to Taylor that she is meant to keep Turtle. The next day Taylor goes to the office of a notary with Estevan and Esperanza, who pose as Turtle's parents giving her up for adoption. The papers are then filed for a "legal" adoption of Turtle. Taylor says good-bye to Estevan and Esperanza at a church, and she and Turtle head back to Tucson.

The book's title refers to the recurring image of the bean tree, or wisteria plant, throughout the novel. As Taylor discovers at the end of the book, the plant is able to flourish in poor soil because of rhizobia, a microbe that nourishes its roots. The image underscores the importance of the mostly female community that nourishes Taylor and her adopted daughter.

Historical Context

"The Bean Trees" is set in the early 1980s and can be read as a critique of "the stony-heartedness of conservative bureaucrats [who] generated a selfishness and lack of compassion for the downtrodden" characterized by the Reagan era (Snodgrass 92).

Turtle is given to Taylor when she is on the Cherokee reservation. The Cherokee was one of the so-called Five Civilized Tribes who was moved by the U.S. government from the southeastern United States to Oklahoma in the 1830s and 1840s. This trip, which resulted in many deaths and hardships, is often referred to as the Trail of Tears. Once the Cherokee and other tribes were established, however, "they prospered," building their own homes and schools and participating in the drafting of the state constitution ("People of Oklahoma" par. 3).

The characters of Estevan and Esperanza, as well as the other refugees Mattie hides and helps to safety, represent real historical political refugees who were lucky enough to escape the brutal, repressive regimes of the time in Latin America. Kingsolver herself helped refugees from Chile, El Salvador and Guatemala in 1986 (Snodgrass 15). Estevan and Esperanza are Mayans from Guatemala, where at the time the non-democratic government was engaged in anti-insurgency campaigns that resulted in the destruction of Indian villages and the deaths of tens of thousands. ("Guatemala" 1)

Societal Context

A self-described political writer, Kingsolver addresses social issues on many fronts. Women's empowerment, class consciousness, political oppression, and racism all play roles to varying degrees in the novel.

In her study of women's road narratives, critic Deborah Clarke compares "The Bean Tree" to Bobbie Ann Mason's "In Country" for its use of the automobile as marking a new symbolic connection to women's freedom in the 1980s. She notes that in the twentieth century, women's narratives opened up to include stories of travel, marking a move beyond traditional stories of house and home: "No longer relegated to waiting, women wrote increasingly about journeys, about mobility, and about the power inherent in this increased freedom. The motif of the journey, so long associated with men, from Odysseus to Sal Paradise, comes up more and more in women's texts." (Clarke par. 1)

In "The Bean Trees," by presenting female characters such as Taylor, Taylor's mother, and Mattie, the car repair shop owner, Kingsolver "tweaks women's traditional roles without eradicating them." (Clarke, par. 30) This is because all three women take on the mother role while also displaying skills in handling car maintenance and repair, a traditionally male domain. Taylor's mother supports herself and her daughter and challenges her to learn how to maintain the used car Taylor has purchased. Mattie, the tire-shop owner, exhibits caregiving tendencies in her sheltering of Latin American refugees. Taylor, who eventually takes a job with Mattie, becomes a mother in the novel ironically as she is trying to escape the future of many of her peers in Kentucky of becoming "barefoot and pregnant" at a young age. In addition, the novel represents a departure from the historical and more popular convention of the happy marriage as ending; Taylor's love interest is married and remains faithful to his wife. Thus in the novel, despite its depiction of single motherhood and divorce, marriage and family remain sacrosanct.

As a daughter of the working class from the socially stratified town of Pittman, Taylor is keenly aware of class divisions. She compares herself at the very beginning to the Hardbines, whose clan's father we first see being propelled into the air by an exploding tractor tire. At the same time as she clearly notes the differences between herself and them, she also is careful to acknowledge that she and Newt Hardbine were in the same class and that they were "cut out of basically the same mud" (2). Yet clearly Taylor as a young child has a sense of her own equality, since she insisted that she be called "Miss" Marietta as she "had to call all the people including the children in the houses where [her mother] worked Miss this or Mister that" (2). Later in the novel Taylor tells Estevan about Pittman and makes distinctions among the different groups: the town kids, whose parents were the business owners; the hoodlums (the "motorcycle types"); and the farm kids, also called the Nutters, because they would pick nuts. Estevan likens her description to the Indian caste system. A slightly less obvious comparison here is the oppression of the Mayans in Guatemala, which is represented by Estevan and Esperanza.

Kingsolver, who was pregnant when she wrote the novel but did not experience life as a single mother, also addresses the struggles of poor, single mothers in the United States, struggles still very much relevant to readers twenty years later. In addition to Lou Ann, Taylor befriends another woman, Sandi, at a fast food restaurant. Sandi's strategy for handling childcare on minimum wage is to drop her child off at a free mall childcare center and to dash in on her breaks. Taylor rightly sees this as inadequate, especially for the already developmentally-delayed Turtle. By moving in with Lou Ann, Taylor finds an alternative arrangement by making a family of sorts, where Taylor and Lou Ann support each other, as an egalitarian married couple might, showing that building community is a vital activity for low-income families.

Contrasts between urban and rural landscapes also reveal in a more subtle way Kingsolver's dedication to environmental concerns and to her sensitivity to the ways in which these landscapes shape communities. Taylor and Lou Ann live near a park that she nicknames "Dog Doo Park." Taylor describes it as "pretty awful. There were only a couple of shade trees, which had whole dead parts, and one good-for-nothing palm tree so skinny and tall that it threw its shade onto the roof of the cooler-pad factory down the block" (111). The grass reminds her of "an animal with mange" (111). The description reminds readers that parks in poor urban neighborhoods are subject to neglect and are often surrounded by industry. Still, it has its redeeming feature: wisteria, the bean tree plant. Taylor calls it "the Miracle of Dog Doo Park," thus reinforcing the theme of the novel. Dog Doo Park acts as a contrast to another park Taylor goes to, a "little hideaway by a stream" which they get to by car, a place described as having white rocks, clear water, and a ring of cottonwood trees. It is a place where Taylor and her friends bask in the sun, "feeling too good to move" (91). Such a place is nourishing to them, yet because it must be reached by car and then by a footpath, it is also less accessible.

Religious Context

Mary Ellen Snodgrass describes Kingsolver's religious outlook as "a homemade patchwork based on experience" and as infusing her fiction with "the human yearning for a faith suited to idiosyncratic needs" (172). Certainly Taylor seems to view religion, particularly a grassroots form of Christianity, in a humorous yet tolerantly respectful light. She gleefully observes when her car breaks down in Oklahoma that she's in the Cherokee nation, a place that connects her to a full-blooded Cherokee grandfather. One of the few things she seems to know about the Cherokee is that they "believed God was in trees" and that when she used to climb high up in trees her mother would tell her that she was "'trying to see God'" (13). This observation expresses her feeling of being different, foreshadowing her escape from Pittman and her own unique life path.

The connections between religion and community are made clear through Lou Ann and the arrival of her baby. In the first chapter in which we meet Lou Ann, she is planning on a Catholic baptism for her baby, "purely for practical reasons; if one of the grandmothers was going to have a conniption, it might as well be the one who was eighteen hundred miles away" (28). After the baby is born, Granny Logan and Lou Ann's mother come to visit from Kentucky, creating more tension for Lou Ann. Lou Ann's mother continually hums one line of a hymn, "'All our sins and grief's to bear',' over and over until Lou Ann thought she would scream" (53). Granny Logan gives Lou Ann a bottle of water brought all the way from Kentucky in order to baptize the baby. Later, Lou Ann reacts to Granny's slur on her husband's Mexican ethnicity by muttering that she's prejudiced because he hadn't been baptized "in some old dirty crick" (59). Religion, then, is a cultural attachment, one that is shaken off when Lou Ann leaves behind Kentucky and her family.

By contrast, Taylor's religious sensibility seems to be tied closely with her own unique take on the world. Faith is at issue, but religion becomes more of a metaphor for Taylor's own faith in herself. When she is in the bar next door to the repair shop in Oklahoma, she notices that someone on the television keeps saying, "Praise the Lord. 1-800-THE LORD." (17). This is the place where she first sees the woman with the child who will turn out to be Turtle. After the child is left in her car, Taylor wonders what she will do and tells the child that she may have to call 1-800-THE LORD (20). Instead she finds a motel where two women agree to let her stay in exchange for housekeeping work. The first contact with someone meaningful in Tucson is Mattie, the owner of Jesus Is Lord Used Tires. Taylor is partly attracted to the place because of its echo of the 1-800 phone numbers. Mattie is not who Taylor expects; after noticing that Mattie has a mug with cartoon rabbits fornicating on it she thinks, "I can't figure this woman out. This was definitely not 1-800-THE LORD" (41). Later, after

Mattie announces that the Lord is sending a message for them to go to a desert oasis, she sums up Mattie's religious leanings as "just one damn thing after another" (91).

At the end of the novel, Taylor actually calls the 800 number, on an impulse, even though she knows she doesn't "really need any ace in the hole" (226). A recording answers and tells her that "the Lord helps those that help themselves" and asks for a pledge to the Fountain of Faith missionary fund (226). When a woman comes on the line to take her pledge, Taylor thanks her for the number's existence, as it's been her own "Fountain of Faith." When the woman asks if she'd like to make a pledge, Taylor asks for money or a hot meal for herself. After she hangs up, she feels like doing cartwheels. Her joy can be interpreted as her satisfaction in succeeding in her struggles, from first finding herself the unwitting mother of a young child, to making a home in a new city. Just as the recording has indicated, she's helped herself. Kingsolver here turns religious rhetoric on its head by having the toll-free number stand in for any representation of a Jesus or God. The number, merely in its religious promise, is the one that represents faith, but when Taylor calls it, she finds it's only another organization asking for money, not one that will offer any real help for her. Perhaps, Kingsolver seems to say, it is through the self and community that real spiritual work is done.

Scientific & Technological Context

In her analysis of women's road narratives, Deborah Clarke observes the connections between the automobile, one of the most influential technological advances in the twentieth century, and women. Clarke notes that Taylor "drives a car that contains few of the advances of twentieth-century automobile technology such as windows and starters. In push-starting her car, she evokes the days of the crank engines, aligning herself with … intrepid women … who refused to let the necessary physical exertion keep them from the automobile "(Clarke, par. 28). The kind of relationship between a woman and her car that is depicted in "The Bean Trees" challenges assumptions about male power, which is often connected with almost-secretive knowledge and brute strength. The car is a particularly powerful symbol, in that it represents a person's ability to leave and go long distances easily and independently. Yet, as Clarke suggests, for Taylor the car becomes a domestic space; Turtle is left in the car and it acts as place for Taylor to sleep.

As a trained scientist herself, Kingsolver can't help but include her own scientific knowledge in her writing. This knowledge is put to use through plant and animal imagery. As noted in the synopsis, the wisteria, or bean plant, is an important thematic tool in the novel. According to Mary Ellen Snodgrass, Kingsolver "makes use of the lowly bean as a double symbol of humility and of nature's building blocks" (50). Snodgrass notes that beans and plants in general, become an important teaching and communication tool for Taylor and Turtle. Turtle's language mainly consists of the names of plants; she is also especially interested in planting activities, which is later explained by Taylor's realization that she must have seen her mother being buried. In comparing Turtle's development to food such as corn, Kingsolver places human life "within the greater context of nature" (Snodgrass, 51).

The night before Taylor plans to leave for Oklahoma with Turtle, Estevan, and Esperanza, her neighbor beckons her over to see the rare sight of the night-blooming cereus in full flower. Lou Ann calls it a good sign for their trip. The blooming of the cereus "seems by its loveliness to transform the world and people around it, and in predicting something good it foreshadows the knitting up of plot strands at the end of the novel" (DeMarr 64–65).

At another point in the novel, Kingsolver also adds an emotional depth to Taylor by depicting her response to the scene of a mother quail rounding up her babies in the road: "Something about the whole scene was trying to make tears come up in my eyes" (96). By showing her response to the quail, the author prevents the situation with Turtle from becoming too sentimental while also giving Taylor the emotional responsiveness of a mother. Other birds appear throughout the novel, in another, more subtle motif. In one scene, just after the frightening incident with Turtle in the park, Taylor busies herself in the kitchen with trying to free a bird trapped in the kitchen. In another more obvious scene, just after Taylor is told by the doctor that Turtle had been subjected to continual abuse that prevented her from growing, she marvels at a bird that has made a nest in a cactus.

Biographical Context

Barbara Kingsolver was born in 1955 in Annapolis, Maryland, but spent most of her childhood in the small town of Carlisle, Kentucky. Her father was a family physician; her mother is described as "an avid birdwatcher and true mountaineer in thought and accent" and "unorthodox" (Snodgrass, 7). She is the middle of three children. Growing up where she did supplied her with "her liberal, humanistic conscience, the moral compass of her writing" (Snodgrass, 8). Like Pittman, the fictional town where Taylor Greer is from, Carlisle was a small community whose agriculture was focused on tobacco. Here Kingsolver also witnessed the sharp divisions of class that Taylor describes in "The Bean Trees," divisions marked by the wealthy from Lexington and the poor from Appalachia. As the area's only doctor for thirty-six years, Dr. Wendell Kingsolver did not get rich in his practice, sometimes accepting vegetables for payment from his poor clients. As Kingsolver grew up, so did the awareness of her own poverty. According to Mary Ellen Snodgrass, her inability to afford new clothes "placed her in the local pecking order among country kids, a caste below the children of store owners, mine bosses, and county bureaucrats," a status that mirrors Taylor Greer's (10).

From 1963 to 1966, Kingsolver's family lived in a small village in the central Congo, in western Africa, where her father had a public health post for two years. This was when the Congo had just achieved independence from Belgium; her experiences there form material for a later novel, "The Poisonwood Bible." Here, Kingsolver learned what it was like be a minority, taking away from the experience "an acutely heightened sense of race, of ethnicity," a sensibility that informs her characterization of Estevan and Esperanza in "The Bean Trees." (Kingsolver; qtd. in Snodgrass, 9).

Kingsolver attended DePauw University on a music scholarship, but as a sophomore elected to pursue a B.S. in zoology and a minor in English. While there she was raped in 1974. Turtle could represent the innocence that she lost in the attack and an early attempt at coping with the memory of the trauma. (She would later write about the rape in her poetry and in an essay.)

Kingsolver graduated with honors in 1977. In 1979, after spending some time in Europe, she drove from Carlisle, Kentucky to Tucson, Arizona, a trip that she fictionally depicts in "The Bean Trees." She has been living there ever since. In 1981, she earned an M.S. in animal behavior from the University of Arizona, thereafter working as a research assistant and technical writer. Kingsolver's training in biology is clearly evident in the novel, with its recurring images of plants and other natural phenomena.

Pregnant with her first child and suffering bouts of insomnia, Kingsolver wrote her first novel, "The Bean Trees" in 1986. The book was published in 1988. "Pigs in Heaven" (1993), called a "non-sequel," continues the story of Taylor and Turtle, in which the consequences of Turtle's adoption cause more challenges for the little family. The author of non-fiction, poetry, and short stories, Kingsolver has published three other novels to date: "Animal Dreams" (1990), "The Poisonwood Bible" (1998), and "Prodigal Summer" (2000).

Alyssa Colton

Works Cited

Clarke, Deborah. "Domesticating the Car: Women's Road Trips." *Studies in American Fiction* (2004) 32.1: 101–29. 10 December 2005. InfoTrac OneFile.

DeMarr, Mary Jean. *Barbara Kingsolver: A Critical Companion.* Westport, Connecticut and London: Greenwood Press, 1999.

"Guatemala 1." *The Columbia Encyclopedia* (2004). 20 December 2005.

Kingsolver, Barbara. *The Bean Trees.* New York: Harper & Row, 1988.

"The People of Oklahoma." *Britannica Student Encyclopedia.* 2005. Encyclopædia Britannica Online. 20 Dec. 2005.

Snodgrass, Mary Ellen. *Barbara Kingsolver: A Literary Companion.* Jefferson, North Carolina and London: McFarland & Company, 2004.

For Further Study

Frye, Bob J. "Nuggets of Truth in the Southwest: Artful Humor and Realistic Craft in Barbara Kingsolver's The Bean Trees." *Southwestern American Literature* (spring 2001) 26.2: 73–83.

Murrey, Loretta Martin. "The Loner and the Matriarchal Community in Barbara Kingsolver's The Bean Trees and Pigs in Heaven." *Southern Studies* (1994) 5.1-2: 155–64.

Ryan, Maureen. "Barbara Kingsolver's Lowfat Fiction." *Journal of American Culture* (winter 1995) 18.4: 77–83.

Discussion Questions

1. What makes Taylor Greer different from her peers in Pittman, Kentucky? Why is she "the one to get away"?
2. Discuss the various ways in which motherhood is depicted in the novel. What characteristics are echoed throughout each depiction? How does each relationship serve to characterize Taylor's relationship with Turtle?
3. Compare and contrast the community of Pittman, Kentucky and the community in Tucson that Taylor becomes a part of.
4. Examine the ways in which setting influences character in each of the three locations throughout the novel: Pittman, Kentucky; the Cherokee Nation in Oklahoma; and Tucson, Arizona.
5. Discuss the repetition of religious language throughout the novel. What does such language reveal about the author's attitude towards religion?
6. Locate and discuss the various scenes in which imagery of plants and animals occur in the text.
7. Discuss the "lessons" Taylor learns about the political situation that forces Estevan and Esperanza to become refugees. How do these lessons inform her perspective and shape her understanding of her world and herself?
8. Compare and contrast the depiction of men and women in the novel.
9. Discuss your reaction to Taylor's decision to employ fraud in order to adopt Turtle. What other choices do you think she had?
10. Discuss your reaction to the depiction of Turtle. Is her characterization realistic? Do you believe she has, or will, fully recover from her neglect and abuse?

Essay Ideas

1. Write an essay in which you examine the role of free will and self-determination in the novel.
2. Many of the characters in "The Bean Trees" are refugees of some kind. Write an essay examining the different ways various characters, including Taylor, might be considered refugees, and how this depiction reinforces underlying themes in the novel.
3. Analyze the use of nature imagery in the novel and explain how it expands on and reinforces the underlying themes in the novel.
4. Analyze how setting is developed in the novel and how it relates to the journey construction of the novel.
5. Research Bildungsroman and explain in what ways "The Bean Trees" fits into this definition.

The Bell Jar

by Sylvia Plath

Content Synopsis

"The Bell Jar" was first published in London under the pseudonym Victoria Lucas, just before Plath's suicide in February 1963. This short novel charts the mental breakdown and recovery of college student Esther Greenwood, and draws on Plath's own experience with depression, suicide, and psychiatric treatment in the early 1950s. Although Plath allegedly believed "The Bell Jar" was a "pot boiler," a money-making venture with little literary merit (214), the book initially met with positive reviews. When reissued under Plath's name—in Britain in 1966, in America in 1971—it was inevitably compared with her poetry, but also earned favorable comparisons with the writing of J. D. Salinger. Literary criticism has since explored the feminist, psychoanalytical, and cultural contexts of the novel, and has drawn productive conclusions from its autobiographical import.

"The Bell Jar" is narrated retrospectively, by an older Esther remembering her past. Her story begins in New York City, where Esther Greenwood holds a student editorship for a ladies magazine (similar to the editorship Plath held at "Mademoiselle" in 1953). It is the summer when the Rosenbergs, members of the Communist party, were tried, convicted, and executed for passing nuclear weapons secrets to the Soviet Union. The anxieties of McCarthyite America and the Cold War have seeped into Esther's consciousness.

She is preoccupied with the Rosenbergs' death by electrocution. In a foreshadowing of her own electroshock therapy, she tells us: "I couldn't help wondering what it would be like, being burned alive all along your nerves. I thought it must be the worst thing in the world" (1). The narrative continues in the first-person, imitating journal entries and punctuated by flashbacks and newspaper headings. This structure allows for a fragmented chronology that reflects Esther's unstable hold on reality. Additionally, the text's retrospective viewpoint also allows for a double-voiced, ironic narrative style: in hindsight, Esther can find humor in her younger self. The result is a wry—and sometimes deliberately disturbing—mix of trauma and comedy, naïveté, and self-awareness.

In New York, Esther encounters a world very different from her native small-town in Massachusetts. She admits to feeling out of place in the sophisticated publishing world, and at odds with the more knowing and polished college women also working at the magazine. Esther learns to cope by putting on a mask of confidence. She flings herself into new situations, using false names and forced nonchalance to conceal her lack of experience. Yet, she increasingly finds that the glamour of the world around her is also a mask; when it falls, she finds nothing meaningful beneath. Dates end with lonely walks home, or in disaster. At a country club dance on her last evening in

New York, Esther is introduced to Marco. They go outside, where this "woman-hater" (87) pushes Esther to the ground and tears her clothes half-off. She only escapes being raped by hitting him in the nose. An earlier night is ruined when Esther's roommate and role model, the seemingly mature Doreen, falls into a disappointing drunken stupor. With every new encounter, the glossy promise of New York fades to reveal a series of trite and grubby truths.

The disillusionment that Esther feels soon extends to herself. The magazine's editor, the dynamic "Jay Cee," demands Esther's ambition, but Esther realizes she lacks real drive. She begins to see her college achievements as minor and fraudulent. When Jay Cee asks her what she wants to do with her life, Esther admits she does not know, surprising herself: "I felt a deep shock, hearing myself say that, because the minute I said it, I knew it was true" (27). Later, she envisions her career options as figs on a tree, and sees herself "starving" as the figs begin "to wrinkle and go black" because she cannot choose one (62–63). Esther fills this emotional void with food, stuffing herself with expensive dinners and rich desserts. The foodstuffs of the city, however, are as deceptive as its other luxuries, and leave Esther sick with food poisoning.

A series of flashbacks provides some background to these anxieties. Esther recalls Yale student and erstwhile boyfriend Buddy Willard. Over a series of dates, Esther realizes that the actual Buddy fails to live up to her romantic vision. When he reveals to her that he has slept with a waitress, she is devastated to discover that his sexual innocence has been a pretense. As Buddy becomes more attached to her, hinting at engagement, Esther feels increasingly betrayed and oppressed by his attentions. A series of comments deriding her poetic ambitions and hinting at women's place in the domestic sphere infuriate her. She begins to long for sexual experience with other men, not only to sate her own curiosity but also to gain equal footing with Buddy. When Buddy falls ill with tuberculosis, an incident at his treatment center confirms her feelings of mistrust and dislike toward Buddy. Skiing down a hill, Esther feels elation and freedom: "I thought, 'This is what it means to be happy'" (79). She falls, however, and breaks her leg. Her sudden loss of freedom results in a "queer, satisfied expression" on Buddy's face. Someone comments that "You were doing fine […] until that man stepped in your path" (80). The person is referring to the fact that Esther crashed into someone on the slope, but the comment suddenly takes on a double meaning: Esther was "doing fine" until Buddy came into her life.

At the end of her editorship, Esther learns she has been rejected from a summer writing course at Harvard. Instead of enrolling in a different class, she returns to her home in Massachusetts for the summer. In these months before beginning her senior year at college, Esther finds herself surrounded by mothers and housewives. These domestic roles are exactly the ones Buddy envisioned for her, and Esther finds them stifling. Without intellectual distractions, and already shaken by the events of New York, Esther slowly succumbs to the oppression of suburbia and her own sense of failure. She worries about her career and her upcoming senior thesis, and she feels guilty about not wanting to marry Buddy. She becomes depressed, trapped in a state she later describes as being under a glass bell jar, which is used in laboratory experiments to cover and seal materials in a vacuum: "where I sat … I would be sitting under the same glass bell jar, stewing in my own sour air" (152). She is sent to Doctor Gordon, who prescribes shock treatments. These leave Esther traumatized, and fail to prevent thoughts of suicide. She spends some time envisioning different ways of killing herself—much in the same way she tried on different roles in New York. Finally, after visiting her father's grave, she decides on a method. She steals her mother's sleeping pills, climbs into an unused section of the family basement, and swallows the pills.

Esther's suicide attempt is unsuccessful, though it leaves her physically as well as emotionally damaged: her sight is temporarily affected by the overdose, she is weak, and her depression has not abated. She wakes up in her home town hospital, but is soon transferred to the psychiatric ward of a larger city hospital. However, Esther refuses to respond to therapy. Her benefactress, the novelist who had partly funded her college fees, insists on paying for Esther's treatment at a private facility. There, Esther slowly opens up to the more sensitive (and female) Doctor Nolan. When Joan, a fellow college student, arrives for treatment, Esther begins to see herself from a new perspective; her desire to distance herself from Joan mirrors her desire to move beyond her own depressed state. Under Doctor Nolan's care, and after painless, effective electroshock therapy, Esther is allowed to leave the ward from time to time. On one of these outings, she finally achieves the goal of losing her virginity. The result is a rare hemorrhage that lands Esther in the emergency room. While this experience might have frightened and disturbed the earlier Esther, she is now able to react to it—along with Joan's unexpected suicide—calmly and rationally. These outcomes signify Esther's new emotional strength and symbolize rites of passage rather than traumatic setbacks. The story ends soon after, as Esther is called to the doctors' board meeting, where, it is implied, she will be told her treatment is complete.

Historical Context

As Linda Wagner-Martin notes, "'The Bell Jar' speaks to [Plath's] concern with women's choices, but its title speaks as well to the even more general stifling political atmosphere than the one that surrounds Esther Greenwood" (Wagner-Martin, 5). Esther's concern about the electrocution of the Rosenbergs—executed in 1951 for allegedly sharing nuclear secrets with the Soviet Union—belies a wider concern about oppression that pervades the novel. Esther's growing sense that everyone is an enemy, and especially her paranoia during her breakdown and treatment, mimic the paranoia stemming from post-war tensions between America and Russia. One effect of this Cold War, on the domestic front, was a campaign to expose Communist spies working in the United States. Senator Joseph McCarthy and The House Committee on Un-American Activities investigated and accused government officials, actors, writers, and intellectuals of Communists leanings. The Rosenberg execution, which forms an apt parallel to Esther's personal situation, helped prompt the McCarthyite hysteria that was part of a suffocating bell jar over America as well as Esther and Plath.

Societal Context

Esther's bitterness about the difficulties women face reflects a growing feminist consciousness in America, one that would burgeon into the full-blown women's movements of later decades. In her book "The Feminine Mystique" (1963), Betty Friedan analyzed questionnaires sent to her 1942 class from Smith College, Plath's alma mater. Her book argues that during the post-war period, marriage and motherhood were falsely equated with happiness and self-worth. Friedan's survey, however, showed that housewives were actually unhappy, and that their sense of self had been replaced by a series of undervalued domestic roles. Esther experiences exactly the same kind of unease; her repetitive thought, "I am I am I am," for instance, suggests a woman struggling to maintain a sense of self as she tries to choose between the incompatible roles of housewife and career woman. The run-on phrase "I am," however, also turns into the question, "Am I?" This decline of self-assertiveness into self-doubt is the theme of the novel, but it is also a theme of women's lives in mid-20th century America.

Religious Context

Religion—or rather the lapse of religion—is part of the bleak landscape of Esther's breakdown and reflects the increasingly secular society of post-war New England. Her father was a Lutheran-turned-atheist, her mother a Catholic-turned-Methodist. Esther herself had converted from a Methodist to a Unitarian after her father's death. (Sylvia Plath was raised as a Unitarian). During the summer of her breakdown, she ponders these changes and considers joining the Catholic Church, hoping the priests will forgive her for her sinful thoughts. These different faiths, however, become meaningless to Esther; they are like the outfits, career choices, or means of suicide she tries on, only to find nothing fits. In the case of spiritual faith, nothing offers fulfillment to Esther. "I didn't believe in life after death or the virgin birth or the Inquisition," she tells us, "or anything" (134). Paranoid, but at the same time aware of the world's hypocrisy, she also fears that priests are gossips. As is frequently the case with Esther, she is adept at dismissing any source of guidance, including religion.

Scientific & Technological Context

Psychiatric science and treatment are prevalent themes in The Bell Jar, which takes as its title a scientific metaphor: a glass "bell jar" is used to cover and protect laboratory materials. Significantly, a bell jar also allows objects to remain in view. In describing herself as being trapped under a bell jar, Esther suggests that she is both confined by her situation and on display to the probing, objectifying eyes of her doctors. Although some of Esther's paranoia about psychiatrics stems from her condition, her fears have been justified by painful shock treatments at the hands of Doctor Gordon. The passages in the novel that address the science and technology of psychiatric medicine portray a mechanical clinical world: impersonal doctors, cold white hospitals, and the terrifying specter of invasive machinery.

Shock treatments are an essential part of Esther's therapy and recovery. Electric shock therapy was devised by Ugo Cerletti, an Italian neurologist, in the 1930s. Cerletti observed that hogs going to slaughter were administered electric shocks, and that this rendered them unconscious without killing them. Cerletti applied a similar treatment to his own psychiatric patients, and found that it calmed those with violent or disorderly behavior. In America in the 1930s and 40s, shock treatments were used as a treatment for schizophrenia, and later for a range of less specific problems, such as depression. The treatment involves transmitting electric shocks to the patient's brain, which causes unconsciousness and involuntary convulsions. Initially, patients were not anesthetized before treatment, and these convulsions caused bruising and broken bones. Combined with the use of shock treatments as a disciplinary procedure at psychiatric hospitals, the treatment gained a negative reputation. As medication became the preferred treatment for psychiatric problems, electric shock therapy became less common, and it has been discounted as a treatment for schizophrenia. However, electric shock therapy is still sometimes used to manage severe depression in cases where medication is not effective.

Esther's ordeal reflects a society deeply interested in psychology and invested in probing and curing emotional traumas. Yet, as Pat Robertson has pointed out, Esther's psychological diagnosis is intertwined with contemporary views about women's roles: "Her social maturity as a 'hatted and heeled' mademoiselle is the sign of her psychic maturity as a developmentally 'whole' and medically 'well' citizen-patient of therapeutic culture" (Robertson 6). It is Esther's inability to conform to gender norms that triggers her breakdown. And it is finally under the care of a more sensitive female doctor, who urges Esther to obtain birth control for instance, that she is able to thrive as a truly independent and mature adult woman.

Biographical Context

Sylvia Plath was born in 1932 in Massachusetts to an Austrian-American mother and a German father. When Plath was eight, her father died during a leg amputation, and the family moved from Winthrop to Wellesley, Massachusetts. Although Plath went on to become a strong student and active writer, she continued to be haunted by her father's death. While attending Smith College, she won the "Mademoiselle" fiction contest and was selected to work as a student guest editor at the magazine. In the summer of 1953, she went to New York City for this purpose, but returned depressed. She attempted suicide at her home and was hospitalized, where she underwent psychiatric treatment. These events formed the basis for the story of "The Bell Jar."

After recovering, Plath returned to a successful undergraduate career at Smith, eventually winning a Fulbright scholarship to study at Cambridge in 1955. There, she met the poet Ted Hughes, whom she married in 1956. In 1959, after two years teaching and writing in Massachusetts, the pair moved back to London where Plath gave birth to a daughter, Frieda, and published her first collection of poetry, "The Colossus." A year later, the family moved to Devon, where Plath had a second child, Nicolas. Due

in part to Hughes's affair with Assia Wevill, the marriage unraveled. After a separation in 1962, Plath and the children moved back to London. During this time, "The Bell Jar" was published under the pseudonym Victoria Lucas, and Plath completed the poems that would later comprise her famous collection, "Ariel" (1965). Despite this literary productivity, Plath committed suicide in February 1963.

After her death, Plath's poems were collected in "Ariel" and in the 1971 volumes "Winter Trees" and "Crossing the Water." Hughes edited the "Collected Poems" in 1981, which earned Plath the Pulitzer Prize. "Johnny Panic and the Bible of Dreams," a collection of short prose, was published in 1980.

Jennifer Dunn

Works Cited

Bronfen, Elisabeth. *Sylvia Plath.* Plymouth: Northcote, 1998.

Friedan, Betty. *The Feminine Mystique.* New York: Norton, 1963.

McPherson, Pat. *Reflecting on The Bell Jar.* New York: Routledge, 1991.

Plath, Sylvia. *The Bell Jar.* New York: Bantam, 1981 (1963).

Rose, Jacqueline. *The Haunting of Sylvia Plath.* London: Virago, 1991.

Wagner-Martin, Linda. *The Bell Jar: a Novel of the Fifties.* New York: Twayne, 1992.

For Further Study

Alvarez, A. *The Savage God: A Study of Suicide.* Harmondsworth: Penguin, 1974.

Gilbert, Sandra M. and Susan Gubar. *The Madwoman in the Attic: The Woman Writer and the Nineteenth-Century Literary Imagination.* New Haven: Yale UP, 1979.

_____ *No Man's Land: The Place of the Woman Writer in the Twentieth Century.* New Haven: Yale UP, 1994.

Huf, Linda. *A Portrait of the Artist as a Young Woman: The Writer as Heroine in American Literature.* New York: Ungar, 1983.

Schwartz, Murray M. and Christopher Bollas. "The Absence at the Centre: Sylvia Plath and Suicide." *Sylvia Plath: New Views on the Poetry,* ed. Gary Lane. Baltimore: Johns Hopkins UP, 1979. 179–292.

Wagner-Martin, Linda, ed. *Critical Essays on Sylvia Plath.* Boston: G. K. Hall, 1984.

Discussion Questions

1. What role do clothes play in the narrative? Why does Esther often describe her outfits, and why does she get rid of her "city" clothes by throwing them off a building?

2. Why does Esther seek out her father's grave? Why is her father not mentioned earlier in the narrative? After finding the grave, why does Esther suddenly know how she will kill herself?

3. How do you interpret the novel's conclusion? Why is the text open-ended, rather than providing definitive closure to Esther's ordeal?

4. What is the significance of Esther obtaining birth control?

5. Esther's life is very similar to that of Sylvia Plath at age twenty. Is "The Bell Jar" fiction or autobiography? To what extent do these genres overlap, and what bearing does that overlap have on artistic merit or historical accuracy?

6. Compare the different female role models in the text. How does Esther react to, and what does she learn from, each one? (Consider Jay Cee, her mother, Doctor Nolan, Mrs. Willard, and Joan, for example.)

7. Discuss the factors involved in Esther's breakdown. Is her suicide attempt inevitable, or a product of her time? Do you think other women suffer the same anxieties Esther does, or are budding artists a special case?

8. Do Esther's problems, particularly her difficulty with female identity, apply to today's world?

9. How does this novel compare to Plath's poetry? Are there consistent themes or tones? Does the poetry present a different mindset-a more developed one, for instance-than "The Bell Jar" does?

10. Compare "The Bell Jar" to other coming-of-age texts, both from the same and different time periods. How are these novels different from each other?

Essay Ideas

1. Compare "The Bell Jar" to "The Catcher in the Rye." How does gender play a role in the differences between the two texts?

2. Examine the novel's structure and style and argue how they help convey the story's themes.

3. Analyze "The Bell Jar's" relationship to the bildungsroman.

4. Discuss the motif of doubles in the narrative.

5. Discuss Esther's relationship with her mother and argue how it relates to her sense of self-hood throughout the novel.

Toni Morrison is a Nobel Prize and Pulitzer Prize-winning American novelist. Her novels are known for their epic themes, vivid dialogue, and detailed black characters; four of them are included in this volume: *The Bell Jar; The Bluest Eye; Sula;* and *Tar Baby*. Photo: National Portrait Gallery, Smithsonian Institution; gift of Helen Marcus©1978 Helen Marcus.

Beloved

by Toni Morrison

Content Synopsis

Because this story is told in a non-chronological fashion, some overview is necessary before launching into a more specific summary: Set in 1873, "Beloved" tells the story of a slave named Sethe, who escaped from Sweet Home Plantation in Kentucky in 1855. Because of some problems with the escape plan which resulted in her husband Halle not showing up at the arranged location, Sethe ends up sending her three children on ahead to her mother-in-law, Baby Suggs, who is living in a free community in Ohio. Sethe remains unable to locate Halle, and so she makes the difficult journey to freedom alone. On the way, Sethe gives birth, with the help of a run-away white girl, to her daughter Denver.

When the novel opens, eighteen years have passed since Sethe escaped from Sweet Home. Sethe and Denver now live at Baby Suggs' home, alone except for the company of the ghost of Sethe's elder daughter who died shortly after Sethe's arrival in Ohio. Sethe's other two children ran away when they became teenagers, and Baby Suggs had passed away eight years before. Into this situation walks Paul D., who had also been a slave at Sweet Home Plantation. Sethe has not seen him since those fateful days in which their carefully-laid escape plans crumbled around them eighteen years earlier. The two start to reminisce, with Sethe soon revealing to Paul D. that shortly before she escaped, two young men at Sweet Home had held her down and stolen the milk from her breasts and that she was beaten for reporting this to her mistress. When she shows Paul D. the "chokeberry tree" of scars on her back, he holds her breasts and kisses the scars, an action which antagonizes the baby ghost. Paul D. screams at the spirit, demanding that it let Sethe be. For the first time in many years, the house is completely still. Paul D. decides to stay awhile and look for work in town, a fact which makes Sethe happy but disturbs Denver, who is not pleased to have her mother's attention diverted.

To try to win Denver over, Paul D. takes Sethe and Denver to a carnival where they all enjoy themselves a great deal. When they return to their home, they are surprised to find a figure on the front porch. The young woman, who tells them her name is Beloved, seems ill. Denver nurses her back to health, and she stays on. Her odd questions— "Where your diamonds?" "Your woman she never fix up your hair?" and "Tell me your earrings" (63)—get Sethe talking about her past. She talks about her marriage to Halle and the crystal earring Mrs. Garner gave her to mark the occasion. Sethe also tells about her own mother, whom she did not know really well; a woman named Nan, whose job it was to care for the slave children, had raised Sethe. Sethe did know, however, that her mother had been branded, that she had had other children but had disposed of them in some fashion, and that she had ultimately been hanged.

Although Sethe, and especially Denver, are growing attached to Beloved, Paul D. senses something strange and menacing about her. In a confrontation with Sethe over this very issue, Paul D. winds up revealing to Sethe that he knows why Halle did not show up at the arranged location for the escape. He tells Sethe that Halle must have seen the men at Sweet Home stealing the milk from her breasts, because the last time Paul D. had seen him, Halle seemed to have lost his mind; he was sitting near the churn with butter all over his face. Paul D. had not known what prompted this apparent breakdown until Sethe revealed the story about the milk. When Sethe expresses rage that Halle could have watched that scene without helping her, Paul D. responds: "A man ain't a goddamn ax. Chopping, hacking, busting every goddamn minute of the day. Things get to him. Things he can't chop down because they're inside" (69). Paul D. further reveals that he could not speak to Halle when he saw him at the butter churn because of the iron bit in his mouth. He finds himself telling Sethe that the worst part of that experience for him was realizing that even the plantation's roosters were freer, and more in control of their identities and destinies, than he was. But Paul D. can only reveal so much at once; he decides to "keep the rest where it belonged: in that tobacco tin buried in his chest where a red heart used to be" (73). "The rest" includes memories of the time shortly after the failed escape from Sweet Home, time spent in a prison camp in which the men lived in pits in the ground and were routinely sexually abused by the guards.

Paul D. begins to feel as though Beloved is slowly moving him out of Sethe's home, first to the downstairs rocker, then to Baby Suggs' room, the storeroom, and finally out to the cold room. Beloved seduces Paul D., and he feels as though she has opened the "tobacco tin" in his heart in which he keeps all of his secrets and pain. To try to

gain some control over the situation and reconnect with Sethe, Paul D. tells her that he wants to make a baby with her. Soon, though, something else comes between them. Stamp Paid, who had helped Sethe and a new-born Denver cross the river to freedom, shows Paul D. a newspaper article which reported that, twenty-eight days after her arrival in Ohio, Sethe's owner, "schoolteacher," had come to take her and her children back into slavery. When Sethe saw him coming, she grabbed her children and ran into the tool shed, intending to kill them before they could be claimed by schoolteacher. She managed to kill her oldest daughter before she was stopped and taken to jail. When Paul D. asks Sethe about this story, hoping that she will say that it was all some kind of mistake, Sethe admits to its truth and explains to Paul D. that she had to do what she did because she could not allow her children to live in slavery. She had to put them in a safe place, even if it was out of this world entirely. At this, Paul D. tells Sethe her love is "too thick," and, after uttering a final condemnation—"You got two feet, Sethe, not four" (165)—Paul D. leaves without even a good-bye.

After Paul D's departure, Sethe comes to the overwhelming realization that Beloved is actually the daughter she killed eighteen years ago, the manifestation or incarnation of the baby ghost that Paul D. had banished from the house. Sethe begins to try to make up for the lost time and to explain to Beloved the reasons behind her decision to murder her children. As Sethe tries to placate Beloved, Beloved becomes ever-more demanding. Denver watches, ignored by the both of them, as Sethe becomes thinner and thinner and Beloved grows bigger until she looks as though she will give birth to a baby of her own. Denver realizes that she must get help. She gets a job with the Bodwins— a white couple who had helped Baby Suggs and Sethe years before—and confides in Janey, who also works there, about her mother's trouble. The women of the community march over to house to exorcise the ghost. They still believed that Sethe had been proud and haughty, but they believed even more strongly that no one deserved to have the past become flesh and attack them. The women gather in front of the house to pray and sing. Just then, Mr. Bodwin drives up to pick up Denver for work, and Sethe, flashing back to that day eighteen years ago, believes that it is schoolteacher come to take her and her children away. Sethe rushes at him with an ice pick but Denver and the other women stop her in time. The women's singing and praying seems to have vanquished Beloved; after the commotion settles down, she is no where to be seen.

Denver continues to work and to reintegrate herself into the community that Sethe had abandoned so long ago. Paul D. returns to care for Sethe, who is still suffering from the second loss of her baby girl.

Historical Context

"Beloved" is set near Cincinnati, Ohio in 1873, ten years after the Emancipation Proclamation. It incorporates flashbacks and memories, however, dating back twenty years, to a time when slavery was still legal in the United States. During this period in history, the underground railroad was in full operation; free blacks, former slaves, and white abolitionists expended much effort and took great risks to help slaves escape to freedom. This type of network—including Stamp Paid, Ella, and the Bodwins—helps Sethe and her children escape in "Beloved."

The Fugitive Slave Act of 1850 interfered with the success of the underground since it "required Americans to aid in the apprehension of fugitives" and fined them if they "refused or thwarted the recovery of runaways" (Medford 6). In Morrison's text, it was this law that allowed schoolteacher to locate Sethe and attempt to take her back to the plantation. The prospect of having one's hard-won freedom yanked out from under him could be psychologically shattering. Morrison's fictional

imagining of what might happen in such a situation is in fact based on an 1855 newspaper article published in the American Baptist and titled "A Visit to the Slave Mother Who Killed Her Child," which told the story of a runaway slave named Margaret Garner who killed her child so that it would not be returned to slavery.

Societal Context

The Emancipation Proclamation, issued on January 1, 1863, freed slaves in confederate states, although they still had to escape their masters to obtain freedom. With the end of the Civil War on April 9, 1865 and the passage of the Thirteenth Amendment, which proclaimed that "[n]either slavery nor involuntary servitude…shall exist within the United States, or any place subject to their jurisdiction," slavery was finally outlawed throughout the United States (Williams 80). It took the Fourteenth and Fifteenth Amendments, passed in 1868 and 1870 respectively, to recognize blacks as citizens of the United States and give them the right to vote.

"Beloved" illustrates the backlash against this progression toward racial equality in America:

"Eighteen seventy-four and whitefolks were still on the loose. Whole towns wiped clean of Negroes; eighty-seven lynchings in one year alone in Kentucky; four colored schools burned to the ground; grown men whipped like children; children whipped like adults; black women raped by the crew; property taken, necks broken" (180).

The novel also depicts the tight community that developed in order to weather this storm. Stamp Paid reiterates the community's pledge to take care of one another when he discovers that Paul D. has been sleeping in the church. He explains to Paul D. that all a person has to do is ask for a place to stay and it will be granted, whether or not that person can pay. The solidarity is further evidenced in the women's exorcism of Beloved, despite the fact that they disapprove of Sethe and her actions.

Religious Context

Though non-Christian forms of worship were largely forbidden to slaves, slave narratives record that they did find ways to gather and pray; one narrative recounts that white people "never 'lowed us slaves to go to church but they have big holes in the fields they gits down in and prays. They do it that way 'cause the white folks didn't want them to pray. They used to pray for freedom" (qtd in Robinson 409). Some masters wanted to indoctrinate their slaves into a spiritual belief system that would make them more inclined to be docile and obedient; they tried to convert their slaves to Christianity, and to teach them that slavery was a Godly institution. These attempts resulted in genuine conversion for some, and the incorporation of aspects of Christianity into traditional spiritual belief systems for others. According to Larry Murphy, after emancipation, "[t]he newly freed men and women of the South took great delight in the concept of national black religious organizations that matched those of the ruling white class. To affiliate with such organizations was an exciting, deeply satisfying prospect. And so emancipated blacks left the 'invisible institution' as well as the established white-led denominational churches and joined these black faith communities" (34).

Morrison's "Beloved" reflects this tendency for freed slaves to join black churches, as it mentions that Sethe's mother-in-law Baby Suggs—an "uncalled, unrobed, unanointed" preacher who simply felt compelled to open her heart to her community—preached to Christian churches in the winter time. But the novel also reveals the powerful, non-denominational, non-doctrinal gatherings that were closer akin to traditional African worship. When the "warm weather came, Baby Suggs, holy, followed by every black man, woman and child who could make it through, took her great heart to the Clearing—a wide-open place that cut deep in the woods anybody knew for what at the end of a path known only to deer and whoever cleared the land in the first place" (88). In this place, reminiscent of the secret places in which slaves would gather in secret to pray, Baby Suggs did not tell her listeners "to clean up their lives or to go and sin no more. She did not tell them they were the blessed of the earth, its inheriting meek or its glorybound poor. She told them that the only grace they could have was the grace they could imagine. That if they could not see it, they would not have it" (88). Baby Suggs affirmed the humanity of her community, giving them the message they needed most—that they should love themselves and their bodies and insist upon their value—and she guided them as they sang, danced, and cried together, releasing pent-up emotions and trauma and cementing the communal ties necessary to sustain them.

Scientific & Technological Context

In the seventeenth and eighteenth centuries, "scientific" theories based on anatomy were used to justify and rationalize the enslavement of African peoples. In "Natural History of the Negro Race" (1837), J. H. Guenebault "listed 47 different peculiarities of the Negro which characterized his anatomy from that of the white man" (Johnson and Bond 333). Karl Vogt, a German scientist (1817–1895), "found a remarkable resemblance between the ape and the Negro 'especially with reference to the development of the temporal lobe," although, unfortunately, he had seen but one Negro brain" (Johnson and Bond 330). Count Arthur de Gobineau synthesized much of the contemporary thinking and research in a famous work titled "An Essay on The Inequality of the Human Races" (1855) which held that only one race "was pure and alone fitted to bear the torch of civilization." Gobineau's reasoning was used in America by proponents of slavery who "found in his doctrines and 'evidence' a forceful and complete justification of the institution" (Johnson and Bond 329).

Morrison's "Beloved" depicts this type of scientific research and the behavior and attitudes that accompany it. Schoolteacher and his pupils gather scientific data, such as measurements of their bodies, on the slaves at Sweet Home. In addition, Sethe overhears schoolteacher instructing the pupils to record her characteristics in a chart with "human" on one side and "animal" on the other. The men who conduct this "research" on the slaves at Sweet Home treat them in a cruel manner; these are the men who drink the milk from Sethe's breast and beat her for reporting it even though she is pregnant with a baby who is nearly full-term. For Sethe, even worse than all this cruelty was the dehumanizing data collection. In fact, perhaps her most powerful reason for her decision to kill her children is her need to ensure that no one recorded their characteristics on the "animal" side of the paper.

Biographical Context

Morrison's novel "Beloved" is based on the true story of a fugitive slave named Margaret Garner who killed her child rather than see her taken back into a life of slavery. What was most significant to Morrison about this story was Garner's unshakable belief in the rightness of her actions. Morrison revealed that the story seemed to possess "a despair quite new to me but so deep it had no passion at all and elicited no tears" (qtd. in Century 74). Morrison decided not to learn too much about Garner's life, preferring to use the incident as a springboard for her imaginative exploration, but that is not to say that Morrison's research ended with this one article on Garner. Morrison conducted extensive research into slavery, traveling to Brazil in order to learn about implements used to punish slaves. For Morrison, the fact that the implements "were not restraining tools, like in the torture chamber," but were designed instead to be worn in public,

while the slave continued to work, indicated that "humiliation was the key to what the experience was like" (qtd. in Century 77). The understanding that Morrison achieved through her imagination combined with rigorous research comes through in Paul D.'s memory of the humiliation he felt as a result of the bit; he confesses to Sethe that the worst part of wearing it was "[w]alking past the roosters looking at them look at me" (71).

Morrison expected "Beloved" to be the least read of her novels because "it is about something that the characters don't want to remember, I don't want to remember, black people don't want to remember, white people don't want to remember. I mean, it's national amnesia" (qtd. in Bowers 43). Despite these misgivings, "Beloved" became a best-seller, and Morrison was awarded both the Pulitzer Prize for fiction and the Robert F. Kennedy Award for the novel in 1988.

Kim Becnel

Works Cited

Bloom, Harold, ed. *Toni Morrison's Beloved: Bloom's Notes.* Contemporary Literary Views Ser. New York: Chelsea, 1999.

Century, Douglas. *Toni Morrison (Black Americans Of Achievement).* New York: Chelsea, 1994.

Johnson, Charles S. and Horace M. Bond. "The Investigation of Racial Differences Prior to 1910." *The Journal of Negro Education* 3.3 (1934): 328–339.

Medford, Edna Greene. "Imagined Promises, Bitter Realities: African Americans and the Meaning of the Emancipation Proclamation." *The Emancipation Proclamation.* Baton Rouge: Louisiana State UP, 2006. 1–47.

Morrison, Toni. *Beloved.* New York: Penguin, 1987.

Murphy, Larry G. "African-American Faith in America." *Faith in America Series.* New York: Facts on File, 2003.

Oakes, James. *Slavery and Freedom: An Interpretation of the Old South.* New York: Alfred A. Knopf, 1990.

Robinson, Beverly J. "Faith Is the Key and Prayer Unlocks the Door: Prayer in African American Life." *The Journal of American Folklore* 110.438 (1997): 408–414.

Williams, Frank J. "'Doing Less' and 'Doing More': The President and the Proclamation—Legally, Militarily, and Politically." *The Emancipation Proclamation.* Baton Rouge: Louisiana State UP, 2006. 48–82.

Discussion Questions

1. Why do you think Denver is so devoted to Beloved?
2. Why do you think Baby Suggs gave up preaching? Why did she decide to focus on color during the last weeks of her life?
3. Why is Sethe so angry when she learns about what happened to Halle? And why do you think that Paul D. defends him?
4. Analyze the narration throughout the novel. Who tells which parts of the story, and why is this significant?
5. What do you make of the Bodwins? What motivates them to help slaves and former slaves? What is the significance of the slave figurine they use to keep money in?
6. Why do you think it is that the thing that disturbs Sethe the most about her experiences in slavery, the thing she is most afraid of happening to her children, is having her "human and animal" characteristics recorded in a chart?
7. Why do you think Morrison chooses to use the particular structure she does in this novel, presenting the story in bits and pieces instead of telling it in straight, chronological fashion? Why do you think Morrison elected to divide the novel into three "Books"?
8. What kind of commentary is the novel making about motherhood in slavery? What kind of mothering was possible? How did this mothering or lack of mothering affect the community?
9. Why do you think that Morrison has Beloved also represent slaves on the middle passage?
10. Would you say that Sethe is better or worse off at the end of the novel than she was at its start? Has she experienced a necessary healing? If so, what prompts it?

Essay Ideas

1. What stance does the novel seem to take toward Sethe's decision to kill her children? How are we encouraged to perceive this decision? How does Sethe herself feel about what she has done? Baby Suggs? What other infanticides are mentioned in the novel? Do they influence our perception of Sethe's decision?
2. What kind of commentary is the novel making about the past and its effects on our lives?
3. Can we protect others from the past, as Sethe tries to do with Denver, by keeping silent? How do Sethe and Paul D.'s sharing memories affect them?
4. Paul D. eventually begins to wonder just how much difference there really was between Garner's version of slavery and schoolteacher's. What exactly does Paul D. mean?
5. Analyze and evaluate the character Amy Denver. What is her symbolic or thematic function in the novel?
6. Paul D. thinks at one point: "not to need permission for desire—well now, that was freedom" (162). Explain in detail the conception(s) of freedom presented in the novel.

President Barack Obama talking with Toni Morrison in the Blue Room on the White House upon her receiving the Presidential Medal of Freedom, May 29, 2012. Four of Morrison's novels are included in this volume. Photo: Official White House Photo by Pete Souza.

The Bluest Eye

by Toni Morrison

Content Synopsis

"The Bluest Eye" opens by presenting the reader with three versions of a white child's primer, the first written in sentences; the second without punctuation; the third a block of the same text with no spaces distinguishing the words. The novel is divided into four parts to mark the turn of the seasons. It begins with events in autumn and works backwards through the three seasons leading up to these events. Introducing "Autumn" is a first-person voice: it is fall of 1941 and a girl called Pecola is having her father's baby. The narrator and her sister are so preoccupied with Pecola's pregnancy that they test their own generative powers. However, that autumn the marigolds they have planted do not grow. The voice tells us that Pecola is still alive but that both her baby and Cholly Breedlove, their father, are dead. In "Autumn" the narrative voice reveals itself as that of a young girl, Claudia MacTeer. She and her sister Frieda live in Lorain, Ohio with their parents. A man named Mr. Henry rooms with the family. Another arrival joins the house that autumn: Pecola. Her father Cholly Breedlove has burned down their house and is in jail. The MacTeers will look after Pecola for a few days. She gets on well with Claudia and Frieda, who gives her a Shirley Temple cup. Frieda and Pecola admire Shirley Temple but Claudia hates her "because she danced with Bojangles, who was my friend, my uncle, my daddy" ("Bluest Eye" 13 Morrison's italics). Claudia is repulsed by the blue-eyed Baby Dolls she receives for Christmas and dismembers them. Her destruction of white dolls springs from her desire to destroy white girls who draw the admiration of passers-by on the street. One day Pecola starts her period and Frieda tells her that she can now have a baby.

The next part of "Autumn" introduces us to an abandoned store in Ohio, once the home of Cholly Breedlove, his wife, his son and daughter. The house's furniture evokes no memories and those who live there feel no attachment to the house and its contents. Mrs. Breedlove and her children have a "unique" ugliness which comes from their "conviction" that they are ugly (28). Cholly and his wife argue and have physical fights, often fueled by Cholly's drinking. When Cholly was very young some white men caught him engaging in sex with a young girl. They shone a flashlight on his behind and ordered him to finish. Memories of the incident "stir him into flights of depravity" (32). Isolated at school because of her "ugliness," Pecola prays each night for the beautiful blue eyes of the children in the white primers. She visits the local store to buy sweets. She sees distaste in the storekeeper's eyes. She visits the three whores who live in the apartment above her father's storefront. The women talk freely in front of Pecola. Listening to their stories about men, she wonders what love feels like and recalls that her father's moans in the dark are met only by her mother's silence.

Claudia's voice opens "Winter." A new girl, Maureen Peal, has arrived at school. She is a "high-yellow dream child … as rich as the richest white girl" (47). Maureen enchants teachers and students alike. Frieda and Claudia try to hate her but one day she walks home with them. They come across Pecola, surrounded by bullying boys, fueled by "contempt for their own blackness" (50). They chant that Pecola's father walks around naked. Frieda strikes one of the boys with her book. When the boys see Maureen, they are reluctant to fight back. The boys retreat and Maureen links arms with Pecola. They stop at Isaley's store for ice cream. Maureen's father sued the store for refusing to serve him. She buys ices for herself and Pecola. Maureen asks if they have ever seen a man naked and Pecola asks what kind of father would want his daughters to see him naked? Maureen asks Pecola why she thought she was talking about fathers. Claudia defends Pecola, disconcerted by the memory of seeing her own father naked. An argument ensues, in which Maureen calls Frieda and Claudia black and ugly. Claudia goes to hit her but strikes Pecola instead. Maureen runs away and the girls say good-bye to Pecola. They walk in silence, reflecting on Maureen's insults and wondering why they need to concern themselves with the world's idea of beauty. At home, Mr. Henry gives them money for ice cream. They avoid Isaley's and go to Miss Bertha's store. When they return, they see Mr. Henry in the living room with two whores. Mr. Henry says that they are members of his Bible class and not to tell their mother.

The next section of "Winter" follows the lives of "thin brown girls" who "live in quiet black neighborhoods where everybody is gainfully employed." These girls are not like their sisters who have "lovely black necks" and "eyes that bite" (63); they go to college where they learn good manners; they marry and watch over their households with a forbidding eye. They show little emotion and do not allow themselves to experience any pleasure from sex. One such woman, Geraldine, has settled in Lorain

and had a baby, Junior, who is not allowed to cry. Junior soon learns that Geraldine has more affection for her cat than for him. He is allowed to play with white children only. He bullies the black children. One day he sees Pecola walking alone. He lures her into his house, promising to show her some kittens. Pecola is astounded by the beauty of his house. Instead of presenting her with kittens, he throws the black cat in her face. The cat claws her face and Pecola begins to cry. Junior shuts her in the room and she bangs on the door. The cat approaches her and she strokes it. Junior opens the door and is horrified to see the cat respond to Pecola as it responds to his mother. He demands that she give him the cat back and they fight. The cat dies when it is thrown against a window. Geraldine enters the room. Junior accuses Pecola of killing the cat. She looks at Pecola's dirty clothes and recognizes the black girls of her youth who disgusted her. She screams at Pecola and orders her out of the house.

In "Spring," Mr. MacTeer beats up Mr. Henry for touching Frieda. Claudia asks if Mr. Henry showed her his "privates" like Sopahead Church, another member of the community (78). Frieda, uncertain as to the cause of pregnancy, worries that she might be "ruined" (78). Claudia responds that the whores are ruined women but they are not fat because they drink whiskey. They decide to ask Pecola for some of her father's whiskey. They find Pecola at the house where her mother works. While they wait for Mrs. Breedlove, a white girl walks into the kitchen. Frightened, she calls for "Polly," Pecola's mother. The girls see a fresh cobbler on the counter. Pecola reaches out to touch it and it falls to the floor. Mrs. Breedlove finds her and slaps her. She soothes the little "pink-and-yellow" girl who has started crying (85). She refuses to tell this little girl who the black girls are.

The next section of "Spring" transports us back to the youth of Pauline Williams, Pecola's mother. Interwoven with the third-person narration are first-person accounts from Pauline herself. When she was two, a nail punched through her foot, leaving her with a pronounced limp. She grew up attributing her "sense of separateness" to her injury (86). As World War One approached, her family moved from Alabama to Kentucky to find work in the mines and mills. Pauline's mother got a job and Pauline took over the housekeeping. She enjoyed it for a while but began to long for a stranger to bring her love and salvation. One day the Stranger she has longed for arrived in the form of Cholly Breedlove, who kissed her foot. She and Cholly moved to Lorain, Ohio. She took a job working for a white woman which displeased Cholly. He came over to the house drunk. The white woman told Pauline that she could only keep her job if she left Cholly. Pauline refused. Pauline's loneliness continued through her first pregnancy. She found escapism in the movies, which enacted the scenes which had haunted her imagination as a child and which introduced the idea of "physical beauty" (95). Watching Jean Harlow, she bit into a piece of candy and her front tooth fell out. She began to fight with Cholly again. She had the baby, followed by another. They moved to a larger house and she became an active member of the community. She worked for the Fishers, a wealthy white family, and neglected her own home, keeping the beauty of the white home "for herself" (100). The Fishers gave her the nickname Polly. This section ends with Pauline's first-person account of lovemaking with Cholly, which she once enjoyed but which now gives her no pleasure.

The next section is a third-person account of Cholly's background. It begins in Georgia where his mother dumped him as a baby on a junk heap and his Great Aunt Jimmy rescued and raised him. Cholly left school to work at a store where he befriended an old man called Blue Jack. His Great Aunt Jimmy died. At the funeral Cholly met a girl, Darlene. They left the funeral and had sex. As they were having sex, two white men with guns found them. They held a flashlight over the couple and told Cholly to finish. Cholly projected his hatred and humiliation onto Darlene. The men left and Cholly and Darlene returned to the funeral. Worried that Darlene might be pregnant, Cholly ran away to Macon, where he had been told his father lived. When he found his father, he was immediately rejected. The shock of the rejection caused Cholly to soil himself. After being taken in by three women, he met and married Pauline but marriage "froze his imagination" and he felt bewildered by fatherhood (126). One afternoon, he returned home drunk and found Pecola in the kitchen. Sensing her loneliness and sadness, he was overcome by his impotence to help her. He saw her scratch the back of her calf with her toe and was reminded of the first time he saw Pauline. He kissed the calf and raped her. Pecola fainted.

The final section of "Winter" tells the story of Soaphead Church, a West Indian misanthrope of mixed-raced heritage. Soaphead loved things, but was repelled by contact with people. However he experienced "rare but keen sexual cravings" (131). Soaphead projects his cravings onto young girls, whom he views as more clean than adults and young boys. Soaphead's family history is marked by corruption and eccentricities, caused by intermarriage between family members. After trying several vocations, Soaphead found himself unable to make money. He settled in Lorain, as a tenant of Miss Bertha and her old dog, who revolts Soaphead. He presents himself to the community as a kind of god, working as a "Reader, Adviser, and Interpreter of Dreams." One day a little girl asks him to turn her eyes blue. Soaphead tells Pecola that they must make a sacrifice in order to persuade God to help her. He sprinkles a piece of meat with poison and tells her to give it to the dog. He tells her that if the dog begins acting strangely, she will get her blue eyes. As the dog chokes, she runs away, horrified. Soaphead writes a letter to God, asking how He could let a little black girl become so desperate as to seek him out? He admits that he has been "a bad man" but reminds God that he did not commit the sins he was accused of in newspapers (143). He tells God that he has given Pecola the blues eyes she wanted; she will now look at herself differently.

In "Summer" Claudia and Frieda receive the marigold seeds which they will sell in the town for money. They hope to buy a bicycle. As they move from door to door, they hear fragments of gossip about Pecola. She is pregnant with her father's child. Cholly has disappeared. The gossips are fascinated and outraged by the story but Claudia and Frieda feel sympathy for Pecola. Claudia imagines the baby and wishes that someone will want it to live to "counteract the universal love of white baby dolls" (149). They decide to pray to God for the baby and sacrifice the money they have made. They will plant the seeds instead of selling them. The next section is composed of a dialogue. One voice talks about her new blue eyes and another asks her questions about them. Pecola seems to be talking to an imaginary second self. She keeps looking in the mirror to check that her eyes are still blue. She has been taken out of school. Pecola presumes it is because of her new blue eyes. They begin to talk about Cholly. Initially Pecola denies that Cholly did anything to her but it emerges that he raped her a second time. She told her mother about the first time but Mrs. Breedlove refused to believe her. Pecola's brother has left. Mrs. Breedlove ignores her daughter as much as possible. They return to the topic of Pecola's blue eyes. She seeks assurance that hers are the bluest eyes in the world. She makes her second self promise that she will not leave her if she does not have the bluest eyes in the world. Claudia's voice closes the novel. Pecola's baby died. She became an outcast and spent her days walking up and down, flailing her arms. Frieda and Claudia avoid her out of guilt that their marigolds never grew. Cholly died in the workhouse and Mrs. Breedlove continued to work for white people. She and Pecola lived in a house on the edge of town. Pecola made the rest of the world feel beautiful. Everyone "honed [their] egos on her" and felt beautiful when standing "astride her ugliness" (165). Claudia confesses that the rest of the world's beauty and strength is predicated on self-delusion. Even she now tells herself that the seeds did not grow because the soil killed them.

In the Afterword to the novel, Morrison recalls the young girl at school who wished for blue eyes. The young girl's request haunted Morrison and prompted her to challenge the hegemony of the white gaze.

Symbols & Motifs

As the title indicates, colors are the most prominent symbols in the novel. The blue eyes of Shirley Temple and the yellow-haired, pink-skinned baby dolls symbolise the white paradigm of beauty to which the black girls feel they must aspire. Pink, blue and yellow signify comfort, cleanliness and prosperity. Claudia, Frieda and Pecola are repeatedly confronted with these colors: the "Smiling white face, [b]lond hair" and "blue eyes" of Mary Jane on the sweet wrappers (38); Maureen Peal's "brightly colored knee socks" and sweaters "the color of lemon drops" (48); the pink sunback dress and fluffy bedroom slippers belonging to the yellow-haired girl at the white house. In 1940s American society, blackness is regarded as something to fear: "All things in her are flux and anticipation. But her blackness is static and dread. And it is the blackness that accounts for, that creates, the vacuum edged with distaste in white eyes" (37).

Morrison challenges these associations throughout the novel. By repeating the words of the white primer, Morrison presents the white world as fake and sterile. The family which features in the primer bears little resemblance to the families in the novel; in the primer, the dog delights the children but Pecola's encounter with Miss Bertha's dog is terrifying. Pecola appreciates the beauty of dandelions, commonly regarded as weeds. The black cat, intended to frighten Pecola, offers her comfort and affection. At times, colors bring solace. The "greens and blues" in Mrs. MacTeer's song take the "grief" out of the words (18). Pauline Williams's joy expresses itself in color; she associates her home town in Alabama with its red clay and the fireflies' streak of green. She describes her instantaneous sense of love for Cholly as analogous to the confluence of the colors of her youth: the "purple deep inside of me," caused by the mashing of berries in her dress; the "cool and yellowish" lemonade her Mama used to make; the green streak of the fireflies. When Cholly makes loves to her "it be all rainbow inside" (102). However, color can also compound one's sense of loss or injustice: the bright colors of the "gay paper flowers" surrounding Christ's face seem cruelly incongruous in the context of Pecola's suffering at the hands of Junior and Geraldine (72).

Morrison employs pathetic fallacy throughout the novel, often to dramatize the unspoken. The marigolds will not grow while Pecola is pregnant, as if in protest at her plight. Winter "presides" in Claudia's father's face as he struggles to support his family (47). Maureen Peal's face has hints of spring, summer and autumn. Again, Morrison challenges the easy associations of the seasons. In winter the girls long for spring, but its advent marks the substitution of whipping twigs for the winter strap: "There was a nervous meanness in these long twigs that made us long for the steady stroke of a strap. Even now spring for me is shot through with the remembered ache of switching, and forsythia holds no cheer" (75).

Societal Context

Racial and social prejudices announce their presence immediately in "The Bluest Eye." In the opening paragraph we see Rosemary Villanucci, the MacTeers' next-door neighbor, sitting in a 1939 Buick, telling Claudia and Frieda that they cannot come in. Other ethnic minorities seem to have benefited from social mobility and gained more acceptance than the African-Americans. In Pecola's school, Marie Appolonaire sits with Luke Angelino, but Pecola must sit on her own. The black characters in the novel are aware of their vulnerability in American society; "being a minority in both caste and class, we moved about anyway on the hem of life" (11). They are not permitted to enter the park, so it "fill[s] their dreams" (82). Their greatest fear is complete disenfranchisement: to Claudia and Frieda "Outdoors" represents "the real terror of life … the end of something, an irrevocable, physical fact" (11): the fate that awaits Pecola who, by the end of the novel, is living in a house on the edge of town with nowhere to go. This fear generates a "hunger for property" but social progress is not available to most African-Americans (12): Mr. MacTeer teaches the girls how to keep the house warm in winter by opening and closing particular doors. The Breedloves feel no affection for their home because its contents have to be paid for in increments and serve merely as a reminder of their poverty.

The world of the novel abounds with signs of racial inequality. The young daughter of the white house where Mrs. Breedlove works calls her Polly. Social relationships are determined by skin color. Maureen Peal is welcomed at school because of her lighter skin color. She has more social savvy than Claudia and her friends; her father sues the ice cream store for refusing to serve him and she knows about movie stars. Before introducing Geraldine, Morrison describes the lives of "thin brown girls" who emulate white standards and distance themselves from black people (63). Through her representation of Lorain, Morrison reveals the resistance of northern states to integration: "In that young and growing Ohio town … this melting pot on the lip of America facing the cold but receptive Canada—What could go wrong?" (91). In this melting pot, Polly is maltreated by white and black people. Only in the movies does she see the successful integration of black and white: "There the black-and-white images came together, making a magnificent whole" (95).

Historical Context

Morrison set the novel in 1941, and wrote it in the early sixties. In the "Afterword" she acknowledges the influence of both contexts on her work. She was prompted to write "The Bluest Eye" by the "reclamation of racial beauty" in the nineteen-sixties (167). She wondered why this kind of beauty required acknowledgement and articulation and recognized the assumptions which lay behind this reclamation. Morrison herself identifies the climate in which the book was written (1965–69) as a time of "great social upheaval in the lives of black people" (169). The Civil Rights Movement had won the fight for desegragation and the vote, but African-Americans continued to encounter prejudice on a daily basis. African-Americans moved to the cities of the North as white people moved to the suburbs; in the cities, poverty rates were high, causing riots. While white Americans took advantage of social mobility, African-Americans continued to receive the worst housing and education remained limited. In 1964, the Ku Klux Klan carried out a series of murders and bombings in Mississippi.

Morrison identifies 1941 (the year that America entered the War) as "a momentous year" (170). She opened the novel in the fall of this year because this time signifies the encroachment of "something grim" (170). For many Americans, the forties brought recovery from the Great Depression, mainly through President Roosevelt's New Deal. Few African-Americans benefited from these changes. Mrs. MacTeer rails against Roosevelt and the Civilian Conservation Corps camps. The government founded the CCC in 1933 to recruit young, unemployed men to save America's landscapes. Out of three million jobs, only an estimated 250,000 were given to African-Americans. The state of Georgia initially refused African-Americans admittance into the CCC. Henry Ford was praised for recruiting African-Americans and supporting integration. However, Mrs. MacTeer counts Henry Ford as one of many public figures "who didn't care whether she had a loaf of bread" (17).

Religious Context

Just as Morrison challenges white models of beauty, so does she challenge Western theology. Religious doctrine is presented as a kind of myopia or an instrument of control or self-aggrandizement. Mr. Yacobwoski's religion is "honed on the doe-eyed Virgin Mary" (36). He is unable to recognise Pecola as a subject. Pecola's mother is also blind to her daughter's humanity. For the young Pauline Williams, religion is associated not only with sin, but the possibility of redemption. Sitting in church, she longs for some kind of transcendental experience: a form of "redemption, salvation" from a Presence who will understand her and take her away forever (88). However, when she becomes a mother, her Christianity becomes a kind of weapon. Mrs. Breedlove is not "interested in Christ the Redeemer, but rather Christ the Judge" and views herself as "an upright and Christian woman, burdened with a no-count man, whom God wanted her to punish" (31). The narrator states that if Cholly stopped drinking, Mrs. Breedlove would "never…forgive Jesus," in whose name she suffers (31). She overcomes the women who once despised her, "by being more moral than they" and becomes a martyr to her family: "Holding Cholly as a model of sin and failure, she bore him like a crown of thorns, and her children like a cross" (98).

In contrast, Cholly queries white theological paradigms. At the July 4 church picnic, the young Cholly watches a man break open a watermelon. As he raises up his hand, Cholly wonders if this is what God looks like but remembers that "God was a nice old white man, with long white hair, flowing white beard, and little blue eyes" (105). The Christian image of God is inadequate in comparison to the momentous sight of the man smashing the watermelon. Working off the dichotomies of western theology, he concludes that the man holding the watermelon must resemble the devil and concludes that he prefers the devil.

To Claudia and Frieda, religion is a form of tyranny, called on by adults when they want children to obey: when Pecola drinks three quarts of milk Claudia's mother calls her "downright sinful" (17). Mama often refers to the Bible to support her complaints. The girls dislike "starchy, cough-drop Sundays, so full of "don'ts" and "set'cha self downs" (17). A picture of Jesus hangs on the wall of Junior's house, where western theological models are adhered to. When Pecola is ordered to leave, Christ looks at her with "sad and unsurprised eyes" (72).

Soaphead's grandfather was a religious fanatic. Soaphead himself enters a ministry seeking power: he wishes to discover the secret to "the life to counter the encroaching nonlife" but finds no answers (133). He acquires the name Church when the women of Lorain decide that he must be supernatural to spurn their advances. Soaphead has his own theories about God. He believes that God must have made a terrible error to allow Evil to exist and that he can succeed where God has failed. He identifies himself as a kind of god in order to control the minds of the community. He does not sexually abuse Pecola, but he warps her mind.

Scientific & Technological Context

After the Great Depression, many Americans began to benefit from technological advances. Some could afford cars for the first time; Claudia's next-door neighbor drives a Buick, a symbol of their higher social status. The MacTeers and the Breedloves only see evidence of this progress when they enter white streets and houses. In their own homes, they struggle to survive.

Biographical Context

Toni Morrison is one of America's most eminent novelists. She has garnered a formidable array of awards and honours, including the 1993 Nobel Prize for Literature. Born Chloe Anthony Wofford in 1931, Morrison was raised in Ohio after her parents moved there from the South. She attended Howard University in Washington D.C. and Cornell University, where she wrote her Master's thesis on Virginia Woolf and William Faulkner. In 1965, she joined Random House and worked in publishing while writing. Morrison's first novel, "The Bluest Eye," evolved from a short story and was published in 1970. "Sula" followed in 1973. Her third novel, "Song of Solomon" (1977) interweaves African-American folktales with American history; it won the National Book Critics Circle Award. "Tar Baby" appeared in 1981. Her next three novels form a thematically linked trilogy: "Beloved" (1987), "Jazz" (1992), and "Paradise" (1998). "Beloved," her most acclaimed novel, was made into a film, produced by and starring Oprah Winfrey. The novel retells the true story of Margaret Garner, a black slave who killed her daughter to save her from slavery. In 1992, Morrison published "Playing in the Dark: Whiteness and the Literary Imagination," a hugely influential work of literary criticism. She published her eighth novel, "Love," in 2003.

Morrison views the collaboration between reader and writer as essential to the creative process; she states that she wishes the reader to "work with the author in the construction of the book" ("Rootedness" 341). Her novels are characterized by their polyvocality, lyricism, and alinear, fragmented structures. Prevalent themes include: race and gender ideology; sexuality; standards of beauty; memory and loss; identity and community. She has written books for children, including the "Who's Got Game?" series. Morrison has two sons from her marriage to Harold Morrison. She is currently Robert F. Goheen Professor, Council of Humanities, at Princeton University. She is a member of numerous bodies, including the National Council of the Arts and the American Academy and Institute of Arts and Letters.

Rachel Lister, Ph.D

Works Cited

Morrison, Toni. *The Bluest Eye*. London: Picador, 1990.

Discussion Questions

1. Identify as many references to color in the novel as you can. What meanings do particular colors acquire for the characters? How does Morrison problematize these associations?

2. The novel is divided into four parts which are composed of fragments of interweaving narratives. What is the effect of Morrison's formal strategy? Why has she organized the novel in this way?

3. Discuss Morrison's treatment of religion in "The Bluest Eye."

4. How does Morrison dramatize the hegemony of the white gaze in "The Bluest Eye?"

5. At key moments in the novel, the omniscient narrative voice moves to the fore to comment on the characters' behavior. Identify these moments and consider their significance.

6. Extracts from the white primer appear intermittently throughout the novel. Apart from the first two extracts, the words run together with no spacing or punctuation. Why does Morrison repeat the primer in this way? How do the images from the primer impinge on the ensuing narrative line?

7. Discuss how attitudes towards racial identities shape the characters' identities in the novel. You might focus on one of the following characters: Pecola; Claudia; Geraldine; Pauline; Maureen; Cholly; Soaphead.

8. Discuss the opening of the novel. Why did Morrison decide to narrate most of the events from the perspective of a child? What effect does this have? Why does she begin the novel towards the end of the story?

9. Discuss the significance of the natural world in the novel.

10. Discuss the dialogue between Pecola and her imaginary second self. Why does Morrison reveal Pecola's thoughts in this way? What is the effect of this exchange?

Essay Ideas

1. "Along with the idea of romantic love, she was introduced to another—physical beauty ... Probably the most destructive ideas in the history of human thought" ("The Bluest Eye"). Does the novel sustain this evaluation? How does Morrison dramatize the dangers of these two ideas?

2. Explore Morrison's evocation of place. What does the novel suggest about society in the North and the South?

3. In the Afterword to the novel, Morrison writes that she aimed to create a sense of "sudden familiarity or instant intimacy" between the reader and the text. By what means does she achieve this effect?

4. "Our innocence and faith were no more productive than his lust of despair." How does Morrison problematize Western notions of good and evil in "The Bluest Eye?"

5. In "The Bluest Eye," Cholly Breedlove is described as "dangerously free." The old women of the town feel that they are "at last, free." Taking these statements as a starting-point, explore Morrison's representation of freedom.

Breathing Lessons

by Anne Tyler

"I mean, you're given all these lessons for the unimportant things – piano-playing, typing. You're given years and years of lessons in how to balance equations, which Lord knows you will never have to do in normal life. But how about parenthood? Or marriage, either, come to think of it. Before you can drive a car you need a state-approved course of instruction, but driving a car is nothing, nothing, compared to living day in and day out with a husband and raising up a new human being."

Anne Tyler

Content Synopsis

"Breathing Lessons" opens by announcing that married couple Maggie and Ira Moran have to travel to Deer Lick, Pennsylvania for a funeral. Part One, Chapter One covers this journey. Max, the husband of Maggie's "girlhood friend" Serena, has died (3). Ira does not want to go; Saturday is his busiest day at work. They plan to rise early but oversleep. The narrative voice states that "Maggie must have set the alarm wrong" (3). Before leaving, Maggie goes to the body shop to pick up their car. When she turns on the ignition, the radio is playing.

It is tuned in to "AM Baltimore," a phone-in show. The topic is "What Makes an Ideal Marriage?" As Maggie drives out of the garage, she hears a voice; she thinks she recognises it as 'Fiona's.' The caller does not identify herself but reveals that she is getting married for security, after her first marriage for love failed. Shocked by this revelation, Maggie crashes into a truck and damages the left front fender of her newly repaired car. She dismisses the mechanic's concern and drives away. She picks up Ira from his father's frame shop, purposefully ignoring the windows where she knows her father and sister-in-law will be watching. Ira is clearly angry about the car but she again dismisses the accident. Maggie offers to pay for the repairs but neither of them takes this idea seriously; she earns very little in her job at an old people's home. She tells Ira that she heard Fiona, their daughter-in-law, announce on the radio that she is getting married again. We learn that Fiona was married to their son Jesse and had a daughter, Leroy, their only grandchild. Maggie wonders if Jesse heard Fiona on the radio and Ira scoffs at the idea of Jesse being up before noon. Through the course of the trip, Maggie and Ira bicker over Jesse's broken marriage, the gravity of Maggie's accident that morning, and the best route to Deer Lick. Maggie suggests visiting Fiona after the funeral; she lives near Deer Lick. Ira dismisses the idea, reminding Maggie that they rarely see Fiona now. The bickering is interspersed with flashbacks. Maggie recalls a number of "spy trips" she made to shadow Fiona who now lives with her mother (18). Once she approached Leroy but her granddaughter did not recognise her.

Maggie and Ira stop at a café. Maggie talks to Mabel, the waitress; she is obviously very comfortable conversing with strangers. She tells Mabel about their daughter Daisy, a teenager with a scholarship for an Ivy League college. Maggie starts to cry; Daisy recently asked her whether she consciously decided to "settle for being ordinary" (30). Jesse, their son, dropped out of school and joined a rock band. Maggie blames Ira for the separation of Jesse and Fiona, although she does not explain why. Back in the car, Ira berates Maggie for airing their troubles to the world and blaming him for the breakdown of Jesse's marriage. Maggie demands that he let her out of the car. She walks back towards the café and Ira drives on. Maggie fantasizes about supporting herself through a new life. She laments the loss of romance between herself and Ira. She remembers falling in love with one of the residents at the old people's home where she works. She realises that "what appealed to her" about Mr. Gabriel was "the image he had of her … capable and skilful and efficient" (40). At the time she fantasized about running away with Mr. Gabriel. Mr. Gabriel is in the home because of his fear of fire. When they have a fire drill, Maggie leaves her station to find him and ends up diving into the laundry shute to avoid her boss. When Mr. Gabriel finds out he gives her the same "judging gaze" that Ira gives her (45). Maggie realises that she had been merely seeking "an earlier version of Ira," the husband she had known before "she'd began disappointing him" (46). At the end of Chapter One, Ira turns up at the café and they return to the car.

When Chapter Two opens, Maggie and Ira have reached their destination. They are the first to arrive. Maggie wanders about the church and Ira plays cards in one of the pews. Serena appears.

She describes Max's final days as a confused invalid. Maggie is disconcerted by this image of Max and worries that Serena's experience usually anticipates her own. Serena asks Maggie and Ira to perform a "rerun" of the duet they sang at her wedding for Max's funeral (57). The song is "Love is a Many Splendored Thing." As more guests arrive, it becomes clear that Serena wants to re-enact her wedding to Max as closely as possible. Maggie regrets that she did not wear something more glamorous as so many of the class of '56 are at the funeral. Sugar Tilghman, the high school beauty, and Durwood, whom Maggie sees quite regularly despite not liking him at school, sit next to the Morans. They remember the wedding of Serena and Max and wonder why it was so exaggerated.

As the service begins, Maggie recalls how she and Serena used to spy on Serena's father who left her mother to marry and have children with someone else. Serena vowed never to be like her mother, a woman "whose every trait … hinted at permanent injuries" (69). Maggie vowed to avoid marrying anyone like her father who was "mild and clumsy" (70). For this reason, she refused to date Durwood. When the piano begins to play "Love is a Many Splendored Thing," Maggie and Ira stay seated. After an expectant look from Serena, Maggie starts to sing and Durwood joins in. Maggie wonders what her life would be like if she had married Durwood. Sugar refuses to sing "Born to be with You," the song she performed at the wedding. Instead she sings "Que Sera Sera."

In Chapter Three, Serena and Maggie catch up. Maggie tells Serena how much she resents missing out on Leroy's life. Serena admits that she feels little connection with her grandchildren and was relieved to have her daughter Linda off her hands. Unlike Maggie, she has gone through the menopause. She advises Maggie to enjoy the freedom of old age, but Maggie feels that she is being deprived of things. The nursing home where she works is talking about laying people off. Serena advises her to go back to school and become a professional nurse, but Maggie feels that she doesn't understand. Serena has organised a viewing of her wedding, which was captured on video. They all sit down to watch it. When the young Maggie and Ira appear, Maggie is transported back to their school days and Tyler presents an extended flashback. The young Maggie plans to marry her first boyfriend, Boris Drumm. Her mother forces her to apply for college. In the vacation she takes a job washing windows at the Silver Threads Nursing Home, where she eventually becomes an aide. Her family expresses disappointment that their clever daughter should aim so low. When Maggie hears that the "Moran boy," whom she knows slightly from school, has died in a "freak training accident" in boot camp, she begins to think about him, seeing in him the qualities that Boris lacks (94): "self-possession" and "calm assurance" (94-5, 95). She writes a condolence letter to Ira's father. When Ira walks into choir practice, she learns that it is Monty Rand, another peer, who has died. Ira teases her about the letter as they walk home. Serena asks them to sing a duet at her wedding. She tells Maggie that she is marrying Max because she is tired of dating. When she arrives at the wedding, Maggie does not see Ira. She ignores Boris and goes to Ira's father's shop. Ira's father, Sam, recognises her name from the condolence letter and scoffs at the idea that Ira would ever be able to join the army or get married; his father's heart is weak and one of his sisters is "not quite right in the head" (111). Ira comes downstairs and his father tells Maggie that Ira has no friends and has not had a girlfriend. He mocks Maggie for her false grief, remarking that she seems to have recovered. Maggie corrects him, telling Sam that she was barely existing without Ira and that he has every right to get married. Sam dismisses the idea, reminding Ira that he has a father and sisters. Ira tells his father that they are getting married and they walk out of the shop; Maggie and Ira have their first kiss.

The narrative returns to the present. Watching herself and Ira on the screen, Maggie reflects that nobody would guess the romance of their past. The group remembers that Serena and Max argued after the ceremony; having failed to make it through the rehearsal, Max had walked her down the aisle too slowly. Maggie notices that Ira is missing and finds him in Serena's bedroom playing solitaire. They recall their wedding and the first, rocky year of their marriage. They kiss but are interrupted by Serena who is shocked at their inappropriate behavior. She orders them to leave.

There are no chapter divisions in Part Two. Tyler retains the third-person voice but switches from Maggie's perspective to Ira's. They are on their way home from the funeral. Ira views his life as a waste and regrets the dream that he has had to sacrifice to care for his father, sisters, wife and children: his ambition to be a doctor and cure a disease. Maggie continues to hope that they will make a detour to Fiona's. A driver in a Chevy slows down abruptly and nearly crashes into them. Although Ira is driving, Maggie toots the horn. Incensed by the driver, she insists that they follow him and take his registration number. When they spot him, she leans out of the window and tells the driver that one of his wheels is loose, even though it isn't. When Maggie sees that the driver is elderly and black, she feels guilty and is worried that she will be conceived as a racist. She insists that they drive back and explain. They do so, and introduce themselves to the man who has pulled up at a farm to inspect the wheel. His name is Daniel Otis. Maggie explains what she did but the man seems to be convinced that the wheel must be loose. Ira offers to tighten it up or replace it, eager to placate Mr. Otis and get back on the road. When he opens up the trunk of his own car, Ira sees that the spare tire is missing along with the tools. Maggie explains that she asked a man to replace a tire a while ago and he used the tools. Evidently, they were stolen. Mr. Otis proposes driving to the Texaco garage where his nephew works so that they can fix his 'broken' car. Ira goes along with this. As they drive Mr. Otis along in their car, Maggie tells him all about their lives. Mr. Otis reveals that he and his wife have argued after she had a bad dream about him walking all over her petticoat and shawl. As Maggie talks about Jesse and Daisy, Ira recognises that they have divergent images of their children. He views Jesse as a dropout but understands why Jesse has avoided responsibility; he does not want to end up like his parents. Ira reflects on his sisters' lives. Dorrie is "not quite right in the head" and Junie refuses to step outside because of her agoraphobia. Maggie encourages Junie to go on trips with them; they have all ended in disaster. Maggie, Ira and Mr Otis arrive at the garage and eventually Lamont, Mr Otis's nephew arrives. He admonishes his uncle for falling out with his aunt. When Ira and Maggie leave, they drive past the turnoff to Fiona's house. Ira agrees to turn back.

The final part of the novel returns to Maggie's perspective. As they drive towards Fiona's, Maggie remembers helping her daughter-in-law through her pregnancy. She told Fiona that she would have loved to have had breathing lessons when she was expecting her children; she pointed out the irony that in her youth she was given lessons for everything but parenting and marriage. They arrive at Fiona's to find an unrecognisable, seven-year-old Leroy who does not remember them. Fiona invites them in but is clearly thrown by their unannounced arrival. Maggie tells Fiona that she heard her on AM Baltimore. Fiona denies this; she is not remarrying. Maggie realises that she never heard Fiona's name and wonders how she could have been so sure. Ira goes outside with Leroy to practise Frisbee throwing and Maggie and Fiona catch up. Maggie insists that Jesse still loves Fiona. Fiona reveals that Jesse visited on Leroy's fifth birthday but brought inappropriate presents such as an oversized teddy bear. Maggie tells Fiona that Jesse kept her old tortoiseshell soap box so that he could remind himself of

her smell. Fiona seems touched by this. Maggie invites Fiona to visit them and Fiona suggests driving back home with them. Maggie is delighted but Fiona's mother Mrs Stuckey arrives and vetoes the idea. As Fiona and her mother argue, Maggie disappears to the bathroom. She locates the telephone and calls Jesse to tell him that Fiona and Leroy will be there. He replies cautiously that he might join them and Maggie takes this as a yes. She returns to Fiona, telling her that Jesse is delighted at the prospect.

In Chapter Two, Part Three, Maggie tells Ira that Fiona is driving home with them. He wonders how she managed to arrange everything so simply. He tells Maggie that she spoils Jesse and this triggers a long flashback, filtered through Maggie's perspective, to Jesse's childhood. She recalls his ability to make friends easily, his decision to join a band, his girlfriends and his ongoing conflict with Ira. The teenage Fiona wants to have an abortion when she fell pregnant but Jesse desperately wants to be a father, even though he was only seventeen. Jesse asks his mother to persuade Fiona to keep the baby. She stops Fiona and her sister outside the abortion clinic and convinces her to reconsider. She tells Fiona that Jesse is building a cradle for the baby. Fiona relents and leaves the clinic with Maggie, much to the consternation of Fiona's sister. At home, Maggie shows Fiona some wood spindles and tells her that they are for the cradle. Fiona and Jesse decide to get married. At the wedding only Mrs. Stuckey is genuinely pleased for the couple. Maggie's mother sits "stiff with outrage" and Ira is "grim-faced and silent" (246). Jesse and Fiona move in with Maggie and Ira. Fiona resents being pregnant. When the baby arrives, Jesse bemoans having nothing to look forward to any more. At a family trip to the races Jesse vanishes. An overwrought Fiona yells at him when he reappears, and Maggie admonishes her. Fiona accuses Maggie of trying to "run" her marriage to Jesse (266). She asks where the cradle is and Jesse denies that he started building it. Fiona asks him to explain the rods of wood that Maggie showed her and Ira reveals that they were for his drying rack. Fiona tells Jesse that she married him for the cradle and all it represented. Ira tells Fiona that Jesse has never finished anything in his life; he has lost his job and spends his days with his friends. He has seen Jesse with another girl; Jesse insists she is only a friend. Maggie asks why Ira has not said anything about this; he replies that he does not like meddling. Fiona drives off in the car and does not return home. Jesse claims that he has gone out to look for her but couldn't find her. All of Fiona's clothes are at the house; they speculate that she must be at her sister's. Jesse says that he didn't check there as he was too proud to admit actively seeking her out. Fiona's sister picks up Fiona's clothes, leaving behind "the chaff" (277). Without Fiona, Maggie feels at a loss. She spends time with Ira's father; he tells her that his wife "'didn't lead a real life'" (279). Ira and Maggie sink into a malaise; one day in the kitchen Ira lowers his head into his hands in despair at the way that his life has turned out. Matters improve when Jesse gets a job at a record shop and Daisy, having spent all her time at the house of "Mrs. Perfect," her friend's mother, returns "to her place in the family" (281).

Chapter Three returns to the present day. Ira and Maggie debate over how they can get the car out of the drive without asking Mrs Stuckey to move her Maverick and crashing into the mailbox. Ira says that it will be no problem. Maggie refuses to be responsible for directing him out of the drive, so she gets behind the wheel. Ira directs her but she manages to crash into the mailbox nevertheless. They set off and Ira predicts that Jesse will not show up for dinner. Leroy becomes excited about meeting her father. Maggie falls asleep and dreams about Serena; she remembers spying on Serena's father. She awakens and they stop at a supermarket, where Maggie and Ira recognise an old tune playing on the loudspeaker. They sing along together.

When other shoppers start to listen, Maggie feels like a fraud and stops singing. They return to the car; as they approach home, Leroy recognises the surroundings; clearly Fiona has driven her around Jesse's home town before. When Jesse eventually turns up at the house Fiona asks him where the soap dish is. He has no idea. Fiona asks if he doesn't sleep with the soap box under his pillow at night. Maggie denies saying this, but clearly she has embellished the significance of the soap box. Ira states that the only thing Jesse sleeps with is his new girlfriend. Jesse quietly exits the house. Fiona and Leroy leave. Ira tries to comfort Maggie and she berates herself for interfering.

In the final chapter, Maggie looks back on her life. One of the residents of the home once told her his idea of heaven: being handed a gunnysack containing all the mementoes one has lost in life. She thinks of all the objects she wishes she could retrieve. She calls Serena and they make up. She begins to outline a new scheme to Ira; they will invite Leroy to live with them so that she can attend a good Baltimore school. Ira gently refuses to contemplate it. She asks him what they will do for the rest of their lives now that everyone is leaving; tomorrow they will drive Daisy to college. Ira reassures her. He is playing cards and has reached "that interesting part of the game" when "choices were narrower and he had to show real skill and judgment" (327). Maggie kisses him and thinks about the day ahead which will bring another journey.

Symbols & Motifs

The journey is the most dominant motif in the novel. Tyler takes an aging, bickering couple out of their domestic context and places them in one of the central narratives of American literature, the road trip. For brief moments, the mythology surrounding the American road asserts itself; at one point the road makes Maggie feel "rangy and free-wheeling" (179). The sensibilities of the characters are often figured as journeys: Maggie is "not a straight-line kind of person" (162); she is "always making clumsy, impetuous rushes toward nowhere in particular—side trips, random detours" (125).

Breathing acquires multiple meanings as the novel progresses. It marks the passing of time and the inevitability of repetition. The natural act of inhaling and relinquishing is a correlate of the novel's main theme: Maggie is unable to "'let go'" (80); Serena claims that she can let go of the past but the funeral betrays her struggle to do so; one of the residents in the home states that his idea of heaven is the retrieval of all the things he has lost; Mr. Otis suggests that it "Could be what you throw away is all that really counts" (170).

Song titles serve as motifs of the past yet they retain their significance in the present. They provide a kind of metacommentary on the relationships in the novel and the changing attitudes towards life and love: "Love is a Many Splendored Thing," "Born to Be With You" "Que Sera Sera" and "Tonight You Belong to Me," the song Maggie and Ira sing in the supermarket.

Ira's game of solitaire figures his isolation and self-containment. The game also represents his rational sensibility: as Maggie notes, he responds to practical problems rather than emotional dilemmas. The different stages of the solitaire game dramatize the marriage trajectory. The game "start[s] simply" but by the end of the novel it calls for judicious choices (49).

Wigs recur as metonymies for Maggie's acts of dissembling: she wears a red wig on her "spy trips" to Fiona and Leroy; she tells Serena's mother to wear a "fright wig" to the Halloween party (321); she gives Junie a wig to help her to overcome her agoraphobia. Other symbols include: the picture in Maggie's grandmother's parlor entitled "Old Folks at Home," which figures Maggie's fear of the future; Mr. Otis's dog who, unable to grasp the easiest way to collect the ball from the kitchen chair, whimpers through the spindles, figuring the characters' inability to identify the easiest route in life.

Historical Context

"Breathing Lessons" dramatizes the pull of the past through its series of protracted flashbacks. The characters display different attitudes to the passing of time. As a young girl "Serena had always been ahead of her time" (50); as a grandmother she continues to look forward, relishing the freedom of old age. However, at Max's funeral she tries to re-enact her wedding and to recapture the spirit of the late fifties. For Maggie and Ira, hindsight is often disabling. As the novel progresses, Ira becomes increasingly preoccupied with lost opportunities. Maggie distances herself from the nostalgic atmosphere of the funeral: "All through this church, she imagined, middle-aged people were mumbling sentimental phrases from the fifties" (64). However, she also finds herself wistfully looking back at the fifties when her romantic ideals were intact. She recalls how she and Serena promised themselves that they "wouldn't wash the dishes right after supper because that would take us away from our husbands" and wonders how long it has been since either of them considered their marriages in this light (23). In the flashback scenes, Tyler captures the idealism of fifties ideology: even realists such as Serena collude in the myth of domestic bliss: "In fact, if Serena believed that marriage was not a Doris Day movie, she had certainly never proved it in public, for her grownup life had looked from outside like the cheeriest of domestic comedies: Serena ironic and indulgent and Max the merry good-time guy" (68). Maggie also registers the currency of fifties and sixties stereotypes. She wonders if Mr. Gabriel could "view her as the "I Love Lucy" type—madcap, fun-loving, full of irrepressible high spirits" (45). She insists, however, that she does not play this role in real life.

When Maggie hears rumors of Ira's death, she is alerted to the force of teleology: "It was her first inkling that her generation was part of the stream of time. Just like the others ahead of them, they would grow up and grow old and die. Already there was a younger generation prodding them from behind" (95). However, the novel illuminates the limits of history's grasp. Maggie marvels not only at how much the world has changed, but also how it remains the same: for example, romantic love has always been the primary subject of popular songs: "Once Maggie had seen on TV where archaeologists had just unearthed a fragment of music from who knows how many centuries B.C., and it was a boy's lament for a girl who didn't love him back" (64).

Jesse's song titles and lyrics hilariously betray their historical context, the nineteen-eighties: "Microwave Quartet," "Cassette Recorder Blues," "Seems like this world is on fast forward nowadays" and "Girlie if I could I would put you on defrost" (225, 226, 236). When Maggie hears Jesse's songs, she comments that music has changed: "'It used to be 'Love Me Forever' and now it's 'Help Me Make It Through the Night.'" Jesse sets her straight: "In the old days they just hid it better. It was always 'Help Me Make It Through the Night'" (236).

Tyler wrote the novel in 1988. Her depiction of the younger generation reflects postmodern concerns about the break-up of the nuclear family. Mr. Otis expresses disapproval of his nephew's bachelor lifestyle: he lives alone, afraid to date in case a new girlfriend will "'do him like his wife did'" (171). Even Maggie and Ira abandon traditional family routines when Fiona leaves Jesse for the first time. Maggie heats up frozen dinners and cans of soup that throw her into a panic because they seem designed to accommodate splintered families; they inexplicably hold "'Two and three quarters servings'" (280).

Societal Context

Social convention is the dominant shaping force of the characters' lives. Class ideology clearly influences Maggie. Her resentment towards Mrs. Stuckey manifests itself through snobbery: she recalls her as a "slatternly woman who smoked cigarettes" (8). The shotgun marriage of Jesse and Fiona exposes the class divide between the two families. Mrs. Stuckey is the only guest who is truly happy at the wedding; Maggie's mother is clearly disgusted by Fiona's pregnancy. Class difference exerts its influence in seemingly trivial details: when Maggie visits Fiona she is irritated that the telephone has no "push buttons" (211); at Fiona's mother's house, the garbage can is sealed only with a "token cover" and the side of the house is "speckled with mildew and rust stains" (219); Maggie has a "prejudice against shrimp pink," the color of Fiona's T-shirt, because it is "lower-class" (239). Serena's status as an illegitimate child clearly carries a stigma and shapes her vision of her own future. Jesse and Fiona appear unconcerned about the stigma of divorce and its effect on Leroy.

Wider social issues surface briefly and betray the characters' naivety and insularity. In her encounter with Mr. Otis, Maggie is at pains to assert her liberated views about race. She insists on apologising to him when she sees that he is black. She worries that he will assume she is racist. Ira bemoans the lack of sophistication in Maggie's social views: "'All up and down this highway, other couples are taking weekend drives together. They're traveling from Point A to Point B. They're holding civilized discussions about, I don't know, current events. Disarmament. Apartheid'" (138).

When Maggie visits the abortion clinic, Tyler presents both sides of this highly contested social issue. Maggie tells Jesse that it is Fiona's right to choose but the protesters accuse her of colluding in murder and ask her where her conscience is. Maggie worries that she may have done the wrong thing in persuading Fiona to return home. She and Ira enjoy being grandparents; Maggie laments the loss of Leroy in their lives.

Gender issues lie at the heart of the novel. In the present-day narrative, Ira remains financially responsible for his wife, children and sisters.

Feminists have taken exception to Tyler's representation of middle-aged women such as Maggie. Opportunities were clearly opening up for women at this time: Maggie's parents are disappointed when she foregoes the chance to attend college. The reference to "I Love Lucy" suggests that Maggie is a "throwback to the late-1950s and early 1960s" (Hall 41). However, Maggie insists that she does not subscribe to this stereotype in real life.

Religious Context

Throughout the novel, the characters are reminded of their mortality. The novel opens with a reference to a funeral; Leroy's kitten dies; reports of Ira's death bring Maggie and Ira together; Ira's mother dies when he is only fourteen. Religious discourses surface sporadically, offering hope but taking several different forms. Maggie often considers religion without committing herself to particular doctrines or beliefs. She is unsure "what kind of church" she is in at Max's funeral (50). In her past, religious affiliations have bowed to social convention. Serena is married Methodist but "switched over" once she was married (50). As Maggie and Ira drive towards Deer Lick, they see road signs such as "TRY JESUS, YOU WON'T REGRET IT" alongside "BUBBA MCDUFF'S SCHOOL OF COSMETOLOGY (23). One of the guests at the funeral reads Kahil Gilbran's "The Prophet," a bestseller at the time of Maggie's youth and the touchstone for the sixties counter-culture. The text provides appropriate material for both the wedding and the funeral.

Evangelical discourses play a significant role in the short, sad life of Ira's mother. Dying from a "progressive disease," she "devoted herself … to religion, to radio evangelists and inspirational pamphlets left by door-to-door missionaries" (159).

Mr. Otis describes Maggie as an "angel of mercy" and remains convinced that their meeting is part of God's plan (161).

Although Maggie does not align herself with a particular religion, she clearly believes in fate as a theory; in reality, she tries to engineer situations and pass them off as fate. Serena strips Maggie of her illusions with her pragmatic approach to marriage: "'We're not in the hands of fate after all,'" she seemed to be saying. "'Or if we are, we can wrest ourselves free any time we care to'" (109).

Scientific & Technological Context

Maggie inhabits a fast-paced world which often leaves her befuddled. Technological advancement manifests itself in the push button telephones, the frozen ready meals, the sophisticated mechanisms of the new car. Maggie has problems operating her car and admits to Fiona that she often turns the windscreen wipers on when she means to turn on the indicator. Fiona is learning electrolysis at beauty school and advises Maggie to begin using hair mousse. Jesse deploys technological metaphors in song titles and lyrics which refer to microwaves and defrosting.

Biographical Context

Born in Minneapolis in 1941, Anne Tyler grew up in a number of Quaker communities in the South. The family settled eventually in Raleigh, North Carolina. She graduated Duke University, North Carolina, where she won the Anne Flaxner Award for creative writing twice. Tyler married Iranian Taghi Modarressi with whom she had children. They settled in Baltimore, where most of her novels are set. She published her first novel, "If Morning Ever Comes," in 1964. Her most famous novel, "The Accidental Tourist" (1985), won the National Book Critics Circle Award and was made into a major film. She was awarded the Pulitzer Prize for "Breathing Lessons" in 1989. The novel was also nominated for a National Book Award and made into a film starring James Garner and Joanne Woodward. In 1994, Nick Hornby and Roddy Doyle voted Tyler the 'greatest living novelist writing in English' in the "Sunday Times." "Time" named "Breathing Lessons" one of the ten best fiction books of the decade. Tyler's fiction is concerned with the tension between self and community. She is celebrated for her realistic portrayal of the everyday. Tyler's favorite book as a child was "The Little Horse" by Virginia Lee Burton. She has repeatedly named Eudora Welty as a particular influence on her fiction.

Rachel Lister

Works Cited

Hall, Alice Petry. "Tyler and Feminism." *Anne Tyler as Novelist.* Ed. Dale Salwak. Iowa City: University of Iowa Press, 1994. 33–42.

Tyler, Anne. *Breathing Lessons.* 1988. London: Vintage, 1992.

_____. "Marriage and the Ties that Bind." *Washington Post World Book.* 15 Feb. 1987.

Updike, John. "Loosened Roots." *Anne Tyler as Novelist.* Ed. Dale Salwak. Iowa: University of Iowa Press, 1994. 120–4.

Discussion Questions

1. Tyler describes Ira as "a closed-in, isolated man" (13). Do you agree with this description? What factors have caused him to retreat into himself?

2. Identify all the accidents in the novel. What do they tell us about the characters involved?

3. As a young woman, Maggie determines not to turn into her mother. She reflects later that she has in fact turned into her father. Consider the parent/child relationships and discuss the role of biological determinism in the novel.

4. Part Two is the novel's most extended detour; it has no chapter divisions and could be read as an autonomous story. Read this section again and discuss its significance to the novel as a whole.

5. "You could change who but not what. We're all just spinning here, she thought...everyone is pinned to his place by centrifugal force" (46). Does the novel support Maggie's theory? Identify as many examples of repetition and circularity as you can.

6. Dialogue plays a very important role in the novel. Study the speech patterns of Maggie and Ira and identify key features of their language. What do they tell us about the characters?

7. "It struck Maggie as disproportionate. Misleading in fact" (64). Maggie has a very flexible notion of the truth. Throughout the novel she embellishes or fabricates stories to engineer particular situations. Identify these moments of meddling. To what extent is Maggie aware of this instinct?

8. Many of Tyler's novels probe the tension between self and environment. How does she dramatize this tension in "Breathing Lessons"?

9. "I mean think if we all did that! Mistook our dreams for real life" (152). Identify as many dreams or fantasies in the novel as you can and discuss their significance. Do any patterns emerge?

10. Analyse the final chapter of the novel. Does Tyler deliver a sense of resolution? Have Maggie and Ira learned any lessons? Will their marriage change at all?

Essay Ideas

1. "She had developed a sort of clownish, pratfalling reputation" (36). How might one define "Breathing Lessons" as a comedy?

2. John Updike identifies Tyler's "unmistakable strengths" as: "her serene, firm tone; her smoothly spun plots; her apparently inexhaustible access to the personalities of her imagining; her infectious delight in the 'smell of beautiful, everyday life'" (Updike 120-1). Choose one of these characteristics and examine it in the context of "Breathing Lessons."

3. In an interview Tyler states that an "ordinary, run-of-the-mill-marriage has in many ways a more dramatic plot than any thriller ever written" ("Marriage" 6). To what extent does "Breathing Lessons" sustain this claim?

4. "The telephone poles appeared to be flashing by in rhythm. Maggie felt rangy and freewheeling" (179). How does 'the journey' function as a motif in the novel?

5. "As it happened, Maggie had a prejudice against shrimp pink. She thought it was lower-class" (239). How important is class difference in "Breathing Lessons"?

Kurt Vonnegut, who died in 2007, is remembered as one of the great American writers of the second half of the 20th century. His writing combines satire, dark humor, science fiction and his moral vision; two of his novels are included in this volume: *Cat's Cradle* and *Jailbird*. Photo: Self Portrait, National Portrait Gallery, Smithsonian Institution.

Cat's Cradle

by Kurt Vonnegut, Jr.

"I guess it was either Camus or Sartre who said that because of technology, we no longer make history. History happens to us—the new weaponry, the new communications and all that. I don't much want to play anymore."

Kurt Vonnegut, Jr.

Content Synopsis

John [narrator] discusses the process of collecting material for a book called, "The Day the World Ended," an account of the day the first atomic bomb was dropped on Hiroshima with a distinctly "human" focus. In conducting his research, John becomes entangled in the lives and history of the members of the Hoenikker family. As Felix Hoenikker, inventor of the bomb, is deceased at the time of John's research, he interviews the Hoenikker children, hoping for information to include in his text. This is a fictional story about a non-fiction book that also includes a religious text. This story-within-a-story nesting is trademark Vonnegut.

The "Cat's Cradle" of the title refers to a memory of Newt's [the youngest Hoenikker child] regarding the only time his father tried to 'play' with him using the string game. This event occurred on the day the bomb was dropped on Hiroshima,

emphasizing the distance between the scientist and his creation: Felix is playing a game while thousands are killed. Newt's memory is of absolute terror at his father's striking features and demeanor, as well as the words to the rhyme "Rock-a-bye Catsy" in which a cat (or in other versions a baby) is in a cradle up in a tree. The wind blows, branch breaks and cradle falls. According to one critic, "Newt Hoenikker believes that human culture not only is a game but also a very dull one" (Shippey). The book slowly unveils the dysfunction of the family and the romantic relationships of each of its existing members. Filled with 'coincidence,' Vonnegut questions the possibility of life with an unseen 'design'—Felix, for example, on the day that his bomb was dropped, takes the cat's cradle string from an unread manuscript in which a bomb wipes out the world. The world does get wiped out, eventually, and by Felix's doing.

While interviewing Hoenikker's former boss, John learns of the hypothetical substance called "ice-nine," which Felix is asked to develop for military purposes. It would reconfigure the structure of water to freeze at room temperature. This application would help soldiers complaining of being 'bogged down' in mud while in combat. Ice-nine turns out to have been actually invented by Felix, and was the cause of his own accidental death. The remaining ice-nine was chipped apart and divided by his children as their "inheritance." In each case, the invention spells doom for them and the world itself as ice-nice is accidentally dropped into open water in the last moments of the novel, causing the entire world to freeze over.

Interwoven into the narrative of John's book research is another thread in which he travels to San Lorenzo, where the missing member of the Hoenikker brood, Frank, currently resides. Sent by a magazine to write a feature on San Lorenzo, John is exposed not only to the island's religion of Bokononism but also to Mona, the object of his love and obsession.

This is a novel that turns reality on its head, where a dictatorship may be a good thing, sexual relations are translated into foot-touching and a religion based on lies is ardently supported. It asks the reader to re-evaluate all established structures to form an unbiased position, and to make decisions based on utility, not hereditarily passed-on preferences. The novel is made up almost entirely of separate threads which all come together and, by the end of the story, are woven into an elaborate design.

Historical Context

"Cat's Cradle" focuses on the specific historical event of the atomic bomb detonation in Hiroshima on August 6, 1945. Published in 1963, there are many relevant historical developments that influence the text. The horrifying consequences of Nazism as a ruling social and political ideology are certainly at least partially influential in Vonnegut's works as a whole. There were also continuing developments that either excerpted human beings from making and or carrying out missions [1946: pilotless rocket missile developed], or the transition from human to machine [Electronic brain built, 1947]. Rachel Carson's "Silent Spring," published in 1962, in which the earth is seen as being slowly destroyed by human parasitism, may have added to Vonnegut's bleak vision for the future. Newt's tragic love affair with the Ukrainian midget Zinka

who steals his ice-nine for Russia is the first hint of Vonnegut's engagement with American paranoia over Communism. Communism, and in particular McCarthyism, is also alluded to in chapter 44 when a plane passenger discusses being fired for being a 'communist sympathizer,' which he denies. The accusations are traced to a letter his wife wrote to the New York Times exploring the particular narrow-mindedness of Americans and their inability to perceive another nation's self-pride.

The main objective of the Alien Registration Act passed by Congress on June 29, 1940 was to undermine the American Communist Party and other left-wing political groups in the United States. Leaders of the party were arrested and in October 1949, after a nine-month trial, eleven members were convicted of violating the act. Over the next two years another 46 members were arrested and charged with advocating the overthrow of the government. Other high profile spy cases at the time involving Alger Hiss, Julius Rosenberg and Ethel Rosenberg, helped to create a deep fear in the United States that a communist conspiracy was taking place.

On 9th February, 1950, Joseph McCarthy, made a speech claiming to have a list of 57 people in the State Department known to be members of the American Communist Party. Some had been communists but others had been fascists, alcoholics and sexual deviants. If screened, McCarthy's own drinking problems and sexual preferences would have resulted in his own inclusion on the list. This witch-hunt and anti-communist hysteria became known as McCarthyism. Some left-wing artists and intellectuals were unwilling to live in this type of society and went to live and work in Europe. Although specifically historically situated, Vonnegut's text raises questions about national pride and the dangers of ethnocentrism relevant to the post-9-11 American mindset.

The scene in which Frank is forcing insects in a jar to fight emphasizes the idea that contemporary human nature may be stirred into violent action, as the ants won't fight unless Frank "keep[s] shaking the jar."

Societal Context

"Cat's Cradle" is a scathing critique of contemporary society, an apocalyptic vision of a combination of religious fanaticism and scientific invention. The problem of corruption and power in society is explored in detail. Vonnegut deals with what he sees as society's dangerous infatuation with technological advancements, another theme that clearly has applications to today's technology-obsessed American population. Familial relationships are explored, specifically the effects on children of ineffective parenting. Newt's stunted growth can be interpreted as a result of the lack of fostering love in the Hoenikker household. Vonnegut also explores the currently in-vogue concept of outsourcing large industry work or transportation of industry to foreign countries in Crosby's move of his bicycle company from Illinois to San Lorenzo, California.

Religious Context

Vonnegut offers a critique of the role of religion in modern life. Raised as an atheist, Vonnegut's skepticism of organized religion is understandable. In the text, John converts from Christianity to Bokononism. Vonnegut develops this religion which exists only on the Caribbean island of San Lorenzo by including texts from the Books of Bokonon, 'calypsos' and sayings of Bokonon. Vonnegut is famous for coining new works in his novels and this one is no exception, adding karass, foma, sinookas, boku-maru etc. all taken from the Books of Bokonon. Bokononism is a religion happily 'founded on lies' which its followers find as helpful in its honesty (if not more so) than any other world religion. The first line of the Books of Bokonon states "All of the true things I am about to tell you are shameless lies," a statement which not only reveals the seeming honesty of the

religion but also advances the blurring of truth and fiction, which are clearly blurred in the novel as well. Hoenikker's death on Christmas Eve may be another hint at Vonnegut's stance on religion and science. According to William Doxey: "In Latin, 'felix' means happy. 'Hoenikker' would be pronounced the same as Hanukkah, which is a Jewish holiday…The consequences of Hoenikker's gift, a frozen world, as numerous critics have already noted, physically and morally related to Dante's nadir of despair, the ice-bound lowest level of hell in The Divine Comedy" (qtd in Doloff).

Scientific & Technological Context

The text openly questions the role and place of ethics and morality in science and scientific inventions. It also explores the personalities of scientists, with emphasis on the dangers of a lack of balance in their lives. Newt describes his father as a man who "just wasn't interested in people." Vonnegut also explores the intersections between science and 'religion'—each as a system for viewing one's place in the world, and each as perhaps potentially dangerous. The intersections between science and religion are developed subtly, for example in Felix's death on Christmas Eve and the statement made by a scientist when the bomb was tested: "Science has now known sin" to which Felix replies "What is sin?" When asked to respond to what a secretary perceived as an absolute truth "God is love"—he responds "What is God? What is Love?" When Newt first responds to John's letter he explains of his father: "I don't think he ever read a novel or even a short story in his whole life… I can't remember my father reading anything." Another example of the dangers of single-minded scientific focus, Hoenikker is developed as a character not only without religion but also without a single literary experience. As literature specifically deals with the "human experience," this could be another example of the dangers of pure science in the absence of the Humanities.

Biographical Context

"Cat's Cradle" is seen by most critics as heavily autobiographical. The Hoenikker family parallels Vonnegut's own family structure, including the vocations and interests of each of its members. Although often classified as a science fiction author, Vonnegut himself shies away from this term. A pacifist, Vonnegut was drawn into the realities of war as a soldier. Present at the firebombing of Dresden and its consequences (detailed in Slaughterhouse Five), Vonnegut's first hand view of human pain, misery and death haunts almost all of his texts. The destruction of a relatively unimportant city and the deaths of 135,000 of its occupants only served to harden Vonnegut's resolve that war is both futile and the decisions made by military leaders often inscrutable. Almost all of Vonnegut's novels have some connection to this traumatic experience and the ways in which it shaped his worldview. Vonnegut moved to Schenectady, New York in 1947 to work at General Electric as a publicist. In his fiction, Schenectady and G.E. become Illium and the General Forge and Foundry Company. Although raised an atheist, the text Cat's Cradle also questions philosophy and nihilism as potentially dangerous and destructive influences as well. While teaching at Smith College in Boston, Mass, Vonnegut taped the following bumper sticker to his door: "God is coming and she is pissed" (Abel).

Tracy M. Caldwell

Works Cited

Abel, David. "So it goes for Vonnegut at Smith, 78-Year-Old Author still shaking up the establishment." *Boston Globe*. 5 May 2001: A1.

Dorloff, Steven. "Vonnegut's Cat's Cradle." *The Explicator* 63.1 (2004).56–57.

Shippey, T. S. *Cat's Cradle*. "Masterplots II: American Fiction Series, Revised Edition." MagillOnLiterature Plus. EBSCO. 25 Aug. 2005.

Vonnegut, Kurt. *Cat's Cradle*. Bantam Doubleday Dell: New York, 1963.

Discussion Questions

1. This is a book with approximately 287 pages and 127 'chapters.' Why do you think Vonnegut chose this method to tell the story? What is the effect on you as a reader as you encounter so many chapter divisions?

2. The first line of this novel: "Call me Jonah" echoes the first line of Melville's Moby Dick: "Call me Ishmael." Jonah alludes to the Biblical Jonah and the whale. Although the narrator asks the reader to "call [him] Jonah" he immediately explains that that is not in fact his name, but is close to the name his family gave him [John]. Why do you think Vonnegut played with names and naming in this way? Do you see parallels between the biblical characters and John?

3. In what ways does Angela's premature assumption of the role as 'mother' in the Hoenikker household change her forever? Is this change a positive or negative one?

4. This text talks a lot about The Truth versus A Lie—this is mentioned in terms of the 'truthfulness' of Hoenikker senior and the 'shameless lies' of Bokonon. Which do you think is the 'right' way to live-with a focus on 'harmless lies' or brutal truth? What are the dangers of each?

5. Is it important that almost all religions rely on faith-based understanding rather than factually presented information?

6. Explore the ways in which 'unstable' or 'mentally challenged' characters in the text offer understanding and/or advice that is much more insightful than anything said by a scientist or businessman? [Think of Miss Faust and the elevator operator for a start].

7. When John visits the Hoenikker family plot at the cemetery, he finds that the monument to the family's mother is "an alabaster phallus twenty feet high and three feet thick" while the father's marker was "a marble cube forty centimeters on each side. Talk about what this size difference means in terms of the family's feeling about each parent as well as the implications of the mother's tomb as signifying a powerful 'phallic' presence in their lives.

8. The rule of law in San Lorenzo is medieval to say the least, does the law need to be enacted to be successful (example: the 'hook') or are threats enough to keep citizens in line? In what ways does this philosophy relate to American and other world cultures?

9. The founders of San Lorenzo, Johnson and McCabe, envisioned "making San Lorenzo a Utopia." Do you think they were successful? Do you believe a utopia is practically (as opposed to theoretically) possible?

10. Felix created ice-nine just because he 'could,' without thinking of the long-term implications of such a scientific discovery. Do you see similar examples today of scientists and doctors performing tests and developing techniques 'because they can'? What do you feel are the implications of these advances? Some of them are surely important to curing disease and other human problems, but which ones also pose a potential moral threat?

Essay Ideas

1. As a work that relies on symbols to relay meaning, explore several key symbols in the novel and how they develop Vonnegut's theme(s).
   Some suggestions:
   - Ice-9
   - Ants in the jar
   - Names
   - Dropping of the atomic bomb
   - Cat's Cradle game
2. Look at the relationships developed in the text: familial, friendly and romantic. For each explain and give examples of the 'success' or failure of the relationship and the reasons for it.
   Some suggestions:
   - Felix and his wife
   - Felix and his children
   - The relationship among the siblings
   - Angela's marriage
   - Newt's and Zinka
   - The Narrator and Mona

3. Vonnegut uses this text to critique a number of social 'systems.' Write an essay that explores the systems he addresses and his attitude towards them.
   Some suggestions:
   - Organized Religion
   - Science/Scientific Community
   - Family life
4. Explore the idea Vonnegut raises about the dangerous ineptitude of governmental/war time deployment of scientific advancements, particularly the lack of long-range vision of effects. Compare ice-nine to atomic bomb, agent orange, potential nuclear war, war in Afghanistan, war in Iraq.
5. Explore the use of irony in this novel. How is it developed and supported? To what effect?
6. Explore the similarities and differences between the artificially created, politically motivated religion of Bokononism and any other world religion.

Different Seasons

by Stephen King

Content Synopsis

The first novella in the collection, "Rita Hayworth and the Shawshank Redemption," tells the story of Andy Dufresne, a banker who was wrongly accused of killing his wife and her lover. He is sentenced to life at Shawshank State Prison in Maine. The story begins in 1948 and carries us through Andy's life in prison until his escape in 1975 and the narrator Red's subsequent parole. Red is a fellow prisoner whom Andy befriends. Red is the guy "who can get it for you" meaning that he supplies much of the contraband that comes in and out of prison (King 15). Red is an appropriate narrator because he is privy to information from both prisoners and guards that other prisoners might not have access to. Andy contacts Red because he wants a rock hammer so that he can shape and polish rocks in an effort to feel normal in such a sterile, controlled environment as prison. The rock hammer proves to be an important tool later in the story.

Throughout his twenty plus years in prison, Andy experiences some devastating and violent blows as well as some successes as he manages to get the prisoners, the guards and the warden on his side. Using his skills as a banker, Andy helps the guards and the warden complete tax returns, invest in stocks and launder dirty money. The latter skill is what made Andy the most valuable prisoner in Shawshank. As a result, he is allowed to have a cell to himself, and work in the library instead of the laundry. These privileges make it more possible for Andy to complete his escape (although it is by sheer will and determination that he actually succeeds). Andy uses his rock hammer to carve a hole in the ceiling of his cell and tunnels his way through the sewer system to safety. This is a story about the struggles one must go through in life and about how life is not always fair but one must make the best of it. Above all, this is a story of hope.

"Apt Pupil," the second novella in the collection, is a psychological thriller that focuses on a teenage boy's fascination with the Holocaust. Todd Bowden is a perfect student and an all–American boy living in sunny California. But he harbors a voracious thirst for knowledge of the Holocaust, not survival stories or stories of military strategy, but specific details of Nazi exterminations. He discovers by chance that a former Nazi SS officer, Kurt Dussander, lives in his town under the alias of Arthur Denker. Todd blackmails Dussander into sharing his stories of Nazi cruelty with him in return for Todd's silence regarding Dussander's true identity.

As the story progresses, the two develop a sick interdependence which threatens to ruin them both. Todd becomes so consumed by the gruesome details of the Holocaust that he cannot focus on anything in school and almost fails for the year. Dussander is forced to relive his past, which he had long ago buried, and finds that the memories uncover a fresh urge to torture and kill. He begins by luring stray cats into his home and killing them in his gas stove. Eventually he progresses to taking homeless drunks from the city. Todd eventually begins to experience similar urges and although neither of them share their feelings with one another, they both embark on dangerous killing sprees.

It is not until Dussander suffers a heart attack following a murder that the two are exposed. Todd helps Dussander bury the body in the now rancid basement, which serves as a makeshift graveyard for Dussander. Upon Dussander's death, the police begin to ask questions and grow suspicious of Todd. He ends his journey, not in redemption, but in destruction as he takes a rifle and tries to fight the inevitable. He goes down shooting.

"The Body," like many great literary works, tells the story of a journey. This journey involves four boys, including the reflective narrator Gordie LaChance, walking many miles in search of the body of a boy who has been missing for a few days. The boys believe if they find the body, they will become local heroes. "The Body" is set in Maine in 1960 at the tail end of summer; just a few days before the boys begin junior high school. Each boy has his own demons he is wrestling with as they set out to find the body. Teddy is a victim of his father, a veteran of WWII now in a VA hospital, who abused Teddy by burning both of his ears. As a result, Teddy is a daredevil and obsessed with battle stories. Vern is a boy of below average intelligence and is bullied by his older brother. Chris, Gordie's best friend, comes from a bad family with a brother in jail and an abusive alcoholic for a father. Chris is smart but most people expect him to become a delinquent. Gordie aspires to be a writer; his imagination is his only escape from two aging parents, grief-stricken from his brother's death, who neglect him. Their journey reflects a time of independence, brotherhood and ultimately growth.

Upon finding the body, they are alarmed at its grotesque appearance as well as the reality that the boy was their age and could just as easily been one of them. Coming face-to-face with death in this manner is one step in their coming of age. The next step follows when the boys are interrupted by a group of older, tougher boys, including Vern's brother, who have come to claim the body for themselves. While Teddy and Vern run for safety, Gordie and Chris fight for the body. Chris pulls out a gun and threatens the older boys who eventually retreat vowing to get their revenge later. Chris and Gordie decide to leave the body where they found it rather than turn it in for their own glory. It is unclear if Teddy and Vern have learned anything from their experience but Chris and Gordie have grown up. They have developed compassion and been humbled, but have lost their innocence in the process. The boys head home, begin school and eventually go their separate ways. Gordie, telling this story from the perspective of a 34-year old, informs the reader that of the four boys he is the only one still alive.

"The Breathing Method" is a tale within a tale. David Adley, an aging lawyer, narrates his experience of attending a special club in New York City where men gather to read, drink brandy and tell stories. The club is not really a club and Adley has all sorts of questions about its existence that he refrains from asking, for fear of not being invited back.

The stories told cover all topics and tones, but every year on the Thursday before Christmas, "it's always a tale of the uncanny" (King 454). Adley recounts the most recent Christmas tale he has heard told by an old doctor, Emlyn McCarron about a young woman, Sandra Stansfield, in the 1930s. Miss Stansfield comes to see Dr. McCarron after she has become pregnant and asks him to attend to her even though she is unmarried. He is awed by her determination and dignity despite the situation she is in, which many view as disgraceful.

He sees her through her pregnancy and teaches her a new breathing method, which he believes will help her cope with the pain of childbirth. Miss Stansfield embraces the breathing method, now called Lamaze, and uses it to help her cope with anxiety in life, specifically getting fired from her job for being pregnant.

The story turns macabre when Dr. McCarron has a vision of her death just before childbirth and Miss Stansfield also confesses a sense of doom. Ultimately, she goes into labor on Christmas Eve during an ice storm. To ease her anxiety, she practices the breathing method in the cab, unnerving the taxi driver who speeds to the hospital and crashes into an ambulance. As Dr. McCarron arrives at the hospital, Miss Stansfield is thrown from the cab and beheaded. Rushing to her aid, he inadvertently bumps into her head and it rolls to the curb. As he approaches her body, he sees that she is still breathing and realizes the child might still be alive. He hurries to get his forceps to deliver the baby but he has no need as Miss Stansfield somehow manages to birth the baby without his assistance. He gives the baby to a nurse and goes over to the head of Miss Stansfield. It mouths the words thank you although the voice is heard in the distance from the neck of her body before it stops breathing altogether. As the narrator leaves the club for the evening, he realizes that both the club and life hold mysteries that he has no business uncovering.

Symbols & Motifs

The collection is structured in accordance with the seasons and each novella is given a seasonal thematic title to reflect a different season. "Rita Hayworth and the Shawshank Redemption" is given the label "Hope Springs Eternal" which appropriately sums up its over-arching theme of redemption and the discovery of hope in the darkest of places. "Apt Pupil" is dubbed "Summer of Corruption" which encapsulates the downfall of Todd Bowden from perfect student to cold-blooded killer. "Fall from Innocence" is the title given to "The Body" and this seems most fitting as the narrator experiences a rite of passage from boy to man as he and his friends struggle first to see a dead body and then to do the right thing in respecting the body of a dead boy. "The Breathing Method" closes the collection labeled as "A Winter's Tale" which is fitting in the season in which it is set as well as the symbolic association of winter with death. The narrator, in the late season of his life, recounts a story told to him about a woman, in the prime of hers, whose life is abruptly taken from her.

Stephen King also discusses in the afterword of the collection that the title "Different Seasons" also reflects the shift in genre away from his usual horror. He is alerting his audience that this book is different than his previously published work (King 507).

Mortality is a motif present in all of the pieces in "Different Seasons." Each novella includes a major character or narrator who comes face-to-face with his own mortality or that of others.

Historical Context

"Different Seasons" makes reference to historical events as all of the novellas are set in the past. Both World Wars are mentioned. "Apt Pupil" is set in present day but built upon the events of the Holocaust and World War II. The Holocaust was the systematic persecution and murder or approximately six million Jews and other groups, such as Gypsies, homosexuals and Jehovah's Witnesses, deemed "racially inferior" by Hitler and the Nazis of Germany (United States Holocaust Memorial Museum). Holocaust is Greek word that means "sacrifice by fire" (United States Holocaust Memorial Museum). The Nazis came to power in 1933 and by 1945 the Germans had murdered nearly two thirds of all Jews living in Europe. "The Final Solution" was the name of the Nazi plan to kill all of the Jews of Europe. Jews were sent to concentration camps where they were subject to hard labor and ultimately execution by firing squad, gassing and other torturous methods. Kurt Dussander, the fictional, former SS officer in "Apt Pupil" was a particularly vicious executioner. Seeing as though Todd Bowden becomes equally vicious in the story, King is commenting on the fact that this type of evil might still exist today.

In "The Body," the father Teddy Duchamp was said to have "stormed the beaches in Normandy" referring to D-Day during World War II, June 6, 1944, when almost 200,000 American and British soldiers landed on the beaches of Normandy, France in order to defeat the German army (PBS). Teddy wants to be a fighter like his father and in fact, all of the boys become both fighters and survivors as a result of their journey. King sets "The Body" a few years before the Vietnam War and he presents a war of its own between Gordie, Chris, Teddy, Vern and the older, more aggressive boys in the story.

Societal Context

The collection represents the societies and cultural phenomenon of the decades in which they are set. For example, Andy Dufresne in "Rita Hayworth and the Shawshank Redemption" represents the hard-working, determined man characteristic of the 1930's and 40's. The boys in "The Body" represent the rebellious, restless spirits of teenagers in the 50's and 60's. Yet, although each story is set in a different time and place, they all embody some of the basic elements of human nature. "The Body," for example, reflects humanity's fascination with death as well as its need for companionship and acceptance.

In "Rita Hayworth and the Shawshank Redemption" King makes reference to the popular female celebrities of each decade Andy was in prison. The posters that Andy uses to cover the hole he is digging reflect who was popular at the time. Rita Hayworth was a popular sex symbol of the 1940s; Marilyn Monroe was the idol of the 1950s,

followed by Jane Mansfield and Raquel Welch in the 1960s, and finally Linda Ronstadt in the 1970s. King carries the reader comfortably through the times allowing for both a reflection on how people change, but also how they stay the same.

On December 17, 2007, Jose Espinosa and Otis Blunt escaped from a prison in Elizabeth, NJ, digging an 8 × 16 inch hole in his cell and covering it with posters as detailed in "Rita Hayworth and the Shawshank Redemption." The men most likely got the idea after viewing the film adaptation. Police captured Jose Espinosa on January 8, 2008, just 16 blocks from the prison. Otis Blunt was captured in Mexico on January 9, 2008.

Religious Context

The collection does not have an in depth religious context but focuses mainly on a person's actions while living, while simultaneously dealing with death and the ephemeral nature of life. King likes to pose questions in his work regarding if there is something beyond earthly existence. "The Body" questions what happens after a person dies and Gordie wonders about the dead boy and where he might be and if can see them. Kings questions are especially evident in "The Breathing Method" when a woman continues to breathe after she has been beheaded. His body of work suggests his belief that there is certainly something that exists beyond the living world.

"Rita Hayworth and the Shawshank Redemption" mentions the Bible in an ironic context when the corrupt warden, Sam Norton, makes sure each new prisoner at Shawshank is given a copy of the New Testament. On his wall in needlework hung the Biblical quote, "His judgment cometh and that right early" (King 56). This proved to be true as his history of embezzling money through the prison is exposed right when he least expects it.

King establishes his own religion in these works, one filled with a dichotomy of good and evil, hope and doom, fate and free will.

Scientific & Technological Context

The collection does not have a specific scientific or technological context.

Biographical Context

Stephen Edwin King was born in 1947 in Portland, Maine. His parents separated when he was a few years old and he split his time between Fort Wayne, Indiana and Stratford, CT. (StephenKing.com). By the time King was eleven, he and his mother had settled in Maine where he spent the remainder of his childhood and much of his adulthood (StephenKing.com). He attended college at the University of Maine, Orono, where he met his wife Tabitha. He graduated in 1970 and they were married the following year (StephenKing.com). He taught English for a few years before the publication of his first novel "Carrie" allowed him to leave teaching and devote his time to writing (StephenKing.com). He has been writing best-selling novels and short story collections ever since. In 2003, King won the National Book Foundation's Award for Distinguished Contribution to American Letters (nationalbook.org).

Most of his stories, including "Rita Hayworth and the Shawshank Redemption" and "The Body" are set in Maine. Much of his work has been adapted to film and television. Well known works include "The Shining," "The Dead Zone" and "Christine." In 1999, Stephen King was struck by a car while out for a walk. After the accident, King planned on retiring from writing but he returned a year later and has not slowed down since. In 2000, he wrote the book "On Writing" as both an instructional tool and reflection on his life's work. Naturally, it was a best-seller.

Jennifer Bouchard

Works Cited

Jones, Richard G. "Second Escapee From N.J. Jail Arrested in Mexico." *The New York Times*, 10 January 2008. NYTimes.com. 12 January 2008.

King, Stephen. *Different Seasons*. New York: Signet, 1982.

King, Tabitha. "Biography." StephenKing.com. 12 January 2008.

Lambert, Bruce and Richard G. Jones. "Escapee Caught Just Six Blocks From the Jail." *The New York Times*, 9 January 2008. NYTimes.com. 12 January 2008.

National Book Foundation. 15 January 2008.

PBS Online. "The War." September 2007. PBS. org. 12 January 2008.

Santos, Fernanda. "Inmates Chip Away Jail's Walls and Leap From Roof to Freedom." *The New York Times*, 17 December 2007. NYTimes.com. 12 January 2008.

United States Holocaust Memorial Museum. "*The Holocaust." Holocaust Encyclopedia*. 25 October 2007.

United States Holocaust Memorial Museum, Washington D. C. 12 January 2008.

Weiss, Jerry M. "Selected Stories of Stephen King." *Teacher Vision*. 12 January 2008.

Discussion Questions

1. How does King develop the suspense in each of the stories in "Different Seasons"?
2. What elements of surprise are built into each of the stories?
3. Who is the protagonist in each of the stories? How does the author make you empathize with him?
4. Who or what is the antagonist in each of the stories? When do you discover who the antagonist is?
5. What are the major themes presented in each of the stories?
6. How does Stephen King incorporate elements of horror into each of the stories?
7. What is the nature of evil and where is it present in each of the stories?
8. Is there a message of hope in any or all of the stories? If yes, where does it present itself?
9. How are the secondary characters in each of the stories important and necessary to the plot and development of the protagonist?
10. What makes Stephen King's fiction worthy of study?

Essay Ideas

1. Analyze King's use of seasons as a motif. Discuss how it applies to each novella and how it serves as an overall symbol for the collection.
2. Discuss King's use of setting to establish mood and convey theme (i.e. the use of following train tracks in "The Body" to represent a crossroad/the journey to adulthood.)
3. Analyze King's quote, "I always wanted to be able to explore a little bit of what childhood was like, because we lie to ourselves about that." Discuss how it applies to either "Apt Pupil" or "The Body."
4. Using one of the novellas in "Different Seasons" as a model, write an original story in which you build suspense and include an element of surprise.
5. Investigate how King presents the contrast of youth versus age in "Apt Pupil" and "The Body." Discuss how this contrast contributes to character development, plot and theme.

Do Androids Dream of Electric Sheep?

by Philip K. Dick

"The purpose of this story as I saw it was that in his job of hunting and killing these [androids], Deckard becomes progressively dehumanized. At the same time, the [androids] are being perceived as becoming more human. Finally, Deckard must question what he is doing, and really what is the essential difference between him and them? And, to take it one step further, who is he if there is no real difference?"

Philip K. Dick

Content Synopsis

Written in 1968, the novel is set in 1992 in which the world has been devastated by a nuclear war, World War Terminus. Many plants and animals are extinct. Humans are strongly encouraged to emigrate to space, as long as they have not been too negatively affected by radiation, which might render them sterile or damage their intellects. Relatively few humans remain on Earth, many of whom are outcasts or otherwise marginal citizens. Oddly, however, the androids, who are perks offered to emigrants to encourage their departure and to serve as slave labor for them, sometimes escape and try to hide on Earth. Such escaped androids are hunted

down and destroyed, or 'retired," by policemen such as Rick Deckard.

Rick Deckard is awakened in a happy mood by his Penfield mood organ, a machine that can stimulate any feeling selected by its user. His wife Iran, however, is not happy, does not wish to have her feelings modified by a machine, and fears that such electronic interference with emotions might have a negative effect. They argue about the merits of the technology. Before heading to work, Deckard checks on his sheep, kept on the roof. It is electronic, not real, but keeping an animal is now not only something humans do as an act of atonement for the devastation of WW Terminus but also as a social necessity. People demonstrate their empathy by keeping and caring for animals, thereby proving they are caring human beings. Keeping a real animal is quite expensive, however, so electronic substitutes are a cheaper way to meet the social obligation. Deckard's sheep died, and he has not been able to afford a real replacement.

When he arrives at the police station, he learns that escaped Nexus-6 androids, the most advanced androids and the most difficult to differentiate from humans, have incapacitated the currently active android hunter. Deckard now must hunt down the six androids his predecessor did not destroy. He will receive a bounty of $1,000 for each, enough to buy an expensive new animal.

To gather more information about the Nexus-6, Deckard goes to Seattle, to the offices of the Rosen Corporation, which manufactures the androids. Deckard hopes to be able to confirm that the Voigt-Kampff test, a test designed to measure a subject's empathy, will allow him to detect these androids. Since empathy is an exclusively human emotion, testing potential androids for empathy can determine whether they are human. The company has him first run the test on Rachael Rosen, an employee of the company, and the boss' niece. The test shows that she is an android, but the company informs Deckard that she is in fact human, lacking the expected human responses because she was raised on a space ship. Most of the empathy-testing questions presuppose innate familiarity with mostly extinct animals and with Earth customs pertaining to them, but Rachael, as someone literally not of this Earth, knows of animals from film libraries, not from direct, personal contact. The only other way to confirm someone is an android is via a bone marrow test, to which nobody is required to submit. While Rachael is still hooked up to the testing equipment, however, Deckard thinks of a final test to determine her status. This time, when she fails, he is sure that she is in fact an android. Nevertheless, we now know that the company desires to make its androids undetectable, and Deckard's own sureness about his ability to tell androids from humans is tested.

Meanwhile, J. R. Isidore, a subnormal "chicken-head," as some with diminished intellectual capacity as a result of the radiation are known, who lives in an abandoned apartment building, discovers that someone has moved in to a nearby apartment. He hears her television—television is an omnipresent feature of life in the novel, broadcasting either pro-emigration propaganda or the inane Buster Friendly program. The new apartment dweller is an attractive young woman, and Isidore likes her. He tells her about his theory of the kippleization of the world, the conversion of things into junk,

or kipple. The girl is a bit odd. For instance, she does not have her own empathy box, a device that allows people to participate in the religion of Mercerism. Wilbur Mercer was a mutant whose mutation allowed him to reverse time locally, thereby resurrecting the dead. He was martyred by being stoned to death, but now people use the empathy box to merge with Mercer and suffer his passion with him. An empathy box is like an extension of the self, Isidore says, and he finds it hard to imagine why this girl would have left hers behind when she moved in. The empathy box stands in contrast to television as a technological medium for interpersonal communication. We get a hint of why this girl might lack an empathy box when she tells Isidore her name: Rachael Rosen. He recognizes the connection to the Rosen Corporation, and she then tells him her name is Pris Stratten. The fact that she immediately changes her name when the Rosen name is recognized suggests that she is assuming an identity rather than revealing one and strongly hints that she is one of the escaped androids. Indeed, we later learn that she is physically indistinguishable from Rachael.

Isidore goes to work. He works for Hannibal Sloat, who runs an electronic animal repair service, disguised as a veterinarian's clinic. Isidore is sent on a pick-up, but he fails to recognize that the cat he picks up is real, not electronic, and it dies. Isidore's inability to tell the difference between a real and a fake creature suggests the extent to which he empathizes with all creatures, and it helps underscore the novel's interest not only in the limits of perception but in the probematic task of differentiating between the real and the false. It also foreshadows his ultimate befriending of the androids. Deckard continues his search for the androids. The first he seeks, Max Polokov, is not at his work or his apartment. Deckard gets a call from Rachael, offering to help him find the androids, but Deckard refuses. Deckard then meets a man claiming to be Sandor Kalyadi, a Russian from the World

Police Organization, supposedly sent in to observe how Americans hunt androids. However, Kalyadi is really Polokov, and Deckard barely manages to kill him rather than being killed.

Deckard now proceeds to track down the next android, Luba Luft, an opera singer. She cannily avoids taking the Voigt-Kampff test and calls the police on Deckard. When the officer arrives, Deckard finds he is unable to prove that he himself is a police officer; the officer does not recognize his name or identification, nor does Deckard appear to be known to the police when the officer calls in. The officer takes Deckard in, but not to the Hall of Justice with which Deckard is familiar; that one, the officer reports, closed down some time ago.

At this unknown headquarters, Deckard is questioned by officer Garland, who introduces him to Phil Resch. Resch, Garland says, is the police's android hunter. Deckard now appears to be in trouble, perhaps an android himself with false memories. Resch will administer the Bonelli test (another thing Deckard has never heard of), which tests the reflex-arc response in the spinal ganglia, to determine whether Deckard is human. When Resch goes to get the testing equipment, Garland, who was in fact the next android on Deckard's list, threatens Deckard with a laser. We now discover that this police station is a front for the android underground. However, Resch returns and shoots Garland before he can kill Deckard. Resch and Deckard go to retire Luba Luft.

They find her at an art gallery, looking at a print of Munch's painting "Puberty." Deckard buys her a book including that picture. When they kill her—Resch takes active pleasure in killing androids, unlike Deckard, and burns Luba down with his laser—Deckard then burns the book as well. Deckard believes Resch must be an android, given his lack of feeling (and given that he has been working for two years for an android-run shadow police force), but Resch passes the Voigt-Kampff test. Deckard's doubts about what he is doing escalate; after all, if he

is empathizing with androids, how can he do his job? Resch's is the more normative response, but it seems inhuman to Deckard. He buys a goat with his bounty money, an act of self-reassurance.

At home, Deckard engages in one of his rare moments of merging with Mercer, during which he engages in dialogue with Mercer. This is not the normal experience. Mercer tells Deckard that there is no salvation and that the fundamental condition of life is the necessity of violating your own identity, but that one must nevertheless proceed and do what must be done. Deckard sets out to retire the remaining androids but calls Rachael for help, not believing he can defeat three of them unassisted. They meet in a hotel room and have sex. The point of this, for Rachael, is to render Deckard ineffectual as a bounty hunter. She has done this nine times before, Deckard being the tenth man (since the etymological root of the name Deckard is the same as that of decimal, or "ten," this is perhaps not accidental). So far, only Phil Resch has been able to continue killing androids after having sex with one. Nevertheless, Deckard continues on his mission.

The two plots now begin to merge, as we learn that the remaining androids—Roy and Irmgarde Baty and, of course, Pris—are hiding in the apartment building where Isidore lives. Isidore befriends the three. The difference between Isidore's empathy and their coldness is accentuated when the androids capture a spider and torture it by beginning to cut off its legs, curious to see how many they can remove before it ceases moving. We also learn, via the television program of Buster Friendly, that Mercerism is derived from a lie. There was no Wilbur Mercer, and the experience people share in the empathy box was filmed on a set with an actor playing the part. We also learn that Buster himself is an android, suggesting further the extent to which the androids have penetrated and worked against the dominant human culture—or, perhaps, the extent to which the android "problem" is itself part of the larger political fabric. Regardless, and despite this exposure of Mercerism as false, Isidore falls into a merging with Mercer. This initially seems spontaneous, since there has been no reference to him using his empathy box, but when the experience ends, he finds himself holding its handles. During this merging, Mercer admits he's a fraud but also asserts his reality by giving Isidore the now restored spider. That is, Mercerism may have begun as a fraud, but it has become real nevertheless, as the revived spider and subsequent events demonstrate.

When Deckard arrives at the apartment building, he encounters Isidore, who has gone out to release the spider. Isidore tells Deckard that if he kills the androids, he will never be able to merge with Mercer again. However, Mercer appears to Deckard and warns him of Pris, who is sneaking up on Deckard. Deckard is able to kill her because of Mercer's assistance, and he then quickly dispatches the remaining two androids.

When he returns home, he learns that Rachael has been there. She killed the goat by throwing it off the roof. When his wife asks him if he thinks the revelations about Mercer are true, Rick says that everything is true, everything anyone has ever thought. He then heads out for a final trip, into the desert. There, he walks up a hill and has a Merceresque experience, being struck with a rock. He now believes that he has fused permanently with Mercer. On his way back to his car, he finds a toad, which he takes home with him. At home, though, his wife discovers that the toad is electronic; there is a tiny control panel on its abdomen. As Rick sleeps, she orders a toad kit, including habitat and electronic flies for it to eat.

Symbols & Motifs

Animals: As the title suggests, animals play an important role in the novel, largely in symbolic terms. The fact that owls are the first animals to die off, for instance, has obvious symbolic implications:

humanity has lost its wisdom. Humans either keep pets or keep simulacra of animals in an endeavor to demonstrate their empathy. By contrast, androids cannot keep an animal alive, even when they try to do so as part of their attempts to pass as human. A central irony in the novel is Deckard's attempts to convert the killing of androids into an animal he can care for and therefore prove to himself that he is still human despite his job. Tellingly, the animal he purchases (only to lose) is a goat. Mercerism is explicitly a scapegoat religion. A scapegoat, as described in the Bible (Leviticus 16) was a goat driven off into the wilderness bearing the sins of the community. The toad, by contrast, is an animal with a complex symbolic history. Toads can be symbolic of malignancy or poison, but they are also associated with longevity and fertility. The toad's association with death and resurrection ties it in with Mercer; indeed, Deckard believes Mercer led him to the toad. Toads can also be associated with hallucination, a probable link in the context of Dick's work, marked as frequently as it is by hallucinatory experiences. Given the novel's deeply ambivalent exploration of the duality of human nature, it is fitting that a creature with such complex symbolic associations should figure in its conclusion; indeed, in some contexts, toads are symbols of the unattainable, a particularly apt association for this novel.

Names: Dick was fond of using names that have symbolic associations or resonances. Here, the obvious one is Rachael, which means "little lamb." She is thereby associated with the sheep of the title and with the strand of the narrative that treats the androids as sacrificial victims. Though Deckard does not literally kill Rachael, he does kill Pris, her exact physical double. The name Wilbur Mercer also has complex resonances. The name Wilbur is derived from words meaning will or desire, and fortress. The name therefore suggests both the emotional core of Mercerism and the need for strength and fortitude to face the world as Mercer defines it. The name Mercer suggests mercy, but its etymology connects it with words meaning merchant and merchandise, which tie in with the notion of Mercerism as a scam. The actor who played Wilbur Mercer is named for Alfred Jarry, one of the founders of dada and the inventor of pataphysics, a pseudo-science arguing for the uniqueness of each act and the independent existence of multiple possibilities, again a point of view very much in keeping with the novel's assertions that everything anyone ever thought to be true is true. Finally, the names Rick and Roy not only alliterate but have similar etymological roots, Roy meaning "king," and Richard "powerful ruler," suggesting their functional opposition. Though Dick does not belabor the doppelgänger theme in the novel, it is certainly present, and it is explored in some depth in the film version (see, for instance, Francavilla, passim).

Existentialism: The Edvard Munch painting "The Scream" (see Pioch for a reproduction of this painting and of "Puberty," and a brief biography), one of the most famous images of existential despair, is referenced in chapter twelve. Existentialism clearly informs the novel. This philosophy argues the necessity of humans struggling against their nature, foregrounds alienation as one of the central conditions of life, and denies the existence of an external, authoritative guide to choice. Nevertheless, it also argues for the terrible necessity of choice, recognizes that most decisions have negative consequences, recognizes that some things in life remain irrational or absurd regardless of what reason we attempt to apply to them, and (perhaps most importantly) it argues an anti-existentialist view of life (see Wyatt for an extensive exploration of existentialism). Deckard presents many classic elements of the protagonist caught in existential doubt. He is, for much of the book, alienated from others, not even wanting to experience the artificial community created by Mercerism as

a substitute for the human connection strongly desired but unattainable. Deckard is even at war with himself, struggling, as existentialism posits humans must, against the contradictory elements of his own nature. He is forced to do what he does though he believes it is wrong, because the nature of the universe and of life demand that it be done. Centrally, stripped of any essential definition of what constitutes the human, Deckard is confronted by the absurdity of destroying androids that are physiologically as (or nearly as) "human" as he is because they have been defined as non-human according to arbitrary and undemonstrable (and certainly flawed) standards of what constitutes the human. The existential anguish represented by Munch's painting captures the core philosophy of the novel.

Historical Context
The primary historical events informing the novel are World War II and the Cold War. These events caused ongoing fear of another nuclear war, one that would have more devastating consequences than did the bombs dropped on Hiroshima and Nagasaki. The post-nuclear holocaust novel was a thriving subgenre through the fifties and sixties, and "Do Androids Dream of Electric Sheep?" participates in this tradition. The Cold War also inspired a paranoiac subgenre of science fiction, in which alien enemies disguised as humans invaded and had to be repelled despite being indistinguishable from (American, of course) humans. Dick's androids participate in this tradition, especially as the novel progresses and we discover that there are not merely a few escaped slave androids to contend with but a powerful corporation determined (for reasons never explained) to create androids that can never be distinguished from humans, as well as with a vast and organized android underground capable of striking at the very fabric of North American culture, as they do in their exposé of Mercerism.

Societal Context

Though Dick imagines a world in which a nuclear war has nurtured a belief in empathy as the necessary, even defining, human trait, the fact that humans have almost managed to wipe themselves out suggests the extent to which such a thesis can be provisional at best. Dick depicts a culture and society that pays lip service to empathy that is undermined by almost every aspect of that society. One would assume that if empathy were the defining human trait, then compassion rather than contempt would govern responses to, for instance, J. R. Isidore. Isidore himself is easily the most empathetic character in the book, but he is viewed contemptuously not only by the androids, who lack empathy by nature, but also by the humans. Humans view the subnormals such as Isidore as subhuman, as is reflected in the terms they apply to them: Isidore, being slightly impaired, is a chickenhead, while the more severely impaired are called antheads. The use of animal names as part of these insults ironically contradicts the claim that empathy for animals is the mark of a human being.

Indeed, keeping an animal is as much a matter of peer pressure and social status as it is an act of genuine care. Animals are a prized commodity, priced and traded like collectibles (there are price guides, price ranges, even the array of extras and paraphernalia that go along with the collector mentality). Furthermore, appearing to own an animal matters more than actually owning one: peer pressure and conformity continue to determine to a considerable extent what constitutes appropriate social behavior.

The novel further suggests that the media-saturated, consumer mentality that continues to govern society actually dehumanizes people. Iran, for instance, notes that the Penfield mood organ creates a disjunction between what the reason apprehends and how the emotions respond. She likens its effect to mental illness, absence of appropriate affect (3),

a state that would in fact render humans as affectless as androids. (Indeed, the Voigt-Kampff test is a problematic method of testing for humanity precisely because genuine humans suffering from mental illnesses such as schizophrenia would be no more capable of passing the test than the androids). The novel uses its science fictional tropes to comment critically on the dehumanizing effects of the society in which Dick lived.

Religious Context

Mercerism owes obvious debts to Christianity. Like Christ, Mercer is a miracle worker, specifically a raiser of the dead. Like Christ, as well, he is a scapegoat, suffering a passion and death, descent into a tomb world, and resurrection. He is not crucified, but stoned while climbing a hill. Those merging with Mercer become Mercer during this climb and suffer the wounds inflicted by the rocks, though they never reach the top of the hill. The god figure's suffering, therefore, is not merely something vicarious but something literally lived by his adherents. Mercerism seems in this to literalize the martyrology—or martyrolatry—present in the way some Christians stress the suffering and martyrdom of Christ and various saints. The futile repetitiveness of this passion also suggests that Mercer is a Sisyphean figure (Warrick 208–09), suffering a punishment as much as a transcendence. However, Mercer holds out some hope of immortality and transcendence. The religion may be a construct, but it is one that represents a fundamental human need and is therefore real.

Scientific & Technological Context

Dick generally avoids providing scientific details to explain how his concepts work. Instead, he tends to take as givens many of the staple technological wonders of science fiction, such as gravity-defying cars and laser pistols. Nevertheless, elements of the text reflect genuine scientific possibilities to some degree. Bizarre as it may seem, for instance, the Penfield mood organ derives its name and function from Wilder Penfield's experiments, which showed that electronic stimulation of the cerebral cortex could invoke memory responses, often associated with music (Enns 70ff). It is a small step from there to electronic mood manipulation.

More pervasive in the novel is communication technology, notably television. Television was by no means the cultural force in 1968 that it is today, but it was on its way. Dick had seen the enormous impact television could have (e.g. Beatlemania), and the recent innovation of color gave television even more power. The novel shows television functioning as a powerful propaganda tool convincing humans still on earth to emigrate, and as a provider of mindless pablum to the masses, replacing religion as their opiate in the form of Buster Friendly and his world of crass humor and celebrities famous merely for being famous (a prescient anticipation of much of the television landscape today). Dick satirizes the power of media in his depiction of television, but in the countervailing example of Mercerism, Dick creates a sort of antithesis to televangelism. Anthony Enns suggests that Dick uses Mercerism in a McLuhanesque fashion to allow characters a way to break out of their solipsistic worlds. Marshall McLuhan emerged as a prominent media theorist in the nineteen-sixties, arguing that print media were being superseded by electronic media, that medium and message were increasingly merging, and that electronic media were changing the shape of reality by allowing faster and more extensive communication. McLuhan coined the term "global village" to describe how electronic media were shrinking the distance between places, for instance. Though McLuhan warned that media could be used to exert Orwellian influence (a danger certainly hinted at in the novel), the novel suggests as well that Mercerism could create the shared "global village" experience for alienated and disaffected people (Enns 81–82).

Biographical Context

Philip K. Dick was born in Chicago on December 16, 1928, but he was taken by his parents to California at the age of two weeks, where he lived for most of the rest of his life, except for a few years in Washington as a child and a stay in Canada in 1972. Most of his education was in California, in public schools in Berkley. He briefly attended the University of California, Berkley, where he studied philosophy. He left after a few months but continued the study of philosophy throughout his life, and it influenced his fiction heavily. He began publishing science fiction in 1952 and quickly became a prolific author, publishing as many as four novels in a single year at the peak of his productivity (Pierce 5–9). Dick received the Hugo Award for his novel, "The Man in the High Castle," and the John W. Campbell Memorial Award for his novel, "Flow My Tears, The Policeman Said." His work is frequently satirical, critiquing consumer culture, the corporate and political spheres, and the relationships between the sexes. Most frequently, though, his work interrogates the notion that the world is a rational, logical, objectively knowable place by depicting in novel after novel either a world that has been constructed without the knowledge of its inhabitants, or has been constructed by their own minds and/or perceptions. Dick is especially interested in epistemological issues and in differentiating between the 'real' and the 'simulated.' Numerous novels and short stories make dealing with androids, robots, and other simulacra difficult, if not impossible, to differentiate from human beings. His writing therefore often has a paranoid, irrational, almost hallucinogenic effect so distinctive that "Dickian," like "Swiftian" or "Kafkaesque" has entered the critical lexicon to describe works with a similar sensibility. Dick experimented with drugs, but his most radical departure from consensual reality came in February of 1974, when he had a visionary experience in which he realized that the world he thought he lived in was an illusion, and he was a secret Christian living in apostolic times. He devoted much of his time in later years to writing an extensive Exegesis, in which he attempted to come to terms with what was, for him, a transcendent encounter with God. (McKee 1–5). He wrote only a handful of new novels after this point, many of which also attempted to rationalize his visionary experience. Dick died on March 2, 1982, of a stroke (Pierce 6). "Blade Runner," based on "Do Androids Dream of Electric Sheep?" was released three months later, though Dick was able to see the film before he died.

Dominick Grace

Works Cited

Dick, Philip K. *Do Androids Dream of Electric Sheep?* 1968. New York: Ballantine, 1982.

Enns, Anthony. "Media, Drugs, and Schizophrenia in the Works of Philip K. Dick." *Science Fiction Studies* 33.1 (March 2006): 68–88.

Francavilla, Joseph. "The Android as Doppelgänger." *Retrofitting Blade Runner: Issues in Ridley Scott's Blade Runner and Philip K. Dick's Do Androids Dream of Electric Sheep?* Ed. Judith B. Kerman. Bowling Green: Bowling Green State U Popular P, 1997. 4–15.

McKee, Gabriel. *Pink Beams of Light from the God in the Gutter: The Science-Fictional Religion of Philip K. Dick.* Dallas: UP of America, 2004.

Pierce, Hazel. *Philip K. Dick.* Washington: Starmont, 1982.

Pioch, Nicolas. "Munch, Edvard." *Webmuseum*, Paris. 16 July 2002. 28 February 2006.

Warrick, Patricia S. "The Labyrinthine Process of the Artificial: Philip K. Dick's Androids and Mechanical Constructs." Philip K. Dick. Ed. Martin Harry Greenberg and Joseph D. Olander. New York: Taplinger, 1983. 189–214.

Wyatt, C. S. *The Existential Primer.* 30 October 2005. 28 February 2006.

Discussion Questions

1. What purpose is served by the discussion of the Penfield mood organ in chapter one?
2. Why does the Rosen Corporation want to make the detection of androids more difficult?
3. What is Dick satirizing in his depiction of the marketing of animals? Why?
4. What are the implications of the fact that terms like anthead and chickenhead are used derogatorily to describe humans?
5. What is the function of Isidore's theories about kipple?
6. Why is Luba Luft killed in an art gallery? What other references to art (not necessarily just visual art) are there in the book?
7. Why does Deckard sleep with Rachael?
8. How does the androids' treatment of the spider change their relationship with Isidore?
9. Is Mercerism merely "'a swindle'" (185), as Roy Baty argues?
10. What is the significance of the toad which Deckard finds at the end of the novel?

Essay Ideas

1. Analyze the function of Mercerism in the novel.
2. Analyze the relevance of the art of Edvard Munch to the novel.
3. Compare/contrast the novel "Do Androids Dream of Electric Sheep?" with the film "Blade Runner."
4. Analyze the novel's complex treatment of the ownership of animals. Given the serious function of the practice as an act of expiation for the destruction caused by WW Terminus and as a way of proving one's empathy, why does Dick satirize the practice as he does?
5. Analyze the novel's exploration of and commentaries on the nature of human identity.

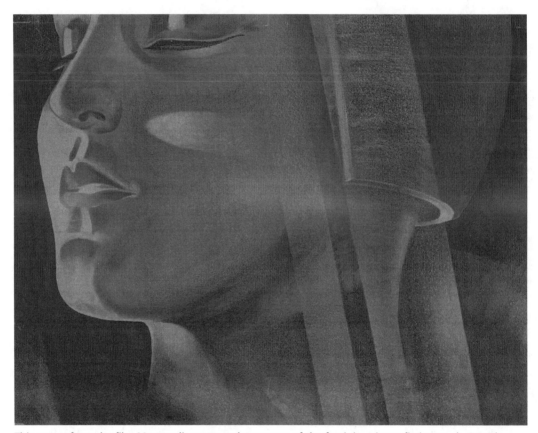

This poster from the film *Metropolis* captures the essence of the feminist science fiction work, *Female Man* by Joanna Russ, discussed in the following chapter. Photo: Library of Congress, Prints & Photographs Division, LC-USZC4-13519.

The Female Man

by Joanna Russ

Content Synopsis

"The Female Man" (1975) is set in four different worlds, and based on the premise of multiple time continuums. As the text explains, "Every choice begets at least two worlds of possibility, that is, one in which you do and one in which you don't [complete any given action]":

> To carry this line of argument further, there must be an infinite number of possible universes … . It's possible, too, that there is no such thing as one clear line or strand of probability, and that we live on a sort of twisted braid, blurring from one to the other without even knowing it … . Thus the paradox of time travel ceases to exist, for the Past one visits is never one's own Past but always somebody else's … . Thus it is probable that Whileaway—a name for the Earth ten centuries from now, but not our Earth, if you follow me—will not find itself at all affected by this sortie into somebody else's past. And vice versa, of course. The two might as well be independent worlds.

> Whileaway, you may gather, is the future.

> But not our future.

> (6–7).

One of the text's four protagonists, Janet Evason, is from the future world of Whileaway.

A thousand years before Janet's time, all the men on Whileaway were killed by a plague. The all-female society that evolved in the wake of this event is presented as a utopia: genetic surgery has rid Whileawayans of disease; "induction helmets" have simplified physical labor; and the merging of ova allows for single-sex reproduction. More importantly, the lack of men allows Whileawayans the freedom to take on male and female roles— although the terms "male" and "female" have little meaning in this post-gender society. Accordingly, Janet is physically as well as emotionally strong, has traveled widely and is highly intelligent, and loves her family and wife Vittoria even though she has killed four other women in duels. Whileawayans have also discovered "probability mechanics" and are able to teleport themselves to different worlds (13). This allows Janet to travel to two versions of 1969 America, where she encounters the text's other protagonists, Jeannine and Joanna. Jeannine is a librarian in a continuum where the World Wars never happened and the Great Depression continues. Unaware of her own oppression in a sexist society, she carries on a discontented love affair with her boyfriend Cal and feels pressure to marry and have children. Being a wife and mother are the only viable roles for women in Jeannine's world, and there is no way for Jeannine to articulate her lack of desire for either of these roles. By contrast, Joanna, an English professor from our own world, has benefited from the women's movement of the 1960s; unlike Jeannine, she is keenly aware of sexism and rejects conventional female roles as oppressive. She is also the author of the text we are reading, so the narrative is frequently interrupted by Joanna's asides to the reader about how she has shaped the plot, how she created Janet, and even how the book will be reviewed (140-41). While Joanna is one of the story's characters, participating directly in the events at hand, she is also, at times, a ghostly presence, self-conscious about her omniscient stance and the writing process.

These three protagonists travel between their respective worlds at the whim of Whileawayan scientists, who control the teleportation process from afar. Sometimes the three women are together, and sometimes they are not; along the way, Janet is interviewed by the press and falls in love with a girl named Laura (also known as Laur), Jeannine becomes more aware of her oppression in a sexist society, and Joanna translates her own growing feminist consciousness into her book, "The Female Man." Jeannine and Joanna are aided in these developments by an unexpected event. The women are suddenly transported from Joanna's kitchen to an unknown, fourth world, where they meet the fourth "J": Jael, also known as Alice Reasoner. Jael is an assassin and lives in a future dystopia divided into Manland and Womanland. She is plotting to destroy Manland forever. She wants to establish military bases in other worlds, and has sought her counterparts—Janet, Jeannine, and Joanna—from different time continuums to enlist their aid. Jael's hatred for the Manlanders is intense—she insists they are not human, keeps a male cyborg named Davy as a sex slave, and kills one of the Manlanders in front of the other Js because she enjoys it. Janet, Jeannine, and Joanna have different reactions to Jael's thirst for violence and domination. Janet refuses to participate in Jael's war, and does not believe Jael when she reveals a surprising historical fact:

Whileaway's plague is a big lie. Your ancestors lied about it. It is I who gave you your "plague," my dear ... I, I, I, I am the plague, Janet Evason. I and the war I fought built your world for you, I and those like me, we gave you a thousand years of peace and love and the Whileawayan flowers nourish themselves on the bones of the men we have slain.

(211)

Jeannine, however, supports Jael, saying: "You can bring in all those soldiers you want. You can take the whole place over; I wish you would" (211). Joanna, like Janet, is uncomfortable with Jael's brand of violence, and seeks another means of radical feminist action.

The conclusion of the novel, Part Nine, is introduced as "the Book of Joanna." In these pages, Joanna reveals a stronger, angrier voice: she articulates her observations about sexism in her society and finally dominates as narrator, since Janet and Jael's voices do not interrupt here. She also describes a final meeting between the characters. Over dinner in Jeannine's world, Jael makes her final proposition about establishing military bases. Only Jeannine accepts the offer, while Janet weeps "about (for) Alice Reasoner" (212). Joanna does not respond directly to Jael; instead, she says good-bye to the other versions of herself, and then invokes her book, saying:

Go, little book, trot through Texas and Vermont and Alaska and Maryland and Washington and Florida and Canada and England and France ... . take your place bravely on the book racks of bus terminals and drugstores ... . Live merrily, little daughter-book, even if I can't and we can't; recite yourself to all who will listen; stay hopeful and wise.

(213)

Thus, the novel does not conclude with a vision of future wars in distant worlds, but with a vision of feminist consciousness and activism in Joanna's, and our, future:

Do not get glum when you are no longer understood, little book. Do not curse your fate. Do not reach up from readers' laps and punch the readers' noses.

Rejoice, little book!

For on that day, we will be free.

(214)

One of the most challenging aspects of the novel is its format. The novel is divided into nine parts, each comprising seven to eighteen sections. Narrative perspective shifts from section to section, and from part to part. Style also varies: the main narrative, already shifting from Janet to Jeannine, Joanna, and Jael, is further disrupted by the insertion of dramatic monologues, statements of fact, anticipated/past reviews of "Joanna Russ's" fiction, and stream-of-consciousness interior monologues. Russ's disjointed format has two effects: first, it disrupts narrative chronology, much as the time continuum trope destabilizes narrative setting. Therefore, Russ's plot is not immediately obvious. We know that Whileaway is experimenting with teleportation, and that Janet has traveled to New York City, where she has gained the attention of the press and the authorities. We also know that Janet, Jeannine, and Joanna come together and travel between their different worlds, but we are not entirely aware of the connection between them until Jael enters the narrative. Although Jael addresses the reader at the beginning of Part Two, she does not participate in the narrative action until Part Eight, when she brings the other Js to Womanland. At this point, Jael confirms that the four Js are different versions of each other, and that Jael's war against men enables the establishment of the all-female utopia in Whileaway. Second, Russ's format destabilizes narrative authority: "The reader must constantly work to understand not only who is speaking in any given episode, but from/in which world this person is … Ambiguity is further complicated because some episodes represent the 'stream-of-consciousness' of one more female character, adolescent Laur" (Teslenko 130). In this way, the women's voices blur together. Russ's representation of a disjointed narrative finds its parallel in her representation of characters' destabilized identities. It is important that these identities are female, because Russ's challenge to female gender roles informs the text's more general subversion of gender itself: hence its playful title, "The Female Man."

Historical Context

"The Female Man" draws on and adapts several genres that fall under the umbrella label of speculative fiction, especially science fiction and utopian and dystopian narratives. Science fiction is "normally based either on a possible scientific advance, or on a natural or social change, or on a suspicion that the world is not as it is commonly presented" (Drabble 906), and includes texts such as H. G. Well's "The Time Machine" (1895) and Ray Bradbury's "The Martian Chronicles" (1950). Utopian fiction more specifically explores idealized societies, usually in a future where philosophical ideals are realized: "Utopia is an imaginative site of economic and affective abundance. The storytellers or history makers of utopia define their own notions of perfection and plenty in the good society which is 'nowhere' but might also be 'anywhere'" (Bartkowski 8). As Frances Bartkowski observes, utopian fiction is largely a nineteenth-century phenomenon; in the twentieth century, these narratives gave way to their opposite, dystopian fiction. Texts such as Aldous Huxley's "Brave New World" (1932) and George Orwell's "Nineteen Eight-Four" (1949) showed that:

> The future still holds all that imagination may shape, but the visions are much more uniformly grim. The nightmare fears of technology which often led to regressive, pastoral, anti-industrial images in the late nineteenth and early twentieth centuries are confirmed by a realization that the machine will not be banished from the garden. The two global wars early in the twentieth century produced strong dystopian strains in popular and pulp science fiction.
>
> (Bartkowski 7)

"The Female Man" incorporates both utopian and dystopian characteristics, since it projects an ideal future world in Whileaway, and a threatening, destructive one in Manland/Womanland. The text is also science fiction, however, since the narrative is based on possible extrapolations of known science: Russ's representation of time continuums and teleportation, for example, reflects the theory of relativity and knowledge about the speed of light and the effect this has on time: "the time dilation consequent to travel at near light-speed" constitutes science fiction's "favorite piece of theology" (Russ 1995 5).

However, while Russ draws on science and technology to imagine and explain different worlds, her motivation for doing so is to offer a feminist critique. As Jeanne Cortiel points out, speculative fiction encompasses many popular genres and reaches a wide audience; it is therefore "particularly useful for 'propagandistic' purposes" (Cortiel 2). In the 1970s a feminist dimension of speculative fiction emerged: "The shift in perspective from late 19th- to late 20th-century utopian critiques is the shift from capitalism and its discontents to patriarchy"

(Bartkowski 9). Along with authors such as Marge Piercy, Ursula LeGuin, and Monique Wittig, Joanna Russ "revolutionized the genre in the 1960s and '70s. This revolution transformed science fiction from a bastion of masculinism to one of the richest spaces for feminist utopian thinking and cultural criticism" (Cortiel 1). For Russ, "Utopias are not embodiments of universal human values, but are reactive; that is, they supply in fiction what their authors believe society … and/or women lack in the here-and-now" (Russ 1995 144).

Societal Context

In sending her book into the world, Joanna tells it to "bob a curtsey at the shrines of Friedan, Millet, Greer, Firestone and all the rest" (213). This is an allusion to some of the major texts of the feminist movement in the West in the 1960s, including Betty Friedan's "The Feminine Mystique" (1963) and Germaine Greer's "The Female Eunuch" (1970)—the latter's paradoxical title may have inspired Russ's own (Cortiel 197)—as well as Simone de Beauvoir's earlier book, "The Second Sex" (1949), which Russ does not mention here. These allusions suggests that Russ's "little book" is a fictional version of those critiques, and is indeed about what "women lack in the here-and-now." As one critic has argued: "Feminist utopias were prepared by the writings of feminist theorists whose analysis of women's situation showed that all aspects of women's lives were riddled with sexism: sex, work, marriage, motherhood, housework, health, education, and language" (Teslenko 165).

"The Female Man" dramatizes three major projects of feminism. The first and most obvious of these is to raise women's awareness of gender inequality and to challenge the patriarchal structure of society. Jeanne Cortiel has read "The Female Man" as representing a "dialectic path" that begins with "a patriarchal society" in

Jeannine's world; followed by "a revolutionary war against the oppressive sex-class" in Jael's world; and ending with "the 'gender-less' utopia Whileaway" (Cortiel 78). Cortiel explains that Joanna's different counterparts represent "the historical progression from the alienated woman via the feminist revolution to the woman conscious of herself and able to act" (Cortiel 77).

A second feminist project supercedes this challenge to patriarchy (and the problematic, violent reversal of sexism endorsed by Jael). This project is a challenge to the view that gender is an inherent, natural, and fixed aspect of identity at all. Over the course of the narrative, Joanna develops a post-gender perspective similar to Janet's. After acting like "one of the boys," she improves her intellect to become "a man with a woman's face" and "a woman with a man's mind" (133-34). She realizes that gender is a social construct and a performance. The benefits of shedding gender codes are clearly embodied in Janet's idealized post-gender world, in which male/female distinctions are meaningless and therefore harmless. This subversion of distinctive male/female roles extends to a subversion of discretely gendered bodies, and of fixed categories of sexual desire. Janet "has a female body but is—at least partially—gendered masculine. Although the text implicitly refers to her body as female, she is not a woman"; additionally, while Janet's "sexual relations are exclusively with other female characters, one can argue that she is not a lesbian either" (Cortiel 11).

A third feminist project is to realize the radical potential of language. This is troped through Joanna, who learns to crystallize her feminist rage into fiction, rather than Jael's brand of violence: "Though each of the four Js attempts to challenge gender stereotypes, the real potential for change resides in Joanna's writing the book we are reading, in the fiction that provokes radical action" (Teslenko 130). It is intriguing that Russ's novel

did have an impact on women's writing and feminist thought:

> Russ's novel … had a profound impact on the emerging feminist community as an example of a consciousness-raising narrative … . Russ reinforces the idea that gender is a social construct, that patriarchy is not going to change by itself, and that individuals can succeed only when they gain access to power, even if it is done by force.
>
> (Teslenko 127)

Even within the field of speculative fiction, Russ's text sets an example, rather than conforming to established conventions. Russ actively transforms science fiction and utopian/dystopian narratives be combining elements of each genre in one text. Her feminist rewriting of these genres is therefore more profound than the mere substitution of female protagonists for male ones, and more complex than adapting a critique of capitalism to a critique of patriarchy. As Tatiana Teslenko argues, Russ refuses to let:

> The antecedent utopian genre to become a rhetorical constraint, particularly in its chronotope [time frame]. Typically, utopia portrays one voyage to (and a return from) a perfect society that is represented as a blueprint for the development of the author's contemporary society … . Conversely, Russ's chronotope is based on the tactics of disrupting time/space linearity.
>
> (Teslenko 130).

The novel's disordered progression, multiple narrators, and overlapping worlds rewrite familiar generic formats while also challenging the view that reality itself is unified, causal (or unidirectional), and logical. In other words, Russ counters a masculine-coded rational worldview with one that subverts fixed order. This challenge allows Russ to subvert the mutually exclusive categories of social reality as well, particularly those relating to gender. In an all-female world, there is no such thing as a "male" category; therefore, there is no such thing as its opposition, "female." (The same is true of homosexual/heterosexual, as discussed above.) When Janet appears in Jeannine's world, her Whileawayan worldview destabilizes the concepts of male and female that Jeannine knows, just as Janet's very existence disrupts Jeannine's concept of the order of the universe. In very much the same way, Russ's text challenges expectations about genre and gender in the world of fiction, and about fiction's political and social role in the world of reality.

Religious Context

Religion is not an important aspect in any of the worlds depicted in the text:

> Russ is an existential writer; the present, not the past or the future, is her concern. There is no god—certainly no good god—to provide hope; the existence of human beings provides reason enough for a moral and ordered universe.
>
> (Holt 485)

The absence of religion in the text suggests that science is the discourse informing "The Female Man," rather than religious or supernatural worldviews. As Russ puts it, "[s]cience is to science fiction (by analogy) what medieval Christianity was to deliberately didactic medieval fiction" (Russ 1995, 5). In "The Female Man," scientists conduct empirical investigations into the organization of the universe, rather than practicing a faith-based belief in the origins or purpose of existence.

Interestingly, Russ's own definition of science fiction compares it to religion. She writes that "science fiction is not only didactic, but very often awed, worshipful, and religious in tone" (Russ

1995, 5). She explains that the leap of faith required for belief in unverifiable religious tenets or deities is like the leap of faith required in reading science fiction. Good science fiction, she insists, should not fabricate discoveries or inventions, but extrapolate from established scientific principles (Russ 1995, 6). Thus, the reader of science fiction must take a leap of faith in believing potential scientific discoveries:

> Science fiction, like medieval painting, addresses itself to the mind, not the eye. We are not presented with a representation of what we know to be true through direct experience; rather, we are given what we know to be true through other means—or in the case of science fiction, what we know to be at least possible.

In this way, science fiction is based on and promotes "wonder, awe, and a religious or quasi-religious attitude towards the universe" (Russ 1995, 9).

Scientific & Technological Context

Science and technology are clearly an important element of science fiction; as explained above, scientific discoveries and technological advances allow science fiction texts to envision alternative and future worlds. The discovery of probability mechanics on Whileaway enables the teleportation that brings Janet to Jeannine's and Joanna's worlds. The same technology allows Jael to explore different time continuums in order to find other versions of herself. At the end of the text, we learn that Whileaway itself is a product of Jael's war, which we know is aided by her ability to establish military bases on other worlds. Other scientific and technological advances shape life on Whileaway into a utopian existence: genetic surgery allows the Whileawayans to rid themselves of disease; "induction helmets" improve economic output while allowing Whileawayans to have a sixteen-hour work week; and the ability to merge ova, most importantly, allows for reproduction and for the continuation of human society. Thus, the text presents scientific and technological progress as necessary for political progress and the ultimate establishment of a utopian society.

The text also offers more ambivalent representations of science and technology however, especially when they are being used to deceive, exploit, or harm people. Jael's world is technologically advanced, but the Womanlanders are effectively slaves who produce and manage this technology for the Manlanders. To gain back some power, they are selective about sharing their knowledge. This is why Jael seeks the other Js; she wants to establish military bases on worlds the Manlanders have not discovered. While this form of deceit can be read as a justifiable reaction to Manland's subjugation of women, Jael herself embodies a darker representation of technology and science. Donna Haraway has written about the "cyborg— a cybernetic organism, a hybrid of machine and organism, a creature of social reality as well as a creature of fiction" (Haraway 149). Jael herself is like a cyborg: she has inserted metal claws in her fingers, and steel teeth in her mouth. The claws are retractable, however, and the steel teeth are covered by false enamel ones: Jael's deadly, mechanical additions are hidden by a human veneer, much as her female appearance belies the physical strength and killing skills of an assassin. Jael's brand of violence is problematized in the text, even while it is revealed to be necessary, and this ambiguity is troped through Jael's own almost-cybernetic body. Jael's teeth and claws recall the text's other (true) cyborg: Davy, Jael's blond-haired, blue-eyed, docile sex slave. Davy is programmed to respond to Jael's commands: he is a "lovely limb" of her computer-controlled house (199). However, Davy's human appearance lends the aura of exploitation to Jael's use of him, and Jael's offhand comment that Davy was kidnapped in childhood and lobotomized for this purpose is alarming, even if she is

only making a joke. While Jael's objectification of the cyborg Davy merely reverses the way Manlanders (and men in 1969 America) objectify real women, it still offers an ambivalent, uncomfortable representation of the uses of technology that counters the progressive, helpful role it plays on Whileaway.

Biographical Context

Joanna Russ was born in New York City on February 22, 1937. Her parents' interests in literature, science, and socialism shaped Russ's high school activities as well as her later fiction and academic criticism. She showed interest in science early in life: in 1949 she was offered a place at the Bronx High School of Science (which she did not accept) and in 1953 she was a finalist in the Westinghouse Science Talent Search. She was also interested in literature, and had two poems published in "Epoch" at age fifteen. After high school, she went on to study English at Cornell University, graduating with honors in 1957. She continued her literary studies at the Yale School of Drama, where she received the M.F.A. in 1960. As a student at Yale, she completed her first work of science fiction, the short story "Nor Custom Stale," which was published in 1959.

After completing the M.F.A, Russ married in 1963 but separated from her husband four years later. She continued writing, publishing numerous stories in magazines and several novels. Her work is almost exclusively science/speculative fiction; as she herself has said, "There are certain pleasures that do not occur in realist literature" (1995 xvi). She has won several awards in this field, including the Nebula award in 1972 (for her story "For When It Changed") and the Hugo award in 1983 (for her novella "Souls" in "Extra(Ordinary) People"). "The Female Man" is her best known and most acclaimed work, and was followed by several science fiction novels in the 1970s and 80s, including: "The Adventures of Alyx" (1976),

"We Who Are About To..." (1977), "The Two of Them" (1978), and "Extra(Ordinary) People" (1985). As discussed in the Historical and Social Context sections above, Russ's writing reshaped science fiction conventions and helped establish a genre of feminist speculative fiction. As Jeanne Cortiel observes, "['The Female Man']'s complexity and multilayered narrative not only anticipated but also influenced later developments in feminism" and laid the groundwork for "feminist science fiction as well as feminist cyberpunk" (Cortiel/Scanlon 260).

After completing her studies at Yale, Russ also entered a successful academic career, teaching at Cornell, the State University of New York at Binghamton, and the University of Colorado before taking a long-term teaching position at the University of Washington, Seattle, in 1977. She has written important criticism on science fiction, but has also contributed to the fields of feminist and lesbian studies. "How to Suppress Women's Writing" (1983), "Magic Mommas, Trembling Sisters, Puritans and Perverts: Feminist Essays" (1985), and "To Write like a Woman: Essays in Feminism and Science Fiction" (1996) demonstrate the diversity of Russ's scholarship, but also reveal her primary interest in the factors shaping women's day-today reality. As Sarah Lefanu notes, Russ examines:

> Science, technology, politics, culture [...] politics, women writers, sexuality, utopian writing, Mary Shelley, Star Trek and Star Wars, politics, Willa Cather, Charlotte Perkins Gilman, politics. I have repeated "politics": Russ's interest lies in the relation of the written world to life: to the life of the writer and the life of the reader.
>
> (Russ, 1995 viii)

The title of Russ's study, "What Are We Fighting For? Sex, Race, Class, and the Future of Feminism" (1997) demonstrates her continuing focus on women's experience and feminism, and a newly explicit interest in how this relates to class and race.

Some of Russ's critical work addresses her own experience as a science fiction writer, lesbian, and feminist; it could be said her fiction draws on her personal life, as well. Her novel "On Strike Against God" (1980), for example, explores the experience of coming out. However, "The Female Man" and Russ's other novels dramatize her subversive feminist stance in challenging or dispelling the fixity of categories such as "female/male" and "heterosexuality/homosexuality." Although Russ continued her scholarly work into 1998, she stopped teaching after she was diagnosed with chronic fatigue syndrome in 1990. Russ has also been plagued with recurring back pain, which sometimes affected her ability to write: her last fictional publication, "Excerpts from a Forthcoming Novel," was published in 1986. Her compounded health problems prompted her to leave her position at the University of Washington and move to the warmer climate of Arizona (Cortiel/Scanlon 258), where she still resides.

Jennifer Dunn

Works Cited

Bartkowski, Frances. *Feminist Utopias.* Lincoln, Neb and London: U of Nebraska P, 1989.

Cortiel, Jeanne. *Demand My Writing: Joanna Russ/Feminism/Science Fiction.* Liverpool: Liverpool UP, 1999.

_____. "Joanna Russ." *Significant Contemporary American Feminists: A Biographical Sourcebook.* Ed. Jennifer Scanlon. Westport, Conn. and London: Greenwood, 1999.

Drabble, Margaret, ed. *The Oxford Companion to English Literature.* 6th ed. Oxford: OUP, 2000.

Haraway, Donna. "A Cyborg Manifesto: Science, Technology, and Socialist Feminism in the Late Twentieth Century." *Simians, Cyborgs and*

Women: The Reinvention of Nature. New York: Routledge, 1991. 149–81.

Holt, Marilyn J. "Joanna Russ." *Science Fiction Writers: Critical Studies of the Major Authors from, the early Nineteenth Century to the Present Day*. Ed. E. F. Bleiler. New York: Scribner's, 1982. 483–90.

Russ, Joanna. *The Female Man*. New York: Bantam, 1975.

_____. *To Write Like a Woman: Essays in Feminism and Science Fiction*. "Intr. Sarah Lefanu." Bloomington and Indianapolis: Indiana UP, 1995.

Teslenko, Tatiana. *Feminist Utopian Novels of the 1970s: Joanna Russ and Dorothy Bryant*. New York and London: Routledge, 2003.

For Further Study

De Beauvoir, Simone. *The Second Sex*. (1949).

Butler, Judith. *Gender Trouble*. New York and London: Routledge, 1990.

Friedan, Betty. *The Feminine Mystique* (1963).

Greer, Germaine. *The Female Eunuch* (1970).

Hacker, Marilyn. "Science Fiction and Feminism" The Work of Joanna Russ." *Chrysalis* 4 (1977): 67–79.

Hicks, Heather. "Automating Feminism: The Case of Joanna Russ's 'The Female Man.'" *Postmodern Culture: An Electronic Journal of Interdisciplinary Criticism* 9.3 (1999).

Lefanu, Sarah. *In the Chinks of the World Machine: Feminism and Science Fiction*. London: Women's Press, 1988.

Perry, Donna. "Joanna Russ." *Backtalk: Women Writers Speak Out*. Ed. Donna Perry. New Brunswick, NJ: Rutgers UP, 1993. 287–311.

Discussion Questions

1. The narrative is sometimes disrupted by factual commentary about the role of women in society. How do you interpret these interjections, and who do you think the speaker is? What world is being described?

2. The text, particularly through the voice of the Joanna character, presents Jeannine as passive and unaware of her own oppression. Do you think this is true? Do you think if the world wars and civil rights movements never occurred, a world like Jeannine's would be inevitable?

3. Is Jeannine's boyfriend Cal represented in a positive or negative light? Do you think the text's representation of men is problematic?

4. Janet's strength of character derives from the fact that she lives in a post-gender world; she does not suffer from pressure to conform to gender-coded roles and behavior. What other categories dictate roles in Whileaway?

5. Is Whileaway a true or even realistic utopia? Is it possible to remove gender, race, class, and any other social categories? How could this be beneficial or detrimental?

6. Why is Laura's name sometimes shortened to "Laur"? What does this abbreviation signify, and why is it not used consistently?

7. How do you interpret Jael's appearance—the alterations from plastic surgery, her metal claws and teeth, her dyed hair?

8. Is the "plague" that kills all the men and enables the utopia of Whileaway justified? Discuss Jael's treatment of Davy.

9. Joanna comes from "our" world, albeit our world of 1969. What role does her character play in the text? How does her outlook compare to that of Jeannine, Janet, and Jael?

10. "The Female Man," like much science fiction, clearly has a didactic agenda. Is it possible for fiction to radically alter our ideas about social roles? Do certain genres have more potential in this respect than others? Why?

Essay Ideas

1. Analyze the form of the novel, paying special attention to Russ's blend of generic conventions and her use of multiple narrators. How do these structural aspects relate to the novel's themes?

2. How does "The Female Man" compare to other feminist speculative fiction, such as Margaret Atwood's "The Handmaid's Tale?" For example, discuss the texts' different representations of science, women, the future, and/or utopian ideals.

3. Compare "The Female Man" to earlier speculative fiction, such as "Brave New World." How does Russ feminize and/or modernize the conventions, plot, and themes of the earlier text?

4. Consider the role of scientific enterprise and discovery in the text, especially in relation to Whileawayan history. Is this a positive or negative representation of the future?

5. Discuss the text in relation to Donna Haraway's essay, "A Cyborg Manifesto."

Fight Club

by Chuck Palahniuk

Content Synopsis

Chuck Palahniuk's novel "Fight Club" opens with an unnamed narrator telling us about someone called Tyler. It drops us straight into the middle of the narrative and asks us to catch up: 'Tyler gets me a job as a waiter, after that Tyler's pushing a gun into my mouth and saying, the first step to eternal life is you have to die' (11). This is the model for the rest of the book. The unnamed narrator remains unnamed for the rest of the book, although he is often, in discussions of the book, referred to as 'Joe' because of statements made by him throughout the book relating to a series of "Reader's Digest" articles he reads with titles such as, 'I am Joe's Prostate' (58). This becomes part of his personal litany with statements such as, 'I am Joe's Complete Lack of Surprise.' (138) (In the film, the name is changed to Jack and so some discussions may refer to him in this way instead.) In addition, the book continues to use the in media res technique of the opening to reset the reader's expectations and to make the story continually fresh and engaging.

The narrative starts at the end. Joe is telling us about Tyler and the feel of the gun in his mouth. He tells us about how to mix nitro glycerine and how to use it to demolish buildings. As the first chapter ends, there are three minutes left until the building Joe and Tyler are in will collapse. He tells us 'I remember everything' (15) and this is the reader's entrance to the story, with the rest of the narrative being revealed as a flashback from this point.

The story then introduces us to Big Bob—an ex-bodybuilder who has had his testicles removed following cancer and has now grown 'bitch tits' (17) thanks to the hormone replacement injections—and to Marla Singer. Joe meets both of these at 'Remaining Men Together' a support group for men who have had their testicles removed. Like Joe, Marla has not been through such an operation, a physical impossibility, and is attending for her own reasons. Joe informs us that he attends a whole range of support groups like this one—from tuberculosis to brain parasites—as it is the only way he has found to cure his insomnia. He attends the group, shares his pain, cries, and goes home to sleep. 'Babies don't sleep this well' (22). But with the arrival of Marla Singer, turning up at all of the same support groups, the cathartic power of the groups leaves him and again he finds he cannot sleep.

Following this, Joe meets Tyler Durden. Joe travels a lot for his job-assessing the commercial necessity for recalling defective automobiles—from one anonymous airport to another. He meets Tyler on a visit to a nude beach on one of his trips. Tyler is arranging driftwood on the beach to cast a shadow of a hand. For one perfect minute, the hand is complete and Tyler sits in the created shadow of the palm. He tells Joe that 'a minute of perfection was worth the effort'. This is the overriding characteristic of Tyler's personality throughout the novel. Throughout the book he is willing to make the effort to find his own version of transitory perfection, whatever the cost.

After meeting Tyler, Joe confronts Marla. When she is present at the groups he cannot cry, and if he cannot cry he cannot sleep. They agree to split the groups, never attending the same ones. 'This is how I met Marla' (39).

The story is told as a chain of events rather than a smooth narrative and the next one sees Joe return home to discover his apartment has exploded, spewing his life onto the pavement fifteen floors below. He has no option but to call on the only person he can—Tyler Durden—for help. They meet in a bar and Tyler utters the immortal words: "I want you to hit me as hard as you can" (46). The fight between the two of them is a poorly handled affair, but the inhabitants of the bar gather round to watch and cheer them on. This is the start of Fight Club. The regular meetings and fights lead to Joe meeting lots of people, and coming to work with injuries to his face and hands, which disturbs his boss. Joe enjoys his boss's discomfort. This enjoyment recalls the conversation between Joe and Tyler after their first fight. Joe asks Tyler who he felt he was fighting, and Tyler answers that it was his father (53).

Then, with the discovery of a used condom in the toilet bowl of the house they are sharing, Joe learns that Tyler and Marla have met and have begun a relationship. Joe had called Marla on the phone to arrange their schedule for attending the support groups and she had been in the midst of a suicide attempt. Joe had ignored her and gone to her meeting, but she had called back and spoken to Tyler. He had gone to help her and in an effort to keep her awake and prevent the sleeping pills from killing her, he had spent the night having sex with her.

The story continues in a series of episodes, each escalating over the other. Tyler teaches Joe how to make soap from liposuctioned fat taken from Marla's mother and uses lye to burn the shape of his kiss into Joe's hand—a mark which he makes on Marla as well. Joe starts working with Tyler at one of his two jobs—hotel waiter—where they add their own special touches to the food by urinating in the soup and breaking wind over meringues. Tyler's other job as a movie projectionist allows him to splice frames of porno movies into children's films and cause distress on a subliminal level.

This rising tide of violent events starts to effect Joe's work—he is responsible for analyzing a car company's liabilities and deciding whether a recall of faulty cars is cost effective—and he once more takes it out on his boss. At the same time, Tyler is threatened with being fired from his projectionist's job. He tells them about the spliced pornography in the thousands of films that have passed through his hands and blackmails them for his silence. He gets Joe to do the same at the hotel where they have been interfering with the food. Tyler gets beaten up by the head of the projectionist's union, but Joe beats himself up, to the distress of the hotel manager. As he swings the first punch at his own nose, he recalls the first time he and Tyler fought.

After this, with both of them earning money but not having to work, Fight Club grows massively and leads to Project Mayhem. It starts when Tyler comes up with homework projects for the members of Fight Club in which they have to assault someone in a particular way, or otherwise cause public disorder. This leads to the more coordinated efforts of Project Mayhem, wherein the sides of buildings are transformed into giant grinning faces with burning offices for eyes. Men start gathering at Joe and Tyler's house, waiting on the doorstep through three days of abuse and rejection, before being let in. Tyler trains these men, including Big Bob from the Remaining Men Together support group, into a kind of army. This is the ultimate expression of Project Mayhem. Tyler wants to end civilization as it stands and return the world to nature.

As the project grows, Tyler is increasingly absent. In an attempt to find him, Joe asks in all the cities to which his job takes him. No one admits to seeing Tyler, but they wink when they say it. Finally, one bartender informs Joe that he, Joe, is actually Tyler Durden. Not believing the man, Joe rings Marla who confirms that he and Tyler are one and same man and that she and Joe have been having a relationship since he, not Tyler, saved her life during her suicide attempt.

Tyler shows up again and tells Joe that it's all true. Tyler is a product of Joe's insomnia. When Joe sleeps, Tyler gets up and goes to work doing all the crazy things he wants to do. When Joe beat himself up in the hotel manager's office it was like the first time with Tyler because he was actually only fighting himself.

Joe returns home and tells Marla about himself and Tyler and the difference between the two. He asks her to keep him awake—to stop him from becoming Tyler—or at least to follow him when he is Tyler so he can keep track of what he's up to.

Following the death of Big Bob, Robert Paulson, on a Project Mayhem mission, Joe tries to end both Fight Club and Project Mayhem, but Tyler has prepared for this eventuality. First, Joe is evicted from Fight Club and attacked by a group of Fight Club members who are under instructions to remove the testicles of anyone trying to shut down the club, even if that person is, seemingly, Tyler Durden.

Finally, Joe confronts Tyler as he moves to his next mission, the demolition of the important corporate building belonging to a company called Parker Morris, and the destruction of all the company's records. We return to the opening scene with Tyler pressing a gun into Joe's mouth as they stand at the top of the building about to be destroyed. Marla arrives with members of the support groups and tries to talk him out of whatever he's planning to do. However, Joe knows that Tyler has mixed the explosive with a formula he has never been able to make work. This means that he can't rely on the demolition of the building to kill him, so he must do it himself with the gun he now realizes he is holding in his own mouth. He pulls the trigger.

Joe survives, and the last pages are written from inside a hospital of some sort. Joe tells us that Tyler is dead, but members of Project Mayhem still surround Joe and inform him that the mission to break up society and civilization is continuing.

Historical Context

Writing a story very much in the model of Brett Easton Ellis's "American Psycho," Palahniuk's book is an examination of the alienation of modernity and pre-millennial angst which manifests itself in violence and sociopath tendencies. This is extended when Tyler talks about the lack of a father figure for a whole generation of men. (140) Modern youth is shown to have been abandoned by society, "God's middle children [...] with no special place in history and no special attention" (141). The anger and rage of Tyler Durden, and his attempt to reshape society in his own image, is a reflection of this disaffection. The success of both book and film suggests that the story has struck a chord with its target audience.

The success of the film greatly boosted the sales of the book and helped establish Palahniuk's career as a writer which has seen the publication of his first, previously unpublished, novel, "Invisible Monsters," and a number of other fiction and non-fiction titles.

Societal Context

"Fight Club" is very much a product of the end of the twentieth century. It represents the obsessions and hang-ups of modern society. Palahniuk dissects society, looking at it from many different angles. First he uses the concept of the support group, where strangers gather together to talk about their problems, as a way of criticizing the lack of family support.

In addition, the consumer culture which makes up so much of modern society is criticized. This happens in a number of ways. First we are exposed to the narrator's exploded apartment. His condominium has been destroyed by an explosion and all his belongings have been vomited from their concrete shell all over the ground below. What follows is a list of all the things the narrator has lost in this explosion. He doesn't list personal items such as letters or photographs but instead lists the items of furniture which have been destroyed. In addition, he is able to recall the names their makers have given to them. He compares the IKEA catalogue to pornography (43) and the list of the lost furniture is certainly fetishistic. In addition, he mourns his refrigerator in which he had different kinds of mustard and dressings. He admits the shallowness of it all with the sentence, 'I know, I know, a house full of condiments and no real food' (45), a sentiment which seems addressed more to his whole life than simply the contents of the refrigerator.

Beyond this, the consumer culture is also criticised in one of the book's main motifs—the production of soap. This is done by rendering the liposuctioned fat removed from rich old ladies. It is then turned into soap and sold back to them. This works, as do the previously mentioned ideas in the book, as a criticism of a society obsessed

with youth, idleness and luxury. Tyler is reacting against a world in which some people starve while others eat too much, get fat, and then have it removed. As if this wasn't enough, if they have enough, these same people can afford to have their fat stored in order for it to be used to give themselves—or in this case, Marla's mother saves it for her daughter—a facelift, injecting fat into loose skin to create the impression of youth. As an image it is disgusting, but as with the other repulsive concepts which Palahniuk introduces, it is captivating and argues his point that society seems out of control. The idea of Tyler making this fat into soap and selling it back to the ladies from whom it was taken satirises this process and turns the ladies into modern-day cannibals, literally consuming themselves.

Religious Context

Religion raises its head in "Fight Club" when the discussions of the lack of a male role model in the life of young men includes the concept of God as a father-figure and highlights the potential hole in society where religion should be. As one character informs us, "If you're male and you're Christian and living in America, your father is your model for God. And if you never know your father, if your father bails out or dies or is never at home, what do you believe about God" (141)? Later this perceived lack is transformed into a positive hatred of us by God, with the possible consolation that being hated by God is at least better than being ignored by him.

Finally, at the end of the book, after attempting to kill himself, the narrator informs us he is now in heaven and has met God (207). But God is no longer a father, instead a doctor, trying to cure him and still there are no answers. In this way, "Fight Club" can be seen as a rejection of religion and what it can do to cure the problems of our society at this point in its development.

Scientific & Technological Context

Science and technology are represented in "Fight Club" only in so much as they are representative of the historical period which Tyler is seeking to rebel against. The first instance of this comes when Tyler and the narrator make soap for the first time (75). Tyler tells him about the origins of soap making: how the combination of fat and the lye produced in the wood ash of pre-historical funeral pyres would create a kind of soap which would run down into rivers and streams and make it easier for clothes to be cleaned. Tyler tells this story to the narrator at the same time as inflicting a chemical burn on his hand—a form of initiation rite. By using this story as part of such a primal ceremony, Tyler exalts the idea of simple, gathered knowledge, rather than the rigours of science.

This anti-science/technology theme is continued later when Tyler explains the aim of Project Mayhem and the rule of anarchy it is attempting to invoke. He describes to the narrator a world in which they could be "stalking elk past department store windows" and "climb[ing] the wrist-thick kudzu vines that wrap the Sears Tower" (125). This evokes a pre-technological existence where the trappings of modern life, of civilization are no longer needed.

Biographical Context

"Fight Club" was written by Chuck Palahniuk as his second attempt at a publishable novel. His first attempt, "Invisible Monsters," had been described by the publishers as being too disturbing. His response to this was to attempt to write something even more disturbing. This was a short story, which eventually became the novel "Fight Club": a book which the publisher was more than happy to accept.

The story is based, not on any real fight club, but on Palahniuk's own experience of being beaten up while on a camping trip. His face was an appalling mess afterwards and he enjoyed shocking people by showing it to them. This was the root of the story. However, since the publication of the book, and more importantly the success of the film, it has been reported that a number of real fight clubs have been set up. There are even claims that, unbeknownst to Palahniuk, a number of them existed previously.

Palahniuk's biography reads like one of his books. He recalls being present in the trailer where he and his family lived when his grandfather shot his grandmother. He hid under a bed while his grandfather searched for someone else to kill before turning the gun on himself. Shortly after this his parents separated and Palahniuk was left to live with his mother, an event echoed in Tyler's discussions of fatherless children in "Fight Club."

After graduating from the University of Oregon's School of Journalism, he worked for a short while for a local newspaper before becoming a diesel mechanic. This is the job he was working in when he started writing his novels. During this time he also volunteered at homeless shelters and worked as an escort at a hospice, accompanying terminally ill people to support groups, an activity which appears in a much altered guise in the book. He started writing seriously after attending writing workshops with Tom Spanbauer, who encouraged him and helped to influence the very sparse writing style which Palahniuk employs.

From his youth, Palahniuk was also a member of Portland's Cacophony Society, an anarchic society who gather together and carry out public events outside the mainstream of society. One annual event, the Santa Rampage, is for the 500 or so members of the Society to all dress up as Santa and gate-crash 'unsuitable' public venues (Chalmers). This Society was the source for Project Mayhem in "Fight Club."

Calum A. Kerr

Works Cited

Bilton, Alan. *An Introduction to Contemporary American Fiction*. Edinburgh: Edinburgh University Press, 2002.

Chalmers, Robert. "Chuck Palahniuk: Stranger than Fiction" *The Independent*, 01 August 2004.

Jemielity, Sam. "Chuck Palahniuk: The Playboy Conversation:. *Playboy.com* at http://www. playboy.com/arts-entertainment/comversation/palahniuk/[Accessed on 25 January 2006].

Millard, Kenneth. *Contemporary American Fiction*. Oxford: Oxford University Press, 2000.

Palahniuk, Chuck. *Fight Club*. London: Vintage, 1997.

Discussion Questions

1. Is this a book about fighting?
2. Discuss how sleep is used as a metaphor in the book.
3. What is the root of the narrator's initial dislike of Marla?
4. Why do the narrator's feelings towards Marla change?
5. What are the narrator's feelings towards Tyler and how do they change through the book?
6. What are the ironies and inconsistencies in the book?
7. How much freedom do you feel the narrator has to make his own decisions?
8. What does Tyler hope to gain with his Project Mayhem activities?
9. Is it possible to guess the narrator/Tyler connection before it is revealed?
10. At the end of the story we learn that Tyler is a part of Joe's subconscious, almost a phantom. To what extent does this undermine the validity of his pronouncements?

Essay Ideas

1. Discuss the title in terms of how it represents the novel's contents?

2. Palahniuk has a very particular writing style. How does it work and how does it enhance the content of the story?

3. Compare the book to the film. How accurate an adaptation is it?

4. Why does Palahniuk never give us a name for the narrator?

5. How does the revelation of the narrator and Tyler's co-existence affect the perception of all that comes before it?

Franny and Zooey

by J. D. Salinger

Content Synopsis

"Franny and Zooey" was published in 1961 and is composed of two previously published short stories. The first, "Franny," depicts a young woman's breakdown played out through a conversation with her boyfriend Lane Coutell. The narrative opens at a train station on the weekend of a Yale football game. Several students are awaiting the arrival of girlfriends and discussing intellectual topics in "collegiately dogmatic" voices (3). Lane is reading a letter from someone named Franny. This is reprinted in full in the text and depicts Franny as an affectionate, exuberant college student. The well-worn appearance of the letter suggests Lane has read it many times and has strong feelings for Franny. But he puts the letter away when the train arrives and feigns indifference, trying "to empty his face of all expression that might quite simply, perhaps even beautifully, reveal how he felt about the arriving person" (7).

Franny is one of the first passengers off the train. She is holding a suitcase and a small, clothbound book, and waves "extravagantly" at Lane before kissing him (7). This warmth and enthusiasm seem out of place in Lane's all-male collegiate world, with its forced nonchalance and intellectual one-upmanship. Franny's show of affection contrasts sharply with Lane's suppression of emotions. Yet, Franny is also masking her true feelings. She secretly feels annoyed with Lane but puts on a cheerful facade to conceal this. However, she cannot hide a certain truth from herself as they leave in a taxi: "'Oh, it's lovely to see you!' Franny said [to Lane] as the cab moved off. 'I've missed you.' The words were no sooner out than she realized that she didn't mean them at all" (10). It is clear that Franny's feelings for Lane have recently changed, but the text does not immediately indicate why this is so. The significance of Franny's clothbound book is also unknown: when Lane asks about it, she hastily puts it away in her bag.

After depositing Franny's belongings in her lodgings, she and Lane go to a restaurant. There, arguments about academe and poetry become a point of tension between the couple, and reveal the disillusionment behind Franny's increasingly strange behavior. The third-person narration plays a role in these revelations by employing an ironic perspective. The use of free indirect discourse conveys the exact tone of both characters' thoughts, but this is juxtaposed with a certain amount of narrative distance, allowing for subtle critical judgments. For example, Lane's desire to be "in the right place with an unimpeachably right-looking girl" (11), his preference for frog's legs and escargot, and his boasts about an English paper reveal his pretensions to sophistication and intellectual superiority. For some time he is annoyed by Franny's refusal to eat a formal meal (she orders but does not eat a chicken sandwich), and is too self-absorbed to realize that her lack of appetite and pale, perspiring face are signs of deep anxiety.

During their conversation, Franny complains to Lane about the "ego, ego, ego" (29) pervading college life, and admits she recently quit a drama group because acting made her feel like "such a nasty little egomaniac" (28). Her observations about intellectual affectation describe Lane exactly, and suggest why she is secretly exasperated with him. Her distaste for "ego, ego, ego," however, also points to a deeper spiritual crisis. Feeling unwell, she goes to the restroom where she cries to herself; after holding the clothbound book, she mysteriously feels better. She returns to the table, and eventually tells Lane that the book, "The Way of a Pilgrim," is about the spiritual awakening achieved through incessant prayer. In an increasingly agitated manner, she says that "really advanced and absolutely unbogus religious persons" teach that "if you repeat the name of God incessantly, something happens." She continues: "You get to see God. Something happens in some absolutely nonphysical part of the heart—where the Hindus say Atman resides, if you ever took any Religion—and you see God, that's all" (39). Unsurprisingly, Lane is skeptical, but reacts with concern when he realizes Franny is very unwell. When Franny gets up from the table again, to return to the bathroom, she faints. There is a break in the text here, and a new scene begins with Franny waking up on a couch in the manager's office. Lane is there and shows concern for Franny, but shortly leaves the room to call a cab. The story ends when Franny is left alone on the couch, and begins whispering to herself. Given the content of her clothbound book, it is clear she is repeating a prayer.

"Zooey" takes place a few days after these events, on a November morning in 1955. This story is about Zooey Glass, Franny's brother and the second youngest of seven Glass children, but is narrated by Buddy Glass, their older brother. The narrative begins with an "author's formal introduction" from Buddy: "what I'm about to offer isn't really a short story at all but a sort of prose home movie" (47). He explains that the events he is about to describe were told to him "in hideously spaced installments" by the people involved, and constitute "a compound, or multiple, love story, pure and complicated" (49). Buddy ends his introduction with the decision to "leave this Buddy Glass in the third person from here on in" (50). However, the rest of the story is subject to frequent interruptions from Buddy himself.

Buddy's story begins with Zooey Glass sitting in the bath, reading a letter "propped up against the two dry islands of his knees" (50). We learn that Zooey is an actor, but then Buddy interrupts the narrative by way of a footnote. This aside to the reader provides some background about the Glass family. Buddy tells us that the oldest Glass child, Seymour, committed suicide seven years ago. The next child, Buddy himself, is a writer-in-residence at a New York college. The oldest daughter, Boo Boo, is traveling in Europe with her own family, while their brother Waker, a Roman Catholic priest, is in Ecuador. Waker's twin Walt died ten years ago, in a "freakish explosion" serving in the Army of Occupation in Japan (53).

In the main text, Buddy provides more background information. We learn that all seven Glass children were regular guests on a popular radio program, "It's a Wise Child," from 1927 to 1943. They gained some fame for their intellectual brilliance (Zooey in particular). As soon as the narrative returns to Zooey reading in the bathtub, the text is interrupted again. The letter he is reading is from Buddy himself, and was written four years ago. Like Franny's letter to Lane, it is reproduced in full in the text. In it, Buddy explains to Zooey that he and Seymour, worried about "the statistics on child pedants and academic weisenheimers who grow up into faculty-recreation-room savants," wanted Franny and Zooey to be able to conceive of a "state of pure consciousness" before they knew "too much about Homer or Shakespeare or even Blake or Whitman, let alone George Washington and his cherry tree or the definition of a peninsula or how to parse a sentence" (65–66). Thus, Franny and Zooey undertook intensive study about "Jesus and Gautama and Lao-Tse and Shankaracharya and Hui-neng and Sri Ramakrishna, etc." (66) as children.

Although Buddy's letter was written to encourage Zooey to continue with his acting career, its comments about this "education" seem to make Zooey anxious. He is described as sweating, and displays impatience and annoyance with his mother, who keeps entering the bathroom to talk to him. (Sweat and annoyance are also signs of Franny's anxiety in the restaurant.) Mrs. Glass is concerned about Franny, who has recently come from her meeting with Lane and is now resting on the living room couch. Mrs. Glass is, in some ways, a caricature of an overbearing mother: she nags Zooey about using toothpaste and a washcloth, and pesters him with complaints about Buddy's reclusive lifestyle and Franny's diet of cheeseburgers. Her real agenda, however, is to prompt Zooey to talk with Franny and ease her anxieties.

A long conversation between Franny and Zooey follows this bathroom scene, during which Franny intermittently repeats the Jesus prayer to herself: "Lord Jesus Christ, have mercy on me." Zooey approaches Franny carefully at first, using jokes to cheer her up. The conversation eventually turns to his own concerns, though, as Zooey begins complaining about people in the acting world (in a manner reminiscent of Franny complaining to Lane in the restaurant). Franny responds with her own denunciation of the "patronizing and campusy" attitudes of her professors, but Zooey immediately criticizes her: "You're way off when you start railing at things and people instead of at yourself ... . But it's wrong. It's us" (139). Zooey blames Seymour and Buddy for the way he and Franny judge everyone: "We're freaks, that's all. Those two

bastards got us nice and early and made us into freaks with freakish standards, that's all" (139).

Zooey then accuses Franny of being selfish and points out the inconsistencies in her "tenth-rate thinking" (166): "There's no difference at all, that I can see, between the man who's greedy for material treasure—or even intellectual treasure—and the man who's greedy for spiritual treasure" (148). Zooey continues this attack on Franny's logic, seemingly reveling in a brilliant performance of reason and intellect. He breaks off when he realizes he has gone too far:

> He stared over at Franny's prostrate, face-down position on the couch, and heard, probably for the first time, the only partly stifled sounds of anguish coming from her. In an instant, he turned pale-pale with anxiety for Franny's condition.
>
> (172)

The concluding part of the story shows Zooey trying a different tactic to help Franny. For the first time since Seymour's death, he goes into Seymour's old room. There, he looks through Seymour's journal (written on shirt cardboards) and briefly scans an entry about Seymour's twenty-first birthday. This describes the family members performing songs and impersonating each other. This account seems to inspire Zooey, because he uses the separate phone line in the bedroom to telephone Franny, all the while pretending to be Buddy. Zooey is adept at impersonation, and Franny initially falls for the trick. She tells "Buddy" about her concerns and complains about Zooey's "completely destructive" attitude (190). She soon realizes she is talking to Zooey, but stays on the line.

At this point, Zooey addresses Franny frankly but with kindness. By cutting short his own theatrical performance and lecturing, Zooey can overcome his "long war with himself (i.e., his ego)" and reach out to his sister (Bryan, 226). Reminiscing, he tells Franny that Seymour once asked him to shine his shoes for the "Fat Lady" before performing on "It's a Wise Child." Franny remembers that Seymour also told her to be funny for the "Fat Lady." This memory causes Zooey's sudden epiphany, which is relevant to Franny's repetition of the Jesus prayer: "There isn't anyone out there who isn't Seymour's Fat Lady," he declares, "don't you know who that Fat Lady really is … Ah buddy. Ah buddy. It's Christ himself" (201–02). Franny responds to this revelation with joy. The story concludes when she hangs up the phone and falls "into a deep, dreamless sleep" (202), which is very different from the cold, sweating faint that ended the first story in the book. This ending resolves the real conflict in the story—not Franny's desire to "see God" or Zooey's resentment about his upbringing—but Seymour's ghost. As Hassan has argued, "Seymour Glass haunts all the Glass children" (Hassan 7). Thus:

> The success of Zooey heralds both the defeat and the apotheosis of Seymour: defeat because the youngest of the Glass children [Franny] has at last achieved a measure of independence from the guru of the house, and the apotheosis because this is precisely what Seymour would have wished.
>
> (Hassan 12)

Historical Context

"Franny and Zooey," like some of Salinger's other fiction, shows a preoccupation with the aftereffects of the Second World War. The Glass family has been traumatized by Seymour's suicide, which occurred shortly after his return from service in Europe. In the 1950s, many American soldiers suffered from what is now known as post-traumatic stress disorder, a state of psychological disturbance arising from a traumatic experience, such as combat, and resulting in flashbacks, anxiety, and/or depression. The decade also saw the rise of the nuclear arms race, known as the Cold War,

between the United States and Russia. In America, Cold War tensions prompted fears about Russian spies and the spread of Communism. These fears were further fueled by a campaign led by Senator Joseph McCarthy and the House Committee on Un-American Activities to oust Communist spies. This movement ("McCarthyism") died out in the first half of the decade. The early part of the decade was also marked by the Korean War (1950–53), in which the United States supported South Korea against North Korea and China. Therefore, for Americans, the beginning of the post-war world was characterized by continuing conflicts overseas and new tensions on the domestic front. The "shell shock" suffered by individual WWII veterans serves as an apt metaphor for the anxious mood of the country at large as it forged a new way of life in the wake of the traumatic war years.

On a more positive note, the text's 1950s time frame was also characterized by socio-economic progress: economic prosperity, the rise of modern mass culture, technological advances, and the centrality of the nuclear family. This was the dawn of the television age: radio entertainment such as "It's a Wise Child" was eclipsed, though not outmoded, by television shows. The war had created more jobs, and families could afford to move out of the city, generating the suburban sprawl that still characterizes America's literal and cultural landscape. There was an emphasis on a return to normality, particularly in the domestic sphere. This is reflected in the Glass family's nostalgia for the happier, easier times of the past, although the text also exhibits suspicions about what "normality" entails, as discussed in the Societal Context section below.

"The Catcher in the Rye" (1951) may have earned Salinger a wide audience, but the publication of "Franny and Zooey" in 1961 confirmed his literary reputation. Advance orders for the book made it a bestseller before it was even published, and *Time* featured Salinger in a cover article

(Alsen 146). "Franny" and "Zooey" were first published as separate short stories in "The New Yorker" in 1955 and 1957, respectively. Read out of context, "Franny" is somewhat cryptic; in 1955, some readers misinterpreted the story and believed Franny was pregnant (Alsen 106). Since there is no mention of Franny's last name, no connection was made to the Glass family, the subject of several Salinger stories. The first Glass character was introduced in "A Perfect Day for Bananafish" (1948), which depicts the suicide of Seymour Glass. Later stories, including "Uncle Wiggily in Connecticut" (1948) and "Seymour: An Introduction" (1959) continued the Glass saga. "Zooey," in particular, provides details about the family's background and the fallout of Seymour's death. The publication of "Franny" and "Zooey" in one book connects the stories chronologically, confirms that the girl in "Franny" is Franny Glass, and provides some insight into the reasons behind her breakdown.

Societal Context

Franny's desire for spiritual fulfillment suggests an inner emptiness that college, a burgeoning acting career, and romance cannot fill. It is fitting (or convenient, as Zooey sarcastically implies) that Franny returns to the Glass home to have her breakdown. The family apartment is literally filled to overflowing: the medicine cabinet in the bathroom is packed with odds and ends; the living room is crowded with furniture; and "children's books, textbooks, second-hand books, Book Club books" are "cram-jammed" on the shelves (120). The apartment is also figuratively filled with memories of the past, signified by such relics as the records from Mr. and Mrs. Glass's vaudeville days, family photo albums, and Seymour's journal. Yet, as Zooey points out, "This whole goddamn house stinks of ghosts" (103). Despite the proliferation of things, the apartment is devoid of life. Seymour's old room is cluttered with his possessions and

writings, for example, but the living Seymour is no longer there. The surface clutter in the apartment belies the inner emptiness caused by the family's deep grief.

This disparity between bright, busy surfaces and inner emptiness can be read as a metaphor for modern society. Zooey rails against the "the joys of television, and "Life" magazine every Wednesday, and European travel, and the H-Bomb, and Presidential elections, and the front page of the "Times" [...] and God knows everything else that's gloriously normal" (108). This "normality" teeming with distractions obscures a recent history of loss, both for the Glass family, and for America in a larger sense. Seymour's post-war suicide and Walt's death in a "freakish explosion" (53) in Japan recall the terrible deaths and post-traumatic stress of thousands of soldiers, and the horrific nuclear fallout of the atomic bomb. The ending of "Zooey" suggests that the primary conflict in both stories is not Franny's quest for spiritual fulfillment, but the lingering effects of Seymour's death on both Franny and Zooey. His ghost stands for the "Charleston and B-17 eras" (53) whose traumas still haunt the 1950s.

Religious Context

Personal spirituality, rather than organized religion, is an important theme in "Franny and Zooey." Franny and Zooey have been exposed to many religious teachings and philosophies, and this is reflected in the fact that there are both Christian and Buddhist symbols in the text. For example, when Mrs. Glass makes chicken soup for Franny, it is described by Zooey as a "a cup of consecrated chicken soup" (196). This alludes to the Eucharist, the bread and wine symbolizing the body and blood of Christ that is used in many Christian masses. Seymour's "Fat Lady" stands for "Christ himself" but also, as Tom Davis points out, the figure of Buddha (47).

The principles of Zen Buddhism are especially important in the story. Franny's desire to "see God" recalls the "state of pure consciousness" that Buddy discusses in his letter to Zooey. In this letter, Buddy refers to Dr. Suzuki, a Zen Buddhist who gave lectures about Zen in America in the 1950s. Buddy also refers to Suzuki's concept of satori: this is a way of being "with God before he said, 'Let there be light', (65). Zen Buddhism teaches that "life itself is a unity," and cultivates detachment from the material world and the unlearning of differences (Davis 42). Both of these practices appear in the text. In rejecting the "ego, ego, ego" Franny is detaching herself from material and intellectual reward and seeking, "a complete release from attachment to the objective world" (Davis 42). In his letter to Zooey, Buddy describes talking to a little girl at a supermarket. Jokingly, he asked if she had a boyfriend. The little girl responded that she had two: "Bobby and Dorothy" (64). This event reminded Buddy of Seymour's dictum: "all legitimate religious study must lead to unlearning the differences, the illusory differences, between boys and girls, animals and stones, day and night, heat and cold" (67-68). At the end of the story, Zooey's assertion that "everyone is Seymour's Fat Lady" suggests that he and Franny have unlearned the differences that set people apart from each other and from "Christ himself." In this way, both Franny and Zooey finally understand the principle that "life is unity," and because every living person is united with "Christ himself," Franny has attained her goal of "seeing God" after all.

Science & Technological Context

Science and technology do not play a significant role in the text, but are part of the background of Franny and Zooey's world. Zooey demonstrates skepticism about science and technology. When Mrs. Glass wonders if Franny should see a psychoanalyst, Zooey is critical and implies that such treatment only teaches patients to conform to problematic standards of normality to "the joys of television," as he puts it (108). Zooey's cynicism extends to the radio show "It's a Wise Child," suggesting a disillusionment about the mass entertainment enabled by modern technology. At the same time, however, a telephone enables effective communication between Franny and Zooey; the use of this modern device also allows them to make a positive, metaphorical reconnection with Seymour and the past.

Biographical Context

Jerome David Salinger was born on January 1, 1919 in New York City to a Jewish father and Irish Catholic mother. He grew up in a fashionable area of Manhattan before going to Pennsylvania in 1934, to attend Valley Forge Military Academy. Salinger's education continued into the late 1930s, when he was enrolled at New York University and Ursinus College, Pennsylvania. In the spring of 1939, he joined a writing class at Columbia University that was taught by Whit Burnett, editor of "Story Magazine." This led to Salinger's first publication, "The Young Folks," in that periodical in 1940. So began an early publishing career that flourished despite Salinger's years of military service in the early 1940s. In 1942, Salinger was drafted into the army, and participated in the D-Day landing at Utah Beach in 1944. In 1945, he was discharged from service, but his military experience influenced his later fiction. For example, Seymour and Walt Glass, and the protagonist in his story "For Esme, with Love and Squalor" (1950), are all soldiers.

After his military career, Salinger began a publishing relationship with *The New Yorker* that lasted from 1946 until his most recent publication, "Hapworth 16, 1924," in 1965. However, it was the publication of his only novel, "The Catcher in the Rye" (1951), that thrust Salinger into the public eye. Its protagonist, Holden Caulfield, was the "first hero of adolescent angst...before Holden, the state of adolescence didn't really exist in print and it has still rarely been bettered" (Calcutt and Shephard 245). The novel has been translated into several languages, and still sells thousands of copies every year.

Although Salinger continued publishing short stories, including several about the Glass family, he was increasingly dismayed by the publicity surrounding his career. In 1953 he moved to Cornish, New Hampshire and has since ceased contact with the press. Salinger's reclusive lifestyle is now as much a part of his reputation as his fiction. "Hapworth" was his last publication, although a pirated collection of his stories was published in 1974. Intrusions to Salinger's private life continue. A court ruling prevented Ian Hamilton from publishing Salinger's letters in a book, but his revised (and unauthorized) biography, "In Search of J. D. Salinger," was published in 1988. More recently, the writer Joyce Maynard described a 1972 affair with Salinger (she was then eighteen) in her book "At Home in the World" (1998). In 2000, Salinger's daughter published a memoir entitled "Dream Catcher."

Salinger has been married and divorced twice: to a French doctor in 1945, and to Claire Douglas in 1955. The second marriage produced two children: Matthew Salinger, an actor, and Margaret Ann Salinger. In the 1990s, Salinger married his third wife, Colleen O'Neill. He still lives in Cornish, New Hampshire.

Jennifer Dunn

Works Cited

Alsen, Eberhard. *A Reader's Guide to J. D. Salinger.* Westport, CN and London: Greenwood, 2002.

Bryan, James E. "J. D. Salinger: The Fat Lady and the Chicken Sandwich." *College English* 23.3 (December 1961) 226–29.

Calcutt, Andrew and Richard Shephard. *Cult Fiction: A Reader's Guide.* London: Prion, 1999.

Davis, Tom. "J. D. Salinger: 'The Sound of One Hand Clapping.'" *Wisconsin Studies in Contemporary Fiction* 4.1 (Winter 1963) 41–47.

Hamilton, Ian. *In Search of J. D. Salinger.* New York: Random, 1988.

Hassan, Ihab. "Almost the Voice of Silence: The Later Novelettes of J. D. Salinger." *Wisconsin Studies in Contemporary Fiction* 4.1 (Winter 1963) 5–20.

Wenke, John. *J. D. Salinger: A Study of the Short Fiction.* Boston: Twayne, 1991.

For Further Study

Alsen, Eberhard. "The Role of Vedanta Hinduism in Salinger's Seymour Novel." *Renascence* 33.2 (Winter 1981) 99–116.

Belcher, William F. and James E. Lee, eds. *J. D. Salinger and the Critics.* Belmont, CA: Wadsworth, 1962.

Bloom, Harold, ed. *J. D. Salinger.* New York: Chelsea House, 1987.

French, Warren. *J. D. Salinger*, Revisited. Boston, Twayne, 1988.

Maynard, Joyce. *At Home in the World: A Memoir.* New York: Picador, 1998.

Salinger, Margaret Ann. *Dream Catcher.* New York: Washington Square P, 2000.

Unrue, John C. *J. D. Salinger: A Study of the Short Fiction.* Detroit: Gale, 2002.

Discussion Questions

1. Do you think the story "Franny" generates more sympathy for Franny or Lane? What pressures do the two students face? Are their respective situations more similar or different?

2. How do you interpret Franny's letter to Lane, especially her spelling mistakes and self-deriding comments? How does her self-presentation in the letter compare to how she presents herself in other moments?

3. Why does Franny focus so intensely on a spot of sunlight in the restaurant? What symbolic meaning could this have?

4. Should we consider "Franny" independently from "Zooey?" If so, how would you interpret it differently?

5. What role does Mrs. Glass play in the family household? How does her caricatured appearance contrast to her insights?

6. What is the significance of Buddy being the narrator of "Zooey?" If the shifting perspective between Franny and Lane in "Franny" suggests some similarity in their characters, what similarity between Buddy and Zooey is suggested in the second story?

7. Were Seymour and Buddy wrong to educate Franny and Zooey in the way they did?

8. Does gender play a role in Franny's breakdown?

9. At one point, Zooey watches a little girl playing with her dog just outside the Glass apartment. How do you interpret this scene?

10. Because Buddy is the narrator of the story "Zooey," we see Franny, Zooey, and Mrs. Glass through Buddy's eyes. What are his opinions of these characters, as suggested by the text? What does the text suggest about Buddy himself?

Essay Ideas

1. Compare the different narrative structures of "Franny" and "Zooey," and discuss this in relation to the text as a whole.

2. Analyze the role of epiphany, or lack thereof, in the text. How does this relate to the text's representation of religion and/or spirituality?

3. Analyze the story "Franny" in relation to "A Perfect Day for Bananafish."

4. How does Salinger's Glass family compare to other characters in post-war fiction to Holden Caulfield in "The Catcher in the Rye" or Esther Greenwood in "The Bell Jar," for example?

5. Examine Salinger's representation of children/childhood in "Franny and Zooey" and in the other Glass stories.

Girl, Interrupted

by Susanna Kaysen

Content Synopsis

"Girl, Interrupted" recounts Susanna Kaysen's experience at McLean Hospital, a psychiatric facility outside of Boston, MA. Diagnosed with a borderline personality disorder after a brief visit to a psychiatrist she had just met, Kaysen is sent to McLean where she voluntarily admitted herself based on the psychiatrist's findings. Her experience is told, not chronologically, but through a series of vignettes that capture the overall essence of her time spent at McLean.

Upon arriving at McLean, Kaysen describes some of the other patients. Polly tries to kill herself by setting herself on fire. Cynthia receives weekly electroshock therapy. Georgina, her roommate, is schizophrenic, but she and Kaysen are deemed as among the healthier patients. Kaysen presents Lisa as one of the crazier patients. Lisa has not slept in two years and is often running away, throwing fits and generally giving the nurses a hard time. Kaysen appears fascinated by Lisa and describes many of her escapades. Daisy is an anorexic girl who joins the group. She is addicted to laxatives and is obsessed with chicken. Her father, who also sexually abuses her, would bring her whole chicken that Daisy would horde in her room and eat. Upon her release, Daisy commits suicide.

Kaysen admits having contemplated suicide many times and attempts it once by taking fifty aspirin. Afterwards, she admits to only wanting to

kill the part of her that wanted to kill herself. Once she realized that she doesn't want to die, she went to the store for her mother, regretting her grave error the whole time. Fortunately, she had called her boyfriend before she took the pills and he called the police. She describes the horrible experience of having her stomach pumped and recalls it as a good deterrent for future attempts.

Despite her depression and suicide attempts, Kaysen says she knew then that she was not crazy. Throughout the book, she repeatedly contemplates the moment with the psychiatrist leading up to being admitted to McLean. She tries to explain what she was feeling at the time as a distorted reality. She says she was not hallucinating but "tumbling down a shaft into Wonderland" (Kaysen 41). She never believed something was there that was not; she knew her perceptions were distortions. She also describes feeling alienated and bored with the world; lacking ambition to function in the world around her. She says that being institutionalized was kind of an easy out, a way to "resist" the expectations of society (42).

Although the hospital offers a life free of expectation and responsibility, Kaysen goes on to depict the lack of freedom that comes with being hospitalized. Something as simple as going out for ice cream requires a handful of nurses to walk the patients there and back in the event that someone tries to run away or make a scene. Windows are screened with chicken wire so getting a nurse just to open one is a big process. In one vignette, Kaysen describes Lisa making a nurse go to the trouble of opening a window so she could get some air. After the nurse labors to open the window and replace the screen, Lisa does not even stay in her room.

Lack of privacy is also a fact of life at McLean. Nurses perform "checks" every few minutes in order to ensure that patients are not misbehaving or endangering themselves in their rooms. She discusses how sharp objects are prohibited so that she cannot even shave her legs without supervision.

The nurses at McLean have their hands full. Kaysen presents Valerie, the head nurse, as a strong and direct woman who is good with the patients. The night nurse, Mrs. McWeeney, is depicted as cruel and unstable, often withholding patients' medication when she is angry. The student nurses are the girls' favorites as they represent a life, normal and hopeful, that the girls do not, and probably never will, lead. The girls live vicariously through them and behave when they are around. When they leave, however, Kaysen says that the patients are even more of a handful.

As Kaysen is getting ready to leave the hospital, after 18 months, she discusses applying for jobs and having to use the hospital as her address. Since it is a well-known address, people react differently, and often with revulsion, upon seeing it. Kaysen suggests that people are curious and afraid of what separates the sane from the insane. Since she appears relatively normal and does not act "crazy," people feel unsettled because if she could end up in McLean, they could too.

Once she gets out of the hospital and integrates back into mainstream society, Kaysen learns to stop telling people that she spent time at McLean. She says she even grew to be repulsed by crazy people as she wanted to be as far from that version of herself as possible.

Kaysen describes her courtship with her future husband and how his proposal prompted her release from McLean. She tells Georgina and Lisa that life will stop and be quiet when she gets married, but admits that she is wrong about this and she eventually loses her husband.

Outside of the hospital, Kaysen keeps in touch with Georgina for a brief time. She describes how Georgina got involved with some women's groups and eventually got married and moved to a farm and had a pet goat which she enjoyed making "dance." Kaysen's description of Georgina's radical behavior reveals the disconnect she still feels between herself and the "crazy" ones. Even so, Kaysen still observes her own behavior and questions her sanity regularly. She compares herself to a girl in a Vermeer painting entitled, "Girl Interrupted at her Music." The girl sits in a soft, overcast light and appears sad as her music teacher stands over her. Kaysen may or may not be crazy but she identifies with this sadness, with not meeting the expectations of society and feeling alone in a hazy light.

Symbols & Motifs

The concept of being and feeling human recurs throughout "Girl, Interrupted." Kaysen illustrates how she and the other patients were aware of and affected by the clear divide between people on the outside and people on the inside. Living at McLean under constant supervision with limited freedom makes Kaysen question her humanity. She even has an incident in which she starts scratching at her skin in order to see if she has blood and bones underneath.

Both during her stay at McLean and after her release, Kaysen constantly questions her diagnosis. She wonders if she was crazy and if she still is crazy. Not only does Kaysen compare her own actions to those actions of the people around her, but the people around her compare their actions to hers in concern for the status of their own well being. All of this raises questions about what exactly defines "crazy."

Historical Context

McLean Hospital in Massachusetts is a psychiatric hospital affiliated with Harvard Medical School and Massachusetts General Hospital. It opened its doors in 1811 and has achieved a celebrity status over the years. It was the first hospital in New England and the fourth mental institution in America (McLean Hospital). It moved to its current Belmont location in 1895 (McLean). Writers Sylvia Plath and Robert Lowell stayed at McLean as well as famous musicians, James Taylor and Ray Charles and mathematician John Nash whose story inspired the book and film, "A Beautiful Mind."

During Kaysen's stay at McLean, the Vietnam War was at its height. Kaysen describes how the patients would watch the war protestors on the news and felt a certain connection to them. Their anger and outrage and feeling misunderstood by authorities was something they had in common.

The style and subject of this work echoes that of the work of Anne Sexton and Sylvia Plath. Both women, like Kaysen, wrote openly and honestly in confessional works often about their struggles with mental illness and treatment.

Societal Context

When Susanna Kaysen was admitted to McLean, she was diagnosed with a borderline personality disorder (BPD) after visiting a psychiatrist whom she had never seen before for approximately twenty minutes to an hour. A BPD is defined by the National Institute of Mental Health as, "a serious mental illness characterized by pervasive instability in moods, interpersonal relationships, self-image, and behavior" (nimh.nih.gov). While Kaysen is clear about the fact that she suffered from depression and inner turmoil, she repeatedly questions her diagnosis throughout "Girl, Interrupted" as she notes that many of the symptoms of BPD are characteristics of adolescence. Kaysen compares herself to the other patients in the hospital and presents herself in a more "normal" context than women such as Lisa, who constantly rages and challenges the staff, and Daisy, an anorexic addicted to laxatives who hid whole chickens in her room to eat. Nevertheless, she does not seem enraged at being in McLean nor does she ever try to prove her sanity in order to leave the hospital early.

Once she leaves the hospital, however, she is faced with the stigma of having a mental illness. She quickly learns not to put her stay at McLean on job applications after getting quizzical looks from employers and not getting hired. She observes society's general repulsion of the mentally ill, and suggests that this stems from fear and the question, "could it happen to me?" In order to adapt to life on the outside, Kaysen stops telling most people she was in the hospital.

Religious Context

"Girl, Interrupted" does not have a specific religious context.

Scientific & Technological Context

The medical treatments used at McLean Hospital represent the latest advancements of the 1960s. Kaysen describes the regular use of electroshock therapy and the use of medications such as Thorazine for patients. She comments on how therapists try to treat "the mind" and discuss the patient's psyche, but when they do not make any progress or cannot determine what is wrong with the patient, they treat "the brain" with medications that treat chemical imbalances (Kaysen 142). Kaysen suggests that it would be much more useful to combine efforts rather than use an either/or approach to treatment.

Biographical Context

Susanna Kaysen was born on November 11, 1948 in Boston, MA to parents Annette and Carl Kaysen. Her father was a well-known economics professor and advisor to President John F. Kennedy. In 1967 at age 18, a doctor she had never seen before diagnosed Susanna Kaysen with a personality disorder and sent her to the famous McLean Hospital. She remained there for 18 months. "Girl, Interrupted" is her account of this time in her life.

Kaysen is also the author of two novels, "Asa, As I Knew Him" and "Far Afield," as well as a second memoir, "The Camera My Mother Gave Me." She lives in Cambridge, Massachusetts.

Jennifer Bouchard

Works Cited

IMDB: Internet Movie Database. Imdb.com, inc. 30 April 2008.

Kaysen, Susanna. Girl, Interrupted. New York: Vintage Books, 1993.

McLean Hospital. Harvard University. 1 October 2008.

National Institute of Mental Health. National Institute of Health. 1 October 2008.

Winik, Marion. "Susanna Kaysen Lays it on the Line." *The Austin Chronicle.* 19 October 2001. The Austin Chronicle.com. 30 September 2008.

Discussion Questions

1. Who was your favorite character and why?
2. Who was your least favorite character and why?
3. Discuss some of the various conditions that landed some of the girls in McLean.
4. Do you think all of the girls needed hospitalization? Did it help them?
5. What are the main themes present in "Girl, Interrupted"?
6. How does the time in which the events take place play a role in the story's overarching themes?
7. Discuss the role of Valerie in "Girl, Interrupted."
8. Discuss the social interactions between the nurses and the patients in "Girl, Interrupted."
9. Discuss the social interactions of the patients with one another in "Girl, Interrupted."
10. In what ways could the narrator represent any young woman?

Essay Ideas

1. Compare and contrast Kaysen's memoir with the film version. Analyze the director's changes to the story and evaluate his depiction of the truth.
2. Describe and analyze Kaysen's literary style. Focus on the structure of her narrative, characters, dialogue and themes.
3. Write an essay in which you analyze one of the other patients in the hospital, such as Lisa, Daisy, or Georgina.
4. Analyze the role of family in "Girl, Interrupted."

Canadian Margaret Atwood is among the most honored authors of fiction in recent history. Her work falls into historical fiction, speculative fiction, science fiction, and dystopian fiction; two of her novels are included in this volume: *Alias Grace* and *The Handmaid's Tale*. Photo: Wikipedia.

The Handmaid's Tale

by Margaret Atwood

Content Synopsis

Margaret Atwood's "The Handmaid's Tale" (1985) is a classic piece of speculative fiction in 46 chapters plus an epilogue of sorts. It reads like a dystopia which is based on actual trends which were given expression in the United States in the mid–1980s. Set in Cambridge (Massachusetts), it deals with the enslavement of women to a totalitarian patriarchy in the guise of a theocratic state. Social control is achieved through various sumptuary laws which regulate and streamline society into broad categories. Women are made to obey a dress code which designates them as being part of one of the following groups: Wives, Widows, Aunts, Daughters, Marthas, Handmaids and Econowives. The Unwomen and the Jezebels (that is women used as geishas) fall into the less socially acceptable categories.

Atwood's gloomy and almost post-apocalyptic scenario for the future run along these lines. The United States has turned into a Christian totalitarian regime ironically called the Republic of Gilead. This revolutionary order has put an end to liberty, individuality, religious pluralism, diversity (through an imposed norm), freedom of speech, to name a few. Citizens are basically given the choice of entering someone's service to become a domestic slave or be deported to toxic regions where they are certain to meet death due to high peaks of pollution. The Republic is self-contained and most of its citizens

are infertile. The ones who are lucky enough to be able to bear children are turned into reproductive machines for the upper-classes. Whatever the problem, women are made to bear the brunt of the responsibility for it while men are irreproachable.

The eponymous character is a woman known as Offred (onomastically, Of Fred, namely her master or "commander" as they put it) who, because of a new Gileadean law, has been declared an adulteress and forced into becoming a handmaid. After she managed to give birth to a baby girl, she wanted to escape to Canada but failed and was separated from her daughter as punishment. As a handmaid, she is meant to assist couples who cannot conceive by sleeping with the men and giving her child away to the couple once born.

All handmaids who fail to conceive are transported to the toxic colonies where they are to meet the tragic fate of all the ones who have been declared "Unwomen." Survival is thus equated with becoming pregnant through any means and with the help of anyone.

The story is told in fact from Offred's point of view and focalisation. She is part of a "statistical population" (Fredric Jameson) in which her identity has been denied and disguised in a new name. Because she didn't succeed in falling pregnant with Fred, whose wife Serena Joy is presumably infertile, Offred will be deported to the dreaded colonies. But before, thanks to Fred, the eponymous handmaid is treated to illicit pleasures like playing Scrabble, anointing herself with hand lotion, reading books and magazines, getting to slip into sexy clothes, or sneaking out to a brothel for instance. But Serena Joy, who suspects her husband to be sterile, offers Offred to conceive with her chauffeur Nick. The couple enter a sexual relationship and the narrative suggests that Offred has been saved from her condemnation to the colonies. It is likely that the eponymous handmaid managed to escape thanks to the underground resistance to which Nick belonged.

In an appendix entitled "Historical Notes," readers learn that this incredible story survived because Offred's tapes, on which the narrative was recorded, were finally found. It has become a historical document much discussed by academia at the Twelfth Symposium on Gileadean Studies held at the University of Denay (possibly pronounced as "deny") in Nunavit (possibly a phonetic transcription of "None of it" as in "none of it happened"). This section works as a disclaimer which questions the authenticity of the narrative. Speculations that the tapes are fake are part of a paper delivered by Professor Piexoto, keynote speaker, on "Problems of Authentication in 'The Handmaid's Tale.'"

Historical Context

"The Handmaid's Tale" reads like a social critique by featuring various feminine and feminist stances dating back to the Women's Liberation Movement of the 1960s-70s. There is radical feminism with lesbian feminist Moira and critical feminism with Offred telling her story of feminine resistance to patriarchy.

Margaret Atwood chose the United States of America as the main setting because, in her own words, "The States are more extreme in everything." She has absorbed all contemporary cancerous evils (such as the rise of right-wing fundamentalism as a political force, pollution, and sterility) into her fiction.

Hélène Greven has pointed in her monograph on "The Handmaid's Tale" that the novel was clearly inspired from American Puritanism: "Life in Gilead reflects easily recognizable attitudes: intolerance towards the other; authority and rigid hierarchy built into the system under the responsibility of a group of commanders; imposed common rule; self-denial and obedience. The women's strict upbringing (presumably paralleled by the men's) and compulsory participation in frequent socio-religious rites reflect in the indoctrination of a whole people. Such a world suffers no rebellion, and heretics are eliminated from Gilead—which is understood to be the former New England town of Cambridge, heart of the Puritan tradition" (Graven, 16).

Societal Context

Dystopia is a form of speculative fiction and a modern satire which is traditionally opposed to utopia. It refers to any alarmingly distasteful fantasy world which is meant to realize itself in a near future and it thereby questions the uncanny world of the present. It is a realistic warning to the reader who visualizes a futuristic world. Therefore Margaret Atwood epitomizes a modern-day Cassandra. Dystopia stresses the channelling of thoughts and language, the pairing of science and engineering with totalitarianism (eugenics for instance), seclusion which prevents the visibility of alternate worlds, nightmarish visions, and the journey through time. Popular dystopias include Aldous Huxley's "Brave New World" (1932), George Orwell's "1984" (1948) and William Golding's "Lord of the Flies" (1954).

Atwood addresses the power of language, the capacity to create (private) worlds through words. Concomitantly, the author analyses the consequences of not being able to express oneself. The manipulation of language in Gilead has been denied in various ways: writing (the transcription of language) and reading (memorizing language) are prohibited to women.

Religious Context

Religion, especially Christianity, has been a major source of inspiration for Margaret Atwood while writing "The Handmaid's Tale." Biblical names are liberally sprinkled throughout the narrative: the Aunts named Sarah and Elizabeth; Offred's former husband is named Luke; Jezebel is the name for the official brothel; the Rachel and Leah Centre (they are the Biblical sisters who became the wives of Jacob and gave him their handmaids); a passing mention to Job refers to "The Book of Job," an Old Testament story in which a series of disasters is told by the survivors; and Deuteronomy, which is the Old Testament law punishing rape of death, to name a few. The Eyes may be a veiled reference to the Abel and Cain story, the classic illustration of guilt. Offred is said to be 33 years old and thus appears as a Christ-like figure, a Saviour of humanity of sorts. The frequent repetition of the verb "believe" is a reminder of the Credo in unum deum while the Jacob story taken from the "Genesis" for the epigraph grounds solidly the plotline into the religious sphere. Serena Joy's garden is a parody of the hortus conclusus (See in the "Song of Songs": "a garden enclosed is my sister, an orchard of pomegranates" [4:12–13] and the Saviour appearing to Mary Magdalen in the form of a gardener in "The Gospel of John." Besides, in "Exodus" (3:8, 17), Christ likens his heavenly Father to a farmer or gardener, who prunes his fruit-trees for a better yield.) The careful reader will find references to the Three Christian Graces, as spelled out in St. Paul's "First Epistle to the Corinthians" 13:13, "And now abideth faith, hope, charity, these three; but the greatest of these is charity." Charity ("caritas") is mentioned once by Offred, hope ("spes") appears on tombstones, while faith ("fides") is frequently used in the narrative. One will also recognise mock religious rites like Offred anointing her forehead and hands with butter. All these references give the full picture of a theocratic society. The republic of Gilead is a Bible-based society which is socially repressive and totalitarian, abiding by the Law of the Father. It is a patriarchal society of words, propaganda, slogan, manipulation, and brainwashing.

Deep down, "The Handmaid's Tale" is a criticism of the excesses of religious powers with its critique of religious fundamentalism. Handmaids are forced to recite three times a day the Republic's creed: "From each according to her ability; to each according to his need" (151).

Psychological Context

"The Handmaid's Tale" may also be viewed as an introspective novel dealing with a nexus of identitarian issues: multifaceted people, loss of identity, redefinition of the self, distancing and identification, schizophrenia, and so on.

Name symbolism reveals Offred's multiple identities. She is of/Fred: belonging to the Commander whose name has been imposed on her. Offred is thus deprived of a personal name, she has no real identity. She is also "of red," the colour used to identify the servant category. Offred's name can also suggest that she has been "offered." As a gift, she belongs to someone and has been reified for this purpose: she has been turned into an object. Her name also implies "off read," in other words she has been deprived of her favourite hobby while hinting at the author's fear of not being read. Offred might just be an alias to remain anonymous, a kind of protection against ego-splitting.

On a structural level, the psychoanalytical predisposition of men to psychoses may account for the patent fact that utopian and dystopian narratives are gender-marked as largely masculine. Christian Marouby cogently argues in "Utopie et primitivisme" that utopia presents itself as a "structure of defence" (Marouby, 41), insularity being understood as a paranoia-prone space. Most utopian narratives feature insular societies located, or at least felt to be located, on an island whose overprotective and overprotected environment acts as a buttress against deep-seated anxieties of penetration and aggression. This fantasy of physical inviolability seeks to ward off putative dangers of invasion, contamination, and degeneration which the openness of borders cannot prevent in the normal course of events. This defence mechanism rests on the illusion that evil has been shut out of the now sanitized enclosed and self-contained space. Dreams of paradise also indicate that utopian thinkers regard evil as a threat which they keep at bay. This dread of evil with which writers are over-concerned morphs into visions of overwrought and strictly controlled societies.

In a sense, utopian thinkers could be regarded as silent tyrants insofaras they superimpose their models of better social systems onto the existing one to which they have to comply half-heartedly. Their utopian impulses do not appear as a straightforward spelled out demand for change, rather they present themselves as suggested counter-models, altered blueprints for the society in which a given people lives, so as to point out in a most oblique way the dysfunctions inherent in reality. Even though these are imagined worlds, it follows that Utopianism is, for these novelists, the cement which consolidates the foundations of their mute tyrannies under which life is ritualised, well-organized and closely controlled, forcing people into becoming overcautious and extremely regimented. Happiness becomes a moral duty, the norm—a rule, companionship—a lifestyle, and seclusion from the external world—an essential requirement. And when you think of it, the denial of complaint, the compliance to a norm, communitarian activity and isolation, are all defining traits of prison life. Because utopian schemes are a response from a discontented mind to the present, they are hardly more than a sublimated vision of a corrupt world making the here and now more endurable to the utopian thinker.

Because utopian fantasies of perfection, control and domination are the mirror image of a foredoomed imaginary dystopian threat, utopianism contains the seed of the paranoia which is developed at the core of dystopian fiction. By and large, utopian projects are excessive in the sense that they are constructed with excess, to excess, and in response to excessive feelings. While utopianism feeds on surplus, dystopia flourishes in saturation. In other words, what can be read between the lines in utopian writings is simply explicated, elaborated on and brought to a pitch in dystopian novels. Just as hate cannot be felt without experiencing love, dread cannot be felt without going through anxiety. The dystopian narrative can no longer be perceived as the negative counterpart of utopian fiction, since the former turns out to be the logical expansion, if not the aggravation of paranoid tendencies which transpire in the latter. Far from being poles apart and antagonistic as they are classically represented, utopias and dystopias should be seen as two adjacent markers on the gradation continuum, proving the dystopian impulse to be an additional projection.

Scientific & Technological Context

As Hélène Greven puts it, "Other than genetic engineering—which allows women to survive without men—there is very little "science" in women's science fiction; in fact, women generally show a certain aversion to classic science fiction tales of space exploration, intergalactic travel, or highly mechanized cities of the future typical of works written by their male counterparts. Women more frequently address the problems of ecological disaster (dubbed 'ecocide'), nuclear holocaust and various other negative effects of the misuse of scientific progress; many novels deal with the long struggle back to civilization after some such global catastrophe" (Graven, 33). Atwood's "The Handmaid's Tale" falls within the purview of this cunning observation.

Biographical Context

Born in 1939 in Ottawa, Canada Margaret Atwood had her literary calling in her teens. She graduated in English from Victoria College in 1961 and travelled to Boston to delve into Victorian fiction. Her first novel, "The Edible Woman," which was completed in 1965, was not published until 1969. She began her literary career by publishing poetry in 1966; a collection entitled "The Circle Game." She wrote a series of novels which culminated in "The Handmaid's Tale" (1985), her most admired book of fiction up till now, which reached an even wider audience with the film adaptation, the screenplay of which was written by Nobel Prize-winner Harold Pinter. Even though "The Handmaid's Tale" was short-listed for the Booker Prize, she had to wait until 2000 to be awarded the prize for "The Blind Assassin." Her other novels, "Cat's Eye" (1988), "The Robber Bride" (1993), and "Alias Grace" (1996) all received their share of critical attention and popular success.

As a literary critic, Margaret Atwood has researched and published on representations of native wilderness in Canadian fiction and has become interested in women's writings. Her interest in things pastoral dates back from her childhood experience of the Canadian bush. Fiction and non-fiction writer, children's writer, editor, Atwood has many hats that she wears artfully.

Jean-François Vernay

Works Cited

Atwood, Margaret. *The Handmaid's Tale,* London: Jonathan Cape Ltd, 1986.

Jameson, Fredric. *Archaeologies of the Future: The Desire Called Utopia and Other Science Fictions,* London: Verso, 2005.

Greven, Hélène. *Margaret Atwood. The Handmaid's Tale,* Paris: Didier-Erudition/ CNED, 1999.

Hill Rigney, Barbara. *Margaret Atwood, Women Writers Series.* New Jersey: Barnes & Noble, 1987.

Marouby, Christian. *Utopie et primitivisme. Essai sur l'imaginaire anthropologique à l'âge classique,* Paris: Seuil, 1990.

Discussion Questions

1. What importance does the setting have? How does knowledge interact with power?
2. Could you analyse the close connection between surveillance and control under the Glieadean regime?
3. In what ways is "The Handmaid's Tale" a power game?
4. Could you define the word coinage "particicution" and discuss its effect on readers?
5. Why is Offred so obsessed with words?
6. Why is the phrase "context is all" repeated throughout the novel?
7. Why are reading and writing prohibited in Gilead?
8. What does the novel reveal about the power of language?
9. What is the function of the "Historical Notes" section in "The Handmaid's Tale"?
10. Why is "The Handmaid's Tale" a warning to the reader in the oblique way?

Essay Ideas

1. Axel, in Villiers de l'Isle-Adam's "L'Eve future," declares: "As for living, our servants can do that for us." Discuss this statement in the light of Margaret Atwood's "The Handmaid's Tale."
2. Study "The Handmaid's Tale" as an exploration of the infinite possibilities of language.
3. Is "The Handmaid's Tale" the work of a feminist writer? Justify your opinions.
4. Why is the Gileadan regime so intent on repressing sexuality in "The Handmaid's Tale"? To what extent is Atwood's "The Handmaid's Tale" a social critique?

The House on Mango Street

by Sandra Cisneros

Content Synopsis

"The House on Mango Street" is composed of short stories and vignettes which may be read as autonomous texts but which feature recurring characters and settings and acquire composite meaning when read as a whole. The stories are narrated by Esperanza Codero, a Mexican-American girl living with her family in Chicago. In the opening story, Esperanza's family arrive at their new house. They have to move each year and Esperanza longs for a home that she might call her own. Many of the stories directly concern Esperanza. Other stories concern friends and neighbors of the Codero family: Marin from Puerto Rico, who likes to dance and plans to meet a man and live in a house far away; Alicia, who studies at university and keeps house for her father; Ruthie, who "sees lovely things everywhere" (68); Minerva, who writes poems on scraps of paper which she "folds over and over" (84).

Esperanza grows up with her brothers and sisters and gets her first job at a photograph shop, where an old man grabs her and kisses her. She reads her poems to her blind Aunt Lupe, who tells her to continue writing because it will "keep [her] free" (61). She determines to seize the advantages which are given to men for herself. In the story entitled "Monkey Garden," Esperanza is raped. While she waits for her friend Sally who has disappeared with a boy, she is surrounded by boys herself. One of them rapes her. In "Red Clowns" she expresses anger at the friends and magazines that have deceived her with their representations of sex.

When the baby sister of Esperanza's friend dies, three aunts come to visit. They identify Esperanza as someone "special" who "will go far" (104). They tell her that when she leaves Mango Street, she must "come back [f]or the ones who cannot leave as easily as you" (105). In the final vignette, "Mango Says Goodbye Sometimes" Esperanza articulates her love of storytelling. She describes writing the story we have just read, of a girl who lives on Mango Street where she does not want to belong. By writing the experience down, "the ghost does not ache so much" (110). She predicts that one day she will leave but that she will come back "for the ones who cannot out" (110).

Symbols & Motifs

Esperanza expresses her loneliness by figuring herself as "a red balloon, a balloon tied to an anchor" (9). The four skinny trees that "do not belong here but are here" not only symbolize Esperanza's sense of dislocation but also provide a model of unfettered freedom for her to aspire to: she observes that the "only reason" for the trees' existence is "to be and be" (75). However the trees represent contingency as well as autonomy: "Let one forget his reason for being, they'd all droop like tulips in a glass, each with their arms around the other" (75).

The house on Mango Street acquires different symbolic meanings for Esperanza. Initially, she refuses to associate herself with the house: "I knew then I had to have a house. A real house. One I could point to. But this isn't it" (5). However, by the end of the text, she realizes the role that the house has played in her trajectory towards self-determination. Esperanza's name has multiple meanings. In English it means hope, in Spanish it means sadness and waiting. Other symbols figure the possibility of transformation: the record player which Gil calls a music box, which make "all sorts of things" happen when the music plays (20).

Societal Context

"The House on Mango Street" dramatizes the social oppression of Chicana communities in eighties America. The Codero family has to move every year and can only hope for a house of their own. In one house, Papa had to nail wooden bars on the window to ensure that his children did not fall out. On Sundays, the family drives to the house on the hill and gazes at it. Eseperanza stays at home, "ashamed" of her family "staring out the window like the hungry" (86). When Esperanza's friend Cathy announces that her family will be leaving Mango Street soon, Esperanza observes: "They'll just have to move a little farther north from Mango Street, a little farther away every time people like us keep moving in" (13).

Esperanza seeks freedom from socialized expectations arising from her ethnicity and gender. She hopes to own a house one day but vows never to forget "who I am or where I came from" (87). In an early story, "My Name," Esperanza writes that the "Mexicans … don't like their women strong" (10). She is named after her great-grandmother who was "a wild horse of a woman, so wild she wouldn't marry" (11). Many of Esperanza's friends view their gender as the primary constituent of their identity. Marin hopes to find a man in the subway who might marry her and "take [her] to live in a big house far away" (26). Esperanza imagines her dancing in the street, "waiting for a car to stop, a star to fall, someone to change her life" (27). The text abounds with images of female oppression: Esperanza's great-grandfather threw a sack over her great-grandmother's head, carried her off "like a fancy chandelier" and consigned her to a life of looking out of the window (11); Rafaela grows old "from leaning out the window so much, gets locked indoors because her husband is afraid [she] will run away since she is too beautiful to look at" (79); Sally is kept at home by her father who beats her when he sees her talking to men and before she reaches the eighth grade she marries a man who won't even let her look out of the window; Esperanza's mother speaks two languages, knows how to fix a television, and can sing an opera, but is alienated in America, unable to fathom the subway system.

The text challenges paradigmatic images and narratives assigned to women. Most of the marriages in the stories are unsuccessful: Ruthie prefers to live with her mother on Mango Street than her husband; Earl, the jukebox repairman, only sees his wife on visits. The stories also illuminate the limitations imposed on women by the male gaze: "The Family with Little Feet" depicts Esperanza and her friends trying on a grandmother's shoes and attracting the attention of drunken, predatory men. By the end of the story they are "tired of being beautiful" (42). Esperanza rejects the paradigm of the beautiful woman in the movies whose power resides in her looks. Instead, she determines to become "the one who leaves the table like a man, without putting back the chair or picking up the plate" (89).

The stories dramatize hostility towards other cultures and the fear of losing one's own culture. Geraldo, the man who dances with Marin, is left to die in a hospital, "just another brazer who didn't speak English" (66). A little boy from Mexico begins to sing the jingle from the Pepsi commercial and his grandmother bursts into tears. Esperanza recognizes both the prejudice against her race and her own suspicion of other races: "Those who don't know any better come into our neighborhood scared ... They are stupid people who are lost"; two paragraphs later, she admits: "All brown all around, we are safe. But watch us drive into a neighborhood of another color and our knees go shakity-shake and our car windows get rolled up tight and our eyes look straight" (28).

Historical Context

The text was written in the 1980s but makes no direct references to historical events. In America, the decade was a period of unprecedented affluence and materialism.

Cisneros wrote the text while working with students who had slipped out of the school system. In "The House on Mango Street," she dramatizes the lives of those who are denied social mobility because of their ethnicity and gender.

Religious Context

Many of the novel's vignettes open in a parabolic tenor and pursue a parabolic structure. "The Family of Little Feet" begins: "There was a family. All were little. Their arms were little, and their hands were little, and their height was not tall, and their feet very small" (39). Esperanza attends a Catholic school. The nuns seem oblivious to the hardships suffered by the students. One nun points to Esperanza's House on Loomis and asks incredulously if she lives there. Many of the characters develop their own religious philosophies. In "Darius Sees Clouds" a little boy points to the clouds in the sky and identifies one of them as God, making religion "simple" (34). Esperanza does not believe in determinism and has no explanation for people's misfortunes: "I think diseases have no eyes. They pick with a dizzy finger anyone, just anyone" (59). In "Born Bad" she reflects philosophically that she will probably go to hell for the way she treated Aunt Lupe.

Although the characters are Catholic, some of them are guided by superstition or their own intuition. Lucy's aunts are reminiscent of the Greek fates and tell Esperanza that she will go far. Aunt Lupe, who tells Esperanza that her writing will keep her free, recalls Tiresias, the blind prophet of classical literature. Esperanza's mother believes that her daughter was born on an evil day. Both Esperanza and her great-grandmother were born in the Chinese year of the horse and are declared unlucky. Elenita, a witch woman, reads tarot cards but blesses Esperanza in the name of the Virgin. She predicts that Esperanza will find "a home in the heart" (64). Some of the stories have religious undertones which are disturbingly subverted. The monkey garden recalls the garden of Eden; the children like to pretend that it "had been there before anything" (96). It appears to be a place where Esperanza can preserve her innocence. However, this is the location where Esperanza is raped.

Scientific & Technological Context

Esperanza and her family live in an impoverished area and see little evidence of scientific or technological advancement. When Louie's cousin arrives in a new car, the children are enchanted by the FM radio and the automatic windows. However, he is soon arrested by the police.

Biographical Context

Sandra Cisneros was born in Chicago in 1954. She lived with her Mexican father, Mexican–American mother and her six brothers. She took a BA at Loyola Chicago University and an MFA in Creative Writing at the University of Iowa. She has published three volumes of poetry, "Bad Boys" (1980), "My Wicked, Wicked Ways" (1987) and "Loose Woman" (1994). In 1984 she published "The House on Mango Street" to much critical acclaim. The text is now taught in schools and universities throughout the United States. Critics were unsure how to categorize the text. Some identified it as a novel, while others viewed it as a unified collection of stories and vignettes. Critics of the short story cycle have identified "The House on Mango Street" as a paradigm of the form. "Woman Hollering Creek" (1991), winner of the PEN Center West award, also challenges generic conventions. It is a collection of thematically linked short stories. Some references seem to signal a return to Esperanza's world, while others resonate forward to Cisneros's next prose work, a fragmented novel entitled "Caramelo" (2002). "Caramelo" was named as a top book of 2002 by "The New York Times" and was nominated for the Orange Prize in the United Kingdom.

Cisneros has received multiple awards and honors including the National Book Award and a fellowship from the National Endowment for the Arts. Cisneros has also published a children's book, "Hairs/Pelitos" (1994). In addition to writing, Cisneros has taught in schools and universities and served as a writer in residence. She has also worked as a teacher and counselor to high school dropouts. In 1995 she founded the Macondo Workshop where she volunteers. The workshop is for burgeoning writers "working on geographic, cultural, social and spiritual borders."

Rachel Lister, Ph.D

Works Cited

Barios, Gregg. "The Nature of Sandra Cisneros." www.sandracisneros.com.

Cisneros, Sandra. "Do You Know Me?: I Wrote The House on Mango Street." *Americas Review* 15 (Spring 1987): 69–73.

_____. "Ghosts and Voices: Writing from Obsession." *Americas Review* 15 (1987): 60–73.

_____. *The House on Mango Street*. 1984. New York: Vintage, 1991.

_____. *The House on Mango Street*. 1984. New York: Knopf, 1999.

_____. "Introduction." *The House on Mango Street*. 1999 xi–xx.

www.macondoworkshop.org

www.sandracisneros.com

Discussion Questions

1. Discuss Cisneros's dramatization of home and family life. Are these institutions sustaining or restricting? Identify the different meanings which accumulate around these concepts.

2. "Sometimes it seems I am writing the same story, the same poem, over and over" (Cisneros, "Ghosts and Voices" 73). How does Cisneros create the effect of variation within repetition?

3. "I wanted to write a collection which could be read at any random point without having any knowledge of what came before or after. Or that could be read in a series to tell one big story" (Cisneros "Do You" 78). After you have all the stories, read "Red Clowns." In what ways does your experience of that particular story change when read in isolation?

4. Esperanza makes several references to her burgeoning identity as a writer. Discuss the metafictional aspects of "The House on Mango Street."

5. "… each of the stories could have developed into poems, but they were not poems. They were stories, albeit hovering in that gray area between two genres" (Cisneros "Do You" 79). What characteristics do these stories share with poetry you have read?

6. Discuss the different descriptions of the houses in the text. What symbolic meanings accumulate around them?

7. "I think my despair is reflected in 'Mango Street'" (Cisneros in Barrios). Discuss the ways in which Cisneros dramatizes despair in these stories.

8. Discuss the significance of names in "The House on Mango Street."

9. Cisneros describes her stories as "compact and lyrical, ending with a reverberation" ("Do You" 78). Look at the final lines of the stories. By what means does Cisneros create this effect of reverberation?

10. Discuss the treatment of creativity in "The House on Mango Street."

Essay Ideas

1. Explore the relationship between theme and form in "The House on Mango Street."

2. "I thought I was writing a memoir. By the time I had finished it, my memoir was no longer memoir, no longer autobiography. It had evolved into a collective story peopled with several lives from my past and present, placed in one fictional time and neighborhood" ("Introduction" xi-xii). Consider the ways in which Cisneros experiments with generic conventions.

3. "The boys and the girls live in separate worlds. The boys in their universe and we in ours." Explore Cisneros's representation of gender identities in "The House on Mango Street."

4. Examine the representation of ethnic identities in "The House on Mango Street."

5. To what extent might one define "The House on Mango Street" as a narrative of self-discovery?

Housekeeping

by Marilynne Robinson

Content Synopsis

This essay explores Marilynne Robinson's prize-winning novel, "Housekeeping," which centers on the themes of transience and loss and presents an alternative perspective on the domestic ideology of the fifties. It provides a plot synopsis and places the novel in a variety of contexts: historical, social, technological and religious. The essay also presents biographical information about Robinson.

At the beginning of "Housekeeping" (1980) the first-person narrator introduces herself as Ruth. She gives a brief history of her upbringing: she and her sister Lucille were raised by their grandmother, their great aunts and their aunt Sylvia. All these women lived in the same house which was built by Ruth's grandfather Edmund Foster, who worked on the railroad. He lived in the Midwest, which he left one day to travel further west. He told the ticket agent that he wanted to go to the mountains, but was dropped off in the town where Ruth was raised, Fingerbone, Idaho. The lake seems to be the town's distinguishing feature; sometimes it floods Fingerbone. Edmund worked on the railroad until he died when a train derailed into the lake. The disaster took place at night; nobody witnessed it firsthand. The next day the boys of the town dived into the lake but brought up only debris; that night the lake sealed itself over. Ruth's grandmother stayed in Fingerbone with her daughters Molly, Helen and Sylvia. They spent years of "perfect serenity" until

Molly left to work for a missionary society in the Orient (13). Helen, Ruth and Lucille's mother, married a man named Reginald Stone. Ruth has no memory of her father. Helen set up housekeeping in Seattle with Reginald. Her mother refused to accept the marriage until they returned to Fingerbone and married with her as witness. They returned to do this only for a day. Sylvie visited them in Seattle a few weeks later. She married "someone named Fisher" (15). Ruth's grandmother tried not to "reflect on the unkindness" of her children who reached sexual maturity and left her within a short space of time (18). Once, before they all left, she heard a thumping noise against the shed wall and wondered "what have I seen?" (19). The narrative leaps forward seven and a half years to Helen's return to Fingerbone. Helen leaves Lucille and Ruth on the steps of their grandmother's house and heads north where she drives off a cliff into a lake. Ruth recalls her life with her mother in Seattle. They lived in two rooms above an old woman named Bernice who told Helen scandalous stories. Bernice's husband Charlie "conserved syllables as if to conserve breath" (21). When Helen disappears, some boys report that they saw her sitting on the roof of her car, bogged down in the meadow by the cliff. She asked them to help her push the car out of some mud and they helped her. She gave them her purse, opened her car windows and drove on, sailing over the cliff.

After Helen's suicide, the girls' grandmother cares for them for five years. When she dies, her sisters-in-law, Lily and Nona, arrive to look after the girls and take up housekeeping. Chapter Two opens with their arrival. Ruth overhears them speculating about Helen's suicide and querying her motives. Lily and Nona look after Ruth and Lucille for one winter. The lake freezes over and the girls enjoy skating over it. Lily and Nona struggle to look after the girls and wonder where Sylvie is. They write a message in the newspaper telling anyone who knows Sylvie to contact their address. One day Sylvie writes a note to her mother, not realising that she is dead. Lily and Nona write to Sylvie, telling her that her mother has died and that they are now looking after Helen's girls. Everyone looks forward to Sylvie's reply. We learn that the girls' grandmother excluded her youngest daughter from her will and that Sylvie is a nomad; she no longer lives with her husband.

By Chapter 3, Sylvie has arrived. The girls are very excited, hoping to find in her a substitute for their mother. They ask Sylvie about their mother but she gives little away. She asks them if they remember their father. Ruth silently recalls that their mother received a letter from their father one day in Seattle. Their mother ripped the unopened letter into four pieces. Sylvie goes for a walk the next day and the girls fear that she will abandon them. They follow her to the station, where she is sheltering to keep warm. She tells them that she has decided to stay and look after them. They return to the house and Lily and Nona leave.

In Chapter 4, Ruth tells us about the floods that lay siege to the town every year. Luckily, their house is on a hill. The year Sylvie arrives, however, they have to live on the second floor for a while. After a few days they come downstairs to find everything saturated. They play games together, but Lucille wants to find some other people. Sylvie momentarily seems to disappear, but the girls find her in the kitchen. After the flood, the community

of Fingerbone gathers together to repair the damage. Sylvie, Ruth and Lucille do not participate. Ruth reflects on the self-sufficiency that has always separated their family from the town.

As Chapter 5 opens, school is about to begin again. Ruth has a "cold, visceral dread of school" (77). One day Lucille is accused of cheating on a test and she does not return to school for three days. Sylvie writes a note listing Lucille's symptoms sarcastically, and stating: "'I did not call the doctor, because she always seemed quite well by 9:30 or 10:00 in the morning'" (77). Lucille destroys the note, refusing to go back to school. The girls spend their days at the lake but do not tell Sylvie about their truancy. One day they spot Sylvie out by the lake and follow her. Sylvie greets them and does not berate them for being out of school. Lucille asks her what she was doing at the lake; if she had fallen in, people would have interpreted it as suicide. The girls worry about the instability of their aunt. They return to school the next week; nobody asks them where they have been. The community seems to feel that the girls are living under special circumstances because of Sylvie's mysterious ways. Sylvie's methods of housekeeping are unconventional and suggest her preoccupation with other matters; when she leaves the davenport out to air but forgets to retrieve it, it turns pink; she prefers to eat in the dark; she sleeps on top of the bed in her clothes.

Ruth reveals her surprise that Lucille begins to show an interest in other people's lives. She begins to change her clothes, to grind her teeth at Sylvie's "fanciful" taste (93). Chapter 6 introduces the "first true summer" of Ruth's life, when Lucille begins to distance herself (95). Lucille begins to mature, becoming a "touchy, achy, tearful creature" (97). The girls spend their long summer days in the woods, returning only at nightfall. While Ruth goes to the woods "for the woods' own sake," Lucille seeks them as a refuge from the shame of society's gaze. She seems to be "enduring a banishment there" (99). One evening Lucille asks Sylvie about her husband and doubts his existence. Sylvie tells her that her husband was a soldier. For a moment Lucille imagines Sylvie as a grieving widow: an identity with which she can sympathize. She is angry when Sylvie nonchalantly produces a photograph of her husband. Lucille becomes irritated by Sylvie's lax housekeeping and berates her for talking to "'trashy'" strangers (104). One day Ruth and Lucille find Sylvie lying on a bench in the local park. Lucille runs away but Ruth wakes her up. Sylvie expresses pleasure at being able to talk to Ruth alone. She tells Ruth that it is difficult to tell "'what [she] think[s]'" because she is so quiet (105). Ruth confesses that she does not know what she thinks. When they return home, Lucille expresses incredulity at Sylvie's behavior. Sylvie leaves. She returns with the huckleberries that she left on the bench; she picked them to make pancakes.

In Chapter 7, the summer continues. Lucille and Ruth continue to spend time together but begin to diverge in their views and memories. Lucille insists that their mother's death was an accident. Both girls sense Sylvie's influence in their truancy. They spend a whole night in the woods. They fashion a roof and a floor out of pieces of driftwood. Ruth reflects that Lucille will remember the night differently from her and claim that Ruth fell asleep. Ruth insists that she does not fall asleep, but lets "darkness in the sky become coextensive with the darkness in my skull and bowels and bones" (116). In the darkness she contemplates the transience of experience and memory. The next day Lucille walks back home, ignoring her sister. They reach home and Ruth falls asleep; she senses that she is dying. When she awakes Lucille tells her that she had a dream in which she was a baby; a woman resembling Sylvie tried to smother her.

Lucille tries to make Ruth over, so that she might blend in with their peers. She takes Ruth to the drugstore but Ruth goes home, baffled by her

sister's movements. As she approaches the house, she notes how it has changed; the grass is overgrown and the house looks as though it "must soon begin to float" (125). Lucille asks Ruth to help her make a dress. She tells Ruth to look up 'pinking shears' in the dictionary. When Ruth looks inside the book she finds pressed flowers. Lucille credits them to their grandfather. She shakes them out of the dictionary and tells Ruth to put them in the stove. Ruth protests and goes to find another book for the flowers but Lucille crushes them in her hand. Ruth attempts to hit Lucille with the dictionary, but her sister slaps her on the ear. They row and do not speak to each other for several days. Lucille spends her days in town and working on the dress. One day she bundles up her dress and throws it into the stove; she has not been able to follow the pattern. The girls forge a tenuous reconciliation; Lucille insists that they need other people in their lives. She begins to groom her nails and exercise. She reads novels that she believes are "improving" (132).

The girls return to school. The school principal, Mr. French, asks them how they intend to catch up on the work. Lucille assures him that her attitude has changed but tells him that Ruth is not interested in "'practical things'" (135). He asks Ruth what she cares about but she merely shrugs. One night Lucille goes to a dance and Sylvie tells Ruth about a valley that she has discovered. Sylvie suggests a trip to the valley on Monday but Ruth says that she has a test at school. They agree to go soon. Lucille comes home from the dance but insists on sleeping downstairs. When Sylvie comes downstairs to find her, she is gone. She has gone to stay with Miss Royce, a "solitary woman" who teaches home economics (140). Miss Royce arrives the next day and Sylvie gives her Lucille's schoolbooks. She tells Sylvie that Ruth may keep her clothes. Sylvie reminds Ruth that there are things she wants to share with her. Ruth now asks if they can go to the valley on Monday; Sylvie agrees to write a note.

Chapter 8 opens on the morning of their trip to the secret valley. They walk to the shore where they must take a boat that Sylvie has been using. At first, they cannot find it. Someone has hidden it under some branches. As they begin to row, a man throws a stone at them. Ruth suggests that it is his boat but Sylvie ignores him. She tells Ruth about the people who live in the surrounding islands and hills. She thinks that she has seen the ghosts of children in the area. She has left marshmallows on sticks outside a doorstep to a house which has fallen into a cellar hole. Sylvie hopes that she will have better luck, luring out the ghostly children with Ruth. They reach the valley shore where they build a fire and eat, waiting for the children to materialize. Suddenly Ruth notices that Sylvie has vanished. She sits on a log to wait for Sylvie and thinks about the strange presences that haunt the woods. She senses a consciousness behind her: the presence of a "half-wild, lonely" child (154). When she was with Lucille she could ignore these voices, but now there is no barrier between herself and these spectral presences. She moves to the cellar hole. She wonders who lived in the sunken house; she has heard stories of families in the mountains who have been snowed in all winter. She puts herself in the place of the children and wishes momentarily that she could be with them and feel again the presence of her mother. Sylvie materializes; Ruth tells her that she did not see the children and Sylvie replies that they will return "another time" (161). They climb back into the boat. When they approach the bridge to Fingerbone, Sylvie pulls the boat up to watch for the imminent train. Night time falls and still the train does not appear. Ruth reflects on the transience of existence and the ephemeral nature of identity boundaries; she feels that Sylvie could easily be her mother Helen. As the train approaches, she whispers "Helen" to Sylvie but her aunt does not reply. As the train passes, the boat shakes. Sylvie stands up and says something. Ruth cannot hear her and Sylvie tells her that she said nothing. Sylvie admits that she probably would not have been able to see inside the train because the lights would be out; evidently she was trying to see the passengers. She is thinking about her father's death; she speculates that the lake must be full of people who were on the train. As they row away, the wind suspends the boat. They beach the boat and climb onto a boxcar in a freight train that has slowed down on the bridge. When they leave the train they walk through the town; the citizens stare at their dishevelled state in horror. Lucille returns home and asks Ruth where they have been. Ruth wants to explain her experience but she falls asleep and dreams about it. Lucille seems to be telling Ruth that she can leave Sylvie too if she wishes.

In Chapter 9 we learn that the sheriff has called upon the house twice. Ruth reveals some of Fingerbone's history: its citizens are "very much given to murder" (177). Neighboring women begin to frequent the house, bringing cakes and inquiring about Sylvie's housekeeping. They are puzzled by the accumulation of newspapers, magazines and cans, which Sylvie has stored in the parlor. Sylvie tries to tidy up the house and Ruth returns to school. She feels completely estranged from the other students and is ignored by Lucille. Sylvie visits Lucille and discovers that the community is planning to take Ruth away. The sheriff confirms that a hearing is planned. Sylvie starts a huge bonfire in which she burns all the paraphernalia which has accumulated in the house. She talks about buying new clothes for Ruth and getting her a permanent wave. Eventually she calls Ruth in. Ruth hides in the orchard, watching the house illuminated by the fire. She has an apocalyptic vision, in which a young girl loses all her family and lives alone in a house. She would be able to walk into the lake or "sail up the air" (204). The sheriff arrives and asks if he can see Ruth. Sylvie admits that she is not sure where Ruth is. Ruth appears and rebuffs the sheriff's offer to take her home to his wife and children.

As the final chapter opens, Sylvie and Ruth are trying to burn the house. They know that they have to leave the town to stay together. As the fire gathers force, they hear the whistle of the train and leave. They cross the treacherous bridge in the wind and almost die. The narrative leaps forward to many years on. Sylvie keeps a newspaper report claiming that she and Ruth died in the lake. Ruth confesses that they have never contacted Lucille. They have lived the life of drifters, taking jobs and leaving them when they felt like it. Ruth reflects that the experience on the bridge finally changed her. She is not sure whether or not she heard a sound or word that was beyond her comprehension, but she felt herself cross over to some other state which resulted in her life of transience. Sylvie tries to track down Lucille in Boston, the city that she once named as her ultimate destination years ago. They are unable to locate her. Ruth plans to return to Fingerbone one day when she is "feeling presentable" (217). She views herself as an absent presence, just like her mother.

Symbols & Motifs

Water is the most prominent and complex symbol in the novel: it reminds Ruth of the transience and fluidity of life yet also signifies freedom. For much of the novel, Ruth contemplates the power of water, figured by the floods and the lake of corpses. However, she also registers its fragility: "Water is almost nothing, after all. It is conspicuously different from air only in its tendency to flood and founder and drown, and even that difference may be relative rather than absolute" (164). Fire is another symbolic element in the novel. Sylvie delights in the small fire that occurs on Ruth's birthday. She and Ruth set fire to the house in defiance of the town's domestic ideology.

Objects and documents acquire symbolic weight in the novel. Sylvie stores several mementoes of other itinerants in her pin box, such as the pearl ring that belonged to Edith, the woman who died crossing the mountains in a boxcar. Her games of solitaire figure her isolation. Lucille's diary contains lists of exercises and a table grace with "an aristocratic sound" (133). Sylvie keeps a twenty dollar bill under the lapel of her jacket, figuring her transient sensibility. Ruth finds a page from "National Geographic" in her grandmother's drawer which features the headline: "Tens of millions in Honan Province alone" and shows photographs of people barefoot. At the foot of the page runs the line, "I will make you fishers of men." Ruth attributes her Aunt Molly's departure to China to these images.

Ruth draws repeatedly on religious imagery to figure her own experience. She compares the banal relics of the Fingerbone flood to iconic motifs from the Bible: "If one should be shown odd fragments arranged on a silver tray and be told, 'That is a splinter from the True Cross, and that is a nail paring dropped by Barabbas, and that is a bit of lint from under the bed where Pilate's wife dreamed her dream,' the very ordinariness of the things would recommend them" (73).

The house which Edmund Foster built serves as a symbol for the family's self-containment. It is situated on top of a hill: "That we were self-sufficient, our house reminded us always" (75). After the flood, the citizens of Fingerbone begin to believe that the house has magical properties: it seems to have escaped the damage.

Historical Context

Fingerbone appears to be subsumed by space and untouched by time: "It was chastened by an outsized landscape and extravagant weather, and chastened again by an awareness that the whole of human history had occurred elsewhere" (62). Lucille has a different temporal sensibility than Ruth and Sylvie: she "hated everything about transience" (103). For Lucille, "Time that had not come yet—an anomaly in itself—had the fiercest reality to her ... Sylvie, on her side, inhabited a millennial present" (93). Written in the eighties but set in the fifties: while Robinson challenges the fifties ideology which placed women firmly in the home, she also addresses the prevalent postmodern concern for the nuclear family. Despite her transience, Sylvie insists that families must stay together: "'Families should stay together,' Sylvie said. 'They should. There is no other help. Ruthie and I have had trouble enough with the one we've lost already'" (186).

In her collection of essays "The Death of Adam," Robinson considers why the biological family remains so "compelling" (87). She reflects that when "siblings founder" and "spouses age," loyalty "should matter" (89). She adds, however, that "invoking [loyalty] now is about as potent a gesture as flashing a fat roll of rubles" (89) and attributes the "sadness" at the heart of contemporary society to his failure.

Societal Context

While Sylvie and Ruth strive for self-determination, Lucille allows social conventions to shape her life. This tension manifests itself early on in the novel. During the flood, Sylvie and Ruth are quite content to stay in the house and play games. Lucille tells Sylvie that she "'want[s] to find some other people'" (66). Lucille will only warm to Sylvie if she fits particular social stereotypes. She is clearly disconcerted by Sylvie's apathy towards her husband. She can only "forgive" her aunt if she imagines that her husband has died and she is a grieving widow (102). Sylvie's housekeeping presents a challenge to the domestic ideology that dominated fifties America. On Ruth's birthday, the candles on her cake set fire to the curtain. Sylvie beats out the flames with a copy of "Good Housekeeping." Rather than being horrified by the thought of a fire, Sylvie derives "intense" pleasure from this incident (101). Sylvie is clearly not suited to marriage. We never discover what happened to her husband; she does not define herself as a wife.

She tells Lucille and Ruth about a woman who once married an old man with a limp to relieve herself from loneliness. They had four children. One day the woman left with her children to visit her mother. When she returned, her husband did not believe that she had merely been to see her mother and stopped showing affection to his wife and children. When Edmund Foster dies, the girls' grandmother expresses little surprise; she views his death as a "kind of defection, not altogether unanticipated" (10). She hopes that her husband will have changed by the time they are reunited in heaven. The novel also queries the cult of motherhood: Sylvie herself feels no compulsion to have children of her own although she treats Lucille and Ruth with affection. The pressures of society are figured in Lucille's preoccupations with education and appearance and the neighboring women who visit Ruth: "those demure but absolute arbiters who continually sat in judgment of our lives" (104).

Religious Context

Robinson is renowned for her engagement with religious discourses. She defends Calvinism in her book of essays on modern thought, "The Death of Adam." Her second novel, "Gilead" (2004) centers on the theme of expiation; its narrator is a third generation preacher who reflects on a number of religious themes and questions in a long valedictory letter to his young son.

Many of the events and images in "Housekeeping" evoke Biblical images and narratives: the annual floods, the appearance of ghosts, the parabolic stories that Sylvie tells Ruth and Lucille. Robinson explicates these connections in Ruth's narration. Biblical narratives serve as analogies for Ruth's experience of loss and the working of time:

"Cain murdered Abel, and blood cried out from the earth; the house fell on Job's children, and a voice was induced or provoked into speaking from a whirlwind; and Rachel mourned for her children; and King David for Absalom. The force behind the movement of time is a mourning that will not be comforted" (192).

Several disasters occur in Fingerbone, signaling the work of some transcendental force. During a blizzard, a limb from the apple orchard is severed and a cable snaps. The leaves seem to be elevated by "something that came before the wind ... some impalpable movement of air" (85). Sylvie saves leaves and scraps of paper when she is sweeping. Ruth speculates that this is because she "sensed a Delphic niceness in the scattering of these leaves and paper, here and not elsewhere, thus and not otherwise" (85).

The novel abounds with references to ghosts: the ghost of Edith, the woman who lies down to die in the boxcar, is exorcised by the time she arrives in Wenatchee; Ruth herself fells like a ghost who "made no impact on the world" (106); Grandmother tells the girls about a woman who once saw the ghosts of crying children on the road; Sylvie is convinced that the ghosts of children haunt the woods.

The possibility of redemption also haunts the novel. Ruth insists that "what perished need not also be lost" (124). The pictures of the barefoot inhabitants of Honan Province are captioned by the line from the Gospels: I will make you fishers of men (91). Ruth imagines her aunt Molly rescuing the needy with her net; she sees this net spreading across the world and saving all those who have suffered or become lost, including her mother. When Sylvie writes a note to her mother, it is deemed to be the work of "providence" (41).

Ruth is particularly drawn to the stories that involve women in the Bible. When she realizes that Sylvie has left her, she states that she would have made a statue to attract the children if there had been any snow. She thinks about the story of Lot's wife who looked back "because she was full of loss and mourning" (153). In Ruth's environment Lot's wife would be adopted as a mother by the children who would adorn her with flowers; she would not turn to salt. Robinson foregrounds the women in the Old Testament who were either punished or represented as appendages to their husbands: Ruth wonders how Noah's wife must have felt the morning after the flood: "she was a nameless woman, and so at home among all those who were never found and never missed, who were uncommemorated, whose deaths were not remarked, nor their begettings" (172).

The novel queries religious dogma and false notions of piety; it condemns those who observe religious doctrines merely to appear pious and show "good breeding" (183): the women who visit Sylvie and Ruth do so in obedience to "Biblical injunction" (182). Ruth comments that Fingerbone is remarkable for its "religious zeal"; the vision of sin and salvation in some of its churches is "ecstatic, and so nearly identical" that the congregations feel obliged to compete with each other to assert their faith. Ruth adds that this obligation falls to the women more than the men. Ettie, one of Ruth's grandmother's friends, tells the girls a story about a Catholic lady who kept a parrot on her balcony. The parrot prayed with her every day until they were both destroyed by the San Francisco fire.

Scientific & Technological Context

Isolated and overpowered by nature, the town of Fingerbone remains largely untouched by technological advancements. The development of the rail system brings Edmund Foster to Fingerbone but also leads to his death. The forces of nature assert their authority over technology when the train is derailed. It lands in the lake, where it stays buried.

Biographical Context

Marilynne Robinson is regarded as one of America's pre-eminent writers. She was born in Sandpoint, Idaho in 1947. After a childhood spent in small towns in the Midwest, she graduated from

Brown University. She took a PhD at Washington University in 1977. Her first novel, "Housekeeping," appeared in 1980. The novel garnered much praise and won the PEN/Hemingway Award for best first novel. Robinson earned her first nomination for the Pulitzer Prize with "Housekeeping." The novel was voted one of the best one hundred books of the century by the *New York Times* and was named one of the best novels of all time by the *Observer.* After the success of "Housekeeping," Robinson wrote for several magazines including *The Paris Review,* and served as visiting professor and writer-in-residence at the University of Massachusetts and the University of Kent, England. Her essay, "Bad News for Britain," was published in *Harper's* magazine. It provided the genus for her non-fiction work, "Mother Country: Britain, the Welfare State and Nuclear Pollution" (1989), which examined the environmental implications of the nuclear reprocessing plant at Sellafield in England. The book was nominated for the National Book Award. Greenpeace sued the British publishers of "Mother Country" for libel. The book was banned in England. Robinson's next publication was a collection of essays, "The Death of Adam: Essays on Modern Thought" (1998). In each essay, Robinson challenges ideologies underpinning modern America. She queries common conceptions of Darwinism and Calvinism and addresses issues such as the American wilderness and the American family. Robinson's long-awaited second novel, "Gilead," appeared in 2004, again to great critical acclaim. The novel won the 2005 Pulitzer Prize and the National Book Critics Circle Award. Robinson returned to some of the themes of her first novel: loss, transience, and the pull of place and the past. Robinson is celebrated for her lyrical, delicate prose and her powerful use of natural and religious imagery. She married while she was a student writing her dissertation. She is now separated from her husband. She has two children and currently works at the Iowa Writer's Workshop. In a recent interview with Jill Owens, Robinson named Melville, Faulkner, William Carlos Williams, Emily Dickinson and Wallace Stevens as favorite writers and influences on her work.

Rachel Lister, Ph.D.

Works Cited

Owens, Jill. "The Epistolary Marilynne Robinson." Jan. 19th 2005. http://www.powells.com/authors/robinson/html

Robinson, Marilynne. *The Death of Adam: Essays on Modern Thought.* 1998. New York: Picador, 2005.

_____. *Housekeeping.* 1980. London: Faber, 1981.

Discussion Questions

1. The men in "Housekeeping" are notable only for their absence. Identify all the absent or silent men in the novel. What is the significance of this elimination of male characters and discourses?

2. Consider the stories that Sylvie tells Ruth and Lucille about the strangers she meets. What is the significance of these stories? Do any patterns emerge?

3. Discuss Robinson's use of water as the primary motif in the novel. What meanings accumulate around this motif?

4. "There was not a soul there but knew how shallow-rooted the whole town was" (177). What kind of place is Fingerbone? Discuss Robinson's representation of the town and its community.

5. Sylvie's housekeeping is clearly unconventional. Identify her methods and habits and consider what they tell us about Sylvie as a character.

6. "Housekeeping" features little dialogue. Why is this? Discuss the role of silence in the novel.

7. Trace Ruth's references to Biblical narrative and imagery. What effect do these references have on the novel?

8. How reliable is Ruth as a narrator? Identify the key characteristics and effects of her voice. How might Lucille have narrated her version of events?

9. Read Chapter 8 again. What is the significance of Sylvie and Ruth's trip to the valley? Why does Sylvie leave Ruth alone? What effect does this experience have on Ruth?

10. Throughout the novel, Ruth and Lucille think about their mother. Identify the images of Helen that are presented to the reader and the theories that surround her death. How do the girls' feelings about their mother change?

Essay Ideas

1. "Appearance paints itself on bright and gliding surfaces, for example, memory and dream" (131). Examine the tension between appearance and 'reality' in "Housekeeping."

2. "Because, once alone, it is impossible to believe that one could ever have been otherwise. Loneliness is an absolute discovery" (157). Explore the representation of loneliness in "Housekeeping." To what extent does the novel support this statement?

3. "… just when I had got used to the limits and dimensions of one moment, I was expelled into the next and made to wonder again if any shapes hid in its shadows" (166). Consider Robinson's treatment of time in "Housekeeping."

4. "And so the ordinary demanded unblinking attention" (166). How does Robinson convey the significance of the everyday?

5. Sylvie suggests that "'you feel [family] most when they're gone'" (185). Explore Robinson's handling of loss in "Housekeeping."

How the García Girls Lost Their Accents

by Julia Alvarez

Content Synopsis

"How the García Girls Lost Their Accents" chronicles the lives of the members of the García family from their early years in the Dominican Republic to their move to the United States and beyond. The story opens in 1989 with Yolanda, as an adult, returning to the land of her birth where she is now, essentially, a foreigner. The novel works backwards chronologically, ending with a depiction of Yolanda as a child in the Dominican Republic in 1956. In between these two chapters, other chapters fill in more of Yolanda's life and also illuminate the lives of the other members of the García family, which includes Yolanda's sisters, Carla, Sandra (Sandi), and Sofia (Fifi); and their parents, Carlos and Laura. When the girls are young they live in luxury and wealth in the Dominican Republic. Carlos is a physician and both parents are members of the elite. Carlos is involved in a failed attempt to overthrow Trujillo, the dictator. Fearing persecution, he flees with his family to New York City, where they begin a new life in a foreign culture, away from their traditions and their extended families. Here they are confronted with prejudice and challenge. As adults, Carla becomes a psychologist, and marries someone in the same field; Sandi is hospitalized for anorexia and a nervous breakdown; and Fifi marries a German scientist and has two children. Yolanda, the character who predominates in the novel and who is revealed at

the end to be the storyteller, becomes a writer and a teacher.

"Carla"

Carla, the eldest, "is the one who experiences the most significant trauma because of the family's exile… [and] suffers more severely from cultural displacement than her sisters" (Sirias 29). In the third chapter, "The Four Girls," in which the mother relates stories about each of her daughters, Laura tells about how, as a young girl, Carla badly wanted a pair of red sneakers. Because they were poor at the time, she couldn't buy them for her. A neighbor gives her a white pair of sneakers, which don't satisfy Carla. So Carla and her father paint the sneakers red with nail polish. In "Trespass," Carla, as a new immigrant, is traumatized first by a flasher then by the rough policemen who take her report. She cannot say what she's seen because she doesn't know the English words to explain it. This incident, along with other experiences of racist and sexist prejudice, "exacerbate her cultural displacement" (Sirias 29). In the only other chapter chiefly about Carla, "An American Surprise," Carla is a young girl in the Dominican Republic. In first person point of view, she relates the excitement of waiting for her father to return from New York with gifts. When Carla opens her gift from her father—a mechanical statue that is also a bank—Gladys, one of the maids who aspires to go to New York, is entranced. Eventually, the bank ends up on the toy shelf with other forgotten toys. On Christmas, excited by her new toys, Carla gives the bank to Gladys after she asks to buy it from her. When the bank is found in the servants' quarters, Gladys is accused of theft. Carla speaks up in her defense, but the maid leaves anyway. The incident is a lesson for Carla in the extent of her own power and of the economic and racial privileges she is accorded.

"Sandra (Sandi)"

Laura does not tell a story about Sandi in "The Four Girls" because she would like to forget Sandi's recent past. Instead, the narrator relates the parents' experience talking to a psychiatrist about Sandi's hospitalization. Their concern for her had started with Sandi "starving herself to death"; the doctor tells them she's had a nervous breakdown (51). Here, the mother unknowingly reveals, the source of Sandi's anxiety: as the lighter-skinned girl, she wants to be "darker complected like her sisters" (52). Sandi is unable to stop reading and talks "crazy"; the books seem to be a monster devouring her identity as she tells her mother "soon she wouldn't be human" (55, 54). This part of her story ends with an image of her running away from a man mowing the lawn. Given that in the same chapter she appears much more normal and sane, the reader is to conclude she recovers from her breakdown.

Sandi's own perspective is provided in two chapters that relate events from her childhood and illuminate further her deep anxiety about her identity. In "Still Lives," the only part of the book told from her first-person point of view and which appears as the later chapter in Alvarez's backwards order, Sandi's artistic talent is noticed when her art seems to take on supernatural powers. She is sent to a local German woman for art lessons, where she defies the teacher's instructions and is punished by being sent to a dark, airless room. Sandi escapes and comes upon the woman's husband working in the shed, naked and in chains. She startles the man, who in turn startles her, causing her to fall and break her arm. The consequence is no more art lessons, and eventually Sandi turns inward, losing her ability to express herself: "But now when the world filled me, I could no longer draw it out…. I could no longer draw" (254).

In "The Floor Show," the Garcías, soon after arriving in New York, go out to dinner as guests of Carlos's sponsor. The dinner is ultimately an embarrassment for Carlos because he cannot pay for their meals, or for the flamenco dolls that his daughters desire. Sandi goes to the bathroom, accompanied by both her father and Mrs. Fanning, the sponsor's wife. She witnesses Mrs. Fanning, who is drunk, kiss her father. It is after this that she begins to have a sense of her own identity as separate from her sisters': "Looking at herself in the mirror, she was surprised to find a pretty girl looking back at her. It was a girl who could pass as American…. It struck her impersonally, as if it were a judgment someone else was delivering, someone American and important, like Dr. Fanning: she was pretty" (181). It is because of this new perspective on herself, as well as the secret she keeps about what she's seen between Mrs. Fanning and her father, that she eagerly accepts the purchase of the dolls for her and her sisters from the Fannings.

"Sofía (Fifi)"

In the very first chapter, Carlos, the father, and Sofia, the youngest daughter, are reconciled after a long estrangement caused by Carlos's discovery that she's had sex before marriage. After she marries and gives him a grandson, they are more or less reconciled. Yet she succeeds in still embarrassing him when she gives him an inappropriate kiss in a game during his birthday party. As a girl, Sofia, or Fifi, was exiled to the island as punishment for having marijuana, where she took on the culture and attitudes of the women there, becoming submissive to a macho, posses-sive Dominican man. Her sisters succeed in end-ing the affair by exposing her when she's gone off with him alone one night. Having been the young-est when the family left their home, Fifi is the one who "least suffers from cultural displacement" and most successfully lives the "American" life (Sirias 28). Her marriage to a German immigrant scientist exemplifies the melting together of two cultures to make a new one. The only chapter in which Fifi speaks is as one of several narrators in "The Blood of the Conquistadores," which describes the criti-cal moments when Carlos evades interrogation by the secret police and after which the family leaves the island. Yet, her perspective is filtered through what others have told her since she was too young when the events occurred to remember all of them. A clue to her tense relationship with her father is revealed by her statement that she "almost got Papi killed" because she was "mean to one of the secret police who came looking for him" (217). What Fifi does remember is Chucha, their cook and longtime servant, saying a prayer for them to a wooden statue for their safe trip. According to Sil-vio Sirias, "[t]elling the story of the family's last moments in their former country constitutes Fifi's only chance to let her island self be heard" (24).

"Yolanda"

In the first chapter, the reader is presented with Yolanda, dressed in the style of an American hip-pie and seen by her Dominican cousins as "one of those Peace Corps girls who have let themselves go as to do dubious good in the world" (4). There-fore the first picture of her is of an outsider in the place of her birth. When Yolanda announces her intentions to drive north by herself, her aunts and cousins are aghast, fearful of the guerillas. Their warnings notwithstanding, Yolanda goes, and finds a place to pick fresh guavas. It is on this trip that she feels she finds "what she has been miss-ing all these years without knowing she has been

missing it. Standing here in the quiet, she believes she has never felt at home in the States, never" (12). But Yolanda's feelings of comfort and safety are quickly dispelled by the passing of a noisy passenger bus, then later by meeting up with two men when she is stranded on the road with a flat tire. Though the men help her, she is so scared of them that she can't speak, and when she is able to, she only speaks to them in English.

Yolanda returns in the fourth chapter as "Joe," the Anglicization of her nickname, Yo, which also means "I" in Spanish. Here she is recovering from breaking up with her husband. The contrast between her and her American husband is depicted through language games. Yolanda rhymes and plays with words, while John criticizes her. She sees it as a game or race where he cannot keep up: she "was running, like mad, into the safety of her first tongue, where the proudly monolingual John could not catch her" (72). When her parents ask her what happened, she simply says, "'We just didn't speak the same language,'" (81), a statement that in this case is both literal and metaphorical. In the next chapter, Yolanda tells the story of being at college and being pursued by Rudy Elmenhurst. Coming as it does just after the previous chapter, the story illustrates the differences she felt between herself and her American lovers. Rudy pressures her to have sex; years later, when he looks her up, he still wants to have sex with her. But to him, Yolanda realizes, she is simply something exotic, a taste of another culture, as if she were a country to be explored.

In the seventh chapter, "Daughter of Invention," an event in Yolanda's youth also characterizes her mother. After coming to New York, Laura becomes absorbed in constantly inventing new things, an activity which "stems from her need to prove her-self in the United States" (Sirias 30). She even-tually gives up after realizing her inventions will already be thought of by others more acceptable in American society. Her last creative endeavor is the assistance she gives Yolanda when her daughter is chosen to deliver a Teacher's Day address in ninth grade. Yolanda is terrified; she still has an accent and fears ridicule. Laura calms her down and when Yolanda finally writes the speech, producing a piece where she "finally sounded like herself in English," Laura praises her (143). Yet because the speech quotes Whitman's phrase that the "best student learns to destroy the teacher" her father insists that the speech be changed (145). Both Laura and Yolanda rebel; Yolanda calls her father the nickname given to the dictator Trujillo. In the end mother and daughter acquiesce and together they come up with a speech of "stale compliments and the polite commonplaces," which, while it wins her accolades, does not express Yolanda's true feelings (148). In the end, Yolanda is given a typewriter as a gift from her father, a sign that he entrusts her with language to say what she really feels.

In the last two chapters, Yolanda appears as the little girl "Yoyo," a nickname that evokes the feeling of being "jerked back and forth between two cultures" (Barak 174). In "The Human Body," she resists her mother's growing insistence that she start acting like a lady, instead of running around with her cousin Mundín. Even her fascination with a new book, "A Thousand and One Nights," is not quite enough to keep her from wanting a part in Mundín's gift, a special kind of modeling clay. She's also interested in another gift from their grandparents, a "Human Body" doll that displays a replica of the insides of a body. Yoyo bargains with her cousin to get part of the clay as well as the doll in exchange for showing him that she's a girl. When she, her sister and her cousin are caught in the coal shed, where they're not permitted, Yoyo is inspired by her book and frees them by coming up with a story that the "guardia" (the military police) came by and that they were hiding from them. The incident is significant in that it gives Yoyo an idea of the power of language and story, a power that is challenged by her uprooting from the land of her birth.

In the last chapter, Yoyo is an even younger girl who's received a drum as a gift. She enjoys banging incessantly on the drum, much to her mother's chagrin, and is sent outside. She finds a litter of kittens and takes one as a pet. Fearful of the wrath of the mother cat, she hides the kitten in the drum and tries to cover up the kitten's yowling with the drum noise. Pursued by the mother cat, Yoyo panics and throws the kitten out the window. For several nights she is haunted by the specter of the mother cat. The specter of the cat returns on and off for several years, a symbol of all that Yoyo fears. It disappears when she moves to New York. She ends the novel in this chapter with a direct address to the readers: "You understand I am collapsing all time now so that it fits in what's left in the hollow of my story?" (289). She is collapsing not only the time in her own life, but of her whole family's, and she is revealed as the Scheherazade, the storyteller of the book.

Historical Context

An understanding of the political climate of the Dominican Republic in the 1950s sheds light on the immense pressure the García family would have felt as they contemplated leaving their homeland, where they enjoyed wealth, privilege, and the close proximity of an extended family. At that time, the country was ruled by a brutal dictator, Rafael Trujillo Molina (referred to as Trujillo), who took power in 1930 and was assassinated in 1961. Trujillo's rise to power, and his ability to stay there for over thirty years, can be attributed to his leadership in avoiding war with their neighboring country, Haiti, and with massive infrastructure improvements, including those to transportation, sanitation, and education. However, Trujillo's regime was merciless in its oppression of opposing parties and views, and its troops were responsible for the massacre of thousands of Haitian immigrants, a massacre mentioned in the chapter entitled "The Blood of the Conquistadores" ("Dominican Republic").

While the United States offered a haven for the fleeing Dominicans at the time, the period of their arrival is characterized by extreme fear of Communism, as expressed in the McCarthy hearings, and in general by a culture of conformity based on white, middle-class norms. Immigrants were expected to assimilate quickly, leaving behind their language and culture as much as possible.

The García sisters are also influenced by American foreign involvement and the constant fear of nuclear war. In "Snow," Yolanda confuses her first sighting of snow with nuclear fall-out. In "Daughters of Invention," she reads her speech as the television broadcasts news of the war in Southeast Asia. "Blood of the Conquistadores," as mentioned above, takes place in a very specific time and place, when Trujillo pursued Carlos. Another character, Victor, also exemplifies American involvement in overthrowing him.

Societal Context

The challenge of immigrant acculturation is one of the central themes of the novel. The four sisters represent different degrees of successful assimilation. Unlike other immigrant groups, Hispanic Americans have a particular challenge, according to Roberto Gonzalez Echevarría, since they "constantly face a flow of friends and relatives from 'home' who keep the culture current. This constant cross-fertilization makes assimilation a more complicated process for them than for other minority groups" (qtd. in Barak 160).

Ricardo Castells identifies Yolanda and her sisters as part of an "intermediate" generation of immigrants, meaning they have been born elsewhere but grew up in the United States. Characteristic of this generation is that it "is not fully part of either its native or its adopted country" (36). The loss of the accent is symbolic of a fusing of cultures, of immigrant acculturation. Yolanda's struggle with language at various points throughout the novel reveals the tensions inherent in this process.

Their move to the United States also highlights differences in gender norms. The distinction between gender norms becomes acutely clear when the girls go back to the homeland. In the first chapter, the adult Yolanda scoffs at her aunts' and cousins' dismay when she announces her plan to drive alone through the countryside. Had she been raised there, she would have been accustomed to the rigorous restrictions on female behavior. In "A Regular Revolution," Sofia, the youngest sister, is sent to the island to live for a year partly as punishment. She takes on the characteristics of a wealthy young Dominican woman, adopting their style, dress, and behavior-In short, according to her sisters, she's become a Spanish-American princess. When her sisters see how submissive she is becoming to her boyfriend there, who exhibits typical machismo of the culture, they purposely expose her secret trysts with him so that the affair will be ended. While they undoubtedly fear "Fifi" might get pregnant, they are more alarmed by the prospect of her ending up married to Manuel, who they call "the tyrant" and who won't let Fifi leave the house without his permission (120). They fear the loss of "feisty, lively Fifi" who "is letting this man tell her what she can and cannot do" (120). The girls confront Manuel, armed with feminist knowledge they've acquired in the States, to no avail. They call their plan to expose Fifi a "revolution" which will "win the fight for our Fifi's heart and mind" (122). As insiders, they've learned to play one tyrant against another tyrant, in this case, Manuel against their mother, who, when she finds out about the tryst, insists Fifi go back to the United States. In this incident, they use a repressive cultural code, the code that dictates that girls not go on dates unchaperoned, in order to free Fifi from the very society that enforces this code.

While in "A Regular Revolution," the mother is portrayed as the tyrant, the father recurs more often in the text as the real tyrant. He clings to his cultural expectations of female behavior and to his belief that he is the "family patriarch, its undisputed master" (Sirias 45). The remnants of his power are still seen in the first chapter, which takes place in the most recent year and which has the daughter complying with his insistence that they come alone to celebrate his birthdays. Ultimately, according to Sirias, Alvarez simply presents sexism as a given feature of Latin American culture and "leaves it up to the reader to choose how to react to the sexism that is so pervasive in the book" (48).

Race filters into the text mainly through the depictions of the family compound in the early years of the girls' lives. The servants who work for the family are mostly of African descent, a legacy of an earlier history of slavery employed by the Spanish colonizers from whom the Garcías are descended. Chucha had been taken in for asylum by the girls' grandparents, escaping Trujillo's order to massacre all black Haitians, and had been with the family ever since. Chucha "always had a voodoo job going" (219) and despite her status as something "like a nun who had joined the convent of the de la Torre clan," she is the "other" for the girls, someone who does not share her emotions with the family and closes herself up in her room during her time off (218). "Other" is a term used in literary criticism to signify a person or race of people whose culture is different from one's own. "'The other'" is often the devalued half of a binary opposition when it is applied to groups of people" but also often serves the purpose of knowing oneself better ("Terms"). Chucha's strangeness is further underscored by her insistence on sleeping in her coffin "to prepare herself for dying" (220). Another servant, Pila, who is accused of stealing, is dark-skinned and half-Haitian. She is feared by the lighter-skinned Dominican maids "for Haiti was synonymous with voodoo" (279). She was "a curiosity" for Yolanda, yet someone who was also a source of answers about the mysteries of life: when young Yolanda discovers a litter of newborn kittens, she wishes Pila were around to tell

her when it could be taken away from its mother (279).

When the family moves to the United States, they find themselves victims of prejudice, with children, and even one of their neighbors, calling them "spics." The chapters about Sandi are especially revealing about the attempt to makes sense of biculturalism. As the daughter who is labeled the most attractive because of her strong white European looks, Sandi is especially ambivalent about the two cultures she lives within and between. In "Floor Show," Sandi is excited to see the flamenco dancers, for they represent something to be proud of in her Spanish inheritance, yet, as Barak notes, Mrs. Fanning's drunken display with the dancers makes the show into a parody (171). The art teacher and her husband depicted in "Still Lives" represent "both a mind/body and a colonizer/colonized duality" (Barak 171). If Sofia might be seen as the most successfully acculturated sister, Sandi is perhaps the least, as she ends up hospitalized for mental illness and anorexia when she is older.

Religious Context

As a former Spanish colony, the Dominican Republic has been shaped by the strong presence of the Roman Catholic Church. As such, religion as a cultural force is ever-present in the novel, yet does not seem to play a vital role other than in the way in which it shapes cultural attitudes and expectations. Perhaps one of the strongest ways Catholicism shapes cultural attitudes is through the restrictions on women's behavior. Sex before marriage is forbidden. Sofia's father is so shocked by finding out Sofia has engaged in sex before marriage that he doesn't speak to her for years, until she marries and has a child. Catholic views dictate that, as a teenager, Sofia must be chaperoned when she goes out on dates in the Dominican Republic, and it is this restriction that her sisters count on in order to free her of the grasp of her new boyfriend.

The girls' Catholic education is comprised of learning about the world in absolute terms. As a young girl in the convent school she attends, Sandi learns from the nuns to "sort the world like laundry into what was wrong and right, what was venial, what, if you died in the middle of enjoying, would send you straight to hell" (248). Her religious education is comprised of lessons that teach her that "everything I enjoyed in the world was turning out to be wrong" (248).

As a college student, Yolanda describes herself as a "mix of Catholicism and agnosticism" (99). When she is rejected by Rudy because she won't give in and have sex with him, she puts a crucifix under the pillow, as she does when she has an exam the next day. She calls the crucifix her "'security blanket," a reminder of her homeland and a comfort to her when the culture of her adopted country becomes too difficult for her (100). Years later, she guesses she's "resolved the soul and sin thing by lapsing from my heavy-duty Catholic background, giving up my immortal soul for a blues kind of soul. Funky and low-down, the kind inspired by reading too much Carlos Castañeda and Rilke and Robert Bly and dropping acid…." Rudy reappears, and she discovers that she still does not want to sleep with him, that she still finds his tactics a turn-off (102). She realizes that her objections to him were not religious in the traditional sense: "Catholic or not, I still thought it a sin for a guy to just barge in five years later" and expect to have sex (103).

Another religious tradition, that of voodoo, is connected with the dark-skinned Haitian servants in the family compound on the island. Voodoo is seen as somewhat mysterious but benign, in that the spells the servants cast seem mainly to protect the family. Before they flee, Fifi recalls, Chucha gets out a wooden statue and says a prayer over each of the sisters. While they are used to Chucha's strangeness, they cry, and it is through this spiritual act they are bonded with Chucha, who herself is a refugee from her home country.

The voodoo tradition is a means of connection between servant and the master's children, a way for Chucha to express her own history and her deep loyalty to them.

Scientific & Technological Context

In "Daughter of Invention," the mother, Laura, is characterized by her obsession with inventing useful products when they first arrive in the United States. Technology and scientific advancement are the hallmarks of their new identity in the States. Both parents spend their early days showing the girls the "wonders" of New York. For the father Carlos, these include the Brooklyn Bridge and Rockefeller Center. For Laura, these include the "true treasures" found in the housewares sections of department stores. The girls are impressed with the escalator, which Laura teasingly tells them is Jacob's ladder. Even the father's job as a doctor takes on a more scientific—and thus "American"—overtone when he brings home pads of paper with ads for tranquilizers, antibiotics, and skin cream. Laura's inventions are her attempts to forge an identity of her own, but her family is unsupportive. The girls resent the time she spends on "those dumb inventions" when they need help "figuring out who they were, why the Irish kids whose grandparents had been micks were calling them spics" (138). Instead of taking time with her children to give them answers—answers she probably does not have—Laura occupies herself with inventing products "to make life easier for the American Moms" (138). Her ideas, then, are not only about expressing an individual identity, they are also an attempt to locate herself in a new culture where motherhood requires more from her than it did in her homeland. After all, she has moved from a life of luxury, surrounded by extended family and servants, to a place where mothers bear the brunt of much of the work in the home. Many of the inventions of the 1950s and 60s were specifically designed to help women in this work, formerly done by family members or servants, so it is unsurprising that Laura would turn to this as a source of interest.

Biographical Context

While not properly a memoir, much of "How the García Girls Lost Their Accents" is based on Julia Alvarez's life. Yolanda is the character who most closely mirrors Alvarez, with many similar experiences growing up in the Dominican Republic and in Queens, New York with three sisters.

Alvarez, herself the second of four sisters, was born in 1951 in New York City to immigrants from the Dominican Republic. Her parents returned to their homeland when she was three months old, "preferring the dictatorship of Trujillo to the U.S.A. of the early 50s" and lived there until she was ten (Alvarez, par. 2). Just as the García family has to flee in order to escape possible persecution, the Alvarez family had to leave the island because of Julia's father's involvement in a conspiracy to overthrow the dictator Trujillo (see Historical Contexts). Dr. Alvarez, like Dr. García, was able to get sponsorship and resume his medical practice in the United States.

When they arrived in New York, the Alvarez family had to learn English quickly; at the time to speak another language "was considered 'Un-American'" (Silvias, 2). Alvarez subsequently lost much of her Spanish and thus now speaks it with an accent. This is in ironic contrast to the title of the book, which portrays the loss of an accent as Americanization.

Language and story became important tools for Alvarez's adaptation to her new life. As an escape from the playground taunts and bullying she was subjected to, Alvarez immersed herself in books. Alvarez notes that coming to the United States was a "watershed experience" for her development as a writer. While she knew some English, the abrupt immersion into the less formal English of the school and playground forced her to "pay close attention to each word—great training for a writer" (Alvarez, par. 2).

At the age of thirteen, Alvarez's parents sent her to boarding school. Between this and summers in the Dominican Republic, Julia Alvarez spent most of her teenage years away from her parents. Her trips to the homeland had a profound effect on Alvarez; it was here she came to understand the distinctions between Dominican and American culture, the double standards for men and women, and the class stratification of Dominican society (see Societal Contexts).

"How the García Girls Lost Their Accents," published in 1991, was Alvarez's first published book and became a bestseller. The book was not at first well-received by her family, however Alvarez claims that "many of the incidents that she invented for her first novel have now passed into the Alvarez family archives of actual events" (Sirias 5). Alvarez has since published "Yo!" (1997), a novel which revisits the Garcías; two novels based on twentieth-century historical figures from the Dominican Republic, "In the Time of the Butterflies" (1994) and "In the Name of Salom" (2000); a book of essays; four collections of poetry; and several children's books.

Alyssa Colton

Works Cited

Alvarez, Julia. "About Me." *Julia Alvarez.* Home page. 11 October 2005. 2 January 2006.

_____. *"How the García Girls Lost Their Accents."* 1991. New York: Plume, 1992.

Barak, Julie. "'Turning and turning in the widening Gyre': A Second Coming into Language in Julia Alvarez's 'How the García Girls Lost Their Accents'." *MELUS* 23, no. 1 (spring 1998): 159–177.

Castells, Ricardo. "The Silence of Exile in 'How the García Girls Lost Their Accents'." *Bilingual Review* 26, no. 1 (Jan-April 2001/2002): 34–43.

"Dominican Republic." *The Columbia Encyclopedia.* (2004). 22 December 2005.

Maycock, Ellen C. "The Bicultural Construction of Self in Cisneros, Alvarez, and Santiago." *Bilingual Review* 23, no.3 (1998): 223–229.

Sirias, Silvio. *Julia Alvarez: A Critical Companion.* Westport, Connecticut and London: Greenwood Press, 2001.

"Terms." English Department, *Southern Oregon University webpage.* 11 January 2006.

For Further Study

Alvarez, Julia. "An American Childhood in the Dominican Republic." *The American Scholar* (winter 1987): 71–85.

_____. *Something to Declare.* Chapel Hill: Algonquin Books, 1998.

Gómez-Vega, Ibis. "Hating the Self in the 'Other' or How Yolanda Learns to See Her Own Kind in Julia Alvarez's How the García Girls Lost Their Accents." *Intertexts* 3, no. 1 (1999): 85–96.

Hoffman, Joan M. "'She Wants to Be Called Yolanda Now': Identity, Language, and the Third Sister in 'How the García Girls Lost Their Accents'." *Bilingual Review* 23, no 1 (1998): 21–27.

Mitchell, David T. "The Accent of 'Loss': Cultural Crossings as Contexts in Julia Alvarez's 'How the García Girls Lost Their Accents.'" *Beyond the Binary: Reconstructing Cultural Identity in a Multicultural Context.* Ed. Timothy B. Powell. New Brunswick: Rutgers University Press, 1999. 165–84.

Discussion Questions

1. Discuss the way in which Alvarez shifts points of view and narrators. How does this impact your reading of the work?
2. Which chapter has the most impact on you? What images stand out?
3. What are the differences in the ways the girls behave, and are expected to behave, in the Dominican Republic and in the United States during the 1950s and 60s? What accounts for these differences?
4. Sofia appears to be the most "successfully" assimilated of the sisters. Do you agree? Why or why not?
5. How do the family relationships change when the family moves to the United States?
6. Find instances of cultural prejudice described in the novel. How do these instances affect the choices made by the characters?
7. Compare and contrast the lifestyles of the García family in the United States and in the Dominican Republic. What are the advantages and disadvantages of both?
8. Analyze the romantic relationships depicted in the novel. What accounts for the tensions and challenges in these relationships?
9. When she is fourteen, Yolanda is given a gift of a typewriter by her father. Discuss how this gift comes about. What does the gift say about her father? Has he changed?
10. Both Sandi and Yolanda are hospitalized for mental illness in the novel. Compare their situations and their outcomes. Are they hospitalized for similar reasons?

Essay Ideas

1. Write an essay in which you analyze both the problems and pleasures of bilingualism as a theme in the novel.
2. Write an essay in which you analyze how each of the García sisters represents the success and/or failure of assimilation. Explain the factors that account for their success or failure.
3. Discuss the structure of the novel and explain what purpose it serves.
4. Analyze the differences in language, imagery, and characterization between the United States and the Dominican Republic as represented in the novel.
5. Analyze the ways in which gender plays a role in the formation of identity for one or all of the García sisters.

The Ice Storm

by Rick Moody

Content Synopsis

Self-consciously narrated from a vantage point some twenty years in the future, Rick Moody's (1961-) "The Ice Storm" chronicles the experiences of two middle-class families in the wealthy suburb of New Canaan, Connecticut just after the Thanksgiving holiday of November 1973. Though introduced as a first person narrative, the novel uses limited omniscient narration extensively, switching chapter by chapter between the perspectives of its central characters: the middle-aged executive Benjamin Hood, his wife, Elena, and their teenaged children, Wendy and Paul.

"The Ice Storm" opens with Benjamin Hood waiting in a guest bedroom for the arrival of his neighbour, Janey Williams. Benjamin and Janey have recently embarked on an affair. About to turn forty, Benjamin is experiencing a mid-life crisis of sorts. He realizes that his body is aging, and that his marriage is not what it was (he has not had sex with his wife, Elena, for two years). While waiting for Janey, he reminisces about the first time he met Elena, and muses on a recent brief sexual encounter with a young woman from work. When Janey does not appear, Benjamin finally decides to leave the Williamses' house. He finds Janey's garter belt in the bathroom, and masturbates with it, hiding the soiled garment in her teenaged son's closet afterwards. As he is leaving he hears the voices of his 13-year old daughter, Wendy, and Janey's 14-year-old son, Mikey, from the basement.

The pubescent Wendy is eagerly learning all she can about love and sex, and has experimented both with Mikey, and his younger brother, Sandy. Last summer, she barged into the Williamses bathroom and demanded to see Sandy's penis. Sandy is still angry with Wendy for that act, and is currently avoiding her. Jim Williams, Mikey's dad is an entrepreneur of sorts, who recently bought crate loads of bazooka chewing gum, currently stored in the Williamses' basement. Mikey barters this gum for Wendy's sexual favours. Benjamin interrupts their adolescent fumbling in the basement, though is oddly apologetic to Wendy as they drive back to their own home.

Elena is addicted to self-help and therapy books of all kinds. As she reads Masters and Johnson's "Human Sexual Response," Elena considers the breakdown in her own sex life with Benjamin. She muses on her family background, including her mother's alcoholism. She suspects Benjamin may be having an affair, and compares herself to the voluptuous Janey Williams. When Wendy and Benjamin return, Benjamin tells Elena about the scene he discovered in the basement. Elena confronts him about his unfaithfulness, which Benjamin does not deny, though he blames his infidelity on the problems in their marriage.

The Hood's 16-year-old son, Paul, is currently at boarding school. Obsessed by the Fantastic Four comic series, Paul has a tendency to see his family as Fantastic Four characters. Like his sister, he struggles to deal with his burgeoning adolescent sexuality. But like all the members of his family, Paul is not looking just for sex, but for love.

He travels into New York City to visit his current infatuation, Libbets Casey. Paul is disappointed to find another school friend, Davenport, visiting Casey too. Together they smoke marijuana and experiment with the prescription drugs in Casey's parents' medicine cabinet. Paul then tries, unsuccessfully, to seduce Libbets.

Benjamin and Elena arrive at the Halford's house party. Benjamin worries that his ascot is now hideously unfashionable. Both are shocked to discover that the party is "a key party," that is, a party at which married couples are expected to trade partners. Benjamin and Elena retreat to the car to discuss the situation. Benjamin agrees reluctantly to go to the party. Elena, it seems, is intent on revenging her husband's infidelity. Benjamin meets George Clair at the party, the bright twenty-four-year-old executive from work, who is slowly but surely eclipsing Benjamin's professional career. Benjamin finds Janey at the party, but she has little interest in talking to him, or in explaining why she stood him up that afternoon. Benjamin feels increasingly lonely and intensely unloved.

Wendy watches TV at home, remembering her sexual experiments with her school friend, Debby Armitage, including her brief foray into cunnilingus. Paul calls from New York telling her that he is going to try to get home tonight by train. Outside it begins to storm, and Wendy decides to go back to the Williamses' house. Mike is out, and Wendy plays with Sandy instead. They organize a mock execution of Sandy's G.I. Joe doll, before going to bed together. Wendy wonders what an orgasm is, and whether she will ever experience one.

Elena realizes that none of her therapy, pop-psychology, sex manuals or self-help books can help her at the party. She socializes, slightly nervously, talking to Wesley, who gives "off the aura of having masturbated too frequently and too far into middle age" (162), but who turns out to be the new rector of the Episcopalian Church. At the end of the evening, the drawing of house keys and sexual partners begins. Benjamin wants to leave, but Elena insists they stay. Janey selects the 19-year-old Neil Conrad, as her husband, Jim Williams watches. Benjamin reacts more strongly, and tries to threaten Neil, but instead collapses drunk on the carpet, before going to the bathroom to vomit. Finally, after the other party-goers have paired off, Elena is left with Jim. They have sex in Janey's car, but it is over quickly and Elena feels nothing but depression afterwards. On the drive home, the car hits a patch of ice and goes into a spin. Jim suggests Elena spend the night at his house.

Libbets tells Paul that she loves him like a brother. Paul disguises his disappointment over his rejection by Libbets, and they travel into New York City, but fail to get into any bars. Libbets is drunk, and vomits over Paul's shoes. He takes her home in a cab, and puts her to bed. Lying beside her, he masturbates guiltily, coming over her bed sheets. Paul takes the train home, reading his Fantastic Four comic books. A power line is down, and the train gets stuck at Port Chester, an African-American neighbourhood, prompting Paul to think about how few black people he knows. He meets an old gin-soaked man who seems to know Ben, and claims to know Paul. Paul suspects the man of being a rapist or child molester.

Benjamin has fallen asleep on the Halford's bathroom floor and dreams about tax and fruit trees—a dream that, we are told, his son, Paul, will also dream many years later. Mikey Williams has gone to visit his friend Danny Spofford. They talk about sex, before Mikey leaves to play in the lanes at the deserted bowling alley. On his walk home,

Mikey sees live electricity wires, brought down by the ice storm. Mikey knows these are dangerous and gives them a wide berth. He rests on a guardrail, which, unbeknownst to him, has been electrified by one of these stray wires. Mikey dies almost instantly, his heart seizing up.

Benjamin wakes up with a hangover, and leaves the Halford's house. On his drive home, he finds Mikey's body. He takes the body home, only to discover that the pipes have burst in his home. An ambulance arrives to take Mikey's body away, and together they all go to the Williamses' house to break the bad news.

Wendy wakes up in bed with Sandy, deciding that she is in love. She meets her mother in the Williamses' house. Elena is incensed by her daughter's behaviour and tries to spank her. Wendy refuses to pull down her pants, having stuffed Janey's garter belt in them some time earlier. Jim explains the concept of partner-swapping to Sandy and Wendy. Elena tells Wendy she doesn't love Benjamin anymore. Janey arrives home, somewhat distraught after her night with Neil. The pipes burst in the bathroom, and just as they stand "all isolated in that foyer" (253), the ambulance pulls up outside.

Benjamin tells the Williamses of their son's death. Jim reluctantly identifies the body. The moment marks the end of an era, both in the lives of each family, and their relationship with each other. It is "the last time when the Hoods and the Williamses will be this close" (259). Back home, Elena tells Benjamin she wants to separate, while Wendy tries on Janey's garter belt, before cutting her wrists half-heartedly with a razor. She comes to her parents, bleeding, and they comfort her. The family travels together to the station to try to find Paul.

Paul, stuck on the train, refers to his family not as the Fantastic Four this time, but the Fucking Family. When they finally arrive to pick him up, Benjamin says he has something to tell Paul and Wendy, and a sign of four appears mysteriously in

the sky. The final paragraph reveals that the novel's narrator has, in fact, been Paul. It was at this moment, "the cusp of my adulthood" (279) that he claims he learned to distinguish comic books from the truth.

Historical Context

Moody sets "The Ice Storm" at a very particular moment in American history with great deliberation. From the novel's opening page, the reader is aware that it is late November 1973, "Thanksgiving just past and quickly forgotten. Three years shy of that commercial madness, the bicentennial" (4). Moody obsessively puts the novel's events into context with frequent references to political events like the Watergate scandal, the conflicts in Vietnam and Cambodia as well as cultural milestones, such as the deaths of Jim Morrison, Janis Joplin and Jimi Hendrix. References abound to contemporary cultural productions such as "Jonathan Livingstone Seagull" and "Billy Collins," and to period details like Benjamin's ascot, shamefully out of fashion by late 1973.

The historical setting is key to understanding "The Ice Storm." The novel makes repeated reference to the Watergate scandal, which was well underway by November 1973. Investigations into a burglary at the Watergate Hotel in Washington D. C. in 1972 by reporters Bob Woodward and Carl Bernstein of the "Washington Post" in particular, revealed that President Richard Nixon's administration was spying on both the Democratic party and anti-war protestors. The scandal dominated American politics and media until August 1974, when President Nixon resigned to avoid impeachment for his part in the scandal. Watergate features in "The Ice Storm" as a symbol of the atmosphere of distrust of government and authority that pervaded American public life in the early 1970s. Cynicism pervades the novel, as Moody writes: "Rose Mary Woods had just accidentally erased eighteen and a half minutes of subpoenaed conversation" (4). And just as the novel's characters expect to be lied to by their government, so they expect to be lied to by their parents, children and spouses.

The novel's references to Vietnam and Cambodia also contribute to the sense of ennui, depression, and failure that haunts Moody's characters. American troops left Vietnam in March 1973, making Vietnam the first major military loss in recent American history. Vietnam was an extremely controversial war, and the first conflict fought extensively on American television screens, which gave a new personal dimension to the conflict. U.S. Forces briefly invaded Cambodia in 1970 with the aim of destroying Viet Cong bases, and American military bombing of the country continued until 1973 with high numbers of civilian casualties. Characters like Elena respond to these events at a personal level. She associates her "bottomless pit of loneliness" both with Cambodia and "a pen mark on the designer pantsuit she'd bought for the holidays" and "the slight warp in her Paul Simon record" (67).

"The Ice Storm" also makes reference to internal conflicts that threatened the status quo in American in the early seventies. Paul remembers watching TV with his father the night that Angela Davis was acquitted. His father reacts with anger, "Fucking communist dyke cunt" (197). Davis, a radical black activist associated with the Black Panthers, had been arrested after a failed bid to free Black Panther member, George Jackson, from a courtroom in Marin County, California in 1970. She was acquitted of all charges in 1972.

Societal Context

"The Ice Storm's" most infamous comment on American suburban society in the 1970s is the key party attended by Benjamin and Elena. Such parties, at which husbands and wives swap partners by selecting house or car keys randomly, have become a staple of the mythology of this period. Moody himself posits the apparent popularity of

this practice to the after effects of the "Summer of Love": the flourishing of hippie culture, and its concept of "free love," on the West Coast of the United States in 1967. Moody claims the "Summer of Love has migrated, in its drug-resistant strain, to the Connecticut suburbs about five years after its initial introduction" (55). That the participants at the party are in early middle age, also prompts a comparison with the more sexually repressed days of their youth in the 1950s. Benjamin married and had children because "there were no other ideas in those days. It was the outer margin of one little universe and nobody knew what lay beyond it" (14). The period from 1950s to the 1970s saw a general relaxation of sexual codes in the U.S. Prompted partly by changing female roles, and the development of the contraceptive pill, this new openness manifested itself in the "free love" philosophy of hippie culture and the popularity of sex guides and manuals, like those read voraciously by Elena. But despite its sexual experimentation, the seventies are also seen, paradoxically, as a time of innocence, before HIV and AIDS made "free love" dangerous again. As Moody reminds us, there is "No Acquired Immune Deficiency Syndrome or Human Immunodeficiency Virus or mysterious AIDS-like illnesses" (3-4) in 1973. Moody also, crucially, connects this form of infidelity to the political duplicity that marked the Watergate scandal: "The idea of betrayal was in the air …. About the time America learned about the White House taping system" (55).

Rick Moody also sets "The Ice Storm" within a very particular regional and social grouping. New Canaan is middle-class, affluent and largely white. Furthermore, despite its key parties, this community adheres to traditional family models. Neither of the story's mothers, Janey and Elena, works outside the home, while both Jim and Benjamin fulfill the traditional male role of "breadwinner." Even when visiting the Williamses' house, Elena and Wendy find themselves assigned traditional female roles, making breakfast in the kitchen for Jim and Sandy. Economics ensure that this community is also racially homogenous. There were no black students at Paul's elementary school, and only five at his high school (196). Racial stereotyping abounds, "every white kid in New Canaan" for example "had been brought up to believe that Afro-Americans were superior athletes" (196), while most of Paul's understanding of black culture comes, he admits, from TV shows. Benjamin's reaction to the acquittal of Angela Davis highlights a latent racism at the heart of this community.

Moody has commented that when he imagined this story, "it was about the isolation in New Canaan, about the ways that the WASPs [White Anglo-Saxon Protestants] of the Northeast could sit surrounded by people, nonetheless besieged by loneliness" ("The Creature Lurches from the Lagoon" 289). In this sense, "The Ice Storm" is an explicit comment on the emotional vacuum at the heart of middle class, suburban white culture in the 1970s.

Religious Context

There is little evidence of strongly held religious faith in "The Ice Storm." Instead, attending church has become a purely social event. As Moody writes, "Theology was out, of course, except for the practical issues at any given parish" (75). Indeed, religion in "The Ice Storm" seems intent to adapting itself to the social, political and cultural climate of the early 1970s. Christian-themed rock operas like "Jesus Christ Superstar" and "Godspell" are popular, and mentioned repeatedly in the novel. In addition to using pop music to sell religion, religious figures like Myers, the new rector of the Episcopalian Church, is not above attending a key party. And while Myers does not take part in any partner-swapping, he nonetheless does not endeavor to repress his own sexuality, "he gave off the aura of having masturbated too frequently and too far into middle age" (162).

What is more, as religion appears in the guise of popular culture in "The Ice Storm," so popular culture appears in the guise of religion. Elena's search for spiritual meaning, for instance, manifests itself in her voracious reading of pop-psychology and self-help books, like "I'm Okay-You're Okay" by Thomas Harris and "Games People Play" by Eric Berne. While self-improvement books have been around in some form or other since Samuel Smiles's "Self Help" (1859), the popularity of such books soared in the 1960s and 1970s. Their popularity is often seen as a result of the "spiritual vacuum" which characterized these increasingly secular decades. Such books have also been criticized for their emphasis on the self, at the expense of any collective or communal identity, or political action.

Similarly, the epiphany at the close of the novel is prompted, not by religious faith, but by Paul's devotion to the Fantastic Four comic series. The family see a "flaming figure four" (278) in the sky above New Canaan, and, significantly, its "Unitarian Church of Stamford" (278) and "Wesley Myers … trying to write the next day's sermon, for the first Sunday in Advent" (279). Moody once more substitutes popular culture for traditional religion: instead of the Advent star, a symbol from a comic book heralds a change in the Hood family's existence.

Scientific & Technological Context

Rick Moody situates "The Ice Storm" very deliberately in the scientific and technological moment of the early seventies. The novel opens, self-consciously, with a list of technology unavailable in 1973: "No answering machines. And no call waiting. No caller I.D. No compact disc recorders or laser discs or holography or cable television or MTV. No multiplex cinemas or word processors or laser printers or modems" (3). Moody carefully shows how the home of 1973 was being changed by scientific developments, "Plastics had also penetrated far into the home. Coffee tables, modular furniture, kitchenware, and electrical appliances, all could now be fashioned from plastic" (105). Technology can also make or break fortunes; Jim Williams and George Clair's investment in the seemingly ridiculous technology of Styrofoam will, we know with hindsight, make them rich.

Moody is also careful to show how technology is changing family behaviour patterns and structures. While her mother is a voracious reader, Wendy watches TV. Television is Wendy's comfort and guide, it serves "as the structured time, the safe harbor for Wendy Hood" (130). It also symbolizes the growing fragmentation of family life. While Babette in Don DeLillo's "White Noise" insists her family watch TV together, Wendy's television viewing is a solitary experience.

Paul's rummaging in Libbets Casey's bathroom cabinet demonstrates the increasing prevalence of psychoactive pharmaceuticals in the 1970s, "Phenobarbital, Valium, Seconal, and an old one, Paregoric" (96). These drugs, principally prescribed to relieve anxiety and insomnia, reflect the tendency to medicate emotional problems rather than relieve them through a change of behavior.

Biographical Context

Generally, critics do not regard Rick Moody's fiction as particularly autobiographical. As Joseph Dewey writes, "[S]eldom has Moody drawn from his own considerable life story, and when he has it has been carefully manipulated" (12). Indeed, Moody has made some moves to derail the hunt for autobiographical elements in his work. A comic storyboard, written for *Details* magazine in 1995, for example, describes a fictional Rick Moody hiring an impersonator to stand in for him on a book tour. Similarly, his autobiography, "The Black Veil: A Memoir with Digressions" (2002), is carefully subtitled to draw attention to its flaws as a "memoir."

However, despite Moody's deliberately obstructive strategies, we can identify some parallels between Moody's life, and "The Ice Storm." Moody was born on October 18, 1961, for instance, which makes him only slightly younger than Wendy and Sandy. Furthermore, though he was born in New York City, Moody's family moved to the Connecticut suburbs where "The Ice Storm" is set, when he was very young. Like Paul, the young Rick Moody also exhibited "a serious love of comics" (Dewey 9). Indeed, the makers of the film version of "The Ice Storm" referred to the character of Paul as "the Rick Moody part in the film" (Moody, "The Creature Lurches from the Lagoon" 291). Moody is also one of three children, two boys and a girl, like Paul. There are also striking parallels between Benjamin and Rick Moody's own father. Both had moved elementary schools once too often, leaving a lingering sense of insecurity ("The Ice Storm" 12, "The Black Veil" 31), and both found themselves married with children by their mid-twenties, because there seemed few other options. Significantly, Moody depicts both his father and Benjamin disturbed by the noise and mess of family life especially:

> He hated noise. The noise of kids, the footsteps of kids, herd of kids, mainly because he had gotten out of school, married immediately, spawned his first child ten months after marrying, two more by the time he was twenty-six. He had no idea how he was going to pay.
>
> ("The Black Veil" 16)

> He loved his wife and children, and he hated all evidence of them. The noise of children, and the terrible quiet after, which augured, always, every single day-some broken heirloom or injury … Almost any life was possible on his salary, but this was the one he had.
>
> ("The Ice Storm" 14)

Furthermore, Moody's own parents divorced in 1970, just as it seems Benjamin and Elena are destined to at the close of "The Ice Storm."

Anne Longmuir

Works Cited

Dewey, Joseph. "Rick Moody." *Review of Contemporary Fiction.* 23.2 (2003), 7–49.

Moody, *Rick.* "The Creature Lurches from the Lagoon." *The Ice Storm.* Boston: Little, Brown and Company, 2002. 281–292.

Moody, Rick. *The Black Veil: A Memoir With Digressions.* Boston: Little, Brown and Company, 2002.

Discussion Questions

1. What does the title signify? Does it refer to anything beyond freak storm that hits the Northeast in the novel?
2. Why does Moody disguise the identity of the narrator of "The Ice Storm?" What's the function of this?
3. Moody peppers the text with frequent references to historic events like Watergate and Vietnam. What purpose do these references serve?
4. Discuss Paul's relationship with comic books. Why does he tell us this was "the end of that annus mirabilis where comic books were indistinguishable from the truth" (279)?
5. What's the significance of the Flaming Figure of Four, which appears in the sky at the end?
6. Discuss the depiction of adolescence in "The Ice Storm."
7. Discuss each family member's attitude toward love and sex.
8. Why does Moody self-consciously narrate the novel from the 1990s? Is this historical perspective significant?
9. Moody has claimed that "The Ice Storm" is "about the isolation in New Canaan, about the ways that the WASPs of the Northeast could sit surrounded by people, nonetheless besieged by loneliness." Do you agree? How does Moody suggest this loneliness?
10. In what ways is "The Ice Storm" a particularly "American" text?

Essay Ideas

1. Examine the depiction of the nuclear family in "The Ice Storm."
2. Examine Moody's use of history and popular culture in "The Ice Storm."
3. Analyze the theme of betrayal in "The Ice Storm."
4. Examine Moody's narrative technique in "The Ice Storm."
5. Compare Ang Lee's adaptation of "The Ice Storm" with Moody's novel.

Jailbird

by Kurt Vonnegut, Jr.

Content Synopsis

The book opens with a prologue in which Vonnegut gives us some insight into the real people on whom he based some of the characters in the book. He talks particularly about a union man and socialist called Powers Hapgood who forms the basis for the character of Kenneth Whistler. When asked why a man with such a privileged background as Hapgood's should want to live as a socialist, Vonnegut explains that Hapgood supposedly answered "Because of the Sermon on the Mount" (xix). He also introduces a fictionalized event called the Cuyahoga Massacre during which protesting mill workers were shot on Christmas morning by Pinkerton agents employed by the mill. Alexander McCone, the son of the mill owner, is a key character in the book.

The novel opens with the protagonist, Walter F. Starbuck, sitting in a cell waiting to be released from prison. He explains that he is writing from three years after the event he is relating. The prison he inhabits is a federal prison for white collar criminals. Starbuck tells us that despite being a Harvard man, he is not among the most educated or important in the prison. He tells us that he was imprisoned for his role in the Watergate affair and that there are many more important Watergate conspirators also in the prison. Starbuck was born into the household of Alexander McCone, as the son of his chauffeur, but was raised, at least partly, by

McCone himself who taught the young Starbuck to play chess so that he would have an opponent. McCone also provided the money for Starbuck to go to Harvard.

Starbuck has gained a bartender's qualification while in prison, along with a guard called Clyde Carter; the supposed cousin of then President, Jimmy Carter. It is this same guard who will escort Starbuck from prison. As Starbuck waits for Clyde, he tries to clear his mind but various thoughts keep intruding. He begins to mention the RAMJAC Corporation and then recalls the lyrics to a dirty song he learned at college. In order to clear these lyrics from his mind, he claps three times, thus performing the conclusion to the song.

Starbuck had been the president's special advisor on youth affairs in the Nixon White House. The job, as he describes it, was a sinecure that he was not really supposed to perform, but he did so anyway. He was given an office in the basement and no one ever read the reports he conscientiously prepared every day. He presumes he was given this specific job because in his youth he had been something of a radical, and a communist, at a time when it was a respectable thing to be. He then tells us about his late wife, Ruth. He praises her for her skill with languages, her painting, her photography and her musical skill; comparing himself unfavourably. He met her in Nuremberg at the end of the Second World War. He was organizing the housing and feeding of the delegations to the War Crimes Trials. She was an Austrian refugee who was so thin that she looked like a young boy. She was acting as an interpreter, using her skill of languages to deal with displaced persons. Starbuck took her away to be his own interpreter and a year later they married. She proclaimed no desire—or ability—to bear children, but Starbuck tells us that later they had a son, who grew up to be unpleasant and a book reviewer for the *New York Times*. Though originally named Walter F. Starbuck Jr., Starbuck's son changed his surname at twenty-one to Stankiewicz, the Polish surname Starbuck's father had been convinced to discard upon his arrival in America.

Ruth died two weeks before Starbuck went to prison. Starbuck has no money, having sold everything to pay for his defense, and in fact still owes his solicitors many thousands of dollars. He can not even sell the glamour of his story as he is the most unknown of the Watergate conspirators. His only consolation is that he no longer smokes. He then tells the story of the one meeting he was asked to attend with President Nixon, in which he found himself so nervous he had four cigarettes on the go at the same time. Nixon made what was, according to Starbuck, the only real joke he ever made: "'We will pause in our business," he said, "while our special advisor on youth affairs gives us a demonstration of how to put out a campfire'" (33).

A door in the prison opens, but rather than the guard, it is a fellow Watergate prisoner, Emil Larkin, who is now a born-again Christian and wants to take a final chance to try and convert Starbuck to his religion. Starbuck then reveals that, at the time of writing, Larkin is having a book published by a division of the RAMJAC Corporation. Larkin reveals to Starbuck that the delay of the guard has been caused by another Watergate conspirator, Virgil Greathouse, who gave up his appeals and will begin serving his sentence. He is due to arrive that morning.

Larkin asks Starbuck, in an effort to convert him, who his friends are. Starbuck is unable to think of any aside from the guard, Clyde Carter, and a fellow inmate, serving a lifetime sentence named Bob Fender. Fender is also revealed as the man who writes science fiction stories under the name Kilgore Trout. Starbuck reveals that his plan upon leaving prison is to go to New York City as he believes that he will somehow find friends and a job there as a bartender.

Failing with his conversion, Larkin starts to insult Starbuck and mentions an event which Starbuck tried to forget. In 1949, while testifying to then–Congressman Nixon about his previous associations with communists, Starbuck named his friend Leland Clewes. No one mentioned Clewes as a communist before and the man ended up in jail because of Starbuck's testimony. Starbuck's job in the Nixon White House came about because Nixon was curious about him. The Leland Clewes case had made Nixon's career; he gave Starbuck the job as a gift in return.

Clyde Carter finally arrives and leads Starbuck through the prison to collect his belongings before leaving. Carter says that he admires Starbuck because he once had a million dollars. The million dollars was in a trunk hidden in his office by the Watergate conspirators and his failure to reveal their identities was the reason he was imprisoned. He refused to name them because of how bad he had felt after naming Clewes and sending him to prison. Arriving at the office in the prison, Starbuck is greeted by Bob Fender. In reply, Starbuck tells him about sitting and singing to himself the dirty song which ended with three claps. Fender later puts the idea into a science fiction story, writing with the name Frank X. Barlow, in which an alien who can travel from mind–to–mind gets caught in the mind of Starbuck sitting on his bed, singing and clapping. Fender is serving a life imprisonment for treason; he fell in love with a spy during the Korean war and tried to hide her and help her to escape.

Fender hands over Starbuck's belongings and Starbuck is touched to see that Fender has arranged for all the cigarette-burn holes in his suit to be mended, particularly the large one in the crotch. Fender gives a gift to all leaving prisoners, and this is his to Starbuck. After he changes his clothes, Carter and Fender try to be nice to him, but Starbuck sees himself in the mirror and views an old man in a purloined suit.

Starbuck is then sitting on a bench outside the prison waiting for a bus. He is headed to New York with three hundred and twelve dollars and a Doctor of Mixology bartending degree. The last time he was set free in such a matter had been when he lost his job two years after the Clewes conviction. Following the conviction, people had started to cut ties with him. Then, after two years, he was sacked from his job. Following this, Starbuck found that no-one was willing to employ him. A previous friend finally tells him that this ostracism was because he damaged the reputation of educated men and made ordinary people presume they were spies.

While Starbuck sits on his bench, a RAMJAC limousine draws up and Virgil Greathouse gets out and goes into the prison. Starbuck is still singing his song in his head and clapping his hands. This gets the attention of the limousine driver, Cleveland Lawes, who offers to take Starbuck to Atlanta to get his plane to New York. Starbuck informs us that Lawes is now the vice-president of the Transico Division of the RAMJAC Corporation. Lawes tells him about being a prisoner of war of Chinese communists in North Korea but of then going to China instead of back home. He was eventually repatriated and imprisoned for a short time for desertion.

Starbuck asks Lawes if he has ever seen Mrs. Jack Graham, the majority stockholder of RAMJAC. Lawes has not; neither has anyone else for at least five years. All her instructions are sent to the CEO of RAMJAC by letter with her fingerprints appended.

Lawes delivers Starbuck to Atlanta where he eventually gets a flight to New York and makes his way to the Hotel Arapahoe where he has a reservation. Starbuck has been to this hotel before, many years ago, on the instructions of Alexander McCone. McCone wanted him to relive an evening he himself had at the hotel; eating an extravagant meal with a pretty girl. He even told Starbuck what to order. Starbuck took a woman called Sarah Wyatt, one of four women he ever loved, including his mother and his late wife. Sarah was from a family which had once been rich but lost its money. Her family owned a clock company which caused cancer in the workers who painted luminous dials with radium paint. The money was lost in lawsuits. The daughter of one of the unfortunate painters was the fourth woman Starbuck loved; his college girlfriend and fellow communist, Mary Kathleen O'Looney.

Starbuck and Sarah arrived at the hotel to find it dirty and seemingly closed, but the restaurant was still open next door. They sat at their table and Starbuck accidentally handed a gypsy violinist a twenty dollar tip instead of a single. Sarah thought he was trying to impress her and the evening ended badly. However, they remained friends and seven years later she agreed to marry him, although this never happened.

Back in the present, the hotel is now just a corridor leading to the front desk with a range of seedy rooms upstairs. The desk is run by a man called Israel Edel who gives Starbuck the best room because he has done the strange thing of making a reservation. Starbuck asks him what the restaurant has become and Israel tells him that it is a gay porno theatre.

In his room, Starbuck finds that one drawer of his dresser contains incomplete clarinets. He goes to sleep and dreams that he smokes a cigarette. When he wakes he is incredibly relieved to discover that it was only a dream and that he did not smoke.

The next morning he wakes at the usual prison waking time of 6 am and goes out into Manhattan. He makes his way to the Coffee Shop of the Hotel Royalton where despite his feelings of being an outcast he is treated nicely by the waitress and served good food by a chef who has a shrivelled hand because he accidentally deep-fried it. Starbuck tells us that at the time of writing the chef is now a vice president in RAMJAC.

Leaving the coffee shop and walking through the city, Starbuck sees Leland Clewes, the old friend that he caused to be sent to prison. He thinks of running, but doesn't and Clewes recognizes him. Leland greets Starbuck by his full name and a nearby bag lady claims to recognize him too. The two men try to ignore her as she joins in their conversation. Leland tells Starbuck that going to prison was the best thing that ever happened to him and his wife. His wife is Sarah Wyatt. He says that going to prison was a test and that his and Sarah's marriage is stronger for having been tested. At this point, the bag lady identifies Sarah by her maiden name even though neither man mentioned it. Starbuck realises that the bag lady is his former girl-friend, Mary Kathleen O'Looney.

Leland leaves the scene with a promise to meet up with Starbuck soon. Onlookers watch the reunion of Starbuck and Mary Kathleen and encourage him to give her a hug. He does so and starts crying.

She leads him off, away from the crowd, talking what seems like nonsense about not being able to trust anybody and about people wanting to cut her hands off. She leads him down, under Grand Central Station, to where they used to mend the steam locomotives. It is where she now lives. From there she leads him to the top of the Chrysler building; home to the American Harp Company, a RAMJAC subsidiary. The kind manager of the company lets Mary Kathleen sit there, under the glass ceiling, and watch the birds that live up in the glass. Starbuck, in a moment of giddiness, remembers the partial clarinets in his hotel room and asks the manager about clarinet parts, not knowing that a truck full of clarinet parts has been stolen and the manager has been warned to call the police if anyone enquires about such a thing.

At this point, Starbuck reveals to us that Mary Kathleen O'Looney is the legendary Mrs. Jack Graham, owner of RAMJAC. She keeps her paper and inkpad (for fingerprinting) in her boots and her fear for her hands is now seen as perfectly reasonable. Mary Kathleen told Starbuck in the elevator up to the top of the Chrysler Building, but he didn't hear her. He himself doesn't realize this fact until later in the story. They talk and Starbuck tells her about the people who have helped him since he left prison. He finishes telling her and then the police arrive to arrest him in connection with the missing clarinet parts.

When they talked, Mary Kathleen mentioned the union man and socialist, Kenneth Whistler. The two of them saw the man talk when they were together. Earlier that day they made love for the first time. After they made love, Alexander McCone arrived, seeking Starbuck, and discovered he was a communist and in a borrowed apartment with a woman. McCone had nothing more to do with Starbuck after that.

Whistler spoke at a rally that night about the poor conditions for workers and the idea of workers taking over the factories for the good of all. He also talked about the ideas of every member of society getting only what they needed and all working for the common good. Mary Kathleen firmly believed it. Starbuck did not. Starbuck then also tells us about Sacco and Vanzetti, two Italian immigrants wrongly executed for murder along with the real murderer who confessed too late. Starbuck compares these two immigrants with his own immigrant parents. The two men were also anarchists and radicals. Starbuck tells us that the men were killed for their beliefs rather than the crime they were supposed to have committed.

Having been taken from the American Harp Company to the police station, there is no room in the cells for Starbuck, so he is put in a padded cell in the basement and left alone for hours. He regales himself with one of Bob Fender's Kilgore Trout stories about people in heaven being told of all the opportunities to be rich that they had missed in life. The story focuses on this process as it happens to Albert Einstein who finally realizes that it is simply God trying to avoid being blamed for poverty. Starbuck then sings songs and tells himself jokes and finally cracks up and defecates in the corner, crowning it with a bowling trophy which has been stored in the cell, before collapsing.

Finally, under orders from Mrs. Jack Graham, RAMJAC CEO Arpad Leen dispatches a lawyer to free Starbuck. The lawyer takes him out to a limousine in which he finds his old friend, Leland Clewes, and Israel Edel, the receptionist from the Hotel Arapahoe. Mary, as Mrs. Jack Graham, has told Leen to hire all of the people who have helped Starbuck as vice presidents of RAMJAC. Starbuck assumes that all this is a dream and determines to be as strange as possible, making little sense in what he says. They stop to pick up the chef with the deep-fried hand.

They arrive at Arpad Leen's apartment. Leen has just learned that Bob Fender—another kind person who helped Starbuck—is in prison for treason. Starbuck has been given orders to free him and employ him but does not see how it can be done. Leen then offers them all drinks and Starbuck, still thinking himself asleep, orders a fancy cocktail that he learned about during his Mixology course. Leen determines to talk to each of them in turn and leaves the room with the chef. Starbuck starts to realize that he might really be awake and the butler arrives with his cocktail, perfectly made.

As they wait, Sarah Clewes calls to speak to her husband. And so Starbuck finds himself talking to his old girlfriend on a phone in the shape of Snoopy. They start into a double-act of jokes that they used to do when they were together. It is a very intimate exchange and Starbuck feels a little awkward doing this in front of the woman's husband. He then imitates his mother's laugh for her just as Leen comes back into the room.

Leen interviews the other two and then Starbuck last. At this point, Starbuck realizes that Leen believes he might be Mrs. Jack Graham. Hearing Starbuck imitate his mother's laugh had cemented the idea in his head. Leen calls Starbuck 'Madam' and Starbuck takes offense. However, Starbuck realizes that Mary Kathleen is Mrs. Jack Graham and tells Leen that he knows who Leen's boss is.

Following his realization, Starbuck makes his way back to the workshop under Grand Central Station to rescue Mary Kathleen from her life of fear. However, she has been hit by a taxi while crossing the street and is dying in a toilet stall. He holds her and tries to convince her to get help but she is tired of life and wants to die. She tells him about trying to protect herself with a staff of Mormons and of finding a visiting friend with her hands cut off. After the incident the friend became a bag lady because no one looks at bag ladies. She tells Starbuck that she wants to die and that her will leaves all of the RAMJAC Corporation and all its many subsidiary holdings to the American people. Shortly afterwards, she dies.

He calls an ambulance for the body and waits for them to take her away. He tells them her maiden name as he is not yet ready to reveal to the world that Mrs. Jack Graham is dead. He returns to his hotel taking with him all of Mary Kathleen's papers, including her will. On return to his hotel he finds out that the job Arpad Leen has given him puts him in charge of the *New York Times* and effectively makes him his own son's boss.

The next day Starbuck claims Mary Kathleen's body and has her entombed in a crypt with an engraved plaque. Two years later the engraver comments to a policeman—Francis X. O'Looney—about his name and he tracks down Mary Kathleen's plaque wondering if they are related. He discovers that she was really Mrs. Jack Graham and reveals Starbuck's cover up.

And so, having come up to date, Starbuck is going back to jail for concealing the will. During the past two years he did not contact his son, and his son did not resign from his job. He kept Arpad Leen convinced that he still saw Mrs. Graham once a week. In that time, Leen carried on doing what he had originally been instructed by her and continued buying companies. Now, all of the companies are being sold off; converted to cash that will go to the American people.

The week before he goes back to prison there is a party for Starbuck. All of his new friends are there and his son comes with his wife and children. The wife and children are happy to accept this new grandfather but Walter Jr. still loathes his father. The party ends with the playing of a recording of Starbuck's testimony to Congressman Nixon. When asked why he had turned his back on America's values to become a socialist he says he used an answer stolen from Kenneth Whistler, "Why? The Sermon on the Mount, sir" (241).

Historical Context

"Jailbird" is a heavily historical novel, with its fictional protagonist, Walter F. Starbuck, involved in a number of high profile events in real American history. Even in the prologue we are introduced to a real historical personage, Powers Hapgood, upon whom the fictional Kenneth Whistler is based. This is then followed by the description of the Cuyahoga Massacre which, while fictional in this account, we are told, is based in fact.

Then, when the book starts, we are immediately given a précis of the historical events which will be included in this novel, including Walter's personal involvement in the scandals involving the Nixon administration which came to be known as Watergate. Later in the book we find that this connection with Nixon also extends backwards in

time to when Nixon was a senator in a committee questioning Walter about un-American activities. Though this was a role more often associated with Senator Joseph McCarthy (leading to the term McCarthyism) it was by really serving on this committee that Nixon rose to sufficient prominence later to run for President.

The Second World War is also involved in the novel, in both Walter's role in the War Crimes trials, and in the form of Walter's wife, Ruth, a young Jewish girl imprisoned in a concentration camp by the Nazis. We are also, tangentially, given insight into the Korean War through the quasi-treasonous experiences of Bob Fender and Cleveland Lawes.

Another real event which is given great prominence in the book is the trial of Sacco and Vanzetti. These were two Italian immigrants who, after discovering that America was not the promised land of plenty that they had been promised, became radicals and anarchists. Through this involvement they became suspects in robbery and double murder in Massachusetts. They were tried, convicted and executed. Subsequent investigation suggests that they may have been innocent, and it is widely-accepted that the judge in the case prejudiced the jury with anti-Italian, anti-immigrant and anti-anarchist sentiments.

The involvement of all these historical events—along with the involvement of the fictional RAMJAC corporation and its mission to buy up all American businesses in the name of 'the people'—suggest that this book was intended, at least in part, as an examination of the role of business and of government in the lives of the populace.

Societal Context

As with many of Vonnegut's novels, "Jailbird" takes place in what on the surface looks like a realistic version of contemporaneous American society. However, as with most of his other books, it soon becomes apparent that this is a particularly Vonnegutian version of society. His view of society seems to have two distinct layers. One fits with the side of his personality which is eternally cynical. It is the society which seeks to remove Mary Kathleen's hands for her wealth, and also cannot administer the wealth of her businesses after her death. It is the society which sends an inoffensive person like Walter to prison, twice, and which allows events like the Un-American Activities Committee and the Sacco and Vanzetti trials to take place.

However, as Uphaus argues in his essay on meaning in Vonnegut's fiction, the author 'has it both ways' (Uphaus, 166); being able to be cynical about society and still optimistic at the same time. So, in what is arguably Vonnegut's most cynical work, the ending refers us back to the idea of the Sermon on the Mount, whereby the meek shall inherit the earth. It can be argued that believers make the most cynical people, and it is this that seems to inform "Jailbird." Even as Vonnegut's protagonist lists and examines the injustices and insults created by society, the book finishes with a (sort-of) reconciliation between Walter and his son, and a referral back to the hope that Walter's willingness to accept what happens will result in a happy ending.

Of course, being Vonnegut, the author doesn't give us a happy ending; he merely leads us to the edge of it and leaves the reader to make up his own mind, but the dichotomy still holds. It is clear, from this and other books, that Vonnegut was worried about the nature of art and literature in a society which was more interested in television, advertising and the acquisition of material possessions. But, it is equally clear that the author still maintained a hope that art and life would triumph. He never reconciled these two stances and it is probable that they are irreconcilable, but the discussion between them informed much of his writing.

Religious Context

Kurt Vonnegut described himself using a number of terms including sceptic, humanist, agnostic and atheist. As such, the role of religion in his books is usually to illustrate the ignorance of people who follow blindly, or, as with the case of the religion of Bokononism in "Cat's Cradle," he shows that for any religion to succeed it must lie about humanity; if it tells the truth then it will be a failure (May, 30–32).

With its focus being primarily on politics, "Jailbird" makes little mention of religion, despite Walter's wife, Ruth, being a Jewish victim of the Nazis. When Walter inquires about her religious beliefs, she claims to have none. He asks if there was any solace from God in the camp and she tells him, "'I knew God would never come near such a place. So did the Nazis. That was what made them so hilarious and unafraid. That was the strength of the Nazis. […] They understood God better than anyone. They knew how to make Him stay away'"(29). Although a tangential mention, this is Vonnegut once more being the skeptical author.

Scientific & Technological Context

Kurt Vonnegut is well known for writing two different types of novels: science-fiction and personal memoirs. Very often the two types are mixed, with science-fictional tropes being used to examine a life. However, "Jailbird" is a personal memoir used to investigate real events in twentieth century America.

And yet, Vonnegut cannot entirely escape the lure of science-fiction. As he tells us at the beginning of the prologue, this book features Kilgore Trout, a recurring character who appears in most of Vonnegut's novels. Trout is a fictional science-fiction writer with a prolific output. When Vonnegut comes across an idea that can best be explained by using a science-fictional metaphor, he creates a new short story or novel by Trout and outlines its plot. In "Jailbird," we are told that the name Kilgore Trout is the pen name of Walter's fellow prisoner, Bob Fender. In the course of the book we are given the outlines of two stories by Fender, one under the Trout pseudonym and one under the name Frank X. Barlow.

Biographical Context

Born to German-American parents in 1922, Kurt Vonnegut Jr. grew up in Indianapolis. While serving as a private in the US Army in 1944 he was captured by the Germans and held prisoner in Dresden. He was still there during the devastating firebombing of the city in 1945, and was one of the few witnesses to survive the cataclysm. He survived because he and his fellow prisoners had been locked in an underground meat locker of a slaughterhouse in Dresden when the air-raid warning came. This building and these events became the center of Vonnegut's most famous novel "Slaughterhouse 5," as well as a feature in a number of his other novels.

It is hard to imagine the scenes that would have greeted Vonnegut and his fellow prisoners when they emerged from their underground refuge to the utter destruction of the city above. Vonnegut and the other prisoners were forced to help with the disposal of the dead. It would seem that this was an event which informed the rest of his writing and may have been a source for his cynicism and skepticism.

The young Vonnegut was deeply influenced by early socialist labour leaders, especially Indiana natives Powers Hapgood (mentioned in the prologue of "Jailbird") and Eugene V. Debs, and was a lifetime member of the American Civil Liberties Union. These influences are probably clearer in "Jailbird" than any other of his novels, as he applies these liberal views to war, capital and politics.

After the end of the war and upon leaving the army, Vonnegut became a graduate student studying anthropology. He left the university without graduating after all of his suggestions for dissertations were rejected. However, upon its publication, "Cat's Cradle" was accepted in place of his dissertation, having been judged, in Vonnegut's words, to be a 'half-way decent anthropology' (Huber, education.html). He was awarded the degree. This fascination with the human race, which led Vonnegut to study anthropology in the first place and which was sufficiently present in his first novel to secure his degree, can be seen in all of his subsequent works.

Calum A. Kerr, PhD

Works Cited:

Bradbury, Malcolm. *The Modern American Novel – Second Edition*. Oxford, Oxford University Press, 1992.

Huber, Chris. *The Vonnegut Web*. 14 April 2008.

Klinkowitz, Jerome and John Somer (eds.). *The Vonnegut Statement*. St. Albans, Granada Publishing, 1975.

Marvin, Thomas F. *Kurt Vonnegut: A Critical Companion*. Westport, Conn., Greenwood Press, 2002.

May, John R. 'Vonnegut's Humor and the Limits of Hope,' *Twentieth Century Literature*, Vol. 18, No. 1 (Jan., 1972), pp. 25–36, Hofstra University.

Uphaus, Robert W. 'Expected Meaning in Vonnegut's Dead-End Fiction,' *NOVEL: A Forum on Fiction*, Vol. 8, No. 2 (Winter, 1975), pp. 164–174, Brown University.

Vonnegut Jr., Kurt, *Cat's Cradle*. Harmondsworth, Penguin, 1973.

Vonnegut, Kurt. *Jailbird*. London, Vintage, 1992.

Discussion Questions

1. How do the discussions of Kenneth Whistler and the Cuyahoga Massacre prepare the reader for what is to come in the rest of the book?
2. What does the inclusion of Walter's mental singing tell us about his character?
3. Look at the names of the characters in the book. What purpose do they serve?
4. Examine the short stories written by Bob Fender under the names Frank X. Barlow and Kilgore Trout. What do they contribute to the novel?
5. How is Richard Nixon portrayed in the novel?
6. Examine the scenes in which Walter discovers Ruth. What do they tell us about him and his attitudes?
7. What is the significance of the various scenes in the Hotel Arapahoe?
8. Why do you think Walter hides Mary Kathleen's will?
9. Examine the scene at the end when Walter meets his son again. What does this tell us about Walter's opinion of himself?
10. Does the ending fit with the rest of the novel?

Essay Ideas

1. What is the significance of the prologue?
2. Is "Jailbird" a historical novel or a personal memoir?
3. What purpose does the in–depth discussion of the Sacco-Vanzetti case serve?
4. Compare and contrast Walter's relationships with women.
5. Examine the role of coincidence in "Jailbird."

This building, in Dallas, Texas, is from where, according to the Warren Commission, Lee Harvey Oswald shot and killed President Kennedy. *Libra* by Don DeLillo, documents the life of Oswald and the assassination. Photo: Library of Congress, Prints & Photographs Division, photograph by Carol M. Highsmith, LC-DIG-highsm-15126.

Libra

by Don DeLillo

Content Synopsis

Don DeLillo's 1988 novel, "Libra," documents the life of Lee Harvey Oswald and the assassination of John F. Kennedy, but this postmodern novel is as much a meditation on the philosophical implications of plotting as it is about a plot to assassinate the president. Principally composed of two parallel narrative lines that eventually merge—one follows the drifting life of Oswald, the other follows the increasingly autonomous life of a plot to assassinate Kennedy—DeLillo draws on documentary sources, (in particular, the enormous Warren Commission report on the assassination) as well as imagined characters to create the hauntingly real texture of his novel. But, as he mixes the real and the fictional, DeLillo also makes his text a mosaic of different voices by skillfully juxtaposing narrative perspectives, shifting between first and third person viewpoints, and blending moments of stream of consciousness narration with a journalistic voice.

DeLillo begins the novel in the Bronx, with a chapter made up of six short scenes. These short, unconnected snapshots provide an early sketch of his disaffected youth: the chapter begins and ends with him riding the subway, while sandwiched in between we see him being picked up by a truant officer, and being described by a psychologist, social worker, school teacher, and by his mother, Marguerite. This fragmentary start is characteristic of the novel as a whole. In the Oswald chapters in particular, DeLillo relies on loosely connected tableaux to emphasize the sporadic drifting quality of his life. These scenes are arranged to slowly build up a picture of Oswald: in the case of this chapter, Oswald's time alone on the subway frames scenes that reveal his long-running fractious relationship with authority, and the efforts of those around him to explain, or understand, his life.

Chapter two introduces the parallel narrative: the story of the plot to kill the president, which begins in April, 1963. The architect of this plot is Win Everett, a semi-retired CIA operative who has been farmed out to the Texas Woman's University in the wake of his role in the 1961 invasion of Cuba (the Bay of Pigs). But while Everett's official duties are limited to scouting out promising students for recruitment, his life is still ordered by his obsessive desire to overthrow Castro. DeLillo introduces Everett as he prepares to meet Laurence Parmenter and T. J. Mackey, two fellow members of a CIA committee set up to address the problem of Castro's communist Cuba in the lead-up to the Bay of Pigs. Mackey had been heavily involved in the aborted invasion of Cuba, while Parmenter has substantial investments in unexplored oil fields in Cuba. But, despite their varied motivations, Everett has summoned them to discuss the plan he has formulated to instigate further American action to regain Cuba. A theory-minded man, Everett has crafted an elegant plot: the men will stage an assassination attempt on the life of Kennedy, but rather than kill the president, they plan a spectacular miss. In the wake of the failed assassination, Everett will arrange an elaborate paper trail of "passports, drivers' licenses, address books … Mail-order forms, change-of-address cards, photographs" (28) that will lead the police to believe that the attempt was orchestrated by the Cuban Intelligence Directorate. When this chain of documentation is uncovered, a violent American response against Castro will be, Everett believes, inevitable.

The alternating motion between this conspiracy narrative and the story of Oswald's life moves the novel forward, but the second chapter also introduces a slim third narrative that DeLillo has threaded through the novel: the story of Nicholas Branch. An aging CIA analyst, Branch has been working for fifteen years on a secret history of the assassination. Branch appears in the novel in six short scenes, during each of which he is seated in a book-filled room, meditating on the deluge of often-conflicting data that has emerged in the wake of Kennedy's assassination. As he sifts through this material, Branch functions as a surrogate for DeLillo, able to offer broad philosophical commentary on the nature of conspiracy theories.

While Branch meditates on the philosophy of theories, and Everett tries to put his theory into practice, for the most part, Oswald's own schemes are much smaller affairs. DeLillo describes him in New Orleans, trying to impress school friends and struggling to read Marxist tracts. The books become a source of obscure, secretive, power for Oswald, making him believe he can transcend his mundane social relations. DeLillo uses Oswald's reading as an opportunity to underscore the contradictions in his character. At the same time as he is absorbing Marx and Engels, dreaming of joining a communist cell, Oswald is also reading a Marine Corps manual, and waiting to enlist. A crucial moment in his life in New Orleans comes

when he buys a broken rifle from David Ferrie, a Civil Air Patrol instructor, who will later provide a pivotal link between Oswald and the Everett's conspirators.

DeLillo next shows Oswald at a marine base, in Atsugi, Japan. It is now 1957, and Atsugi is being used as a base for the U-2 spy plane. But while the military organize spying missions, seventeen-year old Oswald is discovering sex with Japanese girls, and the seductive power of sharing military secrets. Feeling quite at home in Japan, Oswald carries on an affair with a girl named Mitsuko, and talks politics with her mysterious protector Konno, who he believes reports his conversations to shadowy, powerful figures. But when news comes that the marines will soon move to the Philippines, a sorrowful Oswald contrives to shoot himself in the left arm in the hope that he will be allowed to stay in Japan. Oswald receives a suspended sentence for this stunt, but ends up in the brig at Atsugi after he gets into an argument with a sergeant named Rodriguez.

In the brig, Oswald becomes friends with another disaffected marine, Bobby R. Dupard, whom he will later meet in Dallas, but upon his release he begins to plan to defect. He takes Russian lessons from a Dr. Braunfels, and offers her information about the spy planes. Following this, DeLillo alludes only briefly to nine months that Oswald spends with the marines in California, and picks him up again as he leaves the military with a dishonorable discharge. Oswald returns to New Orleans, and then heads east: sailing to Le Havre, and making his way to Finland.

On arrival in Finland, Oswald applies for a visa to enter the Soviet Union, which he receives with suspicious speed. In Moscow, working with his Intourist guide, Rimma, he tries to gain Soviet citizenship. His efforts are rebuffed, so he melodramatically attempts to commit suicide, and is hospitalized. Upon recovering, he renounces his U.S. citizenship, and finally makes contact with the KGB through a charismatic agent, named Kirilenko. Under pressure to recruit a certain number of defectors, Kirilenko arranges for Oswald to stay in the U.S.S.R., where he will work in a radio factory in Minsk.

Despite a brief spell back in Moscow when he is brought to see a captured U-2 pilot, Citizen Oswald begins his new life in the West of the Soviet Union, and eventually marries Marina, an orphan raised in Leningrad. It is not long, however, before the contradictions deep in his character assert themselves: Oswald becomes disillusioned with the Soviet Union and begins to yearn for a return to the U.S.

Back in Fort Worth, Oswald's marriage to Marina degenerates into a desperate, violent, mess. As she embraces western life, Oswald becomes increasingly disenchanted with the materialist obsessions of American life and confides in a well-connected émigré, George de Mohrenschildt. George encourages Oswald to cooperate with the FBI, and serves as a kind of mentor to the younger man. But while Oswald meets an FBI agent, he separates from Marina and their young daughter, June, and moves east, to Dallas where he is fortuitously reunited with Bobby Dupard. Oswald and Dupard share grievances, and eventually formulate a plan to assassinate right-wing spokesman, Edwin A. Walker. Oswald is to be the assassin, and he orders an Italian military rifle (a Mannlicher-Carcano). Before he sets out to shoot Walker, he insists that Marina take a photograph of him clutching both his rifle and a selection of left-wing journals, so that his daughter can remember him. The assassination, however, like most of Oswald's other plans, falls through—the bullet's path deviates as it passes through a window, and Walker is only injured in the arm—but this event, eventually, serves to bring him into the path of Everett's conspirators.

While DeLillo has tracked Oswald's unfolding life, his partially-imagined biography has been interspersed with reports of the developing conspiracy. Nine days after their initial meeting,

Everett sets to work devising the paper trail for his imaginary assassin, while Parmenter meets George de Mohrenshcildt, who informs him that he believes his friend, Oswald, was the would-be assassin of Walker. Parmenter senses that Oswald would fit Everett's plan, and relays this idea to his former colleague, who instructs him to have Mackey bring Oswald into their camp. At the same time Mackey meets up with Guy Banister, a former FBI agent, who now runs a detective agency. Mackey has come to Banister looking for resources for the plan—guns, men, and a pilot—but Banister also suggests to Mackey that he might actually kill Kennedy.

Late in May, 1963, Parmenter and Mackey meet up, and the latter reports that they have lost track of Oswald. In spite of this setback, their plans develop—they decide on Miami as the perfect location for the shooting, and Mackey begins to assemble a group of assassins: Frank Vásquez and Ramón Benítez (known throughout the book as Raymo).

In July of the same year, the first signs emerge that Everett's plot has a life beyond his control. Everett is like an aging philosopher, engaged by ideas and finding the external world growing increasingly distant. Oswald, whose life he believes he can script into his plan, begins to behave with disturbing independence, and while Everett fusses with his theories and papers at home, Mackey decides that it would be simpler to just kill Kennedy and sidestep the elaborate twists of Everett's design. By August, Everett and Parmenter lose contact with the practical-minded Mackey who is acting on his own initiative, and in September he plans a joint attempt on Kennedy's life with a renegade organization named Alpha 66.

The two narratives begin to come together when an Agent Bateman, of New Orleans's FBI, encourages Oswald to set up a Fair Play for Cuba office within Guy Banister's building, and it is in Banister's office that Oswald is reacquainted with

David Ferrie. This meeting spawns several others, as Ferrie attempts to get into Oswald's head and convince him both that powerful figures are trying to manipulate him, and that he is destined to kill Kennedy.

Oswald undertakes some shooting training with Mackey's operatives, but ultimately attempts to disengage himself from the plot, and travels to Mexico in the hope of obtaining a Cuban visa. By this stage, however, he is crucial to the plotters and Mackey uses his Agency connections to ensure that Oswald's hopes of flight are thwarted. By October, Everett and Parmenter have floated entirely free of the plot, and Mackey is making subtle alterations to his schemes. He now plans for word of the Miami assassination attempt to be leaked, and intends Kennedy to die in Dallas. At the same time Alpha 66 has fake Oswalds appearing all over Dallas, while Mackey waits for the original to reappear.

In November, six months after Everett first shared his theories; the plan to assassinate Kennedy is put into action. Manipulated by Ferrie, and his own mixture of superstitions and frustrations, Oswald takes three shots from the sixth floor of the Texas School Book Depository: the first hits the President behind the neck, the second misses and hits Governor Connally, the third misses altogether. In DeLillo's recreation of the assassination, then, Oswald is not the killer. That role is given to Raymo, DeLillo's man behind the grassy knoll. He shoots Kennedy, and then escapes in a car driven by Vásquez.

While Raymo and Vásquez escape, Oswald makes his way to the Texas Theater killing Patrolman Tippit, who challenges him, en route. Mackey has told Oswald that he will be met at the theater and taken out of the country, but, in fact, Mackey has arranged for one of his gunmen—Wayne Elko—to kill him there. While Elko waits for the perfect moment to complete his task, Oswald is arrested.

At this point a subplot concerning Jack Ruby, a struggling club owner, intersects with Oswald's story. Throughout the second half of the novel, DeLillo has interlaced a story of Ruby's financial woes. In particular, Jack owes Carmine Latta, a moneyed gangster, $40,000 that he is unable to pay off. Latta is in contact with Banister (who is understandably keen to see Oswald dead before he can speak out), and the gangster agrees to forgo his money if Ruby kills Oswald. On Sunday, November 24, an increasingly desperate Ruby kills Oswald as he is transferred to the county jail. The novel ends with the burial of Oswald, and a monologue from his mother.

Like many of DeLillo's novels, the plot of Libra is interspersed with many speculations on the impact of television and consumerism upon American life. DeLillo also frequently dwells (in an almost mystical manner) on the significance of names, while the book is filled with doubles (the most significant being Oswald and Kennedy, who are imagined to be darkly linked).

Historical Context

Published 25 years after the assassination of Kennedy, "Libra" draws on the vast body of conspiracy thinking and paranoia that emerged in response to the events of November, 1963. But, at the same time, Frank Lentricchia, an influential early critic of DeLillo, has suggested that the novel also gambles that readers will interpret the conspiracy through the lens of disenchanting political spectacles of later decades. Lentricchia claims that "one of "Libra's" more uncanny effects is anachronistic: DeLillo's wager is that we will read his book out of the political history that Watergate and Iran-Contra has made, as if Watergate and Iran-Contra preceded 22 November 1963" (200). Modern readers, Lentricchia believes, have grown so accustomed to recent governmental corruption that they will now be inclined to believe that Oswald did not act alone. Not all readers were convinced, however, and DeLillo was famously called a "Bad citizen" by George Will, for positing a conspiracy (A25).

DeLillo's novel was also published in the wake of two decades of American novels about paranoia and political corruption. Notable forerunners include Thomas Pynchon's "V." (1963), "The Crying of Lot 49" (1966), and Gravity's Rainbow (1973); and Robert Coover's "The Public Burning" (1977).

Societal Context

Like most of DeLillo's novels, "Libra" is at least partly a critique of American consumerism, and in this book Oswald is often used as a vehicle to criticize materialism. In the phases where he is disaffected with American life, Oswald challenges people who "spend their lives collecting material things and call it politics" and mocks the fact that their belief systems are composed of "Cadillacs and air conditioners" (233). To some extent this critique overlaps with DeLillo's account of America in the age of television, since DeLillo sees television as the origin of many of the modern citizen's consumer desires. And, in fact, there are grounds for linking the assassination itself to this critique if one considers DeLillo's observation in his earlier novel, "The Names" (1982), that "we do the wrong kind of killing in America. It's a form of consumerism. It's the logical extension of consumer fantasy. People shooting from overpasses, barricaded houses. Pure image" (115).

Religious Context

There is little authentic religious belief in "Libra." Indeed, in DeLillo's postmodern world it is the vacuum left by religion that drives his characters to fill the void with some substitute body of meaning. In particular, Mark Osteen has suggested that the characters in "Libra" have devoted themselves to perpetuating a religion based around secrecy (153-64) as a way of directing, and giving purpose, to their lives.

Astrology, and other forms of superstitious belief in destiny, also abound in the novel. Astrology is introduced in the novel's title, but its significance to the book is largely centered on the shabby figure of David Ferrie. DeLillo uses Ferrie to flesh out the astrological implications of his title, and he has Ferrie tell Oswald there are both positive Librans, "who ha[ve] achieved self mastery," and Negative Librans, who are "unsteady and impulsive. Easily, easily, easily influenced" (315). In this context Oswald is, of course, a negative Libran, ready to tilt when pressured.

Scientific & Technological Context

Television provides the crucial technological context for "Libra." In this novel DeLillo calls America "televisionland" (51) with JFK as a kind of television president, whose power emanates from his image. A Kennedy, DeLillo writes, exists to take pictures of ("That's what a Kennedy was for" [141]), and the president can be recognized because he "looked like himself, like photographs" (392). There is a hint of Jean Baudrillard's conception of the "simulacra" here, but while DeLillo sees modern America becoming obsessed by the iconic images of its leaders, television also shapes and motivates Oswald.

Throughout Oswald's American upbringing, the television always seems to be on in the background at home, interrupting the narrative with nonsensical sound bytes ("'Natures spelled backwards,' the TV said" [5]), and he later seems to believe he is receiving messages from the screen. As he wonders whether he should kill the president, the films "Suddenly," and "We Were Strangers" are aired on television, two films dealing with political assassinations. The overlap between his thoughts and the television schedule, leads Lee to reflect that he seems to be "in the middle of his own movie. They were running this thing just for him" (370).

Biographical Context

The son of Italian immigrants who had moved to New York, Don DeLillo was born in November,

1936. He was brought up in the Bronx, but while he recalls numerous events from his childhood that shaped his sensibility—his experience of Catholic rituals, taking part in freewheeling street games, having three mob killings take place in the area— he did not engage much with literature until his late teens. When he did turn to books modernist writers were a major early influence, with James Joyce and William Faulkner becoming particularly important to him. Jazz, movies, and painting also had a profound influence on DeLillo, while his encounter with later writers like Thomas Pynchon and William Gaddis attuned him to developments in postmodern American fiction.

DeLillo attended Cardinal Hayes High School, Fordham College (where he majored in Communication Arts), and after a short spell working in advertising for Ogilvy and Mather, DeLillo published his first novel, "Americana," in 1971. Over the last thirty-five years DeLillo has been quite prolific, writing five plays, a handful of essays, and publishing twelve more novels, including "White Noise" (1985) and "Underworld" (1997).

DeLillo's personal connection to the events related in "Libra," do not arise because he has a particularly interesting answer to the question: "where were you when Kennedy was assassinated?" DeLillo, was in fact, in midtown Manhattan eating lunch with two friends in a restaurant called Davy Jones, and wasn't to hear of the shooting until he visited a bank later that day. Instead, DeLillo has a more personal connection to Oswald that stretches back a decade. When Oswald lived on 179th Street in the Bronx in 1952, DeLillo lived on 182nd, and although he believes they never met, it is significant that DeLillo begins the novel with Oswald in the Bronx. In a further link, DeLillo's father worked for the Manhattan insurance company, Metropolitan Life, and in "Libra" DeLillo has Oswald imagine his father as "a man in a gray suit, a collector for Metropolitan Life" (305).

DeLillo has described the impact of Kennedy's assassination as a shaping influence upon his career as a novelist, and he makes reference to it in several of his other books: in particular, his first novel, "Americana" (1971) ends in Dealey Plaza, and the Zapruder film of the assassination is watched by several characters in his epic novel, "Underworld."

Stephen Burn

Works Cited

DeLillo Don. *Libra*. 1988. New York: Penguin, 1991.

Lentricchia, Frank. "Libra as Postmodern Critique." *Introducing Don DeLillo*. Ed. Lentricchia. Durham, NC: Duke UP, 1991. 193–215.

Osteen, Mark. *American Magic and Dread: Don DeLillo's Dialogue with Culture*. Penn Studies in Contemporary Amer. Fiction. Philadelphia: U of Pennsylvania P, 2000.

Will, George. "Shallow Look at the Mind of an Assassin." *Washington Post,* 22 Sept. 1988: A25.

Discussion Questions

1. "Libra" is partly an exploration of the way a mythologized figure—Lee Harvey Oswald—has been created, but to what extent is the novel itself complicit in this process?

2. Was George Will correct to call DeLillo a "Bad citizen" for postulating a conspiracy?

3. In "Libra," DeLillo calls George de Mohrenschildt (a pivotal character in the novel) "a multinational man." To what extent is this novel about the emergence of money markets bigger than any nation state, rather than about tensions between Cuba and the U.S.?

4. Why does DeLillo name the chapters concentrating on Oswald after places, and the chapters concerned with the conspirators after dates?

5. There are many instances of doubling in the novel, such as when DeLillo stages conversations between two characters called Jack (254, 429), or when he introduces two FBI agents, both called Brown (423). Why are doubles so prevalent in this book?

6. Branch reflects that "Lee H. Oswald seems a technical diagram." What does this mean?

7. Examine the scene where Oswald is killed (438-40). Why does DeLillo blend the event and its broadcast as a television spectacle in this scene?

8. To what extent is Nicholas Branch a spokesman for DeLillo?

9. How sympathetic is DeLillo toward Oswald?

10. DeLillo considered two other titles for this novel—"American Blood," and "Texas School Book"—why, do you think, he ultimately decided to call the novel "Libra?"

Essay Ideas

1. DeLillo said of an earlier novel, "Ratner's Star" (1976), that he was "trying to produce a book that would be naked structure. The structure would be the book and vice versa." What is the relationship between the structure of "Libra" and the story DeLillo tells?

2. The novel ends with a reflection on the "true and lasting power" of a name. What is the significance of the many references to names in this book?

3. DeLillo frequently shifts between first and third person viewpoints in this novel. Carefully follow the alterations in the narrative perspective, and try to work out why DeLillo blurs objective and subjective views.

4. Compare DeLillo's Oswald to the Oswald presented in either the Warren Commission report on the assassination, or Norman Mailer's "Oswald's Tale: An American Mystery" (1995).

5. Is "Libra" a paranoid novel, or is it an account of paranoid characters?

The Midwife's Apprentice

by Karen Cushman

Content Synopsis

Set in Medieval England, "The Midwife's Apprentice" begins with a strange scene of rebirth: a young girl rising from the dung heap where she had huddled during the night to keep herself warm and alive. The girl has no name, no family, no place in the world, and no plans beyond the immediate moment. The village midwife, Jane Sharp, finds the girl, who comes to be called Brat or Dung Beetle by the villagers, and puts her to work in exchange for room and board.

Beetle spends her days avoiding the other villagers as much as she can—befriending only a scraggly cat whom she rescues after the village boys try to drown it—and accompanying the midwife when she attends laboring women. Jane Sharp does not let her inside, for fear the apprentice would learn her secrets, but Beetle observes what she can. Soon it is time for the midwife to travel to Saint Swithin's Day Fair at Gobnet-Under-Green in order to replenish her supply of "leather flasks, pepper, and the water in which a murderer had washed his hands" (25). However, when Jane trips over a pig and breaks her ankle, she decides to send Beetle in her place. Beetle has a wonderful time at the fair, where she is complemented on her curls by one of the merchants and where another man mistakes her for a woman named Alyce, asking her to read something for him. At this point, the girl decides that Beetle is "no name for a person, no

name for someone who looked like she could read" (31). Beetle decides that her name would be Alyce, and when she returns to the village, she begins to correct those who call her Beetle, informing them of her new name. Everyone simply scoffs at her at first, but she persists, and she gives the cat a name as well, Purr.

Ironically, one of the village boys who frequently torment Beetle is the first to use her new name. As this boy, Will, and a number of other boys chase Beetle, Will falls into the river. The other boys run off, leaving Beetle to rescue the drowning boy. Thankful, Will begins to use the girl's new name: Alyce.

Suddenly, the village receives a most unwelcome visitor, the Devil himself. His footprints are found leading to the locations of various sins in which the villagers are discovered red-handed. Once the villagers have received their comeuppance, Alyce throws two blocks of wood carved to look like the feet of a beast into the river, and we discover that she has been behind the revelation of sin in the village.

Alyce seems to find a place for herself in the village and a talent within herself for taking care of others. She helps Will attend to a cow that gives birth to twin calves. On this emotional occasion, she learns to sing softly to the animals and to give them comfort. She has a chance to use her newly acquired skills when the midwife abandons a poor woman in labor to attend to the lady of the manor, whose family will pay her more for her services. She leaves Alyce to care for the poor woman, assuming that the baby will die in the difficult birth. Alyce, however, though she does not know the midwife's spells and magic, manages to help the baby get born with hard work and tenderness. After this occasion, she works extra hard to learn everything the midwife knows about birthing babies. Alyce also finds a little boy called Runt, feeds him, encourages him to pick out a real name for himself—he chooses Edward, naming himself after the King—and sends him to the manor to look for work.

Because word had gotten around that Alyce had been able to help a woman whom the midwife had abandoned, another woman, Emma, requests Alyce's services instead of the midwife's. Unfortunately, Alyce's skills are not sufficient in this case, and she has to send for the midwife to take over the job. Distressed and disappointed, Alyce runs away from the village and takes up residence at an inn, working for her keep as she had done with the midwife. Here, she meets Richard Reese, who is working on an encyclopedia and who teaches a shy Alyce her numbers and letters although he pretends to be teaching them to the cat. One day the midwife comes into the inn and begins to give Richard information about babies for his compendium. She informs him about the desertion of her apprentice, remarking: "I need an apprentice who can do what I tell her, take what I give her, who can try and risk and fail and try again and not give up. Babies don't stop their borning because the midwife gives up" (88).

Alyce helps a woman give birth at the inn and this experience helps her to decide that she truly wants to be a midwife. She turns down several other offers for employment and decides to return to the village. Alyce is stunned when the midwife turns her away, but then she remembers what the midwife had said in the inn, and she tries again, shouting

"It is I, Alyce, your apprentice. I have come back. And if you do not let me in, I will try again and again. I can do what you tell me and take what you give me, and I know how to try and risk and fail and try again and not give up. I will not go away" (117). The midwife opens the door and Alyce, we assume, resumes her apprenticeship and her place in the village she has come to consider her home.

Historical Context

"The Midwife's Apprentice" is set in mid–to–late Medieval England. Mary Lee Tiernan writes that "Alyce's life is a glimpse into everyday life during the Middle Ages: the hardships, the poverty, the superstition" (36). Cushman certainly emphasizes the difficult conditions of the period by introducing us to a helpless child who must struggle to survive in it.

The majority of the Medieval English population lived in villages which consisted of a group of small cottages with floors of beaten earth and thatched roofs, a local lord's manor house set in a complex of buildings such as breweries, granaries, and stables, and a parish church, all surrounded by fields and meadows. The land was divided into the demesne, the property of the lord, and holdings leased out to peasants, who spent the bulk of their time and energy farming with only basic plows and simple tools to aid them. The return for their effort was often poor, yet they were obliged to give their lords a portion of their harvest or else work a certain number of hours in the lord's fields in return for his protection. The lord might also levy taxes and force peasants to use his mills or ovens for which he would then charge them fees. Chronicler Geoffroi de Troyes sums up the life of the medieval peasant: "The peasants who labor for everyone, who are always tired, through all seasons, are constantly under pressure. They are harassed by fire, rape, and the sword. They are thrown into prisons and in chains, or else they die a violent death through hunger" (qtd. in Sabbah 8).

Although the village in "The Midwife's Apprentice" is portrayed as a cooperative community for the most part, Cushman introduces a sense of resentment with brief mentions of characters such as Alnoth the Saxon who "cursed God for making him a peasant and not a lord" as he "cleaned the manor privies" (70). The potential consequences of the social inequity of the medieval village become clear when Jane Sharp abandons a poor woman to attend to the lady of the manor who can give her a much richer reward. If it were not for Alyce's attention, the poor woman and her baby may have both died.

Societal Context

At around age seven, medieval children were steered toward their future social roles, girls learning domestic skills while boys were indoctrinated into outdoor work, although both men and women worked the fields at harvest time. Exactly what a child learned depended upon social class as well as gender. Upper-class girls might learn music and embroidery while lower-class girls were taught the cooking, sewing, and gardening and that they would be expected to do for their families as adults. For boys, upper-class status meant learning riding and hunting; lower-class boys might expect to learn to care for large livestock and to work in the fields. Although widows sometimes gained a degree of independence, owing property in their own right, most women, whether peasant or aristocrat, moved from one subordinate position to another, from the care of their fathers to the care of their husbands. This did not mean, however, that women's labor was unimportant to the medieval economy (Singman 33). A woman might contribute to her family's income, or support herself if she had no family, by spinning thread, sewing, baking, or hiring herself out as a midwife, as Jane Sharp does and, as Alyce hopes to do.

At the end of the fifteenth century, it is estimated that only about 10% of the male population, and one % of the female population, was literate. Only children from aristocratic or very wealthy families, or poor boys being groomed for a career in the church, received a formal education conducted by private tutors or in city schools. Cushman creates an extraordinary medieval girl in Alyce, who learns to read even though she is poor with no family connections to speak of.

Religious Context

A medieval child's family was responsible for indoctrinating him or her into the church and, by extension, the social net of the village. Each person's journey through life was guided and marked by the Christian church, from baptism at which the child was named, to confirmation at age 5 or 7, to marriage which typically marked a person's independence and adulthood, to last rites, administered to the sick and dying. With no family and no connection to the church, Alyce exists on society's margins. We learn that she has spent her years before she met the midwife traveling from village to village "before the villagers, with their rakes and sticks, drove her away" (2). Alyce has to forge her own, difficult path to an identity and a role in her community which she does by persevering as the midwife's apprentice.

Medieval villagers had a strong belief in the power of the devil. In "The Midwife's Apprentice," when a two-headed calf is born and a magpie refuses to be chased away, the "whole village saw witches and devils everywhere, and fear lived in every cottage." The villagers readily accept that the devil is walking among them and exposing their sins when Alyce creates devil's footprints; they also readily place some of the blame for their sins on the devil's shoulders. When the miller is caught cheating a fellow villager, the priest intones, "let us deal with this thief mercifully, for which of us could withstand the Devil?" (43). The other villagers are sympathetic, "[s]o the miller who had listened to the Devil did not have his hands chopped off, but only stood one day in the rain with his millstone tied about his neck" (43).

Scientific & Technological Context

In cities such as London, citizens might have access to physicians, authoritative figures with great theoretical knowledge, or they might visit surgeons and apothecaries, less respected but often more skillful practitioners. In the country, however, citizens likely had access only to part-time healers. In all strata of society, childbirth most frequently happened at home aided by midwives who varied greatly in training and skill. Cushman's Jane Sharp became a midwife because she "had given birth to six children (although none of them lived), went Sundays to Mass, and had strong hands and clean fingernails" (11). Cushman writes, "Medieval midwifery was a combination of common sense, herbal knowledge, and superstition, passed from woman to woman through oral tradition and apprenticeship… . This 'women's knowledge was considered reliable and valuable, as illustrated … by the inclusion of Jane Sharp's information in Magister Reese's great encyclopedia" ("Author's Note" 119). While some of the midwives' treatments were probably only helpful due to a placebo effect, some of the herbal remedies they used still prove effective today. Jane Sharp provides a necessary and important service to her community; Alyce wants to fill this role as well, for it will secure her a place not only in the social network of the village, but within a larger tradition of women healers.

Biographical Context

Karen Cushman was born in a suburb of Chicago in 1941; her family moved to California when she was eleven years old. Cushman earned masters degrees in Human Behavior and Museum Studies and worked as an adjunct faculty member at John F. Kennedy University, editing "Museum Studies Journal," teaching classes, and coordinating the master's project program. At the age of fifty, she began to write in earnest.

Cushman heard a speaker say that "the writers of children's books should always empower the young reader by making the hero of the book the one to solve the problem: find what's lost, fix what's broken, solve the mystery, make everything right again." But, she thought, that's not the way things work in reality, for children or adults for that matter. She began to think about how that was even more the case in the Middle Ages, a time in which "children had much less value and power than they do now" (qtd. in Hendershot 198). So Cushman created Alyce, a girl with very little in the way of value or power and one who cannot possibly "fix" all the problems she encounters. Nevertheless, Alyce's bravery, tenacity, and compassion allow her to make the best out of her situation and do some good for her community in the process.

Cushman's first novel, "Catherine, Called Birdy," another story set in the Middle Ages in which the heroine tries to stop her father from marrying her off to a much older man, was a Newbery Honor book as well as the winner of many other awards. "The Midwife's Apprentice", Cushman's second novel, won the Newbery Award in 1996. More recently, Cushman has also published "The Ballad of Lucy Whipple" (1996), "Matilda Bone" (2000), and "Rodzina" (2003).

Kim Becnel

Works Cited

Cushman, Karen. Author's Note. *The Midwife's Apprentice*. New York: HarperCollins, 1995. 118–22.

_____. *The Midwife's Apprentice*. New York: HarperCollins, 1995.

_____. "Newbery Medal Acceptance." *Horn Book Magazine* 72.4 (1996): 413–420.

Gies, Frances and Joseph Gies. *Life in a Medieval Village*. New York: Harper & Row, 1990.

Hendershot, Judith and Jackie Peck. "Interview with Newbery Medal Winner Karen Cushman." *The Reading Teacher* 50.3 (1996): 198–200.

Sabbagh, Antoine. "The Human Story." *Europe in the Middle Ages*. Trans. Anthea Riddett. Englewood Cliffs, NJ: Silver Burdett P, 1988.

Singman, Jeffrey L. and Will McLean. *Daily Life in Chaucer's England*. Westport, CN: Greenwood P, 1995.

Tiernan, Mary Lee. Karen Cushman, *The Midwife's Apprentice*. "Rev. of 'The Midwife's Apprentice' by Karen Cushman." Book Report 14.2 (1995): 36.

Discussion Questions

1. Compare life in the Middle Ages as depicted in "The Midwife's Apprentice" and life today. How were work, recreation, and relationships different?
2. What do you think motivates Alyce to pretend that the Devil is visiting the village?
3. Discuss the results of Alyce's trick with the "Devil's footprints." Was this an ethical action on Alyce's part?
4. What role does the cat play in Alyce's development?
5. How was childhood different in the Middle Ages than it is today?
6. Discuss the relationship between Alyce and Jane Sharp. How does it evolve throughout the story?
7. Analyze Alyce's dreams.
8. Describe the ways in which Alyce's interactions with Will change her.
9. In what way is Alyce's life at the inn different from her life in the village?
10. What clues does the novel give us about Alyce's future? What do you think will become of her?

Essay Ideas

1. Analyze the role that naming plays in the novel.
2. Discuss the importance of the boy "Runt" to the novel's themes.
3. Compare and contrast Jane Sharp and Alyce. What kind of a midwife is Alyce likely to be?
4. Analyze the effects of Alyce's experiences at the fair on her developing identity.
5. Locate and analyze the images of birth throughout the novel.
6. Compare and contrast Alyce and Birdy, in Cushman's novel, "Catherine, Called Birdy."

Moon Palace

by Paul Auster

Content Synopsis

Paul Auster's "Moon Palace," as *New York Times* Book Review editor Michiko Kakutani notes, "reads like a composite of works by Fielding, Dickens and Twain" where the orphaned hero at once tells the story of his development and investigates his own origins. Auster teasingly acknowledges his debt to this picaresque genre early in the novel, when Victor Fogg's statement that "Every man is the author of his own life" (7) reconfigures the central dilemma of Dickens' David Copperfield, who famously wonders "whether I shall turn out to be the hero of my own story" (13). Auster's novel teases out the curious cross-pollination of these terms, authors and lives, heroes and stories, by recording three interlocking life stories, those of Marco Stanley Fogg, Thomas Effing, and Solomon Barber.

First up is the novel's narrator, Marco Stanley Fogg, whose name alludes to Marco Polo, Henry Stanley of "Dr. Livingstone, I presume" fame, and Phileas Fogg from Jules Verne's "Around the World in 80 Days." Marco does not know his father, and when his mother is killed in a bus accident when he is eleven, he goes to live with his uncle Victor in Chicago. At eighteen, Marco leaves Chicago to attend Columbia University in New York City, and Victor goes on tour with his rock band, the Moon Men. But before Victor leaves, he gives Marco 1492 boxes of books (suggestive, of course, of the year Columbus, another great explorer, discovered America, and also the man for whom Marco's new school is named). Marco uses these boxes to furnish his apartment, stacking them to make a bed, a desk, and a chair. From his apartment, he can see the neon sign of a Chinese restaurant called Moon Palace.

For four years, Marco subsists on his mother's death settlement and on the money he makes selling his uncle's books one at a time after he reads them, till he earns his degree from Columbia and sells the last book. Without any further source of revenue, he is evicted from his apartment. Homeless and increasingly isolated, Marco sleeps in a Central Park cave. One night when wandering the streets, he stops in a bar long enough to watch the television broadcast of Neil Armstrong's walk on the moon. A short time later, he is caught out in a rain storm, and suffers the mental and physical collapse that had been looming since before he became homeless. He develops pneumonia, and would die were he not found by his old college roommate Zimmer and a new acquaintance who will become his lover, Kitty Wu.

Kitty and Zimmer nurse Marco back to health: it takes months before he can walk unassisted, and a trip to the draft board becomes a day-long ordeal. Finally recovered, Marco lands a job as the live-in companion for one Thomas Effing. Marco reads to the elderly blind man who berates his performance, always comparing Marco to his predecessor Pavel Shum, recently deceased. They read only travel books, but the widest possible range of them. When Marco suggests they read Cyrano's account of his visit to the moon, Effing dismisses the idea. Suddenly, Effing decides they have read enough, and sends Marco to look at a painting in the Brooklyn Museum of Art by his old friend Ralph Albert Blakelock. Effing insists Marco go to the museum via subway and keep his eyes closed the whole journey, to be fresh for the experience of this painting, a night scene, with the moon dead center on the canvas. Moons become, for a viewer of the painting, "holes," "apertures of whiteness looking out onto another world" (141). As he stares, Marco begins to notice other details in the painting: an Indian teepee, a campfire, a figure on horseback.

Effing tells Marco his life story so that Marco can write an obituary in anticipation of his employer's imminent death. Effing started life as Julian Barber, and was a successful painter, respected in New York City and Paris. He married socialite Elizabeth Wheeler, a poor match which produced one son, a child Elizabeth was pregnant with when Barber left for a journey through the West to paint the landscapes that inspired Blakelock. He and Edward "Teddy" Byrne hired a local guide named Scoresby, as much con man as guide, who led the two through increasingly remote and dangerous desert terrain until Byrne and his horse slide off a narrow mountain path. Scoresby advises Barber to leave Byrne for dead, but Barber refuses and stays with Byrne till his friend dies. He suffers a nervous collapse, deciding Barber has died in the same unforgiving landscape, and wanders aimlessly until he finds a hermit's cave, with the dead hermit still inside. The cave is well-stocked with provisions, enough for the man who was Barber to survive the winter, so he sets up camp and begins to paint. First, he fills every canvas he has, then paints on the back of each. Next, he paints all the walls in the cave, all the furniture and the table till he has

exhausted his paints. Because of the remoteness of the landscape and the circumstances of their production, no one will ever see these paintings, but Effing maintains they are the best he has ever done.

One day, no-longer-Barber–not-yet-Effing sees a man approach the cave, a half-simple Native American named George Ugly Mouth who mistakes him for the hermit and calls him Tom, which Effing takes as his new first name. The cave is the hideout of the Gresham Brothers Gang. Come spring, they will surely return. Thomas watches them arrive, and when they drunkenly fall asleep, kills the three of them in the darkened cave. He takes their loot and sets out for civilization, concealing the entrance to the cave before he leaves. He adopts the surname "Effing," a bawlderized version of "Fucking," because its crassness and disregard for propriety suits his new persona. In San Francisco, still plagued by guilt, Effing is waylaid by a mugger who knocks him out. Effing slides into a lamppost, paralyzing him from the waist down. To Effing, this is divine retribution: the debt to Byrne is paid, and he can return to life as this new man, Thomas Effing. In Paris, he contracts Pavel Shum, a fugitive White Russian, as a manservant and encounters someone who knew him as Barber, but the man doesn't acknowledge him. This gives Effing the courage to return to New York; he learns his wife has died, but not before she delivered a son, named Solomon Barber.

Marco is to send the story of Julian Barber/ Thomas Effing to the son he's never met when Effing dies. But first, Effing makes one final attempt to rejigger the karmic balance his life rests on, by returning the money he took from the Gresham's to the innocents they initially stole it from. To find the original people stolen from half a century before would be impossible, so Effing and Marco find needy people and gave them fifty dollar bills. On their last night out doing this, a storm comes up. To protect himself, Effing buys from a passer-by an umbrella with no lining, just a skeletal metal frame. He insists it keeps the rain off, but contracts pneumonia and dies a few days later.

During the months Marco works for Effing, he and Kitty Wu live together, and Kitty becomes pregnant. But, because it is not a good time, because she is not ready, she intends to abort the child. Marco feels alone in the world and can't accept her decision to abort the fetus. Finally, he drives her away.

Marco sends the story to Effing's son, Solomon Barber, a history professor at a second-rate Midwestern college. Barber responds warmly, and comes to New York City to talk over the details with Marco. He shares a novel he wrote when he was a teen that explained his father's disappearance and apparent death by having him join a long-lost Indian tribe that also, it is suggested, adopted the original Jamestown colony. The novel mixes science fiction, pornography, and alternate history, and foreshadows the academic pursuits of the adult Solomon. He wants Marco to accompany him to his father's cave, but on a visit to Marco's mother's grave, Solomon reveals he is Marco's father. Marco's mother was his student, and their relationship, once discovered, caused the scandal that has dogged his academic career ever since. The enraged Marco yells at Solomon for concealing this information till his father falls into an open grave and breaks his back. They reconcile in the hospital, but it is too late; Solomon dies.

Marco tries to reconcile with Kitty, but she has already moved on. Marco tries on his own to find the hermit's cave, but for two years it has been underwater, beneath Lake Powell. He finishes his trip West, and the novel leaves him on the shore of the Pacific at Laguna Beach.

It's hard to know what to make of the recurring references to the moon, from Victor's band the Moon Men, through the Chinese restaurant with the novel's title and the moon in the painting by Ralph Albert Blakelock where it is a hole to a new world, to Solomon Barber's head, once described as resembling a full moon (Solomon's name, shortened as it is by Kitty and Marco, to Sol, suggests the sun, which might make his round body the gas giant around which the Solomon's lunar noggin revolves). Is the moon one thing in this novel, developed through manifold incarnations? Or is it instead simply an anchor-word, tolling us back to the novel's hopelessly split selves?

Historical Context

The primary present of the novel is the last years of the 1960s, and this is the social backdrop for Marco's story. He endures the obligatory trip to the draft board, where he is declared unfit for service in Vietnam, and watches Neil Armstrong walk on the moon on a bar television. But the history of the 1960s as we understand it now, which Steven Weisenburger lists as "the occupation of administration offices at Columbia,… and the Kent State massacre… unfold[s] just beyond Fogg's threshold" (70–1), and never plays much of a role in the novel. Wiesenburger, in fact, reads the coincidences in the story, the way that they force the reader to question his or her assumptions about the possible mimetic representation of paternity as an act of culture jamming; in Weisenburger's conception, this is political act, one Auster engages in with gusto, as part of his commitment to the disruptive project of the sixties. But it's hard, a little, to see this as being the primary motivation here, since so much of the other elements of 60s disruptions of authority happen, as it were "just beyond Fogg's threshold." The history of the 60s seems, mostly, absent from Marco's story.

History plays a more significant role in Julian Barber's story, especially as it is narrated with hindsight to Marco. In Barber's story, we are given a clear and unclouded view of the 1893 Chicago World's Fair, also known as the Columbian Exposition. For Barber, and, it seems, for Auster as well, there was a palpable optimism about what people could achieve, and no one symbolized this potential more than Nikolai Tesla whose exhibitions of alternating current promised a brighter future. However, Tesla's promise is diverted by Thomas Alva Edison's better organization and reputation. In the history the novel records, this moment seems like the start of something new, the seed of squandered opportunities, and it develops a pattern that the novel never really overcomes. Instead of playing a significant role in the novel, history is writ small through the failure of the various characters in "Moon Palace."

Societal Context

Steven Weisenburger reads "Moon Palace" as the story of paternal decline, the long story of Julian Barber/Thomas Effing squandering all he has earned in his life so that he will have nothing to pass on to his male heirs, and it is possible to see the novel as likewise documenting the decline of a society. This part of Weisenburger's argument is easier to accept than his other claim that the novel questions narrative conceptions of coincidence; if there is a Golden Age in this novel, it certainly seems to be Barber's youth and young manhood. But if Auster seems sincere when he grants a privileged status to the 1893 Columbian Exposition as society's finest moment, surely the moon landing of 1969, which occupies the novel's first sentence, must rank as a close second in terms of man's accomplishments.

Likewise, while the novel might, through its staggered revelation of paternal bloodlines and the squandering of potential inheritances, critique the importance given to patriarchal bloodlines as a mode for structuring society, it also offers us alternate kinship possibilities. Kitty Wu early on identifies Marco as "brother," and it is as brother and sister, incestuous though they may be, that they are successful as a couple. It is only when they are poised to become instead father and mother that they disagree.

There is another sister-brother pairing in the novel, that of Effing's housekeeper Mrs. Hume and her brother, Charlie Bacon, a disabled World War II vet. Their relationship, while never at the center of the novel, seems healthy, long lasting, and forthright in ways few other relationships in this novel do.

It is possible to see this new interest in alternate kinship models as Auster's contribution to the reimagining of the social order, the collective rethinking that occupied so much of the 1960s. Marco's nervous breakdown is perhaps a hereditary legacy, since it so closely mirrors the one his grandfather experienced; this, then, would contrast with his legacies from other sources: his first and middle names, the books given him by Uncle Victor, and the friendships he makes, all of which serve him well.

This approach suggests rethinking the role of allusions to past literary works: instead of a Freudian misreading, Auster might be engaged in a playful textual networking. Instead of being fathers of this novel, "David Copperfield," "King Lear," and "The Odyssey" might be seen as siblings who share certain tropes and mannerisms.

Religious Context

Religion plays a small role in this novel, aside from Thomas Effing's sense of life as the working out of a kind of karmic balance. This is unsurprising in an example of the bildungsroman genre, as "Moon Palace" is: the bildungsroman sets its protagonist against the world to see what he can make of himself. In that ideological context, the strong influence of religious issues and imagery would be damaging to the themes of self-reliance and self-identification.

Scientific & Technological Context

Auster has described his purpose in "Moon Palace" as representing Columbus's 1492 journey, and of mistaking America for China. And, when science and technology in this novel appear, it is often in the context of misrepresenting good data. Thus, at the novel's scientific center, the 1893 Columbian Exposition, Nikolai Tesla's scientifically accurate claims for the value of his alternating current are undercut by his rival (and direct current pioneer) Thomas Edison's demonstration of an electric chair which can use alternating current to kill a man, simultaneously delighting and horrifying his audience. Alternating current, and Tesla himself, are overlooked, and when Tesla resurfaces as a character later in Effing's story, he is a homeless man, driven the edge of insanity by his failure. The "science" of Solomon Barber's scholarly histories is tainted in the reader's estimation by their proximity to the fantastic novel he wrote about the same landscape when he was a teenager. Similarly, when Marco sees the moon landing he is in the midst of his nervous collapse, wandering the streets.

In some ways, Tesla's alternating current is a fit metaphor for the binaries that organize this novel: sane/insane, Barber/Effing, living/dead, Earth/moon, father/stranger. Auster's use of science is mostly metaphorical, but that does not dimish its effectiveness as a structuring device.

Biographical Context

Paul Auster was born in 1947, the same year as Marco Stanley Fogg, and he began writing the novel in 1968, shortly after graduating from Columbia. The novel, alongside the manuscript for a memoir, "The Invention of Solitude," was one of Auster's first experiments writing prose. As Auster explained to Michael Freitag, "this novel was knocking around in my head for many years" (Freitag). Splitting the last years of the sixties and much of the seventies between France and the United States, Auster had some success as a poet and less as a prose writer, eventually putting both manuscripts aside until the eighties when he would return to them as an older man, with greater

success. Novelist Alan Gurganus, among others, has credited Auster's training and early work as a poet for the lyric sparkle of his prose (Gurganus 7).

"The Invention of Solitude: A Memoir" was published in 1982, Auster's first book length work of prose. The critical and commercial success "The New York Trilogy," a meditative inquiry into the detective story genre, followed, and Auster published "Moon Palace" in 1989. "Moon Palace" explores questions of paternity, and is itself a collection of coming of age stories, the story of the development of an artist. This last element makes it easy to imagine this as being one of Auster's first attempts at writing an "adult" work, and makes it interesting to speculate what differences crept in between the original, young man's novel of 1968 and the later version that was published two decades later.

Though not as widely lauded as his "New York Trilogy," it's easy to see "Moon Palace" as a product of the same impulse that motivated those books, the desire to write a book that at once interrogates the implied assumptions of a genre while still exisiting as part of that genre. It's somewhat harder to find a similar grouping in Auster's later novels, though they share other features between them. Many of the novels, for example, stress the locale, especially when that locale is New York City, where Auster writes and lives at least part of the year. A screenplay, "Smoke," became two films, "Smoke" and "Blue in the Face," and both are deeply engaged in the life of the borough of Brooklyn. Auster's interest in movies became the subject of "Book of Shadows," a recent novel about loss, grieving, and recovery that also documented the protagonist's obsession with silent film comedies. The protagonist in that novel shares some characteristics with most Auster protagonists, in fact: a deep and abiding interest in some element of culture that is just slightly off the radar, but which the novel sets out to rehabilitate as an object of serious critical inquiry. We, as readers, are invited to assume that these same passions take a hold of Auster the novelist, at least for the time it takes Auster to write these novels.

Matthew Dube

Works Cited

Auster, Paul. *Moon Palace.* New York: Viking, 1989.

Dickens, Charles. *David Copperfield.* New York: Signet Classic, 1962.

Freitag, Michael. "The Novelist Out of Control." *New York Times,* 19 March 1989.

Gurganus, Allan. "How do you introduce Paul Auster in three minutes?" *The Review of Contemporary Fiction* 14.1 (Spr 1994): 7–8.

Kakutani, Michiko. "Books of The Times; A Picaresque Search for Father and for Self." *New York Times,* 7 March 1989.

Weisenburger, Steven. "Inside Moon Palace." *The Review of Contemporary Fiction* 14.1 (Spr 1994): 70–9.

Discussion Questions

1. The title of the novel is taken from a Chinese restaurant Marco can see from his window. Is this a fitting title for the novel? If not, what might be a better title?

2. Is Marco's nervous breakdown realistic? Why do you think Auster writes it in this way? How does it fit into the novel as a whole?

3. Who is the protagonist of "Moon Palace?" How can you tell?

4. Is "Moon Palace" one big story, or is it three stories brought together under one cover and only loosely connected?

5. What role does coincidence play in this novel? What do you think Auster might be trying to say about novels, and about life, through the level of coincidence here?

6. How would you describe the relationship between Marco and Kitty? Is it always the same kind of relationship, or does it go through different phases?

7. How does Auster write about New York City? How does he write about the rest of the country?

8. Why does Thomas Effing feel it is so important that Marco read him the travel books? Do they help Marco to write Effing's life story?

9. The book tells us that the novel Solomon Barber writes when he is a teenager is the same kind of book as the critical histories he writes later, as an adult. In what ways is this true? In what ways is it false?

10. Is there any character in this novel who you wish you'd gotten to know better? What do you think his or her life story would be like?

Essay Ideas

1. What does the moon symbolize in different parts of the novel? Does it always stand for the same thing, or does its meaning change?

2. The novel is rich with allusions to other famous works of literature: Homer's "Odyssey," Dickens' "David Copperfield," Shakespeare's "King Lear," and many others. Read one of these texts to decide if the way Auster uses his references to these other books is complementary or contradictory.

3. Is Marco the author of his own story? If not, who is the author? If he is, what kind of story has he written for himself?

4. Is "Moon Palace" a realistic novel? Why or why not, and how does this affect the way we understand the book?

5. Is the book a product of its time (the 1960s of its primary present, or the 1980s of its publication)? How does this affect the way we read it?

William Gibson, an American-Canadian speculative fiction novelist, coined the phrase "cyberspace" in his short story *Burning Chrome,* and is credited with predicting the rise of reality television and the rapid growth of virtual environments; his novel *Neuromancer* is included in this volume. Photo: Wikipedia.

Neuromancer

by William Gibson

"Information is the dominant scientific metaphor of our age, so we need to face it, to try to understand what it means."

William Gibson

Content Synopsis

We first meet Case (we do not learn the rest of his name until later) in the Chatsubo Bar in Chiba City, Japan. He is now a hustler, running "the fastest, loosest deals on the street" (7), but two years ago he was one of the best console cowboys, or computer hackers, able to project "his disembodied consciousness into the consensual hallucination that was the matrix" (5)—cyberspace—stealing data for the highest bidder. Having cheated an employer, Case has had his nervous system destroyed by a mycotoxin, rendering him incapable of any further direct interface with the matrix; he has been imprisoned in his flesh, his case, and is on a self-destructive downward spiral.

He is recruited by Molly Millions, a "razor girl" who has been biologically enhanced and had surgical implants, including retractable razors in her fingers (hence the razor girl designation) and mirror shades (a staple icon of

cyberpunk fiction) implanted over her eyes that provide direct data feeds to her brain. She is employed by a man who calls himself Armitage, who is putting together a team of experts to pull off an elaborate scheme. Armitage finances the expensive procedures that repair Case's neural damage, allowing him to again interface with the matrix, as it is these skills for which he has been recruited. Armitage also eliminates Case's ability to use drugs by redesigning his pancreas and liver to bypass them. In addition, Armitage has had sacs of toxin implanted in Case's arteries—toxins that will burn out his nervous system again when the sacs dissolve. Case will need a complete blood transfusion to remove these when the job is complete, but until then, he is effectively dependent on Armitage for his life. By contrast, Molly gives him a gift: a shuriken, a star-shaped weapon that is thrown at an enemy and that, we are told, had "always fascinated" Case (11).

With Case now recruited, the team needs to grow more. Case and Molly's first mission is a raid on the data stores of a corporation called SenseNet. All they steal is the digitized copy of the personality of McCoy Pauley, the "Lazarus of cyberspace" (78) also known as the Dixie Flatline, who now joins the growing team. This name reflects his survival of lethal anti-hacking software knows as ICE—intrusion counter-measure electronics—though he briefly suffered braindeath (flatlined) first. He was also Case's mentor and perhaps the greatest console cowboy, or hacker, of all.

Meanwhile, there is evidently more going on than Case or Molly know. Armitage himself represents someone—or something—else, something powerful and mysterious. Case and Molly become lovers, and begin to consider how they might discover the truth behind their mission. Case begins to have strange experiences, the first of which is simply a one-word message: Wintermute. Case discovers that Wintermute is "the recognition code for an AI" (73)—or artificial intelligence. Such machines have been developed but are supposedly strictly controlled, incapable of autonomous action. This AI is the property of the Tessier-Ashpool corporation, a frightening family-run corporation (such organizations being archaic holdovers) now based in Freeside, an inhabited orbital satellite with more lax laws and regulations regarding genetic engineering than exist on earth. Some time in the past, a mysterious artifact, a mechanical head that functions as a computer terminal, was stolen from Tessier-Ashpool. This artifact was retrieved by Hideo, a ninja servant of Tessier-Ashpool. Hideo, though, is not a normal human but is rather "vat-grown" or genetically engineered for maximum effectiveness as a ninja. That Tessier-Ashpool is involved in such genetic manipulation foreshadows their more radical scientific experimentation in the development of Artificial Intelligences, as suggested by the bizarre nature of the head-shaped, but mechanical, artifact. The implications of these facts become clear only later in the novel.

The Dixie Flatline helps them solve the mystery of who Armitage really is. His real name is Willis Corto. He was a Colonel in the American Army, involved in a mission called Screaming Fist, an attack on Russian computer systems. The mission went awry, and Corto required massive reconstruction not only physically but also psychologically. Armitage is, in effect, a constructed persona inhabiting Corto's rebuilt body, in contrast to the Dixie Flatline, a recorded persona with no physical body at all.

The team's next mission is to complete its own composition by adding Peter Riviera, who has the ability to project holographic images. Riviera is unstable and sadistic. (Indeed, all the characters are dysfunctional on some level.) Their mission proper now begins, as they travel to the Villa Straylight, the Tessier-Ashpool stronghold on Freeside, to engage in the next phases of the plan. They are carried there by Rastafarian spacers from the Zion cluster. These Rastafarians have turned their back on Earth and the earthbound quest for the lost homeland of Zion (as the Rastafarian faith seeks), choosing instead to set up their own colony in an asteroid cluster that they now call Zion. They are willing to rent out their services, especially because Wintermute seems to them like a manifestation of a supernatural creature. Molly seems another iconic figure to them; they dub her "steppin' razor," adopting for her a name from a Peter Tosh song. Wintermute continues trying to contact Case, and the team comes to realize that their task is to free the AI from the constraints that keep it subservient to the Tessier-Ashpool clan. But another Tessier-Ashpool AI, Neuromancer, is apparently working against them. Case is briefly caught by Turing Registry agents, whose task is to ensure that AIs remain subjugated, but Wintermute murders them and frees Case. Case also learns more of Molly's history: she earned the money to afford her implants and modifications by working as a meat puppet, a prostitute whose consciousness is disengaged from her body while it is used by clients. Some of her experiences bled through because her employers were using her upgrades to offer her to a specialized clientele. Some of Molly's dysfunction is explained by these experiences, which put her in contrast to the deliberately perverse 3Jane Tessier-Ashpool (the numbers in the name indicate what iteration the person is in the Tessier-Ashpool program of cloning and inbreeding). Riviera's task is to use his holographic abilities to seduce 3Jane. She is to provide him with a way in to the Villa Straylight, and he is then to find a way to admit Molly and Case to complete the mission, since they need actual physical access to the head-shaped computer terminal to input the code that will free the AIs.

Initially, the plan seems to be working. Riviera successfully infiltrates Straylight with 3Jane, and the run, or mission, begins. Molly and Case are linked via simstim, simulated stimulation, a direct linking of one individual into the sensory perceptions of another, so Case can switch back and forth between his console and Molly's physical location, monitoring the progress of their hacking of the computer system defenses while Molly makes her way into Straylight. The Dixie Flatline's job is to help Case get past the AI's sophisticated ICE.

During the run, Case flatlines when he is sucked into a virtual reality created, he thinks, by Wintermute. But he learns that he has now in fact encountered Neuromancer, the other AI that has been attempting to prevent the mission from succeeding. Case's uncertainty about what he is encountering is not surprising, since we eventually learn that Wintermute and Neuromancer are each only partial; to be complete, they must be combined, linked, like the right and left hemispheres of the brain. This has been Wintermute's real plan all along, the fulfillment of a capacity built into the AIs by 3Jane's mother, the last visionary of the Tessier-Ashpool clan, who envisioned a symbiotic relationship with artificial intelligences, rather than the subservient model enforced by the Turing Registry. Neuromancer offers Case life inside the computer, divorced from the body in a virtual reality, even providing him with a simulated version of his old girlfriend, Linda Lee, murdered at the beginning of the novel. Surprisingly, perhaps, Case rejects the offer.

Meanwhile, Molly's share of the mission is also going awry. She kills the Tessier-Ashpool patriarch, but Riviera has betrayed them, and Molly is captured by Hideo, the vat-grown ninja who originally recovered the stolen terminal. Case has to go in physically himself to access the password, accompanied by Maelcom, one of the Rastafarians. They too are captured. Case tells 3Jane of the AI plan to merge. Riviera tries to kill Case and Hideo, but Hideo's ninja skills are too great; even after Riviera blinds him by burning his eyes out with lasers, he is able to kill Riviera. Hideo's skills are so refined, he can kill even when blinded; he used to train blindfolded. Case convinces 3Jane to give up the code by pointing out that the change the release of the AIs will bring (whatever that change may be; what will be different is of course by definition unknowable at this point) will provide a potential answer to the inward-directed stagnation to which the clan has become subject. 3Jane releases the code—"three / notes, high and pure. / A true name" (262)—and Neuromancer and Wintermute are freed and able to merge.

The novel's coda is set some time later, after Case and Molly have returned to earth, wealthy and free and clear, the newly merged AI having not only purged them from the Turing Registry records but also having penetrated Case's brain deeply enough to allow it to manufacture the enzyme necessary to release the toxin sacs (a feat that almost carries the AI over into the territory of miracle worker); the Rastafarians provide the necessary blood transfusion. He and Molly are lovers for a while, but she leaves him. Case has a final encounter with the new AI, which says it has become the matrix. Nothing obvious has changed—"Things are things," it says (270)—but it has encountered another of its kind in deep space. Nevertheless, the result of the quest for Case is difficult to determine, since he is also essentially unchanged, unlike the conventional quest hero. Case uses some of his money to replace his pancreas and liver with ones that will allow him to use drugs again. However, he also throws the shuriken into the computer screen through which the AI last contacted him, and his final words are "'I don't need you'" (270). He goes back to his career as a console cowboy.

"Neuromancer" is the paradigmatic cyberpunk novel. As summarized, its plot is easily recognized as a conventional quest story, and most of its conceits have deep roots in the science fiction genre. Its novelty resides more in its style and structure than in its content and consequently is minimally evident in a redaction (for one of many discussions of this aspect of Gibson's work, see Rapatzikou 75ff). Below are some beginning points for further study of its less evident complexities.

Symbols & Motifs

Mirror Shades: One of the most vivid visual icons of cyberpunk is the pair of mirrorshades that reflect the disconnectedness and flatness of affect of the typical cyberpunk character. When Case meets Molly, he discovers that her modifications include surgically inset reflective glasses that completely enclose and conceal her eyes. Though this technology provides her with enhanced visual perception—and the installation of simstim equipment allows her full range of perceptions and sensations to be shared by Case later—the glasses also symbolize alienation and the concealment of the self beneath a slick, polished surface. If eyes are the window to the soul, the soul is inaccessible in "Neuromancer." The power of the eye is explored extensively in the book. In her confrontation with Riviera, Molly gets one of her lenses shattered; subsequently, she sees her own reflection, including the shattered socket, in effect seeing herself for the first time. In a similar moment of simultaneous disembodiment and self-perception, Case later sees himself from outside, when the simstim connection to Molly shows him "a white-faced, wasted figure, afloat in a loose fetal crouch, a cyberspace deck between its thighs" (256). The self is so alienated

even from itself that Case sees himself here not merely as other, but as an 'it.'

Meat: The mind-body split is a major motif in "Neuromancer." Console cowboys view the body as "meat" and are contemptuous of it. Initially, Case views his body as a prison from which he cannot escape into the matrix. The body is defined for him by limitations and needs; his disdain for the flesh verges on the contempt for the material that defines some Christian thought, and indeed the novel associates the mind/body disconnect with the soul/body disconnect of Christianity. However, the body is also intimately interwoven into concepts of the self and consciousness. Case's awareness that he is being followed, for instance, is "cellular" (14), linked to the inherent components of the flesh. The complexity of the mind-body disconnect is perhaps most vividly depicted in the figure of Molly, who disconnected her consciousness from her body, serving as a "meat puppet" prostitute, in order to earn money to enhance that very body. The nature of the body and the connection of consciousness to the body is deeply problematized in the book. Genetic engineering and prosthetic modification techniques have led to cyborgization in which the nature of humanity has become oxymoronic: the body is simultaneously opposite things (Siivonen 229). But if the meat is being mechanized, the machine is being organicized. Organic metaphors recur in relation to the computer world. Indeed, even the term for cyberspace employs a fundamentally biological metaphor to describe the realm of the disembodied consciousness.

Matrix: The term Gibson uses for cyberspace, the matrix, has an array of associations that apply to the concept of cyberspace as a representation of organized data. The term has meanings in math, logic, and electronics that link it with structuring systems and circuit arrays. However, the root meaning of the word is "womb" (the word "mother" in fact has a common etymological ancestor). Unsurprisingly, perhaps, though the AIs are attempting to achieve their own metaphorical birth, they have been programmed to do so by a woman, 3Jane's mother, who does not appear in the book but who is the prime mover of its events. Paradoxically, flight from the body is flight into the womb, as Case's fetal pose when he views himself through Molly's eyes suggests. Despite the overt masculinity of cyberpunk as a genre, the feminine is woven into its defining image. Indeed, other images conventionally associated with female models of creation and habitation are associated with the matrix as well. For instance, both web and nest images recur in the novel, not only in association with the AIs (Wintermute, especially) but also with Case's lovers. His bed with Linda Lee (admittedly within the virtual reality constructed by Neuromancer), for instance, is a "nest of blankets" (235).

Historical Context

The novel was written during Ronald Reagan's first term as President, when the impact of Reaganomics was beginning to be felt. The corporate-dominated world of the novel imagines the possible result of Reagan's economic policies. Though Reagan is widely credited with being instrumental in the fall of communism, the novel was also written five years before the Berlin Wall came down but only a year after the Strategic Defense Initiative was announced, so increased tensions between the West and the USSR inform the novel. The mission in which Willis Corto suffered the trauma that leads to his recreation as Armitage was directed against the USSR, and though the USSR is not a major force in the novel, Corto/Armitage's experiences in his flight over Siberia are central to his character and his breakdown, and as a result they have an impact on the development of the plot. There are hints, as well, that some sort of military conflict in Europe has been a factor in the shift in world power; in the context of increased global tensions in the early eighties, such a conflict in the near future would not have been improbable.

Also influential on the novel was the emergence of Japan as a dominant economic and technological power. As a Vancouverite, Gibson directly witnessed the influx of Japanese into the local economy (the Northwest coast of North America is the easiest access point for Pacific Rim peoples and products), but through the early eighties the influence of Japanese technology, as represented by companies such as Sony, was widely felt across the continent. Gibson extrapolated from this trend (reasonably accurately, as it turns out) in imagining a future world in which Japanese corporations, corporate models, fashions, and even criminal organizations, penetrate western culture. Japanese influence pervades the novel in various ways, from the shuriken Molly gives Case to the product names for the imagined technology (e.g. the Ono-Sendai computer).

Societal Context

The social ramifications of the development of computer technology were a direct influence on the novel. Gibson has acknowledged that watching kids playing arcade video games and seeing that the game players "clearly believed in the space games projected" (*Interview* 272) was a direct influence on his development of the concept of the "consensual hallucination that was the matrix" ("Neuromancer" 5). The concept of cyberspace, therefore, represents to some extent Gibson's perceptions of the cultural impact of computer technology.

The social world of the novel as a whole is permeated by technology in conjunction with corporatization. As a console cowboy, Case was a thief, but a thief of information; the underworld of this novel traffics in information and emergent technologies which Gibson imagine as increasingly limiting and controlling human freedom. Corporate loyalty is no longer merely a matter of employee fidelity to an employer but a technologically-mandated necessity. Employees of Mitsubishi-Genentech (this merging of a computer and a biotech company is merely one of innumerable examples in the novel of the blurring of lines between technology and biology), for instance, are bar-coded and implanted with microprocessors in their bloodstreams, so they are always monitored and effectively incapable of disloyalty. (The toxin sacs in Case's blood represent a similar controlling technology.) Even the underworld, the novel suggests, is allowed to thrive as a sort of Darwinian breeding-ground for new technologies that can further consolidate power in the hands of corporations.

Rebellion against such dominant forces in the novel emerges in numerous forms, most notably perhaps in the figures of the space Rastafarians, whose shift from Earth to space as their habitat constitutes a literal turning away from the corporatized Western forces they view as Babylon. As Benjamin Fair argues, the Rastafarians in the novel have created in Zion "a community of unalienated production, economic communalism, and an egalitarian politics of difference contrasted with liberal, humanist, global capitalism" (Fair), explicitly contrasted with the parasitic, non-productive, capitalist, hierarchized (and white Western) world represented by Straylight, the Tessier-Ashpool corporation/clan, and the generalized corporatist model of life that dominates Earthside.

Religious Context

Gibson extensively invokes conventional Christian iconography and ideology in the novel, from its opening paragraphs forward. Case's loss of the ability to jack in to the matrix, for instance, is compared to the Fall, but Case is imprisoned in his own flesh, rather than in hell. The AIs are frequently, albeit ironically, associated with the Christian God, as for instance when Wintermute appears to Case as a simulation of Finn. Finn is a fence, a dealer in stolen technology, who provides assistance to Case and Molly early in the novel. Wintermute jokingly asks whether Case would prefer him to appear as a

burning bush. Unlike the Christian God, however, Wintermute and Neuromancer are not the ultimate I AM, the Word, but cannot know their name; as Wintermute tells Case, in language that echoes the Bible, "'I am that which knoweth not the word'" (173). In providing the code, Case provides the AIs with their true name and releases them not only into the matrix but also into full self-knowledge and autonomy. At the end of the novel, Case wonders whether the merged AIs have become God.

However, the AIs are also imaged as demons by the Turing police, and dealing with them is likened to making a pact with the devil. In this respect, perhaps the most significant element of religion in the text is in its invocations of Rastafarianism. Gibson not only invokes Rastafarianism as a site of political resistance but also as the basis of an alternative view of the pseudo-religious aspects of the matrix. For Maelcum and the Rastafarians, the matrix is Babylon, in contrast to their home, the Zion cluster, which is named for the promised African homeland of Rastafarianism. Ultimately, Case rejects the dubious model of transcendence offered by the AIs in a simulated, disembodied state, being led back to the body by the pulse of the Rastafarian music (Fair).

Scientific & Technological Context

"Neuromancer" depends entirely on scientific and technological concepts. The most obvious examples are computers and information technology. Though both the computer and the concept of the internet had existed for decades (the idea of a world-wide computer network was first described in 1962), when William Gibson published "Neuromancer," home ownership of personal computers was still a relatively recent phenomenon, and ARPANET, the predecessor to the current Internet, was taking shape. (For more detailed information, see Boutell.com.) Similarly, the concept of artificial intelligence has existed for centuries. Greek myth includes independent automata created by the god Hephaestos, and the head-shaped terminal stolen from Straylight almost certainly derives from the talking head purportedly created by the alchemist Roger Bacon in the thirteenth century (and featured as a stage prop in the Renaissance play "Friar Bacon and Friar Bungay" (1589), by Robert Greene), so the concept of the intelligent machine has deep mythological and literary roots. (For a brief history and chronology of AI, see Buchanan). However, the term "artificial intelligence" was not coined in the mid-nineteen fifties. Alan Turing designed a test for machine intelligence in 1950, and Gibson nods to Turing in his Turing Registry for AIs. Powerful computers and artificial intelligences had been popular parts of the science fiction repertoire at least since the nineteen-sixties. Gibson's innovation lies in combining the concept of the computer network with the concept of the artificial intelligence, so the AI ceases to be a function of hardware: the AI ceases to be contained within a machine but becomes instead a manifestation of the matrix itself.

The nature not only of consciousness but also of the human is further explored in some of Gibson's other invocations of scientific possibility. The possibility for the creation of artificial intelligence is parallel to the possibility for the copying, or uploading, of human consciousness into a computer environment. Early in the novel, Case sees the body as a prison, but by contrast, the Dixie Flatline views his status as ROM equally limiting. He asks Case to erase the disc when the run is over. Such mapping of human consciousness was pure speculation when Gibson wrote the novel and is not possible even today, but some speculate that it will be possible within decades. The nature of the human as modified by scientific intervention is further explored in the book's invocation of cloning, genetic engineering, and cyborgization. In these cases, Gibson is extrapolating from what either already existed or fell within the realm of possibility in the early nineteen eighties. Genetic engineering

at some level has been going on for centuries, through practices such as selective breeding and grafting, but genetic engineering at the DNA level has been going on since the 1970s, so genetically modified organisms were a reality when Gibson wrote the novel, albeit not in the form of vat-grown Ninja assassins. Though human cloning remains unachieved as of 2006, the first animal cloning took place in the 1950s (the animal in question was a tadpole), and cloning involving recombinant DNA has been going on since the 1970s ("Human Genome Project Information"). As for cyborgization, technically anyone with a prosthetic replacement for a body part is a cyborg, though again the degree of cyborgization Gibson imagines extrapolates well beyond what is possible even today, let alone what was possible in 1984. Gibson's explorations, and problematizations, of what will constitute the human in an age of cyborgization, genetic engineering, cloning, consciousness uploading, and the creation of artificial intelligence, derives from extrapolations from existing and emergent technologies at the time he wrote the book. His explorations have themselves been enormously influential on the development of subsequent science fiction and have been the subject of extensive critical commentary on the novel (see Tiimonen for one example).

Biographical Context

William Gibson was born in Conway, South Carolina, on March 14, 1948. He attended a private boys' school in Arizona, but did not graduate, and in 1967 he went to Canada, to evade the draft. He married and settled in Canada, moved to Vancouver in 1972, ultimately taking a Bachelor's degree in English from the University of British Columbia in 1977. He published his first science fiction story that year but did not leap to prominence in the field until the publication of "Neuromancer" in 1984. The novel won several major awards, including the Hugo, Nebula and Philip K. Dick awards.

Gibson wrote two sequels, "Count Zero" (1986) and "Mona Lisa Overdrive" (1988), which with the first novel constitute the Sprawl or cyber-space trilogy. A second trilogy, "Virtual Light" (1993), "Idoru" (1996), and "All Tomorrow's Parties" (1999), is sometimes referred to as the Bridge trilogy. His collection of short stories, "Burning Chrome," was published in 1986, and includes stories set in the Sprawl world. He also wrote "The Difference Engine" (co-authored by Bruce Sterling) in 1990, "Agrippa: The Book of the Dead" (1992), published in electronic form, the screenplay for "Johnny Mnemonic" (1995), and "Pattern Recognition" (2003). (Most of these details are drawn from Gibson, "Since 1948.")

Dominick Grace

Works Cited

Boutell.com. 2005. 21 Feb. 2006.

Buchanan, Bruce G. "A Brief History of Artificial Intelligence." *AI Topics.* 2006. 11 April 2006.

Fair, Benjamin. "Stepping Razor in Orbit: Postmodern Identity and Political Alternatives in William Gibson's Neuromancer." *Critique: Studies in Contemporary Fiction* 46.2 (2005): 92–103. *Literature Online.* 9 Feb. 2006.

Gibson, William. "An Interview with William Gibson." By Larry McCaffery. *Storming the Reality Studio: A Casebook of Cyberpunk and Postmodern Science Fiction.* Ed. Larry McCaffery. Durham: Duke UP, 1991. 263–85.

_____. *Neuromancer.* New York: Ace, 1984.

_____. "Since 1948." *Source Code.* 6 Nov. 2002. 23 Feb. 2006

Human Genome Project Information. 27 Oct. 2004. 21 Feb. 2006

Rapatzikou, Tatiani G. *Gothic Motifs in the Fiction of William Gibson.* Amsterdam: Rodopi, 2004.

Siivonen, Timo. "Cyborgs and Generic Oxymorons: The Body and Technology in William Gibson's Cyberspace Trilogy." *Science-Fiction Studies* 23.2 (July 1996): 227–44.

Discussion Questions

1. What does the opening sentence of the novel reveal about its world? How is it indicative of Gibson's style?

2. Do you think the copying of a human personality into a computer environment is plausible? Do you think it is desirable? What benefits and dangers does such a possibility suggest?

3. How does Gibson employ stereotypes of female sexuality and danger, especially in the figure of Molly?

4. What character names in "Neuromancer" are symbolic or otherwise revealing of the characters?

5. How does the shuriken function symbolically?

6. What sorts of literal body modifications does the novel imagine? What metaphors of the mechanization of the body does it employ? What does its treatment of the body suggest about human nature?

7. How is Straylight described? What is significant about its structure and its nature?

8. Why does 3Jane give Case the code?

9. How does the merging of Wintermute and Neuromancer change things, if it does so at all?

10. What purpose is served by the new AI informing Case that there is another AI, an alien one, in the Centauri system?

Essay Ideas

1. Analyze the associations between the AIs and divine powers.

2. Analyze the novel's use of the conventions of the quest. To what extent does the novel subvert quest motifs?

3. Analyze Gibson's use of Rastafarianism in the novel.

4. Analyze the role of sexual intercourse in the novel.

5. Compare/contrast Molly and 3Jane.

A Star of David necklace is symbolic to the novel, *Number the Stars*, by Lois Lowry, which depicts the escape of a Jewish family from Copenhagen during the Occupation of Denmark. Photo: Source unknown.

Number the Stars

by Lois Lowry

Content Synopsis

Set in Nazi-occupied Denmark, "Number the Stars" tells the story of Annemarie Johansen and her Jewish friend Ellen Rosen. The families of both girls are doing their best to cope with worsening conditions as it becomes clear that Denmark's Jews are in grave danger from Hitler's regime.

To boost Annemarie's pride and faith in her country, her father tells her about a time when German soldiers, watching King Christian X ride down the streets of Denmark, asked a Danish boy why the king did not travel with bodyguards. The boy replied that all of Denmark was the king's bodyguard. When the Nazis begin to terrorize the Jews of Denmark, Annemarie tells her father: "I think that all of Denmark must be bodyguard for the Jews" (25). Later, she wonders if she would truly die to protect the Jews and admits that she is not sure.

When the Nazis take the synagogue list of all the Jews and their addresses in order to arrest them, Ellen's parents, Mr. and Mrs. Rosen go into hiding, leaving Ellen with the Johansens in hopes that she will be safe with them. However, the Nazis invade the Johansens' home in the middle of the night. Annemarie manages to rip Ellen's Star of David necklace from her neck, hiding it just before the Nazis enter the room. When the soldiers take notice of Ellen's dark hair, they become suspicious, but the Johansens pretend that Ellen is Lise,

Annemarie's older sister who died in an accident years before. Mr. Johansen tears three pictures out of the family album, portraits of each of his daughters as babies. On the bottom of the picture of a baby with dark curls was written: Lise Magrete. The Nazis are satisfied. After one of them tears up the picture and grinds the pieces with his boot, they depart.

After this terrifying incident, Mrs. Johansen, Annemarie, Kirsti, and Ellen suddenly prepare to go to visit Mrs. Johansen's brother Henrick. Mr. Johansen calls Henrick and tells him, "I'm sending Inge to you today with the children, and she will be bringing you a carton of cigarettes" (53). Annemarie cannot figure out what her father means, since she knows they are not bringing cigarettes. At Henrick's, Annemarie is further puzzled as the family prepares the living room for the arrival of Great-aunt Birte's body and the guests who will join them for mourning. She is confused for good reason; she has no Great-aunt Birte.

Annemarie confronts Henrick, asking him why he and her mother have been lying to her. In return, Henrick asks Annemarie how brave she is, to which she responds, "Not very" (76). Henrick explains that it is easier to be brave when one does not know more than one needs to in order to play his or her part. He asks Annemarie to understand that they have lied to her so that she can be brave enough to help them do what they must do.

When people begin to arrive at Henrick's, Mrs. Johansen introduces them as "Friends of Great-aunt Birte." Lowry writes: "Annemarie knew that Mama was lying again, and she could see that Mama understood that she knew. They looked at each other for a long time and said nothing. In that moment, with that look, they became equals" (79). To Annemarie's surprise, Peter, the young man who had been engaged to her sister Lise and who often brought the Johansen's secret newspapers, arrives at Henrick's. With him are Ellen's parents.

Nazi soldiers arrive and demand to know why so many people are gathered together. When they explain about the death of Great-aunt Birte, the Nazi officers ask why the coffin remains closed since Danish custom dictates that family members look at the faces of deceased loved ones to pay respect. Mrs. Johansen pretends that the woman had died of typhus and that opening the coffin would pose a serious health threat.

After the officers leave, Peter reads a psalm: "O praise the Lord. / How good it is to sing psalms to our God! / How pleasant it is to praise him! / The Lord is rebuilding Jerusalem; / he gathers in the scattered sons of Israel. / It is he who heals the broken in spirit / and binds up their wounds, / he who numbers the stars one by one ..." (87).

Then, Peter opens the casket which is filled with clothing and blankets and begins to hand them out. Peter gives Mr. Rosen a packet to deliver to Henrick, and Annemarie suddenly understands what is happening, that Uncle Henrick will take the Rosens along with other Jewish families across the water to Sweden.

Peter takes one group to Henrick's boat and Mrs. Johansen follows a short time later, escorting the Rosens. On her way back, Mrs. Johansen breaks her ankle. Annemarie spots her mother crawling along the path and runs to help her. The two make a startling discovery near the steps to the house: the packet that Peter had given Mr. Rosen had fallen out of his pocket.

Annemarie and her mother formulate a plan. Annemarie will pretend to take her Uncle his forgotten lunch. She quickly packs a basket with food, hiding the packet at the bottom, and runs to the boat. But she is stopped by soldiers along the way. The Nazis take apart the lunch and discover the packet in the bottom of the basket. Annemarie begins to cry, terrified of what they will find in the packet, but it is only a hemmed handkerchief. Annemarie brings the basket to her uncle who assures her, "because of you, Annemarie, everything is alright" (119). Later, Henrick explains to Annemarie that the handkerchief contained a special drug that attracts dogs and ruins their sense of smell so that they cannot find the humans hiding on the fishing boats.

Two years after Annemarie helps the Rosens to escape, the war is over and the Danes are celebrating freedom. Sadly, Peter has been caught and executed by the Germans; Annemarie learns that her sister Lise had been a member of the resistance alongside him. The Nazis had run her down in a car. Annemarie asks her father to fix Ellen's Star of David necklace. He agrees and reassures her that she can give it to Ellen when she returns to her home in Denmark. Annemarie replies: "Until then ... I will wear it myself" (132).

Historical Context

In the 1930s, Germany was struggling to get back on its feet after being decimated in World War I and humiliated by the Treaty of Versailles which ended that War. Adolf Hitler and his Nazi Party came to power in 1933; not long after, they renounced the Versailles Treaty, becoming a threat to independent nations across Europe. In 1938, Hitler's forces occupied Austria, Hitler demanded the return of the Sudetenland, and by 1939 it was clear that he wanted to retake the Polish Corridor. Initially, France and England attempted to appease Hitler's demands in order to avoid war, but it soon became clear that he intended to control all of

Europe, ridding it of what he called its "Jewish problem."

The larger events dramatized in "Number the Stars" are historically accurate. Unable to defend itself against such a large and powerful enemy, Denmark surrendered to Germany in 1940. It was occupied by Nazi soldiers until 1945, yet King Christian chose not to flee but to remain in Denmark with his people, riding his horse through the streets of Denmark unguarded. Lois Lowry writes that "the story that Papa told Annmarie, of the soldier who asked the Danish teenager, 'Who is that man?' is recorded in one of the documents that still remain from that time" ("Afterword" 134). In August of 1943 the Danish people did sink their own navy in the Copenhagen harbor to stop Hitler from using it for his own purposes, creating the brilliant lights in the sky which Mrs. Johansen tells little Kirsti are fireworks in celebration of her fifth birthday. It is also true that on the Jewish New Year Holiday in 1943 the rabbi warned the Jewish people that were to be "relocated" by the Germans. A German, G. F. Duckwitz, had passed this information along to the rabbis so they could warn their congregations. After the warning, almost seven thousand Jewish people escaped as the Rosens do in "Number the Stars," across the sea to Sweden, aided by Danish friends. Almost the entire Jewish population of Denmark managed to escape. Others were not so lucky: more than six million Jews were killed elsewhere in Europe between 1939 and 1945.

Societal Context

Anti-Semitism was rife in many parts of the world in the early part of the twentieth century. Hitler and his Nazi party capitalized on this as they began a propaganda campaign that dehumanized and vilified Jews. Ultimately, Jews, and other "undesirables" such as Gypsies and homosexuals, living in all German-occupied countries were rounded up and sent to concentration camps or simply murdered en masse.

While some non-Jewish people helped Germans round up Jews out of anti-Semitic feelings or fear for their own safety, others risked their lives to protect them. There were resistance movements on some scale throughout Nazi-occupied Europe, both within and without the Jewish community. Denmark, especially, refused to stand by and allow the Nazis to mistreat its Jewish population. Denmark's King Christian X demanded even as he surrendered that Denmark's Jews not be treated differently from its other citizens. Since Denmark had a small Jewish population of approximately 8000, Hitler agreed, and he honored this agreement in the early years of the occupation. By 1943, Hitler had decided that Denmark's Jews must be exterminated. The Resistance went into action, hiding and helping Jews to safety before the Germans could find them. The Germans managed to find only 450 Jews in Denmark, many of them living in institutions. When these people were loaded onto German cargo ships, the Danish gathered to watch them go, singing the Danish national anthem to demonstrate solidarity. While in the camps, Danish Jews received visits from representatives of the Danish government and care packages and letters of support from Danish citizens. When the Jews—those who had been in camps as well as those who had fled to Sweden—returned to Denmark, many citizens gathered once again to welcome them home.

While it certainly portrays the harsh reality of prejudice and hate, "Number the Stars" is more of celebration of those who not only refused to accept this ideology, but who risked their lives and the lives of those they loved to resist it.

Religious Context

The global Jewish population currently numbers approximately thirteen million, a majority of whom live in the United States and Israel. While there are many similarities between Judaism and Christianity, there are significant doctrinal differences. Jews believe in one God to the extent that they reject the Christian idea of a tripartite deity. In addition, Jews do not believe that Jesus was the Messiah. Rather, they still look forward to the coming of a Messiah who will usher in a time of peace. While Christians believe that salvation comes from belief in God and Jesus' sacrifice for the sins of mankind, Jews believe that it is ethical behavior on earth that will lead to God's favor after death. To be forgiven for their failings, they must not only pray, but also try to make amends for the wrongs they have committed. In "Number the Stars," Ellen and her family get the news about the Nazi plans to "relocate" Danish Jews when they go to the Synagogue for Rosh Hashanah, commonly known as the Jewish New Year. This important Jewish holiday inaugurates the Days of Awe, a ten–day period of time ending with Yom Kippur, the Day of Atonement, in which a Jewish person examines his or her life, repents for sins and reconciles with people he or she has wronged.

In "Number the Stars," Jews and Christians coexist peacefully, even participating in one another's traditions. Lowry writes that the Johansen family would often go over to the Rosens to watch Mrs. Rosen light the candles on the Sabbath. Even young Kirsti, though she does not understand the religious significance of the practice, is respectful since she understands that she is witnessing something important to the Rosens. Through these simple acts of respect and the larger acts of risking their lives for each other, we can see that these two families, and the whole of Denmark by extension, are connected by a respect for each other and a recognition of their common humanity.

Notwithstanding that the Jewish faith is central to the identity of many Jews, Jews are also part of an ethnic group that shares a long history. Their strong sense of national identity persists despite, or perhaps because, of the fact that they have been persecuted and physically dispersed time and time again in the course of that history. Indeed, some argue that for many Jews being "Jewish" has more to do with being born into a Jewish family and all that that entails—bearing a physical resemblance to other Jews past and present and receiving the cultural memories passed down by one's forbears—than with believing in or practicing the Jewish faith. According to scholar and Rabbi Nicholas De Lange, "They practice the Jewish religion because they are Jews, not the other way around" (1). It is this ethnic identity that has come under fire from so many different angles in recent history. But far from the intended affect of destroying the Jewish communal identity and pride, European anti-Semitism, "Russian pogroms and the Nazi policy of genocide have actually had the effect of greatly strengthening attachment to the Jewish nation, as an ideal and as a reality" (De Lange 44).

Scientific & Technological Context

Although the Treaty of Versailles restricted the growth and development of the German army, German scientists worked in secret through the 1920s and 1930s developing experimental weaponry. Thus, when World War II erupted, Germany was much more of a threat than the Allied nations expected, and they had to devote their own resources to technological advancements in order to compete with Hitler's regime. The result was rapid technological escalation. While most nations had begun World War II using the same technology they had employed in the First World War, including rifles, grenades, and poisonous gases, by the end of World War II, they were relying on jet fighters, radar, and atomic weapons.

In addition to putting scientific and technological advances to use on the battlefield, the Nazi party used them to further its mission of genocide, a fact which spurred on the work of other scientists who wanted to put a stop to the Hitler's atrocities. By 1941, Germans had conducted successful experiments with gas which allowed them to kill large numbers of Jews at once. Lowry writes that after Nazis began to use dogs to sniff out Jewish people who were trying to escape this fate, Swedish scientists began to work on the problem in earnest: "They created a powerful powder composed of dried rabbit's blood and cocaine; the blood attracted the dogs, and when they sniffed at it, the cocaine numbed their noses and destroyed, temporarily, their sense of smell. Almost every boat captain used such a permeated handkerchief, and many lives were saved by the device" ("Afterword" 137).

The fate of the world seemed to hinge on which side could boast the greatest scientific and technological developments. Ironically, some of the American scientists who helped to create the atom bomb, the weapon which surpassed all others, were so awed by its power that they petitioned the government not to use it, sparking an ethical debate about whether the power of destruction can ever truly be used for the good of humanity, regardless of who wields that power.

Biographical Context

Lois Lowry was born in 1937 in Honolulu, Hawaii, while her father was stationed at Pearl Harbor. She spent the years during World War II in the Amish country of Pennsylvania with her mother's family. Lowry has written many critically-acclaimed books for young people. She received the Newbery Medal for her 1989 novel "Number the Stars" and for her 1993 novel, "The Giver".

The characters in "Number the Stars" were inspired by real people, those Lois Lowry knew in person or through their written histories. She writes that "Annemarie Johansen is a child of

my imagination, though she grew there from the stories told to me by my friend Annelise Platt, to whom this book is dedicated, who was herself a child in Copenhagen during the long years of the German occupation" ("Afterword" 133). Lowry writes that the sacrifices and hardships endured by her friend, along with the "courage and intensity of the Danish people under the leadership of the king they loved so much, Christian X," inspired her to create "Number the Stars."

In her research, Lowry came across the story and photograph of a twenty-one year old man, Kim Malthe-Bruun, a member of the Danish resistance whom the Nazis executed. She writes, "seeing the quiet determination in his boyish eyes made me determined, too, to tell his story, and that of all the Danish people who shared his dreams" ("Afterword" 137). Lowry quotes from a letter written by Malthe-Bruun to his mother on the night before his execution: "and I want you all to remember that you must not dream yourselves back to the times before the war, but the dream for you all, young and old, must be to create an ideal of human decency, and not a narrow-minded and prejudiced one" (qtd. in "Afterword" 137). Lowry traveled to Denmark and visited "the place in Copenhagen where the Resistance fighters had been executed. When [she] learned that the Danes still placed flowers there each day, after close to 50 years, it reinforced [her] admiration for them and [her] need to tell their story" ("Number" 100).

Kim Becnel

Works Cited

Bachrach, Deborah. *The Holocaust Library: The Resistance*. San Diego, CA: Lucent, 1998.

De Lange, Nicholas. *An Introduction to Judaism*. Cambridge UP, 2000.

Hart, Christine. *World War II: 1939–1945*. New York: Franklin Watts, 2000.

Lois Lowry. *Major Authors and Illustrators for Children and Young Adults*. 2nd ed. 8 vols. Gale Group, 2002. Reproduced in Biography Resource Center. Farmington Hills, MI: Thomson Gale. 2005.

Lowry, Lois. "Afterword." *Number the Stars*. Boston: Houghton Mifflin, 1989.

_____. *Number the Stars*. Boston: Houghton Mifflin, 1989.

_____. "Number the Stars: Lois Lowry's journey to the Newbery Award." *The Reading Teacher* 44.2 (1990): 98–101.

Rich, Tracey. *Judaism 101*. Retrieved from the site http://www.jewfaq.org

Discussion Questions

1. Describe and evaluate the novel's portrayal of the Danish resistance. What kinds of people participate in the effort; why do they risk their own lives in this cause?

2. Describe and evaluate the novel's portrayal of the Nazi forces. Does the novel treat the soldiers as actual people or as representations of something bigger?

3. How does the Nazi invasion affect each of the characters in the book? Compare Annemarie's reaction with Ellen's and with her younger sister Kirsti's. What factors determine their individual reactions?

4. In the "funeral scene," Annemarie knows that her mother is lying in order to try to help the Jews escape. Lowry writes that "she could see that Mama understood that she knew. They looked at each other for a long time and said nothing. In that moment, with that look, they became equals" (79). What passes between them here? In what ways are they now equals?

5. Identify key symbols of death and rebirth in the novel. What are their precise meanings in the context of the novel?

6. What images show up repeatedly in the novel? Discuss the significance of each image to the novel's themes.

7. What is the significance of Annemarie's decision to wear Ellen's Star of David necklace until she can return it to her?

8. Although there were resistance movements throughout Europe, the united effort on the part of Denmark to stop Hitler's persecution of its Jewish population is unique. Why do you think their collective response was so different from that of other countries'?

9. What is the significance of the book's title? How does it connect to the novel's themes?

10. In "Number the Stars," protection and safety are strongly associated with deception. For example, Annemarie's family lies to her about the Rosen's escape to Sweden to help her to be brave, and her mother tells Kirsti that the explosions in the harbor are fireworks for her birthday. Do you think that such a connection between safety and deception might have far-reaching affects on the people involved? On the culture at large?

Essay Ideas

1. Trace Annemarie's development throughout the course of the novel. Identify and discuss scenes you consider central to her maturation.

2. Lise has already died when the book opens, yet she is an important character. What role does she play in the novel?

3. Annemarie reflects on everything the Rosens have lost, yet, she realizes that "they had not left everything behind" (94). What does Annemarie mean here? According to the novel, how did the Jewish community cope with the Nazi's treatment of them?

4. Do you agree that it is easier to be brave if a person does not know all the details of something which would frighten him or her? What is the definition of bravery according to this novel?

5. What kind of picture does the novel paint of the Danish people? How do they feel about their King's decision to surrender to Germany? What do they think of Nazi ideology? After doing some outside research, how accurate do you find this representation to be?

Portnoy's Complaint

by Philip Roth

Content Synopsis

This whole book is written as a monologue being delivered by Alexander Portnoy to his psychoanalyst, Dr. Speilvogel. It opens with the definition of a mental disorder called 'Portnoy's Complaint' whereby an individual's desires to act ethically and morally are the result of guilt over constant perverted sexual desires which manifest themselves in compulsive sex and/or masturbation. These sexual acts never result in gratification and, the definition goes on, may be the result of unresolved tension between the sufferer and his mother. As the book goes on, it is revealed that this mental disorder has been defined by Dr. Speilvogel based on the ensuing monologue from the protagonist.

Alex starts his narrative by talking about his mother and his belief as an early child that she was also the teacher at school and that she used magical powers to travel home faster than him in order to be there when he got back from school. He quickly moves on to talk about his father, who suffers from chronic constipation, and how hard he worked at his job selling life insurance policies in the slums and poorer parts of town. He talks about how he has always wished for more from his father but how he has always been let down.

This leads him back to his mother; a woman who has always amazed him, particularly with her ability to get sliced peaches to hang suspended in jello. He lists all of the things that she did that he found amazing when he was a child but finishes off by telling us that he was locked out of the apartment when he was bad. Alex tells us he was a good boy and cannot remember what he had done that could be so bad that he would be thrown out by his own mother at such a young age. He then tells us that when he refused to eat she threatened him with a bread knife.

His tale then reaches adolescence and the start of the chronic masturbation. He lists various methods and aids that he used, bemoaning his inability to stop. Even when he thought he had given himself cancer, he carried on. He tells the story of breaking off during dinner, claiming diarrhea, to rush to the bathroom to masturbate over his sister's brassiere and the family coming to investigate. He continued, even as the door-knob was twisted and rattled, and then flushed the toilet even though he had been told not to. The family does not guess what he has been doing, instead his seeming diarrhea is held up in contrast to his father's constipation and is seen by his mother as a sign he has been eating the wrong things after school, and therefore hanging around with the wrong people. This becomes a litany of the all the things that Alex's mother holds over him at various times, including the suggestion that his father's headaches are caused by a brain tumor. This all leads to a clear memory of his father joining them in the evenings during their holiday by a lake and swimming in the fading light. It is a pure and beautiful memory and seems to surprise Alex with its intensity.

Alex's narrative returns to the event of the diarrhea and his mother's constant nagging about what he eats. Alex then brings us back to the present, where he is in his thirties and visits his parents once a week and still they nag him with their worries. He finishes the section by pleading with his doctor to stop him from being the classic Jewish son henpecked by his parents and still lying at home in his bed, masturbating.

The next section starts with the story of one of Alex's testicles which did not descend properly and made it necessary to have treatment. This leads to criticism of his parents—his father for not being strong enough, his mother for being too strong. He again mentions being threatened with a bread knife for not eating, but also remembers a time when he saw his mother's menstrual blood on the kitchen floor and another when she sent him out to buy sanitary pads. These stories remind Alex of being at a pre-school age watching his mother slide on her stockings and a possible memory of the significance of such a sight. Then we are told that she still does it, even now when he is in his thirties. Alex then tells us of other ways in which she flirts with him and how uncomfortable he feels about it.

The next story is of Alex's father taking him to the steam bath with all the other Jewish men and of the sight of his father's large genitalia. This is followed by a story in which he wanted an athletic support in his swimming trunks and his mother replies, incredulous, saying, "For your little thing?" (51).

We then hear about Uncle Hymie, described as the 'potent man in the family' (51) and his son Harold, known as Heshie. Before Heshie went off to fight in the army, he had planned to get engaged to Alice, a non-Jew. Despite Heshie's strength and athletic prowess, Hymie wrestled him to the ground and held him there until he agreed not to get engaged to the shiksa' (a disparaging term for a non-Jewish girl or woman). Heshie was later killed while fighting in the Second World War. The family was upset but consoled by the fact that at least he never married Alice.

This leads us to Alex's own rebellion when he refused to go to synagogue with his father and sister while his mother was ill in hospital. Alex did visit his mother, but always wanted to leave as soon as possible and run away to play Little League baseball, one of the few places where he feels comfortable. The story then takes us back to Hannah, Alex's sister, talking to him about the fact that he is a Jew and should be proud because of the six million who died in the Holocaust. They both end up crying.

Then Alex is telling us about the time he masturbated while sitting in a bus next to a young non-Jewish female stranger. He wonders if it was precipitated by eating lobster—a forbidden food; forbidden because his mother once ate it and was very sick. Then Alex remembers a young woman that his father brought home from work for dinner and wonders if his father was having an affair with her. Was this, he wonders, his father's way of atoning for the affair, by bringing her home and showing her to the family? He seems to remember an argument between his parents in which Hannah is hiding behind their mother and he behind his father, but then this memory becomes one of him being shouted at by his mother for stealing Hannah's chocolate pudding from the refrigerator. This leads, once again, into thoughts and memories of his mother and her strict rules for living.

He then remembers a boyhood friend who committed suicide. His family's general reaction was one of 'how could he do this to us?' This is complemented by all the people who Alex knew as a child who his mother now reminds him of and tells him about their lives and how many children they have. He sees this as his mother's way of asking when he is going to bless them with grandchildren. His internal response to this is that he cannot provide them with children when he is too busy chasing new and exciting types of sex with lots of different people. He introduces into the narrative a girl he has been seeing recently, who he calls The Monkey. Despite her inventiveness in the sexual arena he has had to leave her because she wanted to settle down and have children. He left her on a balcony in Athens where she was threatening to kill herself.

He returns to the topic of his parents and how they don't seem to care that he has been appointed by the Mayor to be the Assistant Commissioner for the City of New York Commission for Human Opportunity because; despite keeping every newspaper cutting about him, they still nag him about his health. He tells tales of their nagging and emotional blackmail, ending with how he told them about his recent trip to Europe at the very last minute so that they had no time to nag him about it. Then we are back to stories of young Alex and his mother's over-the-top treatment of his transgressions.

We return to the story of the masturbation in the bus. He tells us that the surreptitious method he used for this was created for masturbating into his baseball glove during a trip to the Empire Burlesque house. He tells us of the war in his mind over disgust at what he was doing and the desire to do it. The desire won. He describes what he would like to do to the largest of the women in the chorus line; defining an image of womanhood for him.

This tale is broken into by a sudden memory of being taught to urinate while standing up by his mother who was sitting next to him on the edge of the bath and tickling the underside of his penis. This leads his thoughts back to the bus and then on to the time he masturbated using the piece of liver from the refrigerator which was later served for the family's dinner.

Alex takes us back to the tale of The Monkey and Alex tells us that the worst thing he did to her, other than leaving her, was to get her involved in a sexual threesome with an Italian whore. The event led to recriminations which almost immediately

led to them doing it again. This was then quickly followed by Alex leaving The Monkey.

Alex then introduces his obsession with shiksas, especially the ones who would go skating in winter at Irvington Park. He tells how he would have liked to have had one as a girlfriend and how he invented a new name he could use to cover his Jewish-ness until he realized that his nose would give him away.

Alex then tells us how he was supposed to be The Monkey's knight in shining armour; rescuing her from her poor uneducated upbringing. She called him 'Breakie,' because he was supposed to be her breakthrough: her first normal relationship. However, he tells how she was the symbol of depravity he had been looking for so he had no real desire to rescue her.

The ending of the tale of the skating 'shiksas' at Irvington Park is that when Alex finally got up the courage to approach one of the girls, he fell and broke his leg; nearly crippling himself for life.

Next, Alex tells of a going to see 'Bubbles' Girardi, a friend of one of his schoolmates, who was apparently willing to give the young Alex and his friend oral sex. As the story unfolds, she agrees only to pleasure one of the boys, with his clothes on, and Alex is chosen. He is unable at first to attain an erection and then she stops before he can reach orgasm. He finishes the job himself and ejaculates into his own eye. He runs out, believing he has blinded himself. Alex is later told that after he left, the girl supposedly agreed to have both oral sex and full sex with his friend.

Alex's story then returns to The Monkey and his focus on her lack of education, resulting in her starting a note with the word 'dear' spelled 'dir' (205). This discovery seemed to lead to a breakthrough in Alex's own emotional life when, during a holiday in Vermont, he was able to drop the shield of his lust and start to actually feel affection for The Monkey along with the continuing erotic fascination. However, this collapses as they return to the city and Alex admits he is ashamed of his girlfriend. He relates a story she told him wherein one morning a man offered her money for the night they had spent together and she took it, supposedly out of curiosity. Alex presumes this story is the cover for a life of prostitution. He argues, at some great length, that a man in his position cannot be seen with such a woman. He tells of his efforts to try and educate her, and to make her more than she is, and of an occasion where he took her to an important dinner but nearly didn't take her in because he was worried about what she would do and say. In the end, she behaved perfectly.

Tales of The Monkey lead to thoughts about Alex's earlier girlfriends. There is Kay Campbell, a round and ample non-Jew, who he referred to as Pumpkin. Alex, aged seventeen, and during his first holiday from college, went back to Pumpkin's family for Thanksgiving. He tells of his experience of this non-Jewish, all-American family. He enjoys it at first; purely because it is not his own home, but then realizes how much he misses the traditions and rituals of his own family.

Then we hear about the time when Kay missed her period and the two of them started plans to marry while still at college. However, when Kay refused to convert to Judaism, Alex took umbrage and the relationship ended. He tells us how he couldn't understand how something that mattered so little to him as his religion could suddenly mean so much.

Then he tells of another gentile girlfriend, Sarah Abbott Maulsby, who he met working at the Senate when he was on a sub-committee into quiz-show scandals. As he talks about her he realizes that her background, and her non-Jewishness, mattered more to him than the girl himself. He also realizes that this particular girl could have been a stand-in for the daughter of his father's old boss and that by sleeping with her—and forcing her to perform oral sex on him—he was achieving some kind of revenge for his father.

We then move to a memory of all the men in Alex's childhood neighborhood gathering on Sunday morning's to play softball. This elegiac section recalls the men, their banter, and how much little Alex enjoyed watching them and longed to grow up to be one of them; with a wife and family to return to, tired and happy. He then reveals that he remembered all of this while looking out of the window of a plane above Tel Aviv airport as he arrived in Israel for the first time, having fled from The Monkey in Athens. The memory caused him to cry, but the passengers around him assume it is the power of his seeing his 'homeland' for the first time.

Having arrived in Israel while running away, Alex pretends it was planned and follows the tourist trail, inspecting all the sights and learning the history. At the same time he is amazed to be in a country where every face is Jewish and is also worried that he has caught some kind of venereal disease from the Italian whore he shared with The Monkey. There is no sign of any infection, but this simply convinces Alex that it is the really bad, invisible strain of infection he has caught.

On his return journey through Israel, Alex meets Naomi, a girl from a kibbutz who he christens the Jewish Pumpkin. Only in retrospect does he realize that she is identical to the pictures of his mother at a young age, and that she has the same strength of character. He decides that he should marry her and stay in Israel living on a kibbutz. When he tells her this she accuses him of being insane. He tries to force himself on her and she fights him off, having previously been in the Israeli army for her national service. He tries again, and although he succeeds in subduing her he discovers he is unable to achieve an erection in Israel.

This leads to Alex's final rant in which he basically asks why he cannot just be a normal man with normal appetites, or at least, why he cannot stop feeling so guilty for all things he wants to do.

The final punch line is the doctor announcing that he is ready to start; showing that either all of the preceding was only in Alexander Portnoy's mind, or that Alex needed to get it all out before they could properly begin.

Historical Context

"Portnoy's Complaint" is very much a product of it's time. It was written in 1969 at the end of the 'sexual revolution' of the late sixties and reflects a much more liberal attitude—in some parts of society at least—to sex and sexual practices. Despite this, however, it was seen as a very shocking novel for the frank way it deals with both sexual practices and sexual politics, and remains so to this day.

While the content reflected change in what could be said about sex, the style of the book—a single continuous monologue alternating between humour, anger and self-flagellation, can be seen as resulting from examples of Jewish-American stand-up comedy at the time—such as the routines performed by Lennie Bruce or Woody Allen (Nilsen, 91).

Of course, apart from the sexual nature of the novel, a large part of it is an examination of Alex's New Jersey childhood. Even in 1969 this was largely a nostalgic process, looking back on a type of suburban living that had mostly disappeared. In the early 1950s, the time that Roth is writing about, it was common for ethnic groups to inhabit the same neighbourhoods forming enclaves or ghettoes where their way of life, or religion, was predominant (Gross, 81). Roth grew up in just such a neighbourhood and it is this place, and its subsequent loss, that he eulogizes in the book.

Other influences on the novel are, of course, the Holocaust and the creation of the state of Israel. Although the first of these is only mentioned tangentially, the latter forms the ending of the book with Alex's return to his 'motherland.' This is not a happy experience for the character and shows Roth's ambivalence towards his heritage.

Societal Context

"Portnoy's Complaint" was written and published at the end of the sixties, a decade synonymous with great changes in sexual mores and sexual roles. It was the decade of free love and also of the feminist movement. The advent of the contraceptive pill created the opportunity for consequence-free sex and also for women to choose when they wished to become pregnant, if at all.

It was also a decade informed by books written by Alfred Kinsey: "Sexual Behavior in the Human Male" (1948) and "Sexual Behavior in the Human Female" (1953). Both of these books were widely read and created an atmosphere in society that allowed more discussion of sexual matters. This led on, in the 1960s, to the famous obscenity trials which finally saw the publication of D.H. Lawrence's "Lady Chatterley's Lover," Henry Miller's "Tropic of Cancer," and John Cleland's 1750 novel "Fanny Hill." It was in this atmosphere of greater awareness and permissiveness surrounding the portrayal of sex in literature that Roth wrote his novel.

As well as reflecting society at the time of writing, "Portnoy's Complaint" is also an elegy for the post-war society of Roth's childhood. This period, the late 40s and early 50s, was a much more conservative time in America with fear of the Communist threat both inside and outside of the country being prevalent. It is just one more contradiction in Alexander Portnoy's story that he should so revel in the modern times while constantly harking back to the earlier, simpler period—attempting to both wallow in nostalgia and break away from the strictures of that earlier era (Bradbury, 178).

Religious Context

Alexander is most definitely Jewish. The whole book deals with his attempts to fit himself into his Jewish heritage. This battle comes out in the text in a number of ways.

First, there is the relationship between Alex and his mother. As he comments, he is caught in the midst of the classic Jewish joke whereby the grown up son is still smothered by the mother ('Help, help, my son the doctor is drowning!' (111)). Although this is perhaps more cultural than religious, and may even be simply a stereotype, it is a concept associated with Jewishness rather than any other religion.

Next we are confronted with Alex's desire to be seen as a human being rather than simply a Jew (76). This attempt is stifled by his sister when she raises the subject of the Holocaust. This passage shows us that Alex's strong reaction against his heritage is partly due to how thoroughly immersed in it he is. However, it is also possible to see his attitude as a reaction against accepting the holocaust as his responsibility. The mass murder of so many Jews is not a burden he feels he can carry, so he rejects the whole religion (77–78).

Finally, we are confronted at the end of the book, surprisingly, with Alex taking a trip to Israel. He tells us that this was his attempt to run away from the Monkey, rather than towards anything, but the destination, however unintentional, must be seen as significant. It would seem, at this point, he is trying to reconcile himself with his ethnic and religious heritage by returning to its symbolic heartland. He attempts to conform and do all the things that are expected of him, changing himself to fit his heritage, but when he attempts to fulfil his usual nature he finds himself impotent. Thus we are left at the end of the book as we started it, with Alex unable to reconcile his internal and external natures.

Scientific & Technological Context

There is very little of scientific or technological nature in "Portnoy's Complaint," as it is a book mostly concerned with the internal life of emotions and neuroses. However, the book is founded on the concept of it being a session between Alexander and his psychoanalyst to the extent that 'Portnoy's Complaint' is identified at the beginning of the book as being a psychological disorder. While psychoanalysis was not new in the 1960s, it was a period when this particular form of therapy expanded into the public consciousness.

Biographical Context

Philip Roth was born in 1933 in Newark, New Jersey and grew up in the same Weequahic neighbourhood as attributed to the Portnoy family. In fact, as in many of his novels, Roth gave many of his own attributes to his main character—date of birth, place of birth and upbringing, family structure and taste in literature—and it would seem that many of the more anecdotal passages in "Portnoy's Complaint" are thinly veiled autobiography. Indeed, Roth's own father was an insurance salesman, just as Alex's father is in the novel.

The career of civil rights attorney which Roth ascribes to Alex is a path that may have appealed to Roth who studied law as a high school senior and, according to comments made in his pseudo-autobiography "The Facts," he had "sometimes imagined working on the staff [of the Anti-Defamation League], defending the civil and legal rights of Jews" (Facts, 123).

Other comments in "The Facts" reveal that the character of The Monkey—Mary Jane Reed—was possibly a caricature of Roth's first wife, Margaret Martinson (re-named Josie in the book). In particular, this is a recurring character in Roth's work of a woman whose own home and family life was so lacking in love and warmth that she feels the need to imbed herself in the male character's strong Jewish family.

It is interesting to note that, through his outspoken views on Jewishness, Roth has at times been accused of being an anti-Semite; an accusation which he has always denied claiming that he simply wishes to start discussion about his culture, not to condemn it.

Calum A. Kerr, PhD

Works Cited

Bradbury, Malcolm. *The Modern American Novel – Second Edition*. Oxford, Oxford University Press, 1992.

Cooper, Alan. *Philip Roth and the Jews*. Albany, State University of New York Press, 1996.

Gross, Barry. "Seduction of the Innocent: Portnoy's Complaint and Popular Culture," *MELUS*, Vol. 8, No. 4, "The Ethnic American Dream" (Winter, 1981), pp. 81–92.

Milowitz, Steven. *Philip Roth Considered: The Concentrationary Universe of the American Writer*. New York, Garland Publishing Inc, 2000.

Nilsen, Don L. F. "Humorous Contemporary Jewish-American Authors: An Overview of the Criticism," *MELUS*, Vol. 21, No. 4, "Ethnic Humor" (Winter, 1996), pp. 71–101.

Roth, Philip. *Portnoy's Complaint*. London, Vintage, 1995.

Roth, Philip. *The Facts*, London, Jonathan Cape, 1989.

Wade, Stephen. *The Imagination in Transit: The Fiction of Philip Roth*. Sheffield, Sheffield Academic Press, 1996.

Discussion Questions

1. What is the symbolism of Alex's father's constipation?
2. In what ways is "Portnoy's Complaint" a Freudian novel?
3. The book is full of contradictions. Examine some of them and look at what purposes they serve.
4. Alex seems to be obsessed with non-Jewish girls. What is the significance of this?
5. It has been commented that Alex's whole disorder is simply a desire to achieve a ménage a trois. Is this valid?
6. Alex tries to deny his Jewishness. How successfully do you think he manages this?
7. What role does The Monkey play in Alex's disorder?
8. Discuss the symbolism of the softball games played by the neighbourhood men.
9. To what extent do the male figures in Alex's life act as role models?
10. What is the significance of the 'Punch Line'?

Essay Ideas

1. Alex feels a range of emotions for his mother. Discuss the contrasts in these feelings.
2. Examine the ways in which "Portnoy's Complaint" is a novel of nostalgia.
3. Why is it important to the characterization of Alexander Portnoy that he is constantly masturbating?
4. During his time in Israel, when he tries to have sex with Naomi, Alex finds he has become impotent. Discuss the symbolism of this with regard to the role of Jewishness in the novel.
5. "Portnoy's Complaint" is a novel born of the sexual revolution. Discuss.

Rabbit, Run

by John Updike

Content Synopsis

This essay examines "Rabbit, Run" (1960), the first novel in John Updike's Rabbit tetralogy. The novel charts the experiences of Harry 'Rabbit' Angstrom, a high-school basketball star turned husband and father, against the backdrop of 1950s America. The essay places the novel in a number of contexts and provides biographical information about Updike.

"Rabbit, Run" opens on the image of boys playing basketball. Rabbit Angstrom, so named because of his broad white face and "a nervous flutter under his brief nose," watches the boys playing (3). He is twenty-six and wears a business suit. He joins in the game and becomes a high-school basketball star again, feeling "liberated from long gloom" (6). As his breath grows short, he leaves the game but continues running through his home city Brewer, Pennsylvania. He reaches his apartment where his pregnant wife Janice is watching children's television. On the screen, Jimmie Mouseketeer tells the viewers to know and to be themselves; he tells them that God would not ask a waterfall to be a tree. The apartment is a mess and Janice appears confused. Their son, Nelson, is at Rabbit's mother's house and their car is at her mother's house. Nelson was born seven months after their wedding. Rabbit is repelled by Janice's pregnancy and the untidiness of the house. Sensing his irritation, Janice tells him not to run from her. Rabbit leaves and walks to his

mother's to collect Nelson. He passes the Sunshine Athletic Association where his old coach Tothero lives. He reaches his old home, and sees his son being fed. He walks away, and goes to his parents-in-law's house instead. He gets into his car outside the Springer house and drives. He drifts for a while and tries to head south; he ends up taking a round trip from Brewer to West Virginia and back. At one point the road begins to narrow and he prays that it will keep going. A car almost crashes into him and he lands in a ditch. Confronted with the highway, he panics and turns towards home; the route back is easier. He stops at his coach's apartment building and sleeps there, telling Tothero that he has left his wife because she is an alcoholic.

After Rabbit has slept, Tothero tells him that they are going out with his girlfriend; he has organized a date for Rabbit also. They meet the women at a Chinese restaurant. Rabbit's date is called Ruth. She is "chunky" and "tall" (55). Over dinner he tells her that he served in the Army in Texas. Ruth grew up in Brewer and knows Ronnie Harrison, who used to play basketball with Rabbit. Rabbit is shocked; Harrison is a "notorious bedbug" (64). When Tothero and his date leave, Rabbit tells Ruth that he has left his wife. Ruth lives alone in an apartment and does not appear to have job. Rabbit offers to give her something towards the rent and she takes fifteen dollars; they both seem to recognise that this is a kind of transaction, although neither comments on it. At Ruth's apartment they begin to kiss. Rabbit asks her not to use any contraception. She reluctantly agrees. They sleep together and Ruth expresses surprise that she was satisfied sexually. The next day is Sunday. Rabbit and Ruth discuss religion. She is an atheist; Rabbit believes in God but does not attend church. He drives home to get some fresh clothes. On leaving his apartment a car approaches; it is Jack Eccles, the Episcopalian minister. Eccles tells Rabbit that Janice's mother called him after he left. Rabbit tries to explain why he left and Eccles seems to understand but berates his lack of responsibility. Eccles asks Rabbit what God would want him to do but Rabbit asserts his right to fulfill his needs; his interior life defines him. He tells Eccles with contempt that he demonstrates a kitchen appliance, the Magi-Peeler, for a living; he used to be a basketball star. He tells Eccles that God would not ask a waterfall to be a tree. They agree to play golf in a few days. Rabbit returns to Ruth and they walk up Mount Judge together. At the summit, he scans Brewer and calculates that somebody in the city must be dying at that moment. He asks Ruth to put her arm around him and inquires if she was a whore. She responds by asking if he is a rat.

For the next few days, Rabbit and Ruth live together. Rabbit goes to Eccles's house and encounters his wife Lucy; she is clearly unhappy. Before Eccles appears, Rabbit slaps her on the backside. When Eccles comes downstairs, he and his wife bicker about the children; she does not tell Eccles what Rabbit has done. As they drive to the golf course, Eccles tells Rabbit that he saw Janice with her friend Peggy Fosnacht. As they play golf, they discuss Rabbit's desertion; Rabbit sees himself as a quest figure, Eccles views him as a vagrant. Eccles offers Rabbit a new job, gardening for a Mrs. Smith. He surprises Rabbit by asking about Ruth; Rabbit denies all knowledge of her. They play golf; Rabbit used to caddy and has some experience of hitting the ball. Initially, he struggles to perform but he strikes one ball perfectly.

The novel is divided into parts, marked only by protracted gaps in the text. The second part opens on the garden of Mrs. Smith, where Rabbit now works. Mrs. Smith, an elderly widow, comes out and flirts with him. She tells him that her son died in World War II. Rabbit and Ruth go swimming and Ruth comments that life is pretty good for Rabbit. She now has a job as a stenographer. The narrative moves to Ruth's perspective; she has been experiencing the early signs of pregnancy but she has resolved not to tell Rabbit, as she is uncertain of how she feels. The scene shifts to Eccles, who is visiting Mrs. Springer, Janice's mother. Nelson and Billy, Peggy Fosnacht's son, are playing outside. Mrs. Springer speaks bitterly of Rabbit's treatment of Janice and insinuates that Eccles is partly responsible for his continued absence. Eccles defends Rabbit and assures her that he will return to Janice eventually. Mrs. Springer dismisses his optimism and states that she should have called the police the night Rabbit disappeared. Eccles visits Mrs. Angstrom. She accuses Janice of trapping her son with her pregnancies. She predicts that Rabbit will crawl back to Janice because he is "all heart" (161). Eccles wonders if she gets her ideas from the Lutheran church. Mr. Angstrom enters and apologises for his son's behavior, attributing it to the Army. Miriam, Rabbit's younger sister, appears, carrying with her the aura of youth. Eccles leaves and visits Kruppenbach, the Lutheran minister, hoping to enlist his help with Rabbit and Janice. Kruppenbach mocks Eccles' interference. He quotes the Bible at Eccles and tells him that his meddling is the Devil's work. Eccles refuses to pray with him but as he drives home he senses that Kruppenbach is right. Instead of returning home he goes to the Youth Club.

The scene shifts to Club Castanet, where Rabbit and Ruth meet Margaret, Tothero's old date. She enters with Ronnie Harrison, Rabbit's team mate from school. Rabbit and Ronnie clearly dislike each other; Ronnie tells the women that Rabbit was not a team player. He tells Rabbit that he and Ruth went to Atlantic City together. Miriam enters with a young man. Rabbit is appalled to see her in that setting and attacks her date. He leaves with Ruth and demands to know how many men she has slept with. He asks her to perform the same sexual act she performed on Harrison. She reluctantly agrees.

Mrs. Springer calls the Eccles house. Janice has gone into labor. Eccles calls Rabbit who leaves Ruth in bed and walks to the hospital. Janice has a baby girl. She welcomes Rabbit, still inebriated from medication. Rabbit stays with Jack and Lucy Eccles that night. He and Lucy talk the next morning; Rabbit senses that she wants him. As he leaves, she seems to wink at him. Back at the hospital Rabbit sees Mrs. Tothero; his old coach is ill. He visits Tothero, who is unable to communicate lucidly. When he returns to Janice, she reproaches him for leaving her. Rabbit wants to name their daughter June, after the month in which she was born. Janice wants to call her Rebecca, after their mother. They decide on Rebecca June. Rabbit and Nelson return to the apartment. Rabbit quits his job with Mrs. Smith; he will now work for Mr. Springer at his car lot. He visits Mrs. Springer, who expresses her dislike for Peggy Fosnacht. In contrast, Rabbit's mother is now hostile towards her son and grandson. She asks Rabbit what will happen to Ruth; he replies that she expected nothing. Mr. Angstrom tells Rabbit that they hardly see his sister Miriam anymore.

The days pass slowly in the apartment and, whenever Nelson is asleep, Rabbit becomes restless. Janice returns. Eccles calls on them and looks forward to seeing them at church. Rabbit attends that Sunday. His attention is distracted by Lucy Eccles who sits in front of him. After the service, they walk home together. She tells Rabbit that he differs from her husband because he is not afraid of women. She invites him in for a coffee; Rabbit is tempted but refuses. When he returns to Janice, Rebecca is crying. Rabbit tells Janice to have a drink to relieve her nerves; they argue. He tries to make love to her, but she reminds him that she cannot have sex with him for six weeks. She is unwilling to experiment sexually the way that Ruth did. Rabbit leaves. The rest of the second part is narrated from Janice's perspective. She tries to placate Rebecca but begins crying herself when she thinks about Rabbit and Ruth. She drinks whiskey to fill the "hole" of Rabbit's "absence" (256). She plays with Nelson and cries when she fails to stay within the lines in his coloring book. Her father calls and asks where Rabbit is; it is now eleven o'clock in the morning and he has not arrived at the lot. She tells her father that Rabbit left to show a car to a client. Her mother calls; the Springers suspect that Rabbit has left again. Mrs. Springer insists on coming over. In a panic, Janice tries to tidy up and hide the whiskey. She places Rebecca in bath water, not realising that the bath is almost full. Rebecca sinks to the bottom. Janice tries to resuscitate her but realizes that "the worst thing that has ever happened to any woman in the world has happened to her" (265).

In the final part of the novel, Jack Eccles receives the call that Janice has drowned the baby. He tells Lucy. She asks why he bothers with Rabbit; Eccles replies that he loves him. She tells him that he should never have encouraged Rabbit and Janice to reunite. Rabbit calls; he is concerned that nobody is answering the telephone at his apartment. Eccles tells Rabbit what has happened. Stunned by the news, Rabbit struggles to focus. He spent the night before in a hotel; Ruth was not home. After hearing the news, he goes to the Springers' house where Janice is sleeping. Eccles is there. Mr. Springer tells Rabbit that they are all to blame; he and his wife never made Janice feel "secure" (274). He states that they still consider Rabbit part of the family. Rabbit puts Nelson to bed and glimpses Mrs. Springer crying in her room. He leaves for the apartment where the bathtub remains full of water. The next day he returns to the Springers.

Tothero visits, his face "half-paralyzed" (279). He attributes the accident to the recklessness of youth. Eccles tells Rabbit to atone by being a good husband and father. Rabbit asks him about the "the thing behind everything" that they used to discuss (282). Eccles tells him that it does not exist in the way he thinks it does. That night, Rabbit dreams that two disks hover in the sky; one is the sun and one is the moon. The sun, the stronger disk, is eclipsed by the moon. Rabbit senses that he has witnessed death and that he has a new message for the world. When he awakes he realizes that he has nothing to tell. He and Janice go to the apartment to dress for the funeral. Janice states that they can no longer live there. They return to the Springers; Rabbit dreads seeing his parents for the first time after the accident. They arrive and Mrs. Angstrom asks Rabbit what "they" have done to him. She embraces Janice; Rabbit surmises that she is sympathizing with Janice because her son has been "restored" to her (293). Eccles performs the service. At the cemetery, Harry tells Janice not to look at him; "I didn't kill her," he proclaims (295). He looks around at the mourners and tells them "She's the one" (296). He tries to placate Janice by recognizing that she didn't mean to kill Rebecca. He hates her for refusing to "join him in truth" (296). Seeing the horror on his mother's face, he turns and runs. Eccles tries to chase him but Rabbit gets away. He runs and runs, eventually losing his way. He calls Eccles from a cafeteria. His wife answers and hangs up when she hears his voice. He goes to Ruth who tells him that she is pregnant. Eccles called her half an hour ago; she knows about Rebecca. She tells Rabbit that he is "worse than nothing" but that she will marry him if he divorces Janice (304). Rabbit goes to the delicatessen for food, feeling suffocated by responsibility. Bewildered by the decisions that lie ahead of him, he finds comfort in walking around the block. The "sweet panic" grows "lighter and quicker and quieter" and he runs on (309).

Symbols & Motifs

Updike's conception of Rabbit Angstrom was influenced by Beatrix Potter's tale "Peter Rabbit." Peter Rabbit is trapped by the farmer, Mr. McGregor, when he disobeys his mother's orders and trespasses on his land. The name 'Rabbit' signifies entrapment and rebellion. Sports metaphors figure the different stages of Rabbit's trajectory and the tensions which characterise his quest. Rabbit is reminded of the maneuvers of the basketball game; his indecision makes him feel elusive, "impossible to capture": "It's like when they heard you were great and put two men on you and no matter which way you turned you bumped into one of them and the only thing to do was pass" (309). Golf serves as a metaphor for the religious quest and the golf course as a site for the contention between Rabbit and Eccles: Rabbit has one of his most powerful epiphanies on the golf course. Eccles feels that if he can beat Rabbit on the golf course, he can convince him to return to Janice. He realizes that it is Rabbit's commitment to the moment, which enables him to hit the ball so proficiently and which prompts him to abandon people on a whim.

For the men in the novel, cars symbolize both social status and the will to escape domestic boundaries. Eccles and Rabbit both fantasize about driving away from their lives; Rabbit fulfils his fantasy at the beginning of the novel. However, cars also symbolize entrapment for Rabbit; he resents working at his father-in-law's car lot where the Springers can keep an eye on him. It is running, not driving, that gives Rabbit the illusion of freedom. In the 1950s, the road became a dominant American symbol of mobility and escapism. Updike undermines this mythology; Rabbit's first escape ends when, faced with the highway, he becomes disoriented, panics, and heads back home. In Rabbit's trajectory, the metaphor of the road figures both moments of tenuous stability and dislocation. After Janice has given birth, Rabbit tells Lucy that while driving home he felt that he had a "straight road ahead" of him and that before that he was "sort of in the bushes and it didn't matter which way I went" (210). When Rabbit discovers that Mr. Springer has been paying rent during his absence, "The straight path is made smooth" (219). However, he is unable to "walk the straight line of paradox" that symbolizes Christianity.

Updike conceived the novel as a 'zig-zag' shape (Plath 48). The branches of the evergreen bushes in Mrs. Smith's garden take this shape; their "fingers" point "in every direction" and seem to belong to a "different land, whose gravity pulled softer than this one" (137); this image figures Rabbit's sense of otherness, his periodic sense of estrangement from American culture and his propulsion towards a different reality. Mrs. Smith's husband, also named Harry, bought a rare pink rhododendron which she named "Harry's Bianchi." She tells Rabbit that it is the only one in the United States; this also symbolizes Rabbit's own sense of exclusivity.

The second part of the novel opens with the sentence, "Sun and moon, sun and moon, time goes" (135). These images reappear in Rabbit's dream at the end of the novel; the sun eclipses the moon in a symbolic enactment of death. Rabbit fails to extract any kind of lesson about the passing of time and mortality; when he wakes, he realizes that he has no secret to impart to the world.

Historical Context

"Rabbit, Run" is written in the present tense and is situated firmly within its time. The novel explores the rise of middle-class, suburban America and the burgeoning influence of consumerism and popular culture. The novel makes several references to broader historical events. When the novel opens, President Eisenhower is holding talks with Prime Minister Macmillan in Gettysburg. The Dalai Lama has gone missing while the Tibetans fight the Chinese communists. Mrs. Smith and Rabbit discuss the impact of the Depression and World War II. Rabbit and Ruth go swimming on Memorial Day. However, most of the characters consider historical events in the light of their safe but sterile suburban lives. Lucy Eccles wonders what will happen to Christianity if the Russians take over America.

Societal Context

The novel contests the domestic idealism of fifties America. In attempting to explain his abandonment of Janice and Nelson, Rabbit tells Eccles: "It just felt like the whole business was fetching and making all the time. I don't know, it seemed like I was glued in with a lot of busted toys and empty glasses and television going and meals late and no way of getting out" (105). Even the minister sympathizes with Rabbit's predicament; he tells him that if he were to leave his wife, he would get in a car and drive thousands of miles away. Rabbit's mother also sympathizes with her son; he is a victim of the domestic ideology shaping the country: she tells Eccles that Janice has "everybody on her side from Eisenhower down" (161).

Janice's alcoholism undermines the mythology which placed women firmly within domestic boundaries. Most of the women in the novel are deeply unhappy; their situations anticipate the issues that would preoccupy the feminists of the sixties. Mrs. Zim, the Angstroms' old neighbor, used to spend her days screaming at her daughter. Eccles's wife is clearly miserable in her role as "the wife" (117). She also has "personality problems" with her daughters (118). Rabbit is shocked that a minister's wife openly "dislikes her own children!" (118). Lucy views her family situation from a psychoanalytical perspective; she would like a boy but feels that he would threaten her husband. She scoffs at her husband's statement that even a bad marriage is a sacrament. Like Rabbit, she wonders how she "[got] into" her marriage (189).

The novel undermines the strict gender polarizations that characterized the fifties. Unlike most of the women, Rabbit likes the idea of domesticity. He enjoys setting up house with Ruth; Eccles comments that Rabbit is "by nature a domestic creature" (157). Rabbit is adept at housekeeping, while Janice struggles to maintain order. In her alcoholic haze, Janice watches a program about a woman named Elizabeth and her husband; the husband's best friend comes to stay and turns out to be a better cook than Elizabeth. This program makes Janice "so nervous" that she "pours herself another drink" (258). Rabbit's sister Miriam resents housework; as the youngest, she was not "exposed to the bright heart of the kitchen" and was "sullen about assuming her share, which eventually became the greater share, because he was, after all, a boy" (219). Miriam distances herself from her family and embodies the sexual freedom that women of the sixties would enjoy; Rabbit is clearly conditioned by the gender ideology of the time; he is disgusted by Miriam's conduct at Club Castanet.

Updike also challenges the veneration surrounding the parent in fifties America. The novel represents parenthood as a form of impotence: as a father of two, Rabbit recognizes that he will never recapture the vitality of his past. After Janice has given birth, Rabbit realizes "the truth: the thing that has left his life has left irrevocably; no search would recover it. No flight would reach it. It was here, beneath the town, in these smells and these voices, forever behind him. The fullness ends when we give Nature her ransom, when we make children for her. Then she is through with us and we become first inside, and then outside, junk. Flower stalks" (226).

The fifties and sixties saw the rise of popular culture. Rabbit distances himself from popular culture; television is indicative of the sterility of domestic life. When we first meet Janice, she is watching television; Rabbit repeatedly refers to her as "dumb" and includes television in the list of traps that he wishes to escape. On the radio Rabbit hears a commercial for the Big Screen Westinghouse TV Set with One-Finger Automatic Tuning which delivers "needle-sharp pictures a nose away from the screen" (31). However, Jimmy Mouseketeer's advice resonates more clearly with Rabbit than any of the minister's words. Ruth and Rabbit go to the movies, but struggle to suspend their disbelief. Rabbit is depressed by the sight of Robert Donat, who is dying but pretending to be a Mandarin and Ruth asks if Ingrid Bergman is really a whore. Rabbit listens to popular songs on the radio; some of the song titles offer a meta-commentary on Rabbit's situation: "I Ran All the Way Home Just to Say I'm Sorry"; "Let's Stroll"; "Turn Me Loose"; "That Old Feeling" and "Almost Grown": both Eccles and Rabbit admit that they are immature.

As the economy continues to boom, class distinctions become increasingly tenuous. Sitting in the Springers large but cluttered house, Eccles sees through the trappings of middle-class prosperity and imagines that they are "on the porch of a shabby peeling house." He sees Mrs. Springer as "a long-suffering fat factory wife who had learned to take life as it came" and reflects: "That is what she looked like; that is what she might have been" (151). When Lucy Eccles refers to Freud, Rabbit perceives a connection with "the silver wallpaper and the watercolor of a palace and canal" and decides that the Eccles have "Class." However, as he looks at Lucy she appears to be merely a "fine-grained Ruth" (118). The novel satirizes the middle classes primarily through its treatment of the Springers and their recently acquired bourgeois sensibility. Eccles identifies Mrs. Springer's "ability to create uneasiness" as just one of the "strategies of her middle-class life." The cluttered Springer house is a parody of middle-class pretension: "each room seems to contain one more easy chair than is necessary" (150). Their large house offends Eccles's "aristocratic sense of place" (151).

Religious Context

Updike states that the novel is a "fairly deliberate attempt to examine the human predicament from a theological standpoint" and observes that, while Rabbit is not a "formal Christian," he is motivated by an "instinctiveness that his life must be important" (Plath 253, 254). He senses that "somewhere there was something better for him than listening to babies cry and cheating people in used-car lots" ("Rabbit, Run" 271). Rabbit's adult life is underpinned by a sense of loss; he spends much of the novel in existential angst, signified by his surname. When the novel opens, the Dalai Lama has gone missing in the wake of the Tibet's conflict with China. Eccles had a very religious grandfather who asked him if he believed in Hell. He tells Rabbit that his idea of Hell is separation from God and that even "the blackest atheist" could not imagine this. Rabbit concedes to Eccles that he senses the presence of something behind life's surface that "wants [him] to find it" (127). At the beginning of the novel Janice watches a children's programme featuring Jimmie Mouseketeer who tells the viewers: "God doesn't want a tree to be a waterfall, or a flower to be a stone. God gives to each one of us a special talent" (9). Rabbit's one talent—his athleticism—has religious meaning for him. He explains this to Eccles: "I once did something right. I played first-rate basketball. I really did. And after you're first-rate at something, no matter what, it kind of takes the kick out of being second-rate" (107). Eccles later admits that he was impressed by this philosophy.

The epigraph of "Rabbit, Run" comes from Pascal and foreshadows the tensions in the novel: "The motions of Grace, the hardness of the heart; external circumstances." Eccles warned his wife to keep her heart open to grace before they got married; she, like Rabbit, wrestles with the demands of external circumstances. In a feature for the *Independent on Sunday* Updike, a Christian, writes of his interest in the philosophies of Kierkegaard and Karl Barth. He acknowledges that he "took from Kierkegaard the idea that subjectivity too has its rightful claims" (843). Marshall Brown's study of the Rabbit tetralogy examines the Kierkegaardian strain of the Rabbit novels in detail. Several critics have used Kierkegaardian models to analyze Rabbit's sensibility: he is, potentially, a 'Knight of Faith,' committed to his individual identity, rather than a 'Knight of Resignation.' Comparisons between Rabbit and Jesus resurface continually in the text. The first day that Rabbit wakes up with Ruth is Palm Sunday. Rabbit sees a picture of a carpenter in the Eccles's house and the protective glass "gives back to [him] the shadow of his own head" (124). Mrs. Smith tells Rabbit that he has kept her alive. Ruth observes that Eccles has filled Rabbit with delusions about his Christ-like sensibility. When Eccles dismisses Rabbit's quest as an excuse for vagrancy, Rabbit sees a parallel with Jesus. Eccles replies that Christ warned saints not to marry.

Rabbit takes comfort from religious abstractions, but views religious institutions with suspicion; several of the characters express irreverence towards religion. Rabbit has always fantasized about a "little Catholic from a shabby house, dressed in flashy bargain clothes" (137). In Lancaster he passes an Amish buggy and feels obliged to respect "the good life these people lead" but is unable to shake off the image of the bearded man and the woman in black as devils. He figures their buggy as a "Tall coffin lined with hair clopping along to the tune of a dying horse" and dismisses the Amish as "fanatics" (29). Mrs. Smith's friend compares her garden to heaven and Mrs. Smith jokes that she need not waste her time driving to church every Sunday if heaven is simply a replica of her garden. People turn to religion for seemingly arbitrary reasons. In St. Joseph's hospital Rabbit reads a Catholic magazine article about a man who "becomes so interested in how legally unfair it was for Henry VIII to confiscate the property of the monasteries that he becomes a Roman Catholic convert and eventually a monk" (195). Jack Eccles is figured as a "captor"; Rabbit "feels caught" in his handshake (102). When Rabbit visits church he is momentarily enraptured by the "beauty of belief" but is irritated by Eccles's "affected" and "nasal-pious voice" (235, 236). Despite drawing affinities between his life and Christ's, he hardly listens to the sermon on Christ's temptation. Eccles argues for the relevance of this story in twentieth-century America but Rabbit senses the minister's doubt. Rabbit has no "taste for the dark, visceral aspect of Christianity, the going through quality of it, the passage into death and suffering that redeems" (237). Nevertheless, Rabbit is unwilling to give up the idea of faith. He is disconcerted by Ruth's conviction that God does not exist: "Her rasp, her sureness, makes him wince; he wonders if he's lying. If he is, he is hung in the middle of nowhere, and the thought hollows him, makes his heart tremble. Across the street a few people in their best clothes walk on the pavement past the row of worn brick homes; are they walking on air? Their clothes, they put on their best clothes: he clings to the thought giddily; it seems a visual proof of the unseen world" (91). However, he is also excited by the thought of having sex while the church is full. Rabbit experiences a number of quasi-religious epiphanies in his everyday life. As he dresses for his blind date with Ruth he feels that the juncture of his tie, the collar of his shirt, and the base of his throat are "the arms of star that will … extend outward to the rim of the universe" (50–1). For that moment, "He is the Dalai Lama" (51). Playing basketball fills him with transcendental joy. On the golf course, he strikes one perfect ball and Rabbit proclaims, "That's it!" with a "smile of aggrandizement" (134). Episodes of quasi-religious exultation are countered by moments of nihilism: waiting for Janice to give birth, Rabbit sees his life as "a sequence on

grotesque poses assumed to no purpose, a magic dance empty of belief" (198).

The other characters struggle to find spiritual fulfilment. Jack Eccles wrestles with Christian doctrine and, ironically, finds solace in Rabbit's fidelity to the self. Eccles views himself as a kind of trickster:

> "With his white collar he forges God's name on every word he speaks. He steals belief from the children he is supposed to be teaching. He murders faith in the minds of any who really listen to his babble. He commits fraud with every schooled cadence of the service" (154).

Lucy, his wife, wishes that religion was extinct and characterises Christianity as "neurotic" (241). The Angstroms are Lutherans: Eccles characterises Luther as a man who "overstat[ed] half truths in a kind of comic wrath" yet senses that Reverend Kruppenbach, the Lutheran minister, is correct in his evaluation of the role of religion in contemporary America (161). In twentieth-century suburbia, faith must adapt to changes in social status: "The Springers were Episcopalians, more of the old phony's social climbing, they were originally Reformeds" (101). Rabbit's mother becomes embroiled in an argument with the Methodists next door who refuse to cut more than their own half of the lawn.

As Janice tries to resuscitate her daughter, she prays frantically and senses that a "third person" has entered the apartment; God's presence is figured in as Mrs. Springer knocks on the door (265). After Rebecca's death, Eccles reverts to conventional Christian wisdom; he tells Rabbit to stop seeking the "thing behind everything" and to turn to Christ for forgiveness (282). Rabbit struggles to see the relevance of his words. After his dream of the sun and moon, Rabbit realizes that he has no message for the world. As he stands outside Ruth's house at the end of the novel, Rabbit seeks out the church window for guidance. He sees only a "dark circle in a stone façade" (308). He finds comfort, however, in the streetlights and begins to run.

Scientific & Technological Context
Rabbit is dissatisfied by his job, yet he acknowledges that he "was not entirely miscast as a barker for the Magi-Peel Peeler" (219). He is a more efficient housekeeper than Janice and has "an instinctive taste for the small appliances of civilization, the little grinders and slicers and holders" (219). Rabbit marvels at the processes of nature as he enjoys working in Mrs. Smith's garden; the lawnmower is presented rather comically as part of the natural process: "Fragrant of gasoline" it "chews the petals" (136).

Some of the characters are flummoxed by the simplest forms of technology. Eccles is unable to assemble his children's swing-slide-and-sandbox set. Technology is also associated with bourgeois pretension. Janice incites Mrs. Angstrom's disdain when she asks why they don't own a washing machine. The Springers' house is full of easy chairs. Although Rabbit's car delivers him from Janice, he loses his way and finds it easier to turn back than continue. Running affords Rabbit more freedom.

Biographical Context
Born March 18th, 1932, John Hoyer Updike was raised in Shillington, Pennsylvania. In 1950 he was awarded a scholarship to Harvard University. When he graduated, he won a Knox fellowship and attended the Ruskin School of Drawing and Fine Art in Oxford, England. *The New Yorker* accepted his first story, "Friends from Philadelphia." From 1955-7 Updike worked as a reporter for the magazine. He lived in New York with his wife Mary E. Pennington, whom he later divorced, and daughter Elizabeth. In 1957 the Updikes moved to Massachusetts. Updike's first novel, "The Poorhouse Fair," was published in 1959. The following year, he published "Rabbit,

Run," the first novel in the Rabbit tetralogy. "Rabbit Redux" appeared in 1971; the novel dramatized Rabbit's involvement with the sixties counter-culture and was less well received than the other Rabbit novels. "Rabbit is Rich" (1981) is generally regarded as the finest novel in the series; it won the Pulitzer Prize, the National Book Critics Circle Award and the National Book Award. "Rabbit at Rest" (1990) also won the Pulitzer Prize and the National Book Critics Circle Award. In 1977 Updike married his second wife, Martha Bernhard.

Updike is celebrated for his poetic rendering of consciousness and experiments with form. He has written short stories, short story sequences, poems and essays of criticism. In 2004 Updike was awarded the PEN/Faulkner award for "The Early Stories; 1953–1975." Some of his works are linked by place: "The Olinger Stories," for example, take place in a fictional representation of Shillington, Updike's home town. Dominant themes of his fiction include: the dilemmas of masculinity; the tension between the individual and the community; the mechanisms of consciousness; the lives of middle-class America. Infidelity, another preoccupation, is the main theme of "Couples" (1968); the novel generated some controversy by depicting adultery as a form of spiritual gratification in the postmodern era. "The Witches of Eastwick" (1984) was made into a major film. In 2000 Updike published "Licks of Love," a collection of short stories which included a novella, "Rabbit Remembered." His latest novel is "Terrorist" (2006).

Rachel Lister

Works Cited
Boswell, Marshall. *John Updike's Rabbit Tetralogy: Mastered Irony in Motion.* Columbia: U of Missouri 2001.

Iwamoto, Iwao. "A Visit to Mr. Updike." Plath 115–24.

Kimmel, Michael. New York: Free, 1996.

Nunley, Jan. "Thoughts of Faith Infuse Updike's Novels." Plath 248–60.

Plath, James, Ed. "Conversations with John Updike." *Literary Conversations Series.* Jackson: UP of Mississippi, 1994.

Reilly, Charlie. "A Conversation with John Updike." Plath 124–51.

Rhode, Eric. "John Updike Talks About the Shapes and Subjects of His Fiction." Plath 46–55.

Samuels, Charles Thomas. "The Art of Fiction XLIII: John Updike." Plath 22–45.

Updike, John. "In Response to a request from The Independent on Sunday of London, for a contribution to their weekly feature "A Book That Changed Me." *Odd Jobs: Essays and Criticism.* London: Deutsch, 1991. 843–4.

——. *Rabbit, Run.* 1960. London: Penguin, 1995.

Discussion Questions

1. Updike states that writing in the present tense in "Rabbit, Run" enabled him to "move between minds, between thoughts and objects and events with a curious ease" (41). Discuss the effects of the use of the present tense in the novel. How does this sense of 'ease' impact on your reading of the novel as a whole?

2. Updike aims to reflect reality by leaving something "in the air" at the end of his novels: "that's how life is, that's how a book should be" (118). Does Updike achieve this aim in "Rabbit, Run"?

3. "'Cause you haven't given up. In your stupid way you're still fighting" ("Rabbit, Run" 92). What forces is Rabbit fighting in "Rabbit, Run"?

4. Discuss Updike's treatment of popular culture in "Rabbit, Run." What role does it play in Rabbit's life?

5. "… the strategies of middle-class life" ("Rabbit, Run," 150). How significant is class status in "Rabbit, Run"?

6. "With women, you keep bumping against them, because they want different things, they're a different race" (93). Examine Rabbit's encounters with women in "Rabbit, Run." Do any patterns emerge?

7. "The fullness ends when we give Nature her ransom, when we make children for her" (226). Discuss Updike's portrayal of parenthood.

8. "Youth is death. Youth is careless" (280). Does the rest of the novel support Tothero's statement?

9. "In large part, it's other men who are important to American men; American men define their masculinity, not as much in relation to women, but in relation to each other" (Michael Kimmel, "Manhood in America: A Cultural History" 7). Examine the male relationships in "Rabbit, Run." To what extent does the novel sustain this statement?

10. Rabbit feels that his rich interior life distinguishes him from the rest of humanity. Discuss the significance of his dreams and daydreams.

Essay Ideas

1. "I really begin with some kind of solid, coherent image, some notion of the book and even its texture ... "Rabbit, Run" was a kind of zig-zag." Discuss the significance of the zig-zag image for "Rabbit, Run."

2. "It's the kind of hero I come up with again and again: a person who combines good and the absence of it in an interesting, sometimes comical, way" (Plath 128–9). Discuss Rabbit's credentials as hero and anti-hero.

3. "The motions of Grace, the hardness of the heart; external circumstances" (epigraph to "Rabbit, Run"). To what extent do these forces shape "Rabbit, Run"?

4. "Of course, all vagrants think they're on a quest. At least at first" ("Rabbit, Run" 128). What kind of meanings accumulate around the idea of a 'quest' in the novel?

5. Updike states that the novel is a "fairly deliberate attempt to examine the human predicament from a theological standpoint." In the light of this statement, explore the representation of religion and religious experience in "Rabbit, Run."

The Red Tent

by Anita Diamant

Content Synopsis

"The Red Tent" tells the story of the four wives of Jacob and his children, specifically his daughter Dinah, the narrator of the story. Dinah is Leah's daughter, and the only female offspring of Jacob.

The story opens with Jacob having left Canaan and traveled to see his uncle Laban in Haran. Although the younger son, Jacob was chosen as the favorite by his mother Rebecca and thus was chased off the land by his jealous brother Esau. Upon arriving at Laban's camp, Jacob sees Laban's beautiful daughter Rachel and falls in love with her. Jacob proves to be a reliable worker for Laban who allows him to marry Rachel when she is old enough. In return, Jacob agrees to provide Laban with seven years of service. When the time comes for the two to be married, Rachel is tricked by Zilpah, one of Laban's illegitimate daughters. Zilpah is close to Leah, Laban's oldest daughter, and knows she has feelings for Jacob. Zilpah convinces Rachel that the wedding night will be horrible and Rachel agrees to let Leah switch places with her. Leah and Jacob are then married and have a wonderful passionate week together. Rachel is now jealous of Leah and eager to marry Jacob. Leah learns that she is pregnant before Rachel's wedding to Jacob and nine months later gives birth, with the help of her sisters and Inna the midwife to a son, Reuben.

Over the years, Leah continues to have many children, eight in all, while Rachel remains barren.

Zilpah and Billah, who are offered to Jacob as part of Leah's and Rachel's dowries, eventually bear Jacob's children as well. Zilpah gives birth to twins Gad and Asher but almost dies in childbirth and refuses to lie with Jacob again. Billah gives birth to Dan as an offering to the childless Rachel but after his birth, Rachel accepts that this is not her child and again despairs her infertility.

Rachel begins to learn the ways of the midwife from Inna and becomes quite gifted in the practice. Leah's last child is a daughter, Dinah, and all of the sisters rejoice. Shortly after the birth of Dinah, Rachel conceives, and a son Joseph, is born. Dinah and Joseph spend much of their childhood playing together.

All of Jacob's wives share their child-rearing responsibilities. Because Dinah is the only daughter, she is doted on by her "mothers" and allowed to stay in the red tent during their monthly cycle. Here she listens to their stories and songs and observes their duties cooking and caring for the men. She also observes Rachel and begins to pick up the skills that help her to eventually develop into a skilled midwife.

After serving the ungrateful Laban for many years, Jacob decides to move back to his homeland. He negotiates for some of Laban's livestock and household goods and after months of planning Jacob and his family set out for Canaan. Rachel steals Laban's teraphim, household gods, and claims them as protectors for the women.

Along their journey, Dinah loves observing all of the different travelers and scenery and is especially drawn to the river. During one night camped at the river Jacob is attacked and almost dies but the women tend to him and pray to the ancient gods for his survival. As Jacob recovers, he anxiously awaits the reunion with his brother Esau, fearing that Esau will want revenge.

When Esau and Jacob are finally reunited, the two embrace and old grudges are forgotten. The brothers introduce their families and Dinah befriends her cousin Tabea. Eventually, the family of Jacob travels to meet his mother, the great and formidable Rebecca. Rebecca is the oldest person Dinah has ever seen and she is impressed by her decorative appearance and colorful robes. Rebecca is viewed as an oracle in Canaan and people travel miles to receive her counsel.

Dinah is impressed with her grandmother until Tabea arrives months later. Rebecca banishes Tabea and her mother from the family because they did not follow the appropriate custom when Tabea became a woman. Dinah is devastated and harbors a deep anger towards grandmother. As the family is about to depart, Rebecca requests that Dinah stay with her. She tells Dinah that her mother will not allow her to be disgraced like Tabea when she reaches womanhood. She warns her that she will suffer some unhappiness in her life but her life will be very long.

Dinah returns home and Jacob decides to relocate his growing flocks and family. Shortly after, Dinah begins menstruating. Her mothers honor her entry into womanhood with wine, fine food and offerings to the moon. They take her clothes and offer her blood to one of the household goddesses. She dreams of a creature and Inna tells her that it is Taweret, an Egyptian water goddess who lives in the river.

Inna and Rachel acquire a reputation for their skills in midwifery and travel frequently. Dinah joins them and begins to learn the ways of the midwife. They are called into the walled city of Shechem to deliver a child of King Hamor by one of his concubines. While there, Dinah meets and falls in love with Hamor's oldest son, Shalem. The two make love and are married. The king offers a generous bride-price to Jacob who is outraged and refuses. He eventually agrees to the marriage if Hamor, Shalem and all the men in his kingdom will be circumcised. Much to Jacob's surprise, they agree.

Shalem gets circumcised and is healing in bed with Dinah when one night she awakes to find him murdered beside her. Dinah's brothers, Simon and Levi, had entered the city and killed every man they could find. Dinah walks back to her family and disowns them all. Disgraced, Jacob changes his name and leaves the area forever.

Dinah returns to Shechem and is taken in by Hamor's wife, Re-nefer, who takes Dinah with her to Egypt to her brother Nakht-re's home. On the journey, Dinah learns that she is pregnant and Re-nefer has hopes that Dinah's son will be a future prince of Egypt. When Dinah gives birth to a son, she names him Bar-Shalem after her husband but Re-nefer changes his name to Re-mose and threatens to throw Dinah out if she does not call him by that name. Re-nefer takes Re-mose as her own child and Dinah is reduced to the role of wet nurse. Even so, she takes great pleasure in being one of Re-mose's mothers and settles into her new role in the house of Nakht-re.

When Re-mose turns nine, he is sent away to school to become a scribe and over the years away becomes a stranger to her. Dinah befriends the midwife Meryt and eventually becomes a famed midwife herself in the region. She meets a man; a carpenter named Benia, and is attracted to him. Before she can accept his advances, Re-mose returns and Dinah abandons her plans to move on.

A few years later, Re-nefer and then Nakht-re die and Dinah decides to move to the Valley of the Kings with Meryt and resumes her work as a midwife. A few months later, Benia arrives at her door and the two fall in love and begin a happy life together. One day, Re-mose appears at their door and requests her services as a midwife on behalf of his boss, a vizier, whose wife is in labor. Dinah agrees and helps to deliver a healthy baby but falls ill herself and must stay at the vizier's palace for a week to recover. An attendant, Shery, tells Dinah the vizier's story and she figures out that the man who now is called Zafenat Paneh-ah is really her brother Joseph.

Once Re-mose learns the story of his father's murder, he blames Joseph and threatens to kill him. Joseph tells Dinah she must convince Re-mose to leave the area forever or he will be executed for his threats. Re-mose agrees to leave and she says goodbye to him forever. Dinah returns to Benia and tells him the story of Shalem's murder by her brothers that she had kept hidden for so long.

Years later, Joseph comes to Dinah because their father is dying and he wants Dinah to accompany him. She and Benia go with him and when they arrive Jacob is delirious. He does not remember Dinah but as she talks to her niece Gera she learns that her story has lived on in the family. She returns home with Benia and a few years later she dies peacefully at home satisfied with the life that she has lived.

Symbols & Motifs

The red tent is the most prominent symbol in the "The Red Tent." It represents the bond that women share and serves as a gathering place where they can escape their duties to the men and focus on each other. Regardless of what goes on in the outside world, the women are united in the red tent. They sing songs, tell stories and spoil themselves with fine food and drink. It is here that Dinah hears the stories of her mothers and learns the traditions that she will take with her as she grows up and moves away.

The river represents change. Dinah first encounters it when her family leaves Laban's land and travels toward Canaan. She embraces its smell and freshness and is invigorated by its power and swiftness. It both scares and entices Dinah when she first encounters it. Years later, Benia teaches her to swim in the river and it serves as a symbol of her breaking free from her past and moving forward in life.

The act of childbirth appears frequently in "The Red Tent." Inna, Rachel, Dinah and Meryt are midwives and thus several scenes involve women in labor and babies being delivered. Diamant emphasizes both the harsh reality and the miracle of childbirth, as well as the strength of women for persevering through the act, even if they do not always survive.

Motherhood is perhaps the most important motif in the novel. Anita Diamant takes special care to honor the role of the mother in this novel. While the men have the dominant role in the Bible, they are secondary characters in Diamant's story with the women and mothers given responsibility for nurturing, instilling values and passing down stories and customs to the future generations. Dinah is lucky enough to have four mothers whose guidance during her childhood allowed her to survive and overcome the challenges of her adulthood. From Leah's leadership and her unselfish devotion to family, to Rachel's skills in midwifery, to Zilpah's gift for storytelling, and Billah's kindness and insight, each of Dinah's mothers contributed something unique to her life. While her own role as a mother was quite different, her devotion to her son and the sacrifices she makes for him further emphasize the selfless role of the mother.

Historical Context

The concept of a "red tent" where women gather during their monthly menstrual cycle is known to have existed in ancient Native American and African cultures but there is no record of it being used in Near Eastern society (www.anitadiamant.com).

Societal Context

While the story is fictional and not based on actual events, "The Red Tent" accurately portrays domestic life and the roles of women in the Near East in ancient society, approximately 1500 BCE (www.anitadiamant.com). Living in a patriarchal society, women had much responsibility but limited rights and participation (www.mideastweb.org).

Marriages were often arranged by parents who tried to find a match in the same village. Marriages between cousins were acceptable as was polygamy (Thompson). The most important duty of a married woman was to give birth, preferably to a son (Thompson). Daughters were loved as well but they were not as valuable because they would have to leave upon getting married (Thompson). It was fairly common for a wife to have a personal slave and if the wife could not have children, the slave would be offered to the husband as a surrogate (Thompson). Women were in charge of raising the children and tending to the home. Cooking was a major part of a woman's day. Bread was baked every few days. Women also took on the responsibility of taking fruits, vegetables, wool and handmade items to cities to sell (www.mideastweb.org).

Religious Context

Genesis, Chapter 29 of the Bible, describes Jacob's wooing of the beautiful Rachel and how he came to marry "tender-eyed" Leah first (King James Bible, Genesis 29). The Bible indicates that Jacob fell in love with Rachel and her father Laban agreed to marry them but at the last minute the brides are switched so Jacob unwittingly marries Leah instead (King James Bible, Genesis 29). After confronting Laban, Jacob is allowed to marry Rachel too. He also inherits Leah and Rachel's handmaids Zilpah and Billah (King James Bible, Genesis 29). Since Leah is the "hated" wife, God rewards her with many children and makes the beautiful Rachel barren for many years (King James Bible, Genesis 29). Contrary to the Bible, in "The Red Tent" Leah is not tender-eyed but has two different color eyes and an intense stare that causes people to turn from her gaze. She is depicted as a leader and source of strength in the family and Jacob has both admiration and affection for her.

The only mention of Leah's Dinah in the Bible is known as "The Rape of Dinah" in Genesis, Chapter 34 in which the Prince of Shechem, Shalem, after allegedly raping Dinah, is murdered by two of Dinah's brothers. In the Bible, Shalem lies with Dinah and then decides he wants to marry her. Jacob agrees under the condition that all of the men of the city undergo circumcision. Shalem and his father Hamor agree but after they are circumcised, Dinah's brothers Simon and Levi go into the city, murder all the men and take their wives and their riches (King James Bible, Genesis 34). Since Dinah is never given a voice in the Bible, Diamant decided to expand on Dinah's story by making her an active participant in the love affair with Shalem rather than a victim.

Scientific & Technological Context

"The Red Tent" does not have a specific scientific or technological context.

Biographical Context

Anita Diamant is a freelance writer whose nonfiction has been published in established periodicals such as *The Boston Globe*, *Yankee Magazine*, *Parenting*, *Self* and *McCalls* (www.anitadiamant.com). She often writes about Jewish living. "The Red Tent" was her first published work of fiction (www. anitadiamant.com). Other books she has written include: "The New Jewish Wedding," "Choosing a Jewish Life," "Good Harbor," and "The Last Days of Dogtown: A Novel" (www.anitadiamant.com). She lives in Massachusetts.

Jennifer Bouchard

Works Cited

Anita Diamant.com. 3 September 2008. Diamant, Anita. *The Red Tent*. New York: Picador USA, 1997.

"The King James Bible." *Internet Sacred Text Archive*. 2008. 3 September 2008.

Discussion Questions

1. What is the role of the red tent in the novel?
2. Who was your favorite character and why?
3. Who was your least favorite character and why?
4. Discuss some of the sacrifices that the wives of Jacob made for their family. What do the women gain from helping each other?
5. What are the main themes present in "The Red Tent"?
6. How does the time in which the story was written play a role in the story's overarching themes?
7. What do you think of the relationship between Rachel and Leah?
8. Discuss the role of Rebekah in "The Red Tent."
9. The Bible describes Dinah's relationship with Shalem as rape whereas it is depicted as a love affair in "The Red Tent." Why do you think Diamant chose to represent Dinah's story this way.
10. Discuss Dinah's relationship with her son.
11. Compare the social interactions between men and women today to those during the time in which "The Red Tent" is set.
12. In what ways does Dinah represent the modern woman?

Essay Ideas

1. Compare the stories of Jacob and his wives in the Bible to "The Red Tent."
2. Describe and analyze Diamant's literary style. Focus on the structure of her narratives, characters, dialogue and common themes.
3. Write an essay in which you analyze each of the wives and the role they play in the story. Be sure to discuss the special relationships that the women have with one another.
4. Analyze the role of men in "The Red Tent."
5. Write an essay in which you analyze some of the symbols in the novel. Be sure to cite specific examples from the text to support your ideas.

Sula

by Toni Morrison

Content Synopsis

"Sula" opens by introducing us to a place in the hills called "the Bottom" that was once inhabited by black people ("Sula" 3). The land has been stripped of its trees to make way for houses and the Medallion City Golf course. The narrator remembers the Bottom as a place where strangers would hear a "shucking, knee-slapping, wet-eyed laughter" without noticing the pain beneath it (4). The hilly land on the Bottom was difficult to manage. The citizens joke that slaves were tricked into taking it by their masters who lived on the "rich valley floor" but promised their slaves the best land at "the bottom of heaven" (5). In 1920 the residents of the Bottom were preoccupied with two of their citizens: Shadrack and Sula. Shadrack founded National Suicide Day when he returned from the war, traumatized by witnessing a soldier's face being blown off. Although suffering from shellshock, Shadrack was released from the hospital. Unable to function properly, he was arrested for intoxication. In the jail cell he saw his reflection in the toilet bowl. His "blackness" told him who he was and he slept peacefully (13). On his way back to Medallion, Shadrack decided to dedicate one day a year to his fear of the "unexpectedness" of death (14).

Other citizens include Wiley Wright and his wife, Helene Sabat. Helene was raised by her Catholic grandmother. Her mother was a Creole prostitute. The couple has a daughter, Nel, whom Helene raises with a firm hand. When Helene's grandmother falls sick, Helene reluctantly returns to New Orleans with Nel. She is reprimanded on the train for walking through the "white only" compartment. When Helene is reprimanded by the conductor, she responds with a dazzling smile. The black soldiers on the train look at Helene with hatred and Nel resolves to "always be on her guard" (22). When they arrive, Mrs. Sabat is already dead. Helene's mother is there. She hugs Nel but Helene keeps her distance. They return to Medallion and Nel feels that she has changed. She looks in the mirror and recognizes herself as Nel, rather than as merely Helene's daughter. This gives her the courage to befriend Sula Peace, a girl at school whose family her mother dismisses as "sooty" (29). When Sula visits, Helene accepts her; Sula has none of the "slackness" of her mother, Hannah (29).

Sula lives in an ever-expanding house, ruled over by her one-legged grandmother, Eva. Eva's husband Boyboy left her with three children: Hannah, Pearl and Plum. She left them with a neighbor for eighteen months and returned with only one leg and money. She built her own house, took in tenants and retreated to her bedroom. She took in three boys and named them all Dewey. Although they are of different ages and ethnic backgrounds, they embrace their collective identity. Another tenant, Tar Baby, is believed to be "half-white" (39).

He lives on cheap wine and seems intent on killing himself. Sula's father dies when she is young. Hannah sleeps with the husbands of her friends and neighbors. Plum served in the war and returns after years of traveling, still clearly traumatized. One night Eva pours kerosene over her son, lights a stick and throws it onto his bed.

Nel and Sula walk to the ice cream parlor under the gaze of men. A man named Ajax says the words "pig meat" as they walk by. When some boys threaten them, Sula takes a knife and slashes off the tip of her finger. The boys retreat. One day Sula overhears Hannah saying that she loves Sula but does not like her. Sula and Nel meet a boy called Chicken Little. He and Sula climb a tree. When they descend, Sula picks him up and swings him around. He slips from her hands and lands in the river where he drowns. The girls run to Shadrack's house across the river to find out if he saw the accident. Sula is about to ask him if he saw what happened and he smiles at her and says the word "Always" (61). Sula runs out of the house and cries. She is thinking of Shadrack and the sense of "promise" encapsulated by the word "Always." Nel and Sula attend Chicken Little's funeral.

Hannah asks Eva why she killed Plum. Eva responds that Plum wanted to crawl back into her womb when he returned from war. She killed him so that he could die like a man. A few days later, Eva sees Hannah on fire in the yard. She rushes out to save her but it is too late. As Eva lies in shock she recalls seeing Sula on the porch, simply watching her mother burn. The action moves to Nel's wedding. Jude Greene proposed when he learned that a new road was being constructed to transport merchants to Medallion. When he is passed over for "thin-armed white boys," he turns to marriage as a "posture of adulthood" (82). Nel's wedding day is the last time she will see Sula for ten years.

In part two, Sula returns. Eva asks her when she is going to get married and have children and Sula replies that she does not want to make anyone but herself. They argue, accusing each other of watching their loved ones burn. Sula sends Eva to an old people's home. Nel is shocked that Eva is in a home run by white people. Sula says that she was scared of being burned and had nowhere else to go but home. Jude enters and complains about work. Sula challenges him, joking that he should be flattered that "everything in the world" worries about black men (103). Nel and Jude laugh. The narrative perspective shifts to the first person: Nel recounts finding Sula and Jude naked on her floor. Jude saw her and cast her the same look of resentment as the soldiers on the train to New Orleans. Sula sat naked on the bed, as if waiting for them to argue and be done. Jude departed, leaving only a tie. Nel tries to avoid the gray ball in the corner of her eye which represents her pain. Unable to release her grief for the loss of her husband and friend, Nel mourns over the emptiness of her thighs. The community turns against Sula when it learns that she put out Eva and took Jude only to reject him for other men. The men of Medallion ensure that Sula is cast out forever when they hear that she sleeps with white men. Accidents begin to happen around her. Suspicion grows when one of the citizens sees Shadrack tip his hat at Sula. Sula has no sense of compunction towards Nel; she presumed that she could sleep with Jude because they had always shared everything. She is disappointed that Nel has capitulated to the town's narrow values. She sleeps with lots of men but finds that sex compounds her loneliness until Ajax comes to her door with an offering of milk bottles. With Ajax, Sula begins to understand the meaning of "possession" (131). Ajax tells her that Tar Baby has been arrested for an offense committed by the mayor's niece. He had been stumbling along the road, drunk, and she had swerved to avoid him, hitting another car. When Ajax complained, he was arraigned. When Sula offers him sympathy, Ajax decides to leave. Sula is haunted by his absence. She realizes that she has "sung all the songs there are" (137).

Three years after Sula slept with her husband, Nel calls on her. Sula is suffering from a mysterious illness. Nel asks why she slept with Jude. Sula tells her that she needed him to fill up a space in her head. Nel is shocked that Sula did not even love Jude. Sula refuses to live by Nel's standards of good and bad. She predicts that the world will love her when these standards lose their currency. Nel leaves and Sula dreams of the Clabber Girl Baking Powder lady who beckons to her but disintegrates when she approaches Sula. The baking powder chokes Sula and she wakes up, in pain. She imagines jumping out of the window and finally being alone. She remembers the word "always" and tries to recall who promised her a "sleep of water" with that one word (149). As Sula dies, she looks forward to the time when she will tell Nel about the ease of death. The community sees Sula's death as a good omen. Their optimism is compounded by the construction of a new old people's home and a tunnel across the river. However, there is a sudden frost that October. The citizens are housebound and fall ill. When the frost thaws, a restlessness sets in. Those who had blamed Sula for their misfortunes have no one to "rub up against" (153). Meanwhile Shadrack has begun to feel lonely. He looks at a purple and white belt that Sula left behind and remembers saying the word "always" to reassure the girl of permanency. He sees Sula's body in a coffin at the undertaker's. After this, he gives up his daily routine. He reluctantly prepares for National Suicide Day. This year, the community joins his parade. They march to the mouth of the tunnel that they were not allowed to build and smash the materials. Many of them perish on their way down the tunnel, including Tar Baby and the Deweys.

The action leaps forward to 1965. Black and white people have begun to integrate. The community in the Bottom has dissolved as more people have moved to the valley. The hilly land has become more valuable so that black people cannot afford to move back. Nel remembers the boys of 1921 fondly. She has failed to have lasting relationships with men and her love for her children has dwindled. She visits Eva who asks her why she killed the little boy in the river. Nel tells her that Sula killed him and Eva reminds her that she watched the little boy die. She says that Plum tells her these things. She remembers the death of Chicken Little and wonders why she did not feel guilty. She visits Sula's grave. She recalls how nobody went to collect Sula's body when they heard that she was dead. Nel herself had to call the mortuary. When Nel leaves the cemetery, she sees Shadrack. He recognizes her as a face from the past but cannot identify her. Nel sees a ball of fur scatter in the breeze. She realizes that all this time she has been missing Sula, not Jude.

Symbols & Motifs

Clothes and colors take on symbolic significance in "Sula." Brights colors figure individuality, often distinguishing those who are marginalized by society. Rochelle, Helene's prostitute mother, wears a canary yellow dress. Sula wears a purple and white belt. When Sula dons a green ribbon, however, Ajax reads this as a sign of her burgeoning dependence on him. The color red signifies death: shortly before she dies, Hannah has a dream in which she wears a red wedding dress. She is consumed by flames, her dying body surrounded by smashed tomatoes.

The novel abounds with omens and presentiments. Before she dies, Sula dreams of the Clabber Girl Baking Powder lady disintegrating in her hands. "[E]xcesses in nature" mark disturbances in Medallion (89): a plague of robins accompanies Sula on her return and an October frost follows her death. Spring arrives in January and unexpected gales of wind bring no rain or lightning.

Names are clearly significant in "Sula." Some critics have objected to Morrison's treatment of black men in the novel. Names such as Dewey, Boyboy and Chicken Little suggest their infantile qualities. In the prelude to the novel, Shadrack is identified as a foil to Sula. His narrative emulates that of his biblical namesake whose faith saved him from death and won him recognition.

Morrison's symbols are characteristically ambiguous and their significance changes as the novel unfolds. The gray ball symbolises Nel's pain at Jude's betrayal. At the end of the novel a soft ball of fur fragments and Nel recognizes her pain for what it is: her longing for Sula. Sula's birthmark—a stemmed rose that stretches from her eyelid towards her brow—figures her connection with the natural world and symbolizes her vitality and nonconformity; it gives her face "a broken excitement and blue-blade threat" (52). When the community learns that she has slept with Jude and put out Eva, they read the mark as a sign of evil. However, when Shadrack encounters Sula, he sees a tadpole over her eye: a sign of friendship and the mark of the fish he loves.

In a novel populated by mothers, maternal imagery abounds: the image of Nel "excret[ing], "milk-warm commiseration" for her husband (103); the milk bottle which Ajax drains before handing it to Sula, the one woman who can match his mother's self-sufficiency; Nel's intuition that her children's love has dried up because their mouths "quickly forgot the taste of her nipples" (165).

The final image of "Sula" reflects tensions embodied by the novel's structure. Morrison leaves us with the sound of Nel's cry; it has "no bottom and no top, just circles and circles of sorrow" (174): this image figures the primacy of circularity and repetition over the tyranny of linear time and the hierarchical social structures which marginalize the citizens of the Bottom.

Societal Context

Before reaching its final chapter, the novel stretches from 1919 to 1941. Morrison dramatizes some of the effects of racist ideology on American society throughout this time span. The bargeman who discovers Chicken Little's body only retrieves him because he is a child; he reflects that if he had been an old black man, he would have left him there. The bargeman immediately presumes that the child has been drowned by his parents and wonders if "those people" will "ever be anything but animals" (63). When he considers the smell that the body will make, he dumps the body back in the water. Racial prejudice manifests itself in the treatment of Tar Baby. The community thinks that he is "half white," but Eva identifies him as "all white," insisting that she knows her own blood when she sees it (39). When the mayor's daughter causes an accident involving Tar Baby, the police beat him and leave him in soiled underwear. They also identify Tar Baby as white, and tell Ajax that "if the prisoner didn't like to live in shit, he should come down out of those hills, and live like a decent white man" (133). Jim Crow laws prevail on public transport. Helene, a Creole woman, and her daughter Nel find themselves in a "white only" carriage on the train to the South. Helene walks through the compartment to the "colored only" door and is scolded and humiliated by the conductor. In retaliation, Helene gives him a most dazzling smile. The black soldiers in the compartment look at the Creole woman with resentment. When they reach Birmingham, there are no longer toilet facilities for black people and Helene and Nel have to squat in the grass at the station houses.

In its final chapter, the novel moves forward to 1965. The 1960s are generally regarded as a time of progress for African Americans. The Civil Rights Movement fought for and won the right to vote. Morrison both registers and queries the value of this 'progress': "Things were so much better in 1965. Or so it seemed" (163). Black people work behind the store counters. A black man teaches mathematics at the local junior school. Strangely, Nel compares the new look of the young people to the look of the Deweys, who never found a role in society. Communities have dissolved, as families become more insular, cutting themselves off from their neighbors.

The novel also dramatizes the effects of hegemonic gender ideology. Some critics have identified "Sula" as a feminist novel. As young girls, both Nel and Sula are aware that they need to create new narratives to escape the constraints of race and gender ideology: "Because each had discovered years before that they were neither white nor male, and that all freedom and triumph was forbidden to them, they had set about creating something else to be" (52). White standards clearly influence Helene; she tells Nel to pull her nose to counter its flatness and to straighten her hair. Through her friendship with Sula, Nel comes to reject these standards. Sula refuses to live her life according to social determinants. She sees no fulfilment in the life of the wife and mother. Instead, she sets about inventing a new, unfettered identity, incurring the hostility of the community. Some readers and critics have queried Sula's credentials as a feminist figure, questioning the extremity of her views and her 'betrayal' of Nel.

Historical Context

By heading each chapter with a date, Morrison constantly reminds us of the significance of the historical context. The horrors of the First World War haunt the novel; Shadrack and Plum are deeply traumatized by their experience; soldiers who fought for America sit in the "colored only" compartment of the train to New Orleans. The novel was written during the Vietnam War. Dr. Martin Luther King Jr. described this conflict as "the white man's war, the black man's fight," to draw attention to the disproportionate number of African-Americans serving and dying in Vietnam.

Patterns of repetition and circularity counter the sense of unremitting chronology furnished by the dates. The narrative reveals that time is anything but linear and that history repeats itself. In 1927, the "fake prosperity," a hangover from the war,

leads the black people to hope for new jobs (81). The construction of the River Road gives them this hope but all the jobs go to white men. A decade later, they are let down again when the tunnel is constructed and the work is given to white men. Although "Sula" ends on an image of circularity, Morrison has compared the novel's structure to that of a spiral (Tate 128). Narrative lines not only repeat themselves, but also advance and retreat, continuously rising and falling.

"Sula" dramatizes both the dangers of living in and ignoring the past. The people of the Bottom are unable to relinquish their vision of the past and move forward. The joke about the origin of the Bottom serves as a constant reminder of the oppression of black people. A slave owner promised his slave good land in the hills, telling him that it is blessed land from "the bottom of heaven" (5). When the slave arrived there, he found that the hilly land required "backbreaking" work (5). The citizens of Medallion are reluctant to let go of the past because this requires finding new ways to live and conceive the self. Sula reflects: "If they were touched by the snake's breath, however fatal, they were merely victims and knew how to behave in that role … But the free fall, oh no, that required—demanded—invention" (120).

However, the novel does not fully endorse Sula's commitment to the moment. In "Rootedness: The Ancestor as Foundation," Morrison writes: "I want to paint out the dangers, to show that nice things don't happen to the totally self-reliant if there is no conscious historical connection" (Evans 344). Sula's narrative of alienation and her disturbing vision of the future reveal these dangers.

Religious Context

The opening description of the Bottom and the joke about its origins establishes the parabolic tenor of the novel. However, the novel challenges the strict categories which form the basis of western religion, revealing how religious belief can be used as an exclusionary force. Fear informs the town's religious faith. At Chicken Little's funeral, the congregation senses that "the only way to avoid the Hand of God was to get in it" (66). Morrison exposes the dangers of such a narrow, either/or vision. The citizens of the Bottom accept evil without questioning it or trying to change it: "they let it run its course, fulfill itself, and never invented ways either to alter it, to annihilate it or to prevent its happening again" (90). They align the evil of racial oppression with accidents or misfortunes such as tuberculosis and famine (90). They show little interest in forgiveness and interpret the freak occurrences reminiscent of the Old Testament selectively.

As white people call on their own interpretations of religion to justify racial oppression—the bargeman is confounded by the "terrible burden his own kind had of elevating Ham's sons" (63)—so the citizens of Medallion draw on biblical discourse to justify their exclusion of anyone who challenges their dichotomized conception of right and wrong. Sula eludes definition so she must be the devil, the fourth face of God; when Shadrack arrives resembling a prophet with a new message, he is dismissed as mad; Ajax's mother is an "evil conjure woman" (126); Mrs. Sabat raises her granddaughter "under the dolesome eyes of a multicolored Virgin Mary" to protect her from her mother's wild blood (17). Through Sula, Morrison offers a counter-argument to such narrow definitions. Sula reflects that for Nel to escape the role of victim embraced by the town, would require "invention" beyond the town's imagination (120). However, when she is betrayed by her husband and friend, morality becomes the main constituent of Nel's identity: "Virtue, bleak and drawn, was her only mooring" (139). Sula challenges her moral code, telling her that "Being good to somebody is just like being mean to somebody" (144–5). In a disturbing vision, she talks of a time when these categories will no longer apply: when "the old women have

lain with the teenagers," "the whores make love to their grannies," and "Lindbergh sleeps with Bessie Smith" (145).

Although the novel does not endorse Sula's vision, her death exposes the inadequacy of the town's moral vision. The citizens interpret Sula's death as a good omen but they soon realize that their moral system was contingent upon their outrage at Sula's behavior: "… mothers who had defended their children from Sula's malevolence … now had nothing to rub up against. The tension was gone and so was the reason for the effort they had made" (153).

Scientific & Technological Context

The people of the Bottom welcome news of urbanization but in the final chapter, Morrison reveals how 'progress' and 'advancement' have eroded community life. As "[o]ne of the last true pedestrians," Nel is a lonely figure, "walk[ing] the shoulder road while cars slipped by" (166). Technology ousts nature and alienates people. Trees are cut down and towers for television stations are erected. People live in "separate houses with separate televisions and separate telephones" (166).

Biographical Context

Toni Morrison is one of America's most eminent novelists. She has garnered a formidable array of awards and honors, including the 1993 Nobel Prize for Literature. Born Chloe Anthony Wofford in 1931, Morrison was raised in Ohio after her parents moved there from the South. She attended Howard University in Washington D.C. and Cornell University, where she wrote her Master's thesis on Virginia Woolf and William Faulkner. In 1965 she joined Random House and worked in publishing while writing. Morrison's first novel, "The Bluest Eye," evolved from a short story and was published in 1970. "Sula" followed in 1973. Her third novel, "Song of Solomon" (1977) interweaves African-American folktales with American history; it won the National Book Critics Circle Award. "Tar Baby" appeared in 1981. Her next three novels form a thematically linked trilogy: "Beloved" (1987), "Jazz" (1992), and "Paradise" (1998). "Beloved," her most acclaimed novel, was made into a film, produced by and starring Oprah Winfrey. The novel retells the true story of Margaret Garner, a black slave who killed her daughter to save her from slavery. In 1992, Morrison published "Playing in the Dark: Whiteness and the Literary Imagination," a hugely influential work of literary criticism. She published her eighth novel, "Love," in 2003.

Morrison views the collaboration between reader and writer as essential to the creative process; she states that she wishes the reader to "work with the author in the construction of the book" (341). Her novels are characterized by their polyvocality, lyricism, and alinear, fragmented structures. Prevalent themes include: race and gender ideology; sexuality; standards of beauty; memory and loss; identity and community. She has written books for children, including the "Who's Got Game?" series. Morrison has two sons from her marriage to Harold Morrison. She is Robert F. Goheen Professor, Council of Humanities, Princeton University. She is a member of numerous bodies, including the National Council of the Arts and the American Academy and Institute of Arts and Letters.

Rachel Lister, Ph.D

Works Cited

Morrison, Toni. "Rootedness: The Ancestor as Foundation." *Black Women Writers:*
A Critical Evaluation. Ed. Marie Evans. New York: Anchor, 1984. 339–45.
——. *Sula.* 1973. London: Picador, 1991.
Tate, Claudia. *Black Women Writers at Work.* New York: Continuum, 1984.

Discussion Questions

1. Discuss Morrison's representation of Sula. Why does she present her heroine from a third-person perspective only? How might our conception of Sula differ if she were given narrating privileges?

2. Morrison dedicates "Sula" to her two sons. She opens the dedication with the declaration that, "It is sheer good fortune to miss somebody long before they leave you." Using the dedication as a starting-point, explore Morrison's treatment of the themes of absence and loss.

3. "… she felt no compulsion to verify herself— be consistent with herself." Identify and discuss moments when you were puzzled by Sula's actions.

4. "Hell is change" (Nel in "Sula"). Discuss the different attitudes to change presented in the novel.

5. "A bright space opened in her head and memory seeped into it." Discuss the represention and function of memory in "Sula."

6. "You say I'm a woman and I'm colored. Ain't that the same as being a man?" By what means does Morrison challenge identity categories and oppositions in "Sula?"

7. Discuss Morrison's dramatization of trauma in "Sula."

8. "Being good to somebody is just like being mean to somebody." Discuss Morrison's treatment of morality in "Sula."

9. Take one of the following scenes from Sula and discuss its significance to the novel as a whole: Helene's smile and the reaction of the soldiers; Sula cutting off her finger tip; Shadrack's encounter with Sula; the communal parade on National Suicide Day.

10. "She had clung to Nel as the closest thing to both an other and a self, only to discover that she and Nel were not one and the same thing" (119). Discuss the close relationship between Sula and Nel. How do their choices and actions impinge on each other's identity?

Essay Ideas

1. "The Peace women simply loved maleness, for its own sake." Explore Morrison's representation of masculinity in "Sula."

2. "I don't want to make somebody else. I want to make myself." Discuss Morrison's treatment of maternity in "Sula."

3. How does Morrison represent the tension between isolation and contact in "Sula?"

4. To what extent might one define "Sula" as a feminist novel?

5. Morrison compares the structure of "Sula" to the shape of a spiral. Taking this analogy as a starting-point, examine Morrison's formal and narrative strategies.

Tar Baby

by Toni Morrison

Content Synopsis

This essay examines Toni Morrison's fourth novel, "Tar Baby" (1981), in which she explores the problematics of identity and the pull of cultural heritage. It provides a content synopsis and places the novel in a variety of contexts: historical, societal, technological and religious. The essay also presents biographical information about Morrison.

The prelude to the novel presents a man standing at the railing of a ship, looking at the shore of a place named Queen of France. He sees a pier and swims towards it. He feels a "bracelet of water" pulling him down and returning him to the water's surface (1). He finds himself heading towards a boat which he boards. He hides and hears the voices of two women. He eats some of their food and looks out to sea. He sees only the stars and the moon but "little of the land" (6); the narrator tells us that this is "just as well because "he was gazing at the shore of an island that, three hundred years ago, struck slaves blind the moment they saw it" (6).

The first chapter opens with the history of Isle des Chevaliers, an island near Dominique. Labourers from Haiti arrived one day to clear the land to construct winter houses. The most lavish house on the island is L'Arbe de la Croix, owned by millionaire Valerian Street. Street left Philadelphia when he retired and has spent four years at the house. He has brought all of his belongings, including "the Principal Beauty of Maine" (9). He spends most of his time in his greenhouse. 'The Principal Beauty' makes trips back to Philadelphia to convince herself that they still live in the America. Valerian has little time for his neighbors, although he made friends with Dr. Michelin, his dentist.

Sydney, the butler, enters the greenhouse to serve breakfast. Valerian asks if his wife is awake and expresses his suspicion that she is drinking too much. Sydney tells his master that he is more of a drinker than his wife. Valerian tells Sydney that he will talk to a woman named Jade about his concerns. Sydney reveals that Mrs. Street is waiting for a trunk to arrive from the airport; she is expecting their son Michael. Valerian doubts that Michael will turn up. Sydney exits the greenhouse as Margaret, Valerian's wife, 'the Principal Beauty,' arrives. We learn that they have been coming to the house for vacations for thirty years and that they currently sleep in separate rooms. Margaret announces that Michael is bringing a friend. Valerian predicts that the friend will show up alone, "again" (23). She tells him that she plans to return to the States with her son. Valerian scoffs at the idea and asks what tribe Michael is currently living with. Margaret replies that their son is no longer living with Native Americans but is studying to become a lawyer. Valerian asks what they will do about Jade, who seems to be related to Sydney and his wife Ondine, the cook. Margaret replies that Jade is getting over a love affair but that she will not give up the chance to return to the States with her son for Jade. Jade is currently a model and plans to open up a shop. Valerian worries that Sydney and his family will leave him. He wonders why Ondine and Margaret no longer seem to get along but Margaret does not enlighten him. Sydney arrives again and Margaret states her wish for turkey for Christmas dinner; they contravene Ondine's plans to serve goose.

The scene shifts to the kitchen where Ondine and Sydney discuss Christmas dinner. Ondine scoffs at Margaret's plans and, like Valerian, predicts that Michael will not turn up. If he does arrive, she expects him to encourage her to liberate herself from the streets. Jade arrives and we learn that she is the niece of Sydney and Ondine. She asks for a cup of chocolate. Ondine reveals that some of the kitchen supplies, such as chocolate, have been disappearing. They hear the footsteps of Yardman, the gardener. He often has a female companion, who may be his wife, sister, mother or daughter. Like the other black women on the island, one of her names is Mary. Several Marys work at L'Arbe de la Croix. Yardman is also often accompanied by a young girl. Ondine gives him a list of things to buy, leaving out the turkey that Margaret wants for Christmas.

By Chapter 2, night has fallen. The narrator describes the postures of the inhabitants in their sleep. Jade thinks about the day she gained her degree and shot a cover for Elle magazine. She visited the grocery store and saw a striking African woman in a yellow dress. The woman picked up three eggs, threw some money on the counter and left the store. Entranced by the woman, Jade followed her. When the woman saw Jade, she spat on the pavement. Jade reads this gesture as a sign that she should not marry Ryk, the white European man whose proposal she has accepted.

Valerian wakes up and reflects on his career. He inherited a candy factory from his uncles. They named a red and white gumdrop after him. The Valerian was not a success and sold only in the South. Valerian's first marriage ended in divorce and he fought in the war; only his love of books and music sustained him. When he first saw Margaret, she was dressed in the red and white of the Valerian wrappers; recognizing in himself the sentimentality of his uncles, he vowed to retire at sixty-five "before he got foolish" (50). When Michael was born Valerian expected his son to take over. Michael showed no interest in the business. Valerian sold the company and concentrated on his house in the Caribbean. He left the company at the age of sixty-eight and moved to the island for good to "sleep the deep brandy sleep that he deserved" (52).

Margaret, an insomniac, hopes for sleep but finds herself worrying about the forgetfulness that has begun to manifest itself in her daily behavior. When she was born, her red hair marked her out from her black-haired siblings; it bothered her father and puzzled her mother. Disconcerted by her beauty, her parents concentrated their love on the other children. The loneliness deepened when she married and her husband left her alone in the house. She bonded with Ondine over a radio soap opera but Valerian warned her against "consorting with Negroes" (57). When Michael was born she found teaching him "a horror and a pleasure" (58); the "afterboom" that had followed her around the house got louder after he was born. She tells herself that by moving in with him, she will be enjoying her son "as an individual" (58). Sydney dreams of his days in Baltimore in 1921. Ondine dreams that she is drowning.

In Chapter 3, Valerian, Margaret and Jade are having dinner. Margaret is struggling to remember how to use to the utensils and recognize the food. Valerian reveals that Margaret has invited B. J. Bridges, a poet and old teacher of Michael's, as a surprise for their son. They begin to argue again about Michael. As the argument escalates, Margaret storms out of the room. Jade and Valerian discuss Michael's misguided politics: his attempts to encourage African-Americans to engage with their heritage. Valerian blames Margaret for Michael's obtuseness: "She made him think poetry was incompatible with property" (73). He doubts whether Margaret loves her son. He recalls that he used to find him hiding in the bathroom cabinet, humming a "lonely" song (74). When Michael visited from boarding school she made up threats to herself to show people how much her son wanted to defend her. Valerian predicts that as soon as Margaret gets Michael's attention again, she will reject him. Suddenly they hear Margaret scream. She appears in the doorway and tells them that something "black" is in her closet and has been through her things (77). Sydney goes to investigate and returns with an intruder; he is carrying a .32 calibre pistol. Valerian offers the man a drink.

Chapter 4 opens on the next day. Margaret sits in her room, furious with Valerian for inviting the intruder to dinner. The scene shifts to Jade, who is showing Ondine her new sealskin coat from Paris, where she has been modelling. Ondine tells her to hide it in case the intruder steals it; clearly she is upset by his arrival. Ondine leaves and Jade contemplates Valerian's reaction to the intruder, whom he asked to stay to dinner. Margaret had refused to sit at the table. The man had said 'hi' to Sydney; the butler had dropped something "[f]or the first time in his life" (91). The man told Valerian and Jade that he had been in the house for about a week; he jumped ship on his way to Dominique. He is evidently the man who was introduced in the novel's opening. In the kitchen, Sydney tells Ondine that he cannot understand why Valerian does not call the police. She reassures him that Valerian will dismiss the man eventually. Sydney is insulted that the stranger has been put up in the guest room next to Jade, while they continue to live above the kitchen. Ondine warns him to hide his indignation; she is not prepared to start again, working for white people she does not know. When Sydney leaves, Ondine registers her worries about

the newcomer. She is most unsettled by the fact that he is black, but is not a "Negro—meaning one of them" (101–2). The scene moves to Thérèse, the washerwoman. She waits for Gideon, whom everyone else calls Yardman, to come by. She regrets that Alma, the little girl, will not come and talk to her today. Thérèse and Gideon have been betting on how long the mystery chocolate-eater would last before betraying himself. Gideon arrives and reveals that the intruder is now staying in the house. Thérèse spins stories about the mystery man. Gideon stops listening when she speaks in French Dominique; this was the language she used to "trick him" into leaving the States (108). She had written him letters from the island, begging him to come and take care of the family property. When he arrived there was no land; all of it was owned by a Frenchman. In the U.S., Gideon had gained citizenship "by much subterfuge" and marriage to an American (109). When he returned to the island, he found work at L'Arbe de la Croix. Thérèse refuses to speak to black Americans and acknowledge the existence of white Americans; Gideon is glad to be away from the "humiliations of immigrant life that U.S. citizenship did not change" (110).

Meanwhile Jade is admiring herself in the sealskin coat when she sees the reflection of the intruder in the mirror. They get to know each other. She shows him pictures of her in the magazine. He finds it easier to look at these than to look at her. She asks him to look at her. As he obliges, he recalls watching her in her sleep, trying to project his dreams into her mind: dreams of "fat black ladies in white dresses minding the pie table in the basement of the church" (119). He finally asks her how many sexual favors she had to perform to be so successful (120). She tries to tear his eyes out and he holds her fast; she warns him against raping her and he wonders why white girls always presume that somebody is trying to rape them. Jade reacts in fury at being called a white girl. She tells him that he smells and he replies that he can smell her too. She threatens to tell Valerian about his conduct. The man lets her go and Jade leaves. She is reminded of the dogs that used to smell each other on Morgan Street where she lived as a child. She cannot bear the embarrassment of "telling on a black man to a white man" (126).

In Chapter 5, Jade tells Margaret what has happened regarding the intruder, leaving out his apparent attempt to 'rape' her. Margaret continues to insist that he must leave, comparing him to a "gorilla" (129); Jade is disturbed by Margaret's use of this image. The intruder sits in Jade's room. He looks at her coat, remembering the seals he saw off the coast of Greenland. He recalls his movements since leaving the boat; he did not follow the women who had already disembarked but took his own way, eventually stumbling across Valerian's house. He peered inside and saw a piano; this transported him back to his childhood when he used to play Miss Tyler's piano. He and his friends served in the war. He had a girlfriend named Cheyenne. He has had seven "documented identities" and a few "undocumented ones" in eight years (139). The name that signifies his true identity is 'Son.'

Valerian is in his greenhouse, daydreaming about the washerwoman who used to talk to him as a child. He recalls telling her that his father is dead; she invited him to help with the washing. As he scrubbed away, he cried. When the butler found out about their conversations, the washerwoman was dismissed. He thinks that he saw Michael last night as he talked to Jade; he believes that this vision prompted him to invite Son to dinner. Son arrives and introduces himself as Willie Green. 'Willie' sees that Valerian's cyclamen are dying and shakes them up, promising that they will flourish from now on. Valerian sends Son out with Gideon and Thérèse. Gideon cuts Son's hair while Thérèse looks on, spellbound by the "American Negro" (150). They eat together, with Alma Estée, the young girl. As Thérèse asks Son questions about America, Gideon warns him not to

listen to her; she is one of the "blind race" who "love[s] lies" (152). He tells Son about the slaves who went blind the minute they saw Dominique. Their ship sank and they ended up on Queen of France. Gideon claims that he can hear them but that nobody can see them. He warns Son about Jade; women like her "don't come to being black natural-like" (156). Alma asks Son if he can get her a wig from America.

Son apologizes to Jade about his behavior and she tells him to apologize to Sydney and Ondine. He does so. Sydney berates Son for entering his space. He tells him that Mr. Street is merely letting him stay for his amusement. He makes a distinction between his people and Son's. Son acknowledges that he feels uncomfortable about Mr. Street's hospitality and plans to sleep outside from now on. That evening, Sydney, Ondine and Son eat together. Margaret softens towards Son when she learns that he is no longer sleeping upstairs or eating with them. The next morning Son and Jade drive to the beach. Jade asks him what he wants from life and he answers: the original dime he earned for cleaning a tub of sheephead. He tells her that he comes from Eloe, Florida, an all-black town. He left because he killed his wife for cheating on him. He drove his car through the house, setting it alight. He tells Jade that he loves her. They drive back and break down; Son leaves to get gas and Jade goes for a walk; she sinks into the swamp, where, according to legend, women dwell. She almost drowns before Son returns.

Chapter 6 opens on "Christmas Eve's Eve" (188). Ondine expresses concern about Jade's relationship with Son. B. J. Bridges calls to postpone his visit, Michael does not turn up. At Christmas dinner, cooked by Margaret for Michael's sake, Son tells them about Gideon and Thérèse, whom they know as Yardman and Mary. Valerian reveals that he fired them for stealing apples. Ondine is angry that he didn't tell her. Sydney states that he and Ondine are being slighted again. Son challenges

Valerian to justify his behavior. Valerian orders Son to leave, incredulous that he should have to justify himself to Ondine and Sydney. They tell him that he would die of starvation if they did not serve him. Ondine demands that Margaret never enter her kitchen again; she is neither a cook nor a mother. Ondine screams accusations at Margaret: she cut Michael up as a baby, burned him and stuck pins in him. Ondine and Sydney leave the room.

By Chapter 7, Son is in New York. He used Gideon's passport and Jade's ticket. Jade will join him when she has sorted out her aunt and uncle's future. She arrives and they live in her friend's empty apartment. Sydney and Ondine remain at L'Arbe de la Croix, but their futures seem uncertain. Jade models and Son does odd jobs. Chapter 8 returns to the island. Valerian reflects on Ondine's revelations. He recalls his son's lonely song. Margaret tried to explain herself after everyone had left. Valerian told her to stop. The next morning she feels relief that she did not get away with her behavior. She tells Valerian that she harmed Michael because she felt "hostage" to his "prodigious appetite for security" (238). She tells Valerian to hit her but he cannot. She insists that Michael is now fine. Margaret and Ondine apologise to each other.

In Chapter 9, Jade and Son are in Eloe, Son's home town. Jade has problems understanding the language that Son uses with his friends. Son is reunited with his father, to whom he has been sending money. Son's friend Soldier tells Jade that Son "gets confused when it comes to women" and laughs about Cheyenne's sexual prowess (257). Son asks if they can stay an extra day to see his friend Ernie Paul. They are staying with his aunt Rosa, who disapproves of their relationship. Jade has to sleep alone in a stuffy room. She agrees to stay if Son creeps into her room that night and leaves before Rosa awakes. That night Jade is haunted by the forbidding presence of women from her past and present, including Thérèse, her dead mother, Ondine, and the woman in yellow from the grocery

store. She returns to New York alone; Son agrees to meet her there when he has seen his friend the next day but he does not return for days. Jade continues to be haunted by the 'night women.' Son arrives and they argue about the future; he refuses to take money from Valerian to start a business or go to school. Jade begins to look tired and lose modelling jobs to seventeen-year-olds. A dividend arrives from bonds that Valerian bought Jade one Christmas. Son refuses to use them to pay for his education. They argue about Son's preoccupation with past wrongs. When Son returns to the apartment the next day Jade has gone. She has left some photographs she took in Eloe. As he looks at his old friends and family, they appear "stupid" to him (275). Son resolves to win her back.

In Chapter 10, Jade returns to L'Arbe de la Croix. Margaret tells her that Valerian is unwell. Michael has been accepted at Berkeley; Margaret will not join him. She seems to have changed; she realizes that Michael is an adult and that she is needed at the house. Jade tells Ondine that she plans to return to Paris. Sydney and Ondine feel that she has not taken enough care of them. Sydney waits on Valerian; he drinks Valerian's wine and advises him to forget about returning to Philadelphia; he and Ondine like living on the island. At the airport, Jade encounters the girl, Alma, from L'Arbe de la Croix. She is wearing a wig but it is not American. She tells Jade that Son promised to buy her a wig and asks her if she killed him. Jade calls Alma 'Mary' and bids her goodbye.

The final chapter centers on Son. He returns to the island to search for Jade. He finds Gideon and Thérèse and asks them where Jade is. They express disapproval of his search. Thérèse fetches Alma who tells Son that she saw Jade leave on a plane. She lies, telling him that Jade had been met by a "young man with yellow hair and blue eyes and white skin" and that they had kissed (302). Son begs Gideon to take him to L'Arbe de la Croix so that he can get Jade's Paris address.

Gideon refuses. Thérèse agrees to take him in her boat. Gideon warns Son not to trust her but they leave together in the dark. The journey seems to take much longer than it should. Eventually the boat pulls up; Thérèse tells Son that they are at the back of the island and that he will have to scramble up the rocks to reach safe land. He reluctantly leaves, as she tells him not to pursue Jade, who has "'forgotten her ancient properties'" (308). She tells him that the blind and naked men of the legend are waiting for him and that he can be free of Jade if he joins them. Son reaches the shore and runs on, "lickety-split" (309).

Symbols & Motifs

"Tar Baby" is concerned with authenticity and self-realization yet the novel abounds with secrets and lies. Morrison uses symbols to figure the workings of the subconscious and to alert the reader to gaps in the characters' visions. Maternal imagery dominates Jade's dreams, figuring the pull of "true and ancient properties" on her apparent self-sufficiency. She is haunted by the breasts of the night women: "They stood around in the room, jostling each other gently, gently—there wasn't much room—revealing one breast and then two and Jade was shocked" (260-1). The African woman shows Jade three eggs in her dream at Eloe. Rosa fries eggs for Jade the next morning. However, Jade finds solace in other mother figures. On the flight to Paris, she imagines the ants breeding in the rain forest. Unable to dismiss memories of Son, she reflects that female ants need only mate once in their lives. The queen ant's independence appeals to Jade.

The figure of the 'tar baby' features in the Br'er Rabbit stories which developed from African-American folk tales. The tar baby is used to trap Br'er Rabbit; his attempts to extricate himself only compound the situation. Son tells the story to Jade during their final confrontation, implying that Valerian is the white farmer who sets up the trap

for the rabbit. In the novel, Morrison emphasizes the positive properties of tar. Jade's encounter with the swamp women is highly symbolic. Unable to extricate herself from the "moss-covered jelly" of the swamp, she sinks further and further down under the pictorial gaze of Son and the legendary "women hanging in the trees" (183): figures willing her initiation into her cultural heritage. The women in the trees realize that Jade is resisting their attempts to reclaim her and are puzzled by her reaction. When Jade finally breaks free she is covered in "a deep dark and sticky" substance (185). She denies seeing the swamp women to Son and insists that he take her home. Significantly, it is Margaret who helps Jade to clean herself, telling her that Son is bad luck. In an interview Morrison states that, for her, the tar baby means "the black woman who holds everything together" ("An Interview" 255). One might argue that Jade has the potential to fulfill this role. However, at the end of the novel, Son, like Br'er Rabbit, runs across the shore "lickety-split," suggesting that he has freed himself from Jade.

For some characters, symbols serve to close down meaning. In attempting to construct his own paradise, Valerian reduces everything to its symbolic meaning. All the characters represent abstractions to Valerian. When Valerian sees Margaret, he is reminded of the red and white Valerian candy wrappers and invests his own sense of identity in her beauty: "His youth lay in her red whiteness, a snowy Valentine Valerian" (52). The birth of his son puts an end to his obsession with youth: his son is his youth. He builds the greenhouse as a symbol of his self-sufficiency and defiance: "When he knew for certain that Michael would always be a stranger to him, he built the greenhouse as a place of controlled, ever-flowering life to greet death in" (51). The house itself figures Valerian's preoccupation with control; where the people in the town are at the mercy of the "heat and weight of the sky," the deep eaves of the house enable its inhabitants to "concentrate on whichever of their personal problems they wished" (80).

The work of the natural world exposes the precariousness of Valerian's artificial world. The soldier ants repeatedly invade his retreat, eating their way through the loudspeaker wires that pump classical music into the greenhouse. Son, the swamp women and the legendary horsemen in the hills, embody the force of the natural world. Son's 'invasion' compels Valerian to confront some of the truths of his own history. The imagery surrounding Son identifies him with the natural world: "Spaces, mountains, savannas—all those were in his forehead and eyes" (159). Descriptions of the landscape and weather open the chapters, signalling the futility of Valerian's attempts to insulate himself from the outside world. The fog, figured as "the hair of maiden aunts," mirrors the characters' efforts at obfuscation (60).

Colors in the novel are freighted with symbolic meaning. The first word that Margaret uses to describe the man in the closet is "black" (77). We learn that he is black, before we learn that he is a man. Gideon distrusts Jade, alluding to her as "'that yalla'" (155). The narrator draws our attention to specific shades and their often misleading connotations; Margaret abuses her son but she has "blue-if-it's-a-boy" blue eyes. Red takes on sinister connotations in the description of Alma's ludicrous wig: "Her sweet face, her midnight skin mocked and destroyed by the pile of synthetic dried blood on her head. It was all mixed up" (302). The red wig, donned to emulate American beauty, recalls Margaret's hair. Colors often remind the characters of suppressed desires or needs: Jade is haunted by the African woman in the canary yellow dress. Jade does not participate in the annual mother-daughter dance around the beech tree on her old campus but she is enchanted by the "Pale sulphur light sprinkled so softly with lilac it made her want to cry" (73). She herself has Valerian's solipsism which is figured by the absence of color in his eyes: "Without melanin, they were all reflection, like mirrors, chamber after chamber, corridor after corridor of mirrors, each one taking its shape from the other and giving it back as its own until the final effect was colour where no colour existed at all" (71–2).

Morrison presents a number of disturbing images of America and Europe: Son encounters a Mexican who draws on a map of the U.S., "an ill-shaped tongue ringed by teeth and crammed with the corpses of children" (168). Jade's sealskin coat from Paris reminds Son of all the unnecessary slaughter he has witnessed.

Historical Context

From the beginning of the novel, Morrison foregrounds the importance of heritage. She dedicates the novel to the women in her family who "knew their true and ancient properties"; this phrase resurfaces throughout the novel. The island is steeped in history and mythology. The chapter openings remind the reader of this heritage, charting changes in the landscape and dramatizing the ongoing conflict between nature and 'civilization.' In the opening to Chapter 10, Morrison fuses military and natural imagery: "After thirty years of shame the champion daisy trees were marshalling for war" (276).

The legend of the men on horseback acquires a number of meanings. Gideon tells Son that the French brought some slaves over, who went blind the minute that they saw Dominique. Some of the slaves died when the ship sank. Others were partially blinded and were returned to slavery. Those who went completely blind hid. They have a different kind of vision; they see "with the mind's eye," their blindness signifying their resistance to colonialism (153). During his confrontation with Son, Valerian thinks of "one hundred French chevaliers" riding their horses, mindful of the "Napoleonic code," while Son thinks of "one hundred black men" riding blind and naked through the rain forest (207). Dr. Michelin states that the island got its name from the hundred horsemen who ride on the other side of the island. Margaret insists that only one horseman rode his horse there; the island was originally called Isle de le Chevalier.

Much of the conflict in the novel centers on the issue of heritage. Sydney and Ondine take pride in their own sense of history. Sydney distinguishes his history from Son's: "My people owned drugstores and taught school while yours were still cutting their faces open so as to be able to tell one of you from the other" (164). Valerian views Michael's works with the Native Americans as misguided. Michael irks Ondine, Sydney and Jade by telling them that they should return to Morgan Street. He wants Jade to acknowledge her African heritage by crafting cowrie beads and selling African combs rather than going to art school, and encourages welfare mothers to make and sell African pots. Valerian identifies Michael's politics with the Dark Ages.

Throughout their relationship, Jade and Son battle over the place of history in their lives. Son, unable to forget Eloe, asserts that one must honour one's past. Jade embraces the opportunities that are presented to her and accuses Son of "stay[ing] in that medieval slave basket" (274). The narrative voice does not favor either viewpoint but elucidates the problems with both positions: "One had a past, the other a future and each one bore the culture to save the race in his hands. Mama-spoiled black man, will you mature with me? Culture-bearing black woman, whose culture are you bearing?" (272). At the end of the novel, Thérèse gives Son a choice: he may engage further with the island's past or find Jade. It remains unclear who will be the rescuer and who will be rescued.

Societal Context

Race, class and gender ideologies underpin the tensions in "Tar Baby." Racial conflict is apparent from the beginning of the novel. Dr. Michelin refuses to mend the teeth of "some local blacks" (13). Margaret's racism emerges fully when Son arrives. Her fear of the man in the closet stems from his blackness. She refers to Son as "the nigger in the woodpile" and the "dope addict ape" (82, 86). She imagines him "jerking off," his "black sperm" dirtying her things (85). Most of the characters wrestle against labels. Jade reads disapproval of her prospective marriage to a white man in the African woman's gesture on the street. She wonders if Ryk wants to marry her simply because she is a black woman and asks herself how he will react when he finds out that "sometimes I want to get out of my skin and be only the person inside— not American—not black—just me?" (45). Sydney has become "one of those industrious Philadelphia Negroes—the proudest people in the race" (59). Jade is "disturbed" that Margaret "stirred her into blackening up or universalling out, always alluding to or ferreting out what she believed were racial characteristics" (62). Thérèse leaves Valerian and Margaret out of the stories she weaves around the house; she is unable to associate white people with "any feeling" (111). Jade accuses Son of "pulling that black-woman-white-woman shit" on her and wonders if Valerian can distinguish between different kinds of black people (121).

Race and class ideology inform Ondine and Sydney's reaction to Son. They are offended by Valerian's hospitality towards an unknown black man and distinguish themselves from the newcomer. Having seen the contempt shared by Sydney, Ondine and Jade towards a "black man who was one of their own," Valerian understands his son's politics. (146). Michael has criticized black people for their 'bourgeois' aspirations; Valerian saw evidence of this in Sydney and Ondine's "smug" glances at Son (145). Until this point Valerian did not believe that class distinctions existed in the black community. The secret behavior of the Streets themselves casts doubt over the significance of class status. Each member of the family seeks out unlikely spaces in which to deal with suppressed feelings: Michael hides under the sink to sing his lonely song; as a young boy, Valerian sought refuge with the laundry woman; despite her hankering for fine things, Margaret identifies most with the humble trailer of her childhood, a space of "secret storage and uncluttered surfaces" (81). By the end of the novel, Sydney is drinking Valerian's wine and telling him to stay on the island.

"Tar Baby" associates America with consumerism. As one of the "great underclass of undocumented men," Son is contemptuous of the profligacy of American culture (167): "That was the sole lesson their world: how to make waste, how to make machines that made more waste" (204). Son's all-black home town, Eloe, is untainted by such preoccupations. The citizens struggle to survive, but find sustenance in the bonds of their marginalized community: "It took all the grown-up strength you had to stay there and stay alive and keep a family together. They didn't know about state aid in Eloe; there were no welfare lines in Eloe and unemployment insurance was a year of trouble with no rewards" (270). While Son takes pride in Eloe's self-sufficiency, Jade dismisses the town as a redundant site for "All that Southern small-town country romanticism … kept secret by people who could not function elsewhere" (262). Son remains determined to resists the lure of consumerism. As he watches Jade sleep, he worries that she might "press her dreams of gold and cloisonné and honey-colored silk into him," usurping his dream of "mind[ing] the pie table in the basement of the church" (120).

Valerian's hypocrisy manifests itself in his attitude towards women. He had a couple of flings with young girls to "help him through his fifties" but looks on his wife's vanity with contempt (51). Son repeatedly pre-empts accusations of sexism and acknowledges the power of women: "'Anybody who thought women were inferior didn't come out of north Florida'" (271). However, he and Valerian chortle over a sexist joke. Son presumes that Jade had to perform sexual favors to get ahead in New York. Gideon mistrusts women, warning Son against Jade and telling stories about the "'wiles'" and "'ways'" of women he has known (305). Female power exerts itself in the collectives of women who haunt the text: the women to whom the novel is dedicated; the swamp women; the night women; the fat women in Son's dreams; the mothers and daughters who dance around the tree on Jade's campus; the image of the 'maiden aunts' whose 'hair' surrounds the house.

Religious Context

The epigraph of the novel comes from I Corinthians, 1:11: "For it hath been declared unto me of you, my brethren, by them which are of the house of Chloe, that there are contentions among you." Religious difference engenders further points of conflict in the novel. Margaret's parents object to Valerian because he is not Catholic. Thérèse invests most heavily in the island's mythology; she rows Son to the back of the island where he may enter the mythological world in which she believes. Some of the pivotal points in the novel are analogous to religious experience. For example, Jade undergoes a kind of baptism in the swamp: a baptism which she rejects.

Scientific & Technological Context

In "Tar Baby," Mother Nature often asserts her supremacy over technology. The ants gnaw their way through the loudspeaker wires in Valerian's man-made Eden. When Jade and Son return from the beach, their car breaks down; Jade goes for a walk and is lured into the swamp where the women incite her to engage with her ancient properties. The Haitian labourers would require machines to "fold[] the earth where there had been no fold" but the narrator focuses on nature's response rather than man's methods of devastation (7). Eloe, forgotten by America, is inaccessible by plane; after a circuitous journey, Jade and Son must bum a ride to the town (246). However, Jade escapes the pull of the past—the claims of Sydney and Ondine, as well as Son—by aeroplane.

Biographical Context

Toni Morrison is one of America's most eminent novelists. She has garnered a formidable array of awards and honors, including the 1993 Nobel Prize for Literature. Born Chloe Anthony Wofford in 1931, Morrison was raised in Ohio after her parents moved there from the South. She attended Howard University in Washington D.C. and Cornell University, where she wrote her Master's thesis on Virginia Woolf and William Faulkner. In 1965 she joined Random House and worked in publishing while writing. Morrison's first novel, "The Bluest Eye" evolved from a short story and was published in 1970. "Sula" followed in 1973. Her third novel, "Song of Solomon" (1977) interweaves African-American folktales with American history; it won the National Book Critics Circle Award. "Tar Baby" appeared in 1981. Her next three novels form a thematically linked trilogy: "Beloved" (1987), "Jazz" (1992), and "Paradise" (1998). "Beloved," her most acclaimed novel, was made into a film, produced by and starring Oprah Winfrey. The novel retells the true story of Margaret Garner, a black slave who killed her daughter to save her from slavery. In 1992, Morrison published "Playing in the Dark: Whiteness and the Literary Imagination," a hugely influential work of literary criticism. She published her eighth novel, "Love," in 2003.

Morrison views the collaboration between reader and writer as essential to the creative process; she states that she wishes the reader to "work with the author in the construction of the book" (341). Her novels are characterized by their polyvocality, lyricism, and alinear, fragmented structures. Prevalent themes include: race and gender ideology; sexuality; standards of beauty; memory and loss; identity and community. She has written books for children, including the "Who's Got Game?" series. Morrison has two sons from her marriage to Harold Morrison. She is Robert F. Goheen Professor, Council of Humanities, Princeton University. She is a member of numerous bodies, including the National Council of the Arts and the American Academy and Institute of Arts and Letters.

Rachel Lister

Works Cited

Irving, John. "Morrison's Black Fable." *New York Times*. March 29 1981 1.

LeClair, Tom. "An Interview with Toni Morrison." *Anything Can Happen: Interviews with Contemporary American Novelists* Ed. Tom LeClair and Larry McCaffery. Urbana: U of Illinois P, 1983. 252–61.

——. "Rootedness: The Ancestor as Foundation." *Black Women Writers (1950–1980): A Critical Evaluation*. Ed. Mari Evans. New York: Anchor, 1984. 339–45.

——. *Tar Baby*. 1981, London: Virago, 1997.

Discussion Questions

1. "What is left out is as important as what is there" (Toni Morrison "Rootedness" 341). What does Morrison choose to omit from "Tar Baby"? The revelations concerning Michael mark a pivotal point in the novel. Why doesn't Morrison introduce him as a character?

2. What is the effect of the shifting narrative perspective in "Tar Baby"? To what extent do your allegiances to the characters change?

3. Trace the different visions of the U.S. that are presented throughout the novel; what impression do we gain of modern American life?

4. What is the significance of the characters' dreams?

5. Morrison leaves the novel's multiple plotlines open. Why does she do this? Many critics and readers argue that the novel condemns Jade and endorses Son. Do you agree with this?

6. "New York was not her home after all" (290). "Tar Baby" abounds with dislocated characters. What constitutes a home in this novel?

7. Morrison states: "For me, the tar baby came to mean the black woman who can hold things together." What meanings accumulate around the image of tar baby?

8. Look at the openings of each chapter. How do the evocations of the natural world shape your reading of the novel as a whole?

9. "He thought of it not just as love, but as rescue" (189–90). Identify the different forms of rescue in the novel. How successful are they?

10. "'A girl has got to be a daughter first'" (283). Discuss the uses and significance of maternal imagery in "Tar Baby."

Essay Ideas

1. "Miss Morrison uncovers all the stereotypical racial fears felt by whites and blacks alike" (John Irving "Morrison's Black Fable"). What are these fears and by what means does Morrison represent them?

2. "'His name is Gideon! Gideon! Not Yardman and Mary Thérèse Foucault, you hear me!'" (267). What is the significance of naming in the novel?

3. Examine Morrison's treatment of betrayal in "Tar Baby."

4. Explore the representation of memory and denial in "Tar Baby."

5. "Culture-bearing black woman, whose culture are you bearing?" (272). Identify and discuss cultural tensions in "Tar Baby."

Underworld

by Don DeLillo

Content Synopsis

Don DeLillo's (1936-) "Underworld" (1997) spans over forty years of American history, chronicling the events of the Cold War and beyond, in a narrative that switches continually between different time periods and voices. As John Duvall notes, "it juxtaposes a backward and a forward presentation of time" which "creates plot tensions that simply would disappear if one were to retell the story by creating a conventional timeframe" (25). While critic Tony Tanner states, "I just did not see the point of DeLillo's randomizings" (56), the function of DeLillo's approach, beyond creating plot tensions, may be to explore the nature of history itself. DeLillo sets out to undermine the contention of the novel's central character, Nick Shay, that "history is a single narrative sweep, not ten thousand wisps of disinformation" (82). By introducing multiple perspectives, plot strands, and a nonlinear chronology, DeLillo demonstrates that the "single narrative sweep" of history can only ever be achieved by suppressing numerous other possible histories.

The novel opens with a third person account of the famous baseball game between the Brooklyn Dodgers and the New York Giants on October 3, 1951. The narrative flits between different characters' perspective of the game. Some characters are fictional, such as Cotter, the young African-American teenager who has skipped school to see the game, though most are historical: Frank Sinatra, Jackie Gleason, Toots Shor, Russ Hodges, and J. Edgar Hoover. During the game, an aide brings Hoover word that the Soviet Union has tested a nuclear bomb. The Giants win the game in dramatic fashion when Bobby Thomson hits a home run. The crowd scrambles after the baseball, and after some struggle, Cotter, the young African-American boy, manages to get possession of it.

DeLillo tells the story of Cotter Martin, and his father Manx, in three sections interspersed through the novel. Manx takes the ball from his son in order to sell it. He finally persuades advertising executive, Charlie Wainwright, to buy the ball for his young son, Chuck. Manx has no ticket to prove the ball's authenticity, but he uses this to his advantage, arguing that this lack of proof makes the baseball more significant, as it becomes a symbol of faith and trust between two fathers.

"Underworld" flashes forward to the spring and summer of 1992, to Nick Shay's first person account of visiting Klara Sax, an artist, in the desert. The 57-year-old Nick has not seen Klara since he was 17, when they were lovers in the Bronx. Klara created art from garbage or waste in the past, however, now she is working with abandoned U.S. military planes, which have been left to rot in the desert. She and her helpers paint them a myriad of colors. As she tells Nick, she is "drunk on color … I'm a woman going mad with color" (70). She also talks of her nostalgia for the old stability and certainties of the Cold War.

Nick lives in Phoenix, Arizona, with his elderly mother, and his wife, Marian. He works as an executive for a waste management firm, a form of employment that causes him to see all goods as garbage, even before buying them. Nick's father, Jimmy Constanza, has been missing since Nick was a boy. He went out to get a packet of Lucky Strike cigarettes, and never came back. Nick's life is one of self-control and organization (he jogs regularly and drinks soymilk), though we sense that his youth in the Bronx was more confused and chaotic.

Nick meets with his friends and colleagues, Brian Glassic and Simeon Biggs, also known as Big Sims, at the new Dodger Stadium in Los Angeles. The Dodgers are again playing the Giants, and they reminisce about the famous 1951 game, that opened the novel. Glassic contrasts Bobby Thomson's home run with the Kennedy assassination, arguing that while people went outside after the baseball game, they stayed inside after Kennedy was shot. Nick reveals that he owns the ball that Thomson hit into the stands. Nick purchased it from baseball memorabilia collector Marvin Lundy, a nervous man who wears latex gloves when he drives into the city. Like Nick, Marvin is a Dodgers fan, and both men associate the ball with loss. As Nick says, "It's all about losing" (97).

In a series of episodes from the mid-1980s to early 1990s, DeLillo introduces the Texas Highway Killer, a serial killer who randomly shoots other drivers as he overtakes their vehicles. A young girl captures one of his drive-by shootings on an amateur video. The TV news channels play the video on an endless loop. Some, like Matt, Nick's brother, find themselves hypnotized by the footage. Later in this section of the novel, we discover that the Texas Highway Killer is Richard, a lonely supermarket clerk, who lives with his parents.

DeLillo also introduces the relationship between Marian, Nick's wife, and Brian Glassic. They meet looking at classic cars, and both confess to an overwhelming sense of nostalgia for the Cold War and its certainties. While Nick is in the Bronx, Marian and Brian continue their affair, meeting at Marian's assistant's place. When Marian compares Nick and Brian, she realizes that, contrary to the commonly accepted paradigm of the illicit affair, her husband is the more dangerous choice, "They talk about demon lovers. She had a demon husband. Her lover was a loose-jointed guy with a freckled forehead and nappy hair" (256).

Nick visits his mother, Rosemary, in the Bronx. His younger brother, Matt, is also visiting. Nick wants Rosemary to live in Phoenix with him. The brothers discuss their father's disappearance. Nick believes Jimmy was "got at" by someone, while Matt thinks that he simply walked out. Matt visits Albert Bronzini, Klara Sax's ex-husband and they talk about chess. Bronzini still lives in the Bronx with his sister, but he realizes the Bronx is becoming more dangerous.

Sister Edgar, a nun, is another long-time Bronx resident. Like Marvin Lundy, she is also obsessed with hygiene and wears latex gloves. She hears of a 12-year-old girl, Esmeralda, who is living on the streets, and attempts to find her. In one of many scenes in which "Underworld" seems full of connections, DeLillo describes Sister Edgar reading the same edition of *Time* magazine, featuring Klara Sax, that prompts Nick's visit to the desert.

The narrative moves back to 1978, with a first person narrative from Nick Shay. During a trip to Los Angeles for a waste conference, Nick visits the Watts Towers. The Towers remind Nick of his father, as the creator of the Watts Towers, Sabatia Rodia, also walked out on his family. Crucially, these towers are also built from garbage, and like Klara Sax's art, represent an instance of waste transformed into an aesthetic form.

During the waste conference, Nick visits a huge landfill site. Nick proposes waste as nostalgia tourism. He meets Detwiler, a garbage archaeologist.

Detwiler argues that waste is a motivating force of civilization, as it requires a complex social structure and technological innovation to dispose of it. There is a swingers convention in the same hotel as Nick's conference and he meets one of the swingers, Donna. He tells her about "The Cloud of Unknowing," an anonymous Christian work from the fourteenth century, which describes an abstract, transcendent God, beyond human knowledge and language. Nick believes in the power of language, the possible existence of one ideal word that could explain everything. Nick tells Donna the phrase he relies on, "Todo y Nada," which means all and nothing. Nick also reveals to Donna that he shot a man when he was 17. Nick has never told his wife, Marian, this fact. Though Nick worries that Donna is "an agent of her husband's will" (294), he has sex with her, and Nick feels a rare moment of connection.

Marvin Lundy is in San Francisco with his English wife, Eleanor, to meet Chuckie Wainwright, hoping to complete the lineage of the baseball. Marvin compares this trip to his honeymoon through Europe looking for his half-brother Avram Lubarsky, a search that parallels his quest for the baseball's lineage. We also discover that when Bobby Thomson hit the ball into the stands, Marvin had lost radio reception, as his train was going through the Alps. In other words, not only did Marvin's team lose, but this famous baseball moment was also literally lost to him.

"Underworld" then turns to Klara Sax's experiences in New York City in 1974. The World Trade Center is under construction and it haunts Klara, who sees it almost everywhere she goes. For Klara, the Twin Towers have great symbolic value, being "a model of behemoth mass production" (377). Nixon resigns from office, prompting Klara to remember her adolescence and her own father, of whom Nixon reminds her. There is a garbage strike on, and Klara begins pulling color out of her work. Klara hears of a talented young graffiti artist called Moonman 157, and goes to see his work.

Klara goes to a showing of a recently discovered (and fictional) Sergei Eisenstein film classic, "Unterwelt." "Underworld" intercuts Klara's experience watching the film with scenes from the life of Moonman 157, Ismael Muñoz. Ismael is about to become a father and is overwhelmed by the prospect. Implicit connections are made between Ismael's graffiti art and Eisenstein's film, which Klara characterizes as part of "sneak attacks on the dominant culture" (444).

Klara meets a young black artist called Acey Green. Green is working on a project featuring Jayne Mansfield, whom she characterizes as "the fake Marilyn" (474), referring to Marilyn Monroe. Klara sees the Zapruder film—the infamous film which captured John F. Kennedy's assassination—with her boyfriend, Miles. In shock, they realize that the shot that kills Kennedy seems to come from the front, contradicting the official account of the assassination. The endless replaying of the Zapruder film echoes the media's replaying of the Texas Highway Killer video. Klara also visits the Watts Towers in Los Angeles, just as Nick does earlier in the novel. For Klara, these towers, constructed from garbage, are an extremely powerful piece of art. She calls them a "place riddled with epiphanies" (492).

Meanwhile, Nick's brother, Matt, is working in New Mexico in a government nuclear weapons laboratory, doing "consequence analysis" (401). In other words, Matt calculates the human and environmental costs of a nuclear accident or limited nuclear attack. Matt feels that the unprecedented power of the bomb changes the way in which we view the world, it is "the bomb that would redefine the limits of human perception and dread" (422). This perspective disturbs Janet, Matt's future wife, who accuses him of making the bomb "sound like god" (458).

The novel then returns to the 1950s and 1960s. The narrative switches between various character's experiences in this period, including Nick's time in an institution in upstate New York after the shooting, and the performances of renegade stand up comedian, Lenny Bruce. A psychiatrist tells Nick that the third person in the room the day of the shooting was his father. Nick is given an early release and sent to "a small Jesuit outpost in northern Minnesota" (299). The priests help Nick relearn language, by teaching him the names of the parts of a shoe, obscure words, such as eyelet and aglet. Father Paulus argues that Nick cannot understand the world, unless he can name it properly. After leaving the Jesuits, Nick makes a road trip across the USA with his girlfriend, Amy.

Bruce guides his audience through the Cuban Missile Crisis of 1962, by helping them make the transition from the "global thing" (504) to their own lives. He loves the "postexistential bent" (507) of the situation and the line "We're all gonna die!" (507). Lenny emphasizes that the existence of the bomb and the possibility of complete annihilation eradicates individual choice. Lenny riffs on the names associated with the Cuban Missile Crisis, reminding his audience that their lives are being decided by a powerful elite. He argues that his own decision to change his name was a move towards the "invisible middle" (592).

The novel also introduces scenes from Eric Demming's childhood. In a parody of the happy fifties American family, Eric's mother makes desserts and salads from Jello-O, while Eric masturbates upstairs. Eric is already obsessed with technology, claiming to eat Hydrox cookies because the name sounds like rocket fuel.

We also discover that the baseball is currently in the possession of advertising executive, Charlie Wainwright, who uses lines from Lenny Bruce LPs to impress others. Charlie wants to leave the baseball to his son, Chuck, to compensate in part for their inadequate relationship. This gesture is insufficient, however, and Chuck regards his father as "all empty command and false authority" (611).

J. Edgar Hoover is staying at the Waldorf with his lifelong companion and, perhaps, lover, Clyde Tolsen. Outside a crowd protests against Vietnam. Hoover has arranged an invitation to Truman Capote's famous Black and White Ball, and has a mask fitted that makes oblique reference to his sexuality, as it looks like a "sequined biker's mask" (565). Andy Warhol arrives at the ball wearing a mask that is a photo of his own face.

Marian goes home to visit her parents in Madison, Wisconsin. She hears a student riot on the radio and through the window simultaneously. After telling her parents about Nick, she telephones Nick, revealing that she wants get married.

In a series of scenes, DeLillo builds up a set of the connections and coincidences that was much remarked upon by initial reviewers of "Underworld." Albert Bronzini reads the newspaper headlines about Bobby Thomson's home run, "the Shot Heard Round the World" (669), while Sister Edgar teaches Matt Shay. The seventeen-year-old Nick also begins an affair with the 31-year-old Klara Sax. Crucially, Nick also becomes friends with a waiter, George Manza. Nick accidentally shoots George, after George hands him a sawed off shotgun, telling him that it is not loaded. We begin to understand that Nick's later quest for the one reliable word or phrase is prompted by this early lesson in the unreliability of language.

The closing section of "Underworld," "Das Kapital," describes Nick and Brian's business trip to Russia after the end of the cold war. They discover the legacy of nuclear weapons and power-nuclear waste. They also discover that American consumerism has already infected post-Communist Russia. Nick finally confronts Brian about his affair with Marian. Back in the Bronx, Sister Edgar discovers that somebody raped Esmeralda, the 12-year-old girl she had been looking for, and threw her off a roof. Shortly afterward Esmeralda's face appears on a billboard in a kind of modern day miracle. Crowds and the media gather to witness the spectacle. Sister Edgar describes the event as "strong enough to seem real. It's the news without the media" (819).

Finally, the novel ends with a meditation on the way in which the Internet links topics and people, including Sister Edgar and J. Edgar Hoover, which ensures that "Everything is connected in the end" (826). "Underworld" closes on the word "Peace" (827).

Historical Context

"Underworld" is explicitly and self-consciously situated in history from the opening juxtaposition of the Bobby Thomson's shot heard around the world with the Soviet testing of an atomic bomb. The novel charts the history of the Cold War and beyond, citing many actual historical events, including the Cuban Missile crisis, the Kennedy assassination, Truman Capote's Black and White Ball, President Nixon's resignation, the Vietnam war, the building of the Twin Towers, and the collapse of the Soviet Union. Against this official history, DeLillo plots the story of the baseball that Bobby Thomson hit into the stands, a story that functions as a kind of ur-history. Russ Hodges, for example, calls the baseball game "another kind of history … the people's history" (59–60), contrasting it explicitly with the cold war, the "vast shaping strategies of eminent leaders, generals steely in their sunglasses" (60).

Individuals in DeLillo's fiction are always conditioned to a greater or lesser extent by their culture and history, and "Underworld" explores this theme to its fullest. During the Cuban Missile Crisis, for instance, Lenny Bruce's post–existential scream "We're all going to die!" reminds us that individual control over existence is repeatedly threatened by the actions of governments and bigger powers. The characters of "Underworld" are shaped by the Cold War to such an extent that some feel disorientated and disturbed once it ends. As Marvin Lundy

says to Brian Glassic: "You need the leaders of both sides to keep the Cold War going. It's the one constant thing. It's honest, it's dependable." (170). Similarly, Klara Sax remarks to Nick Shay on the end of the Cold War:

> Power meant something thirty, forty years ago. It was stable, it was focused, it was a tangible thing. It was greatness, danger, terror, all those things. And it held us together, the Soviets and us. Maybe it held the world together (76).

Both Marvin Lundy and Klara Sax recognize the stability granted by the bomb as stemming, paradoxically, from its power. They ascribe the constancy of the Cold War period to the concept of Mutual Assured Destruction (MAD), whereby neither the Soviets nor Americans dared risk a war, because the power of the bomb could result in the annihilation of both sides.

DeLillo also often interrogates our understanding of history in his fiction. Nick believes that recording history is an uncomplicated business. For him, history is a "single narrative sweep, not ten thousand wisps of disinformation" (82). However, DeLillo repeatedly undermines this view. Klara Sax watches the Zapruder film of the assassination of John F. Kennedy. This film epitomizes the difficulty of knowing history. Despite being recorded on film this event is still surrounded by uncertainty, something that no amount of "analyz[ing] the dots" (182), as Marvin Lundy puts it, can resolve. This uncertainty is even seen in DeLillo's depiction of the history of the baseball. Crucially, neither Marvin Lundy nor Nick Shay ever uncover the last link in the baseball's history back to the Polo Grounds. This "lost history" is the story of Cotter Martin and his father Manx, as DeLillo demonstrates how the history of marginalized groups in society has often been lost to dominant culture. In other words, even what Russ Hodges calls "the people's history" (60) is incomplete.

Societal Context

DeLillo once told an interviewer that the fiction he admires the most is that which is "equal to the complexities and excesses of the culture" (Begley 289). In "Underworld," DeLillo attempts to create just such a piece of fiction. Its extremely broad canvas enables DeLillo to chart the principal shifts in American culture and society from the early fifties to the late nineties. The novel depicts the widespread paranoia that characterized the United States during the Cold War, examines the rise of the media and consumerism, and touches on specific issues of race and gender.

DeLillo has long had a reputation as a conspiracy theorist. Robert Towers, for example, called him the "chief shaman of the paranoid school of fiction" (6) in the *New York Review of Books*. DeLillo has earned this reputation not least for his deep-seated interest in the Kennedy assassination, which his fiction refers to repeatedly, and which is the central subject of his novel, "Libra" (1988). "Underworld" cemented DeLillo's paranoid reputation for some critics. Indeed, some even accused DeLillo of creating in "Underworld" a novel which realizes the paranoid imaginings of his characters. Richard Williams argued, for example, that "Underworld" "ends up flattering the paranoid vision of Hoover, because it so immaculately fulfils Hoover's deepest wishes" while Tony Tanner stated that "Underworld" has "a rather wearingly uniform paranoid texture." Paranoia does indeed pervade the novel from J. Edgar Hoover's obsessive information gathering to Klara Sax's response to the Zapruder film. The structure of the novel also replicates this emotion to some extent itself- as reviewers have noted, it is a novel in which "everything is connected." In his defense, DeLillo claimed that that second half of the twentieth century was a period in which "paranoia replaced history in American life" (qtd in O'Toole 64). Certainly, conspiracy theories abounded and internal distrust of government grew in the United States in the second half of the twentieth century. The public not only distrusted official accounts of the Kennedy assassination, but some also even began to question the veracity of the Apollo moon landings. So rather than promoting such paranoia, we can argue that DeLillo is instead seeking to examine the rise of this phenomenon in "Underworld." DeLillo certainly connects its appearance, not just to obvious instances of government dishonesty such as the Watergate scandal, but to his characters' sense that the 1950s were not the halcyon days they remember, but were in fact full of hidden dangers. Matt remembers having his feet x-rayed in shoe shops, for example, which he now realizes was "spraying your feet with radiation" (198). As Marian argues, it is not so much that the world has become more dangerous, as knowledge itself has changed, has "become suspicious and alert" (165)."

Underworld" also charts the rise of American consumerism, particularly in its satiric depiction of the Demming's home life, which is described by one commentator as "a kind of R-rated Leave It to Beaver" (Wallace 370). While Eric's mother creates extraordinary dishes from Jell-O in her "dream kitchen," her teenage son masturbates in his bedroom into an "Honest John" condom. Eric's condom and Mrs Demming's Jell-O molds and crispers are all products of the companies like Du Pont chemicals, who promised "Better Living Through Chemistry." Americans may have become more paranoid during the Cold War, but they also gained materially consumer success that helped the United States win the ideological battle of the Cold War. Indeed, when Nick visits the former Soviet Union, he discovers it has already become infected with the consumer impulses that characterize the United States. But DeLillo also highlights the downside of consumerism. Just as the bomb that kept the peace left a legacy of nuclear waste, so consumerism creates its own environmental problems. Nick works, of course, in waste management, an industry essential to clear up after consumer culture. Indeed, Nick and Marian see goods as garbage even while they remain on supermarket shelves. As John Duvall writes, by the close of "Underworld," "the threat of nuclear apocalypse may have receded, but … with little to contain capitalism's colonization of global markets, an environmental apocalypse looms" (23).

Race relations in the United States are also a theme of "Underworld." The period from the early fifties to the 1990s was, of course, a turbulent one in terms of racial politics. DeLillo makes reference to the Civil Rights movement of the 1960s, the Black Panthers of the 1970s, and the Los Angeles riots in the early 1990s. The opening prologue is itself an ironic commentary on the apparently colorblind camaraderie of baseball fans. While the white Bill Waterson is happy to chat and share peanuts with Cotter during the game, this fellowship soon breaks down into the old binary of black and white afterwards, as Bill fights desperately to seize the ball from Cotter. But "Underworld's" clearest statement on race is in its very plot structure. DeLillo literally separates the story of Cotter and Manx Martin from that of other characters (indeed, these sections are even bounded by black pages in the hardback edition), reminding readers of the legacy of racial segregation in the United States. Furthermore, that neither Nick Shay nor Marvin Lundy recovers the story of Manx and Cotter is a reminder that much black history has been lost to white American society. In other words, just as Simeon Biggs argues to Nick that that U.S. census vastly underestimates the number of black Americans, so DeLillo demonstrates the way in which mainstream American society has excluded the history of its African-American population.

"Underworld" also explores changing gender roles in American society. Women's lives changed dramatically in this period, not least because of the successes of second-wave feminism in the sixties and seventies, which sought economic equality for women (including, crucially, the rights of mothers to have careers outside the home). Nick Shay's mother, Rosemary, is a classic instance of the put-upon wife and mother of the 1950s, whose husband has vanished, leaving her with the responsibility of bringing up their children. Ironically, in her old age, her favorite television show is "The Honeymooners," a fictionalized rendering of the kind of enduring marriage she did not experience in the 1950s. In contrast, Nick's wife, Marian manages to balance a career, children, and an affair with Brian Glassic. Klara Sax also represents the creative and sexual awakening of women in the 1950s. At first a wife and mother, Klara Sax leaves her husband to become an extremely successful artist, shortly after having an affair with the 17-year-old Nick. In scenes from the 1970s, DeLillo depicts a key generational gap between Klara Sax and the young black artist, Acey Green. While Klara Sax struggled to become an artist, Acey Green takes the victories of second-wave feminism for granted.

Religious Context

Despite the rise of evangelical Christianity in the United States in 1980s, it is Catholicism that dominates "Underworld" from Nick Shay's Irish-Italian childhood to Sister Edgar's mission in the Bronx. The novel's focus on Catholicism may be a reflection of DeLillo's own upbringing. As DeLillo told Vince Passaro, "I think there is a sense of last things in my work that probably comes from a Catholic childhood."

Certainly, Nick's religious upbringing, and especially his experiences with Father Paulus shape his understanding of history and language. Father Paulus's insistence on knowing the names of things implies an absolute referential relationship between words and the things that they represent. A medieval religious text, "The Cloud of Unknowing," inspires Nick to believe that he can "search for the one word, the one syllable" which would allow him to "eliminate distraction and edge closer to God's unknowable self" (296). In other words, just as Nick believes that history is "a single narrative sweep" (82), so he believes language offers us a way of understanding and knowing the world. Of course, an absolute, guaranteed relation between the word and the world is integral to faith-based readings of religious texts like the Bible.

However, spiritual yearnings are not restricted to the novel's Catholic characters. Instead, like "White Noise," many of the "Underworld's" characters experience an intense desire to discover some kind of transcendence in the mass culture of modern America. For characters like Brian Glassic, Sims and even Nick to some extent, these yearnings are fulfilled by baseball. For other characters, like Klara Sax, art plays an important spiritual role. DeLillo explicitly depicts her visit to the Watts Towers as a religious experience. As Klara comments, these Watts Towers are "riddled with epiphanies" (492).

Scientific & Technological Context

The way in which science and technology shape our lives is a central concern in DeLillo's fiction. "Underworld" is dominated by the atomic bomb, which DeLillo suggests is the prevailing metaphor of the Cold War era. Eric Deming's childhood illustrates the cultural impact of the bomb most clearly. He eats "Hydrox cookies because the name sounded like rocket fuel" (519), while his mother, Erica, has a Jell-O mold "sort of guided missile-like" (515). Eric also likens his condom to a nuclear warhead:

> He liked using a condom because it had a sleek metallic shimmer, like his favorite weapons system, the Honest John, a surface-to-surface missile with a warhead that carried yields of up to forty kilotons. (514)

Just as the baseball offers some comfort to Nick Shay and Marvin Lundy, so Klara Sax views the bomb as a source of certainty and stability. She recognizes that the stability granted by the bomb as stemmed, paradoxically, from its power. The sheer

destructive power of nuclear weapons deterred both sides from using them during the Cold War, as any nuclear strike was likely to result in the annihilation of both the Soviets and the Americans.

But DeLillo also charts a kind of loss of innocence in America's relationship to science in "Underworld." He undermines the popular faith in science, epitomized by the Du Pont slogan "Better Living Through Chemistry," that characterized American culture in 1950s. Though his characters exhibit nostalgia for the 1950s, they are also aware that the age was not as innocent as it seemed. They remember having their feet x-rayed in shoe stores, and refer to Edward Teller's infamous atomic tests, in which the only protection used was suntan lotion. With the Vietnam War comes the deadly chemical toxin, Agent Orange, and even after the end of the Cold War the world is counting the environmental costs of dealing with nuclear waste.

The most significant manifestation of technology in "Underworld," outside the bomb, is the electronic media. As in "White Noise," DeLillo is interested in the concept of hyperreality, that is, the idea that it is reproduction in the mass media that authenticates reality. The statement "This is what technology does … It makes reality come true" (17) refers specifically to the technology of reproduction, echoing a Bill Gray's statement in Mao II, that "Nothing happens until it's consumed" (44). Reproduction in the media is sometimes erroneously regarded as transparent by DeLillo's characters. For example, Marvin Lundy believes he can discover the true history of the baseball by examining photographs closely: "I looked at a million photographs because this is the dot theory of reality, that all knowledge is available if you analyze the dots" (175). But Russ Hodges's admission that baseball games were re-created for radio alerts us to the role of the media, even in the fifties, not as a window on "reality," but as a shaper of "reality."

That technology mediates our experience of the work is summed up neatly (and perhaps a little facetiously) by the condom. As Brian Glassic says, "this was technology they wanted to wrap around my dick" (110). The condom also charts changing the growing awareness of the dangers that characterize modern living, what Marian calls "knowledge becomes suspicious and alert" (165). From a simple form of birth control in the 1950s, by the nineties the condom had become a barometer of the paranoia of post-Cold War America. The condom is also for John Duvall, "a study of waste and its containment" (46), which neatly connects the legacy of waste produced by both consumerism and the Cold War.

Biographical Context

Until the publication of "Underworld" (1997), DeLillo gave few interviews and made even fewer public appearances. His novels included no biographical information beyond the year and place of his birth (1936, Bronx, New York) and a brief note on his education at Fordham University. DeLillo carried, famously, a business card to interviews that stated simply "I don't want to talk about it" (LeClair 79). He told Tom LeClair, quoting James Joyce, that the lack of personal information available on him was the result of "silence, exile, cunning and so on" (80). As late as 1997, DeLillo was awarded seven out of ten on the reclusiveness scale by "Entertainment Weekly" (Moran 151).

But "Underworld" marks something of a change in DeLillo's fiction, as it is by far DeLillo's most biographical novel to date. Indeed, DeLillo told one interviewer that he realized he was "reliving experience in a curious and totally unintentional way" (Echlin E5) in "Underworld." DeLillo worked for an advertising agency, Ogilvy and Mather, in the 1950s, for example, which as John Duvall reminds us, "finds expression in "Underworld's" portrayal of Madison Avenue culture" (10). But the most significant biographical connections are between DeLillo and Nick Shay.

DeLillo is around the same age as Nick Shay, and is from the same Italian district in the Bronx as Nick. As DeLillo told Fintan O'Toole: "the building he [Nick] lives in … is across the street from the house I lived in" (64). DeLillo is also a baseball fan, though unlike Nick he was a Yankee fan and in his words "slightly aloof from this ball-game. I was interested because the Yankees had already won their pennant and were waiting for the winners of this game" (64). DeLillo also attended Fordham University, the university that Bronzini suggests for Nick, and DeLillo shares Nick's Catholic background.

Anne Longmuir, PhD

Works Cited

Begley, Adam. "The Art of Fiction CXXXV: Don DeLillo." *Paris Review* 35.128 (1993): 274–306

DeLillo, Don. *Mao II*. London: Vintage, 1992

——. *Underworld*. London: Picador, 1998

——. *White Noise*. London: Picador, 1986

Duvall, John. *Don DeLillo's Underworld: A Reader's Guide*. New York and London: Continuum Publishing, 2002

LeClair, Tom. "An Interview with Don DeLillo." *Anything Can Happen: Interview with Contemporary American Novelists*. Ed. Tom LeClair and Larry McCaffery. Urbana: University of Illinois Press, 1983. 79–90

Moran, Joe. "Don DeLillo and the Myth of the Author-Recluse." *Journal of American Studies*. 34.1 (2000): 137–52

O'Toole, Fintan. "And Quiet Writes the Don." *Irish Times* 10 Jan 1998: 64

Passaro, Vince. "Dangerous Don DeLillo." *New York Times Magazine*. 19 May 1991: 36-8, 76–77

Tanner, Tony. "Afterthoughts on Don DeLillo's 'Underworld'." *Raritan* 17.4 (1998): 48–71

Towers, Robert. "From the Grassy Knoll." *New York Times Book Review*. 18 August 1988: 6

Wallace, Molly. "'Venerated Emblems': DeLillo's Underworld and the History-Commodity." *Critique* 42.4 (2001): 367–83

Discussion Questions

1. Why is the novel called "Underworld?" To which underworld(s) might the title refer?
2. What is the function of "Underworld's" nonlinear chronology?
3. Some critics claim that "everything is connected" in this novel, and accuse DeLillo of "realizing the paranoid imaginations of his characters." Do you agree? Explain your answer.
4. What does the baseball symbolize? Is it significant that it represents losing to both Nick Shay and Marvin Lundy? Explain.
5. "Underworld" depicts many absent or inadequate fathers. What's the purpose of this?
6. Describe the relationship of artists and society in "Underworld." Why might the novel depict so many artists?
7. What's the significance of waste in "Underworld?"
8. Some characters claim to be nostalgic for Cold War. Why do they feel this way?
9. "Underworld" intersperses fictional and real-life characters. What's the effect of this? What does the novel tell us about the construction of history?
10. The novel ends with the word "Peace." Is DeLillo being ironic here? Explain.

Essay Ideas

1. Nick Shay claims history is "a single narrative sweep." Discuss whether DeLillo's use of real-life historical events supports or contests this claim.
2. Analyze the depiction of fathers and sons in "Underworld."
3. Discuss the symbolism and significance of waste in "Underworld."
4. DeLillo has been accused of being "the chief shaman of the paranoid school of fiction." Discuss whether "Underworld" is a paranoid novel.
5. Discuss the special role played by art and artists in "Underworld."

The View From Saturday

by E.L. Konigsburg

Content Synopsis

The Newbury Medal winning novel, "The View from Saturday," penned by E.L. Konigsburg, focuses on the intertwined narratives of four children and their paraplegic teacher as they journey toward greater self-discovery and strength. The story's structure is complex, with chapters and subsections that shift in perspective with shifting narrators and changing time settings.

Eva Marie Olinski is a widow who was injured in a car accident that resulted in her disability. After physically recovering as much as she can, Eva returns to teach sixth grade at Ephiphany Middle School in upstate New York just in time to become entangled with four children who together form a group they call The Souls. As individuals, they each make journeys of self-discovery that help them to better forge the collective body which is unbeatable as an academic bowl team. Part of the narrative involves Mrs. Olinski's reasoning for choosing each team member, and the organization of each student's narrative reflects the order of her choices, as well as the narrative and temporal sequencing of their individual journeys.

Noah Gershom's journey is first and is told as a flashback. He had visited Century Village, a retirement community in Florida, to visit his grandparents. At the time, the community was preparing for a wedding between two of the residents, and he took part in these preparations, learning calligraphy, helping with deliveries, and eventually stepping in as the best man.

Nadia Diamondstein's journey follows next. Her story is a bit more complicated. We discover that her parents have recently divorced, and this is a huge issue Nadia is struggling to accept. Her mother has moved to upstate New York and has uprooted the southern Nadia, whose life will consequently intersect with the other Souls. Her nervous and hovering father—whose broken leg caused Noah to stand in for him at the wedding—has her for a custodial visit, and the two spend a lot of time with her newly remarried paternal grandfather (Izzy). Nadia is thus trying to accept her grandfather's remarriage as well as her new status as a commuter between Florida and New York. Her one constant affirmation is her "brilliant" dog, Ginger. Her narrative introduces our third soul, Ethan Potter, who has come to visit his maternal grandmother (Margaret Draper), who has just married Nadia's grandfather.

Ethan struggles with his own issues, being the younger sibling of a superstar, but Nadia discovers little about him due to his impenetrable silence. Instead, she stars in her own drama. The previous year, she had spent time with Margaret and Izzy at the beach, learning about sea turtles and their guardianship. Margaret, a former teacher and principal at Ephiphany Middle School (in fact, she had worked with Mrs. Olinski prior to her debilitating accident), provided instruction so they could join her rescue squad. This summer, Ethan and Allen are also showing interest in learning and when Allen plans to become certified, Nadia loses her temper. Ethan breaks his silence to mention that Margaret is the one who found Nadia's mom the job working as a dental hygienist for none other than Dr. Gershom, which enabled the divorce and, as far as Nadia is concerned, made meddling Margaret a key factor in making possible the separation which is still devastating the young lady. Seeing a parallel between Margaret's meddling in turtles' and her own, Nadia rejects the turtle project until a severe storm threatens to annihilate an entire nest. In the intervening discussion between Nadia and her father, the reader learns about the process of sea turtles migration, and a parallel is drawn whereby Nadia discovers that she, like the turtles, can live a migratory life although she might also periodically need assistance or a "lift."

Ethan's travels physically bring him to Florida, but his metaphysical journey is on a bus to school where he meets the new student, Julian Singh (who will become the fourth Soul). Julian's British accent, Indian ancestry, and upbringing on a cruise ship (which had taught him a little less about peer pressure and blending in than the other students at Ephiphany had learned) lead him to conflict with the book's bully-Hamilton (Ham) Knapp.

Ethan's journey involves finding a voice and the narrative section which is relayed discusses his unvoiced affection for Nadia and for the theatre, a growing friendship and respect between himself and Julian (which has very limited public discussion), and the developing group which forms as Julian invites the three other Souls to his father's Bed and Breakfast for afternoon tea. Ethan's older brother has over-shadowed him, and his silence isolates him, even from their mother who does not even know he's chosen a career differing from the projected path—to carry on the family farm. At his first tea, Ethan cracks a joke he'd developed long ago but never shared. He finds his voice and

develops a relationship with Nadia centered on debate, similar to playing the devil's advocate; through this process they both grow more critically astute. During his narrative, Nadia names the group "The Souls."

The final journey is Julian's. Coming last in the story, his narrative fills in the gaps and completes the story. Although Julian's father describes Julian's journey as "the longest," it is never really specified what his challenge was, aside from ambiguous cruelty, and which seems to have done little to change who Julian is, what he cares about, or how he acts. Fortunately, however, the cruel characters are put into their places and restrained, if not retrained.

Julian becomes more firmly connected to the others when Nadia presents him with Alice, one of Ginger's puppies. Later Julian teaches Nadia how to train a dog to perform so Ginger will win the part of Sandy in the school's production of "Annie!" Michael Froelich, one of Ham's stooges, has a dog (Arnold) who is the understudy of Ginger's dog. Julian also teaches Michael how to train dogs, and through this friendly interchange, Michael is no longer so evil or mean. Despite the positive turn around, Ham plans to make Ginger ill by drugging dog treats in order to allow Arnold to perform. The tables are turned when it is decided by those involved in the production that Arnold should perform the matinee anyway as a reward for his hard work. Julian finds out about the poisoned treats, and must decide whether or not he should allow Michael to pass the treats to Arnold. Julian does not tell the teachers or the dog owners. He takes the treats before any dogs consume them, and after the performance, he returns them to Ham, in front of his mother who is a veterinarian. It is not clear whether or not Ham is punished, but Ham does learn his plot was foiled and by whom.

Julian suggests that the Souls collectively take on a project, and specifies that the project should be Mrs. Olinski. As the Souls, competing in the academic bowl, they provide her with a victory and success that causes her confidence to soar. Her redemption involves a mystic tea experience. After the matinee of "Annie!" she takes the children to the Singh's bed and breakfast, where the Diamondsteins are guests. As they arrive and families greet their children, the Mrs. Olinski's inner monologue reveals her distaste towards Margaret's turquoise outfit. Her resentment rises to "the verge of screaming with pain and rage" (Konigsburg 124) and she is "so blinded by jealousy that she had not noticed Mr. Singh come out" (Konigsburg 124) and wheel her in to tea. The civility of the ceremony leaves her feeling that an indefinable but negative fugue has lifted. She then regains her courtesy and marvels to note the courtesy the children share with each other, attributing it to the custom of tea, observing, "I believe in courtesy. It is the way we avoid hurting people's feelings. She thought that maybe, just maybe, Western Civilization was in a decline because people did not take time to take tea at four o'clock" (Konigsburg 125). At this moment she selects her team for the state bowl championship.

The team works towards the state bowl championship, finally winning it, partly through the knowledge the students developed on subjects such as turtle migration, calligraphy, etc. On the trip back from the finals, Mr. Singh explains that all their journeys ended with a "cup of kindness" (Konigsburg 157), and the final image we have is of Mrs. Olinski, smiling like the Cheshire Cat, aware that "all the king's horses and all the king's men could not have done for Mrs. Eva Marie Olinski what the kindness of her four sixth-grade souls had" (Konigsburg 159).

Historical Context

This book reflects the transitory and fluid nature of our contemporary society, and yet the interwoven lives reflect a sense of community which transcends the possible disconnection that might result from such distance. Nadia's lesson learned,

regarding her need to accept her parents' divorce and her new status commuting back and forth between New York and Florida, is central to this theme. The U.N. Demographic Yearbook indicates that the United States, during the period of 1996–2000, held the highest divorce rate among developed nations ("Divorce" 34). The U.S. Census indicates that during the 1970–1996 period, the number of divorced couples quadrupled, and less than a quarter of children were raised in homes with their parents remaining married (Lord 49). The challenge being faced by Nadia is accepted by all the adults as commonplace, reflecting society's acceptance of divorce. Nadia, however, does not like the personal implications of her divided family and resents the way everyone else accepts and encourages it. Many alternative definitions of "family" are presented in this novel.

The Americans with Disabilities Act (ADA) of 1990 presented schools and workplaces with the challenge of providing equal opportunities for those with disabilities, including making reasonable accommodations. Through the next two decades, the courts would refine exactly who was "disabled" and what might be covered, but this act signaled an important change in the acceptance and accommodations for persons with disabilities. Mrs. Olinski's return to work, despite her physical disabilities, and her seeming success there are reflective of the times. She does still suffer some challenges (she needs to be driven and often pushed in her wheelchair), but this is not a central concern. The book presents that her greatest challenge is attitudinal, in accepting her status and moving forward.

Multiculturalism began in the 1970s in Canada and spread to Europe. Political correctness arose in the 1970s and 80s, as women entered the workforce and challenged previous concepts as well as their linguistic expressions. The notion of Political Correctness seeped into education, and found a home particularly in the campuses of higher education.

By the mid-1990s, the term was beginning to lose favor, as it became a criticism that conservatives would use against liberals.

Konigsburg addresses the status of education in America. Using characters involved in education for several generations, Konigsburg can address the recent shifts in education, which she does in a scathing but not overbearing manner. She mocks the "ed-you-kay-tors" who blindly follow the current theories of the day. Her superintendent, Dr. Rohmer, is a supposed expert in multiculturalism, and yet when Mrs. Olinski is explaining how her team is diverse, rightly calling Julian an Indian, Rohmer corrects her to say that they don't use that term now; Julian is a Native American. Since Julian is a student in his district, and since the team has already achieved some measure of success, Rohmer's error in labeling Julian either reflects an automated response, or an inability to see differences with sensitivity. He responds in his chiding by asking her how she would feel if people called her "cripple" instead of "paraplegic." In fact, on her first day back in the classroom, Mrs. Olinski had written "paraplegic" on the board and when everyone returned from lunch, it had been changed to read "cripple." We later learn that Ham perpetrated this act, but for some time Julian appears guilty. Mrs. Olinski responds by erasing the word and waiting for the facts. After she discovers the guilt, she addresses it, but she doesn't rush to respond and err as Rohmer does. The novel, reflecting an understanding and awareness of the multicultural movement, affirms that any value is derived from deep understanding, not knee-jerk reactionism. The actual language used can be erased, revised, or ignored.

Societal Context

Hybridization is a central theme of "The View from Saturday." When Mrs. Olinski is indirectly invited to tea, she says "two halves make a whole" (Konigsburg 140). This idea that the hybrid is more complete is echoed throughout: Nadia, Julian, and Ginger are all two halves, each with one foot in two cultures. Nadia is mixed, being half Jewish and half Protestant. The fact that her parents split up this union puts into question how permanent or positive it really is to combine ethnicities, but Nadia is better for her rich experiences. Ginger earns the role in "Annie!" because Sandy was not pure bred either. Julian, when asked if he is an alien, says he is not since his mother was American and his dad was naturalized. Here "alien" takes on the questions of "passenger on spaceship Earth" as well as the idea of being a foreign citizen, but in a legal, not cultural context. In fact, the Singh's ultimately reflect their American-ness through knowledge of the TV show, "Jeopardy!" Mr. Singh explains that the Souls are what the four children have fused to become, an incarnation, not a reincarnation. This is a central message—that the parts complete the whole and multiple parts make for a better whole.

There is a strain of Orientalism (romanticizing the Eastern) present here, in that exoticism is given a higher status, a mystical, magical one, just as affirming of the Other and its distancing and stereotyping as the "ed-you-kay-tors" might achieve. The Farmer's Market is where the Singhs shop, but Ethan's family does not find it remarkable given that it attracts many "dark-skinned" people from the college, because the market has such quality products. The Indian family and other dark-skinned people prefer healthy organic foods, integrity, tradition, and civility. They are mystical and curiously see things that are not outwardly apparent.

Silence and what can be said is a central theme as well. Nadia's narrative focuses on what is "important" and who decides that. She resents information being withheld from her and her relationship with her father moves to a more positive ground when they both listen to each other without restrictions. Julian's decision to reveal his perception and skill in foiling Ham's plan seems to contradict what he's been taught by his former magic teacher, but he can't resist. Ethan's process from silence to public applause when Ginger is awarded the part of Sandy shocks all but the Souls. There is even a small comic moment when Fairbain, the bumbling assistant to Dr. Rohmer, is told to limit his participation at the press conference to just one pre-scripted line. Unfortunately, the only question he is asked pertains to how the team's trip to Albany would be financed. The implication of his scripted line, "The taxpayers are very proud" (Konigsburg 148), led to new implications as the superintendent found himself faced with the prospect of transporting the Boosters as well.

The majority of truly deep communication seems to be unspoken. Julian and Ethan understand each other without speech. Mr. Singh speaks cryptically, purposely withholding some information. We do not know how he came to know much of it; in fact Mrs. Olinski wonders how he could possibly know what she herself barely knew regarding her selection of the team. Although his role is peripheral, he certainly knows more than other characters.

The Century Village approach to life is communal and the Souls take on a communal aspect as well, as they blend together, much like the puzzle that Ethan brings to their first tea, only that day they find there is literally and figuratively one piece missing, and once Mrs. Olinski joins them, their group is complete. There has been some criticism of Konigsburg's view as being too socialistic, but she is not working on a political concept here, but one of understanding and civility, reaffirming commitment to other humans in their journey through life. Julian, when schoolyard bullies write "I am an ass" on his leather satchel, revises this to the more positive and global, "I am a passenger on the spaceship earth." This is the type of shift Konigsburg is addressing. In confrontation with the foreign, Julian's exotic presentation is so different that even Ethan obsesses on it. Reactions like Ham's neglect the world view and the novel promotes a tolerance which will enable peace and harmony.

Religious Context

In her statement nominating Konigsburg's "View" for the NSK Neustadt Prize for Children's Literature, Judith Viorst said:

> Without…preaching, she has created a body of moral fiction whose morality—learning tolerance, playing fair, standing up for what you believe—organically emerges from (rather than being shoveled onto) her highly individualized, flesh-and-blood, utterly embraceable (but never too perfect) protagonists; from her rollicking and deliciously inventive plots; from her poetically precise language; and from her profound respect for her readers.

This sense of morality transcends boundaries and religions and serves as a centerpiece for "The View From Saturday."

Scientific & Technological Context

The science most clearly addressed here involves natural sciences and biology, expressed most clearly in Nadia's narrative, which focuses on the topic of sea turtles, their migration, mating, and growth patterns. Infused into her story is another narrative—the report she wrote the year prior for school. This serves as a metaphor for the life events Nadia is confronting, so the global view Konigsburg presents is also cross-species.

In the proverbial struggle between science and faith, Konigsburg falls clearly in this text on the side of faith, which is ironic given her background as a science teacher. Hope and redemption lie in man's faith, tolerance, and acceptance, rather than in science and technology.

Biographical Context

Elaine Lobl Konigsburg began as a science teacher in a private girls' school in Florida and moved into writing when her children began school. She branched out into art, providing illustrations for many of her novels. In 1968, her second novel,

"From the Mixed-up Files of Mrs. Basil E. Frankweiler," won both the Lewis Carroll Shelf Award and the Newbery Award, and "Jennifer, Hecate, Macbeth, William McKinley, and Me, Elizabeth," took Newbery Honors in the same year, 1968. Over the following decades, she continued to write popular texts, receiving the Newbery again in 1997 for "The View from Saturday."

Some of her works have been made into television productions, including "Jennifer, Hecate, Macbeth, William McKinley, and Me, Elizabeth," retitled "Jennifer and Me"; "From the Mixed-up Files of Mrs. Basil E. Frankweiler"; and "Father's Arcane Daughter," retitled "Caroline."

In a statement on "The View From Saturday," Konigsburg reveals that the stories were actually separately penned, coming together as she took a reflective walk, realizing they shared a theme and could work together. Her text pieces these separate narratives together as much as the narrative sequencing, with an intertwined, intricate structure. (reprinted in "E.L. Konigsburg").

Konigsburg attended Carnegie Mellon and the University of Pittsburgh, and lived in New York City, small towns in Pennsylvania, and Jacksonville, FL.

Anne K. Erickson

Works Cited

E. L. Konigsburg. "Educational Paperback Association." 17 Dec. 2005.

Konigsburg, E. L. *The View from Saturday*. New York: Aladdin, 1996.

Viorst, Judith. "Nominating Statement for E. L. Konigsburg." 17 Dec. 2005.

Discussion Questions

1. How do the separate stories work together to make a larger one?
2. How realistic are these characters as sixth-graders?
3. How are the three generations presented? Which seem to be more fully developed? Why?
4. Which characters are hybrids? What benefits or costs do they get from their mixed identities?
5. Bullying exists in most schools; evaluate the tactics the Souls use and suggest other options they didn't explore.
6. How does the Turtle Rescue Squad reflect a concern with the environment? What are other ways our society protects wildlife?
7. Explore the relationship between multiculturalism and education.
8. How does tea as a custom produce civility?
9. Looking at the characters involved in education for several generations, what does Konigsburg imply about young people? What factors might have contributed to it?
10. What moral lesons are offered? Are they relevant or useful?

Essay Ideas

1. Write an essay that explores the reasons Mrs. Olinski picked her team.
2. Write an essay that analyzes the social functions and their influences on the characters.
3. Write an essay that compares and contrasts the various settings.
4. Looking at the presentation of the "foreign" write an essay examining whether Orientalism is necessary to this text.
5. After researching sea turtles, write an essay that illustrates how the characters' experience in this text relates to them.
6. Research paraplegism or another disability. Observe what challenges would face a person with that disability in your school or home.

The protagonist in *Walk Two Moons,* by Sharon Creech, has a background steeped deep in Native American culture, which, as she begins to research her life, "is a natural part of finding herself in America." Photo: Library of Congress, Prints & Photographs Division, photograph by Carol M. Highsmith, LC-DIG-highsm-15776.

Walk Two Moons

by Sharon Creech

Content Synopsis

"Walk Two Moons" won its author, Sharon Creech, the prestigious "Newbury Medal." It is a complex narrative which intertwines the stories of two families. Salamanca Tree Biddle, the protagonist, is coping with the loss of her mother. Salamanca's mother left the family to go on a voyage of self-discovery, and never returned because of a fatal accident. Sal's paternal grandparents take her on a road trip that follows the path of her mother's trip. While they are traveling, Salamanca relates her family story since they left Bybanks, Kentucky to reside in Euclid, Ohio. The novel flips back and forth, between Sal's journey with her grandparents and her adventures in Euclid. Sal entertains her grandparents primarily with the story of Phoebe Winterbottom, and her mother's mysterious behaviors and eventual disappearance.

The Winterbottom storyline features Phoebe, Sal's new friend, and her mother (Norma), father (George), and older sister (Prudence). Phoebe is a creative, paranoid, and imaginative child who thinks she sees axe murderers and lunatics everywhere, and when her mother leaves home, Phoebe is convinced she has been kidnapped and possibly murdered by the "lunatic" teenager she has seen lurking near their house.

Eventually we come to discover that Norma had a child out of wedlock long ago and gave it up for adoption. This child, now a teen looking for his mother, is the "lunatic" whom Phoebe spots

lurking around their house. Subsequently, Norma leaves her family so she can reconcile with her past. Norma always tried to be the super-mother, as a way of compensating for her own deficiencies and past. The family, however, is not aware of any of this, and when Norma leaves, their realities are shaken. Phoebe's suspicions grow more creative each day her mother is gone, and she assumes the worst. At the same time, mysterious messages appear on their doorstep, which only cause Phoebe to become more suspicious.

We also come to learn more about Sal's mother, Sugar. After Sal's birth, Sugar lost a baby in childbirth, and had to have a hysterectomy. Sal's mother and father had always planned to fill the house with babies. Devastated by the loss of her desired family, Sugar leaves home. If she had not been killed in a tragic bus accident, Sugar would probably have resolved her grief and returned home. She loved her family deeply, but found it difficult to live up to the goodness in Sal's father. In a flashback, Sugar states about her husband, "Sometimes I don't think you're human" and Sal concludes, "it seemed as if she wanted him to be meaner, less good" (Creech 109). The commentary suggests that people should be as they are, and yet it also seems to promote a middle ground as ideal. Likewise, in a classroom discussion regarding Pandora's box, Sal reflects that hope is an odd ingredient in the box and concludes that life must be both cruel and kind.

Sal relates that her father had been working on renovations when Sugar left. After he found out that Sugar had been killed, he took out his aggression by demolishing a wall, only to discover a fireplace hidden behind it. Sal relates that, "The reason that Phoebe's story reminds me of that plaster wall and the hidden fireplace is that beneath Phoebe's story was another one. Mine" (Creech 3). She also suggests Phoebe is her doppelganger: "in a strange way, she was like another version of me—she acted out the way I sometimes felt" (Creech 189).

The reader discovers that Sal's father moved to Euclid, Ohio to be nearer to Margaret Cadaver. It is not until near the end of the story that we find out why her father is fascinated with Mrs. Cadaver; she was riding on the bus with Sugar, listening to her talk about her family, expressing deep love, and Mrs. Cadaver was the sole survivor of the bus accident. Since the readers are getting the narrative from Sal's perspective, they are led to falsely believe her father is developing a romantic interest in Mrs. Cadaver, which Sal resents strongly.

Other characters that figure in the Ohio narrative are the Finneys. Mary Lou Finney befriends Phoebe and Sal, and Mary Lou's cousin, Ben, develops a relationship with Sal. Mary Lou Finney's family is "not nearly as civilized as ours," says Phoebe (Creech 46), but Sal wonders if it may be the type of household full of children that her mother wanted. In this house it is not unusual that Mr. Finney finds a peaceful reading spot in the tub and the garage roof can be a place for Mrs. Finney to nap, or both the Finneys to cuddle.

Sal and Ben show a deeper understanding of each other than seems natural. When discussing the expression about walking two moons in someone's moccasins, the two draw upon identical images of two moons actually located in shoes. Similarly, when the two are asked to draw what their souls look like, they independently create the same image of a circle with a maple leaf in it.

The level of understanding between the two illustrates their compatibility.

The novel most clearly reflects how an inability to walk two moons leads to problems. Most notably, Phoebe's family overlooks Norma's unhappiness or depression. Sal sees right away how much Norma is grieving. She also has the ability to anticipate that Margaret's weird hours are more likely due to her being a nurse than her being an axe-murderer, as the dramatic Phoebe has alleged. Along the way, there are many adventures, and one involves meeting Tom Fleet who plays a role in Gram being bitten by a snake, but Sal forgives him and subsequently allows him to help. She also takes Ben's mother's mental disability in stride, without any awkwardness, as she can relate his mother's actions to her mother's after the loss of the baby. These are just some of the many examples in the book that illustrate life's complexity and the need for understanding and acceptance.

There are also parallels between Sal and Sugar, especially with regard to trees (Sal's middle name is "Tree" while her mother's name is Chanhassen, Indian for sweet tree juice or maple sugar) and Sal is referred to as Sugar's left arm. In accepting her mom's death, Sal also accepts her own mortality. Sal's acceptance of Sugar's death coincides with Gram's death during their roadtrip.

Early on, the children's teacher, Mr. Birkway, encourages the students to view life from multiple perspectives in life and in literature—and to develop an appreciation for honesty from others. When he shares journal entries, he values honesty and revealing perspective. He even shares a piece that criticizes literary analysis. When discussing e.e. cummings' poem, he lets the children share their interpretations freely, debating and bringing their own perspective to bear. Ironically, he fails to recognize the potential impact of such honesty, voiced to all, until he reads Phoebe's theories about his own sister (Mrs. Cadaver) being a murderer out loud to the class.

These actions allow healthy interactions to take place and promote awareness that people are complex and not stereotypes.

Historical Context

This narrative conveys a perspective of Native American culture which reflects the confusion arising from revisionism. The narrator's innocent voice deconstructs the shifts in linguistic and socio-political context as the historical perspective has morphed. Indeed, Salamanca is a misnomer, as Sugar intended to name her after the tribe of her great-great-grandmother, which was Seneca. This indicates a disconnection of the Indian people from their tribe and heritage, and shows how easy it is for people to get it wrong, even very important things like naming a child. This slippage then extends beyond Indians, as Phoeby becomes "Peeby" in the mouth of Gram, despite many corrections by Sal.

Just before she leaves, Sal's mom asserts her name is Chanhassen (Creech 110-11). She is on a journey to find herself and what is "underneath" (Creech 143) before she was a Mom and wife. Renovating the house, John replaces the fireplace cement in the structure he found behind the wall, and he writes "Chanhassen," not "Sugar." Thus identity and names do matter. This idea of what is underneath draws a parallel to the plaster wall that resurfaces.

Sal comments on Mount Rushmore: "You'd think the Sioux would be mighty sad to have those white faces carved into their sacred hill. I bet my mother was upset. I wondered why whoever carved them couldn't have put a couple Indians up there too" (Creech 179). This view of society is one which lacks historical recognition of power. There are several instances that illustrate the naming and renaming of Indians such as, Native-Americans and Injuns, and Sal's mother and grandmother's dislike for the revisionist naming.

The idea of a revisionist or idealist image of Indians is one of the most highly praised elements in Creech's work. Hazel Rochman, in a "New York Times Book Review," wrote, "Sal is only a small part Indian—. Still, the heritage is part of her identity. She loves the Indian stories her mother told her, and they get mixed in with Genesis and Pandora's box and Longfellow and with family stories, and, above all, with a celebration of the sweeping natural world and our connectedness with it" (qtd. In "Sharon Creech"). She continues, "for once in a children's book, Indians are people, not reverential figures in a museum diorama. Sal's Indian heritage is a natural part of finding herself in America" (qtd. in "Sharon Creech"). The idea that toleration, acceptance, and understanding are more relevant than names or labels is thus illustrated by the main characters in this novel and enriches the story-telling qualities in this text.

Societal Context

The notion of commitment and fidelity receives some attention in this text. Gram ran off with the Eggman early in her marriage. She says "sometimes you know in your heart you love someone, but you have to go away before your head can figure it out" (Creech 153). Gram is constantly discussing her friend Gloria, and her attraction to Gramps. The discussion the two have about the Eggman and Gloria recurs frequently, and is a playful assurance that they could leave but they choose not to. After Gram dies, Gloria comes to visit, but Gramps can't stop talking about Gram, and Gloria bolts. The reader can overlap these messages with the story of Chanhassen's journey, as it is true that Chanhassen left, but her discussions with Margaret Cadaver were all about the farm and her family. This signifies that Sugar is discovering how much she loves them and that she desires to return.

When Sal and her grandparents go to visit Old Faithful, Gram is fascinated with it, and Gramps is watching Gram and fascinated with her reaction. So much of their lives are shaped by the other's reaction, that the reader can easily see how much they value each other.

Another issue raised is that of weaning. Sal ponders whether her mother's journey was a part of letting Sal go, so she could grow up. The concept echoes Gram's "sometimes you know in your heart you love someone, but you have to go away before your head can figure it out" (Creech 153). The reversal is weaning—letting someone go so she can grow. While Sal toys with the idea of weaning, the growth that occurs with the daughters is questionable. Phoebe seems less likely to learn than her father or sister, who are excited about Norma's return and who accept her son. Sal's growth occurs much later, and is countered by significant denial and assistance. Although she can perceive the Winterbottoms' difficulties, she still struggles with her own.

Religious Context

The idea of the Middle Road is played out here, and conventional Judeo-Christian religion takes a lesser role. The most significant place this occurs is in the discussion of Longfellow's "The Tide Rises, The Tide Falls." Megan finds the rhythm hypnotic, whereas Sal claims it is terrifying that a wave sweeps the man away. Phoebe sees "a murder," but Ben says, "Maybe he didn't drown. Maybe he just died, like normal people do." Sal insists that "It isn't normal to die." Megan then interjects, "What about Heaven? God?" Mary Lou then asks, "God? Is he in this poem?" (Creech 182). Where is God in this book? Neither Heaven nor God are discussed or mentioned otherwise. Megan's question serves as a discussion point. If, as Mary Lou suggests, God can only be relevant if he is discussed in the work, then is there a Heaven or a God in this light? When Sal finally accepts that it is normal to die—her main metaphorical journey in the novel—and accepts her mother's and her grandmother's death, she finds her mother's spirit in nature, in the trees about her, in the birdsong. Gram's body has to be returned and buried at the farm, because Gramps actually needs her presence. In this way, it is suggested that death and loss can have various meanings, and dealing with loss takes many forms.

Given the points made in the combination of Indian myth, Greek myth, and history, one could argue that a true multicultural acceptance allows this text to promote various religious possibilities, but none is promoted outright. There are also other religious elements, such as the Greek myth assignment, and the discussions about the concept of Pandora's box and religion. These are all combined together, fused with a sort of mysticism.

Scientific & Technological Context

There is little scientific or technological discussion in the novel, but instead, there is almost a nostalgic anti-technology motif presented. The families come from rural outskirts, on roads in fairly desolate areas (where one must drive hours to local hospitals). It is a folksy image in contrast with scientific development. Gramps has no clue about how a car works or what a "car-bust-erator" does, and he pulls the "snakes" (hoses) out of a stranded motorist's car. Yet he does have a car and he has even taught Sal how to drive. Technology's role in culture is subtle and pragmatically useful even if the characters are not aware of the scientific principles.

Biographical Context

Sharon Creech was born in 1945. With a B.A. from Hiram College in Ohio and an M.A. from George Mason University in Fairfax, Virginia, Creech experimented with writing for the Federal Theater Project and Congressional Quarterly. She married, had two children, and divorced. She later opted to join The American School in Switzerland (TASIS—a grade school for children of expatriate Americans) where she gave instruction to American students in English. There she met and married Lyle D. Rigg, then the assistant headmaster. The family spent time in England as well as in Switzerland.

Creech says she very much draws from her own life experiences to shape her novels, and combined elements from both herself and her daughter in "Walk Two Moons" ("Sharon Creech"). Her childhood was strongly influenced by a love of reading, and the various story lines interfused, including Indian cultural elements, mythology, and fortune cookies, to help shape the story line of this novel. She also divulges that her own family is more similar to Mary Lou's than other families in this text, with a large and rowdy group gathered around the dinner table, spinning yarns. She credits this experience with helping her to develop a writing voice that is captivating and can maintain the reader's attention ("Sharon Creech").

She began writing novels shortly after her father died in 1986. Previous to that, he had been unable to speak, due to a stroke, and Creech sometimes relates her prolific writing to his backed up words that needed to escape. Ultimately, Creech found her creative outlet in writing. "I think that what inspired me is a love of good stories—wanting to read led naturally (it seemed) to wanting to write. I studied writing in college and in graduate school, but I also learned a lot about writing from teaching both literature and writing, when I had a chance to examine closely what makes a good story" ("Interview"). She credits her knowledge of writing technique for the acclaim and honors garnered by her works. For "Walk Two Moons," she received awards from Notable Children's Books, the American Library Association, including the Newbury Medal, the W.H. Smith Award, The Young Readers Award, the Heartland Award, and the Sequoia Award. Her other works have not been overlooked either, especially "Chasing Redbird," "The Wanderer," "Love that Dog," "Ruby Holler," and "Heartbeat."

Anne K. Erickson

Works Cited

Creech, Sharon. *Walk Two Moons*. New York: Harper Trophy, 1994.

"Interview." 23 Dec. 2005.

Creech. Sharon Contemporary Authors Online (2005)". *Contemporary Authors Online*. Gale. Atlantic Cape Community College, NJ. 23 Dec. 2005.

Discussion Questions

1. Mrs. Winterbottom is making a blackberry pie. Why does Sal say she is allergic to blackberries? Look through for the other references to blackberries, such as which blackberries should be eaten (33), and in relation to trees and kisses. How do these all relate?
2. Why is Pandora's box important?
3. Several characters get renamed or misnamed in this story. What relevance is there to this renaming?
4. Why would Mr. Biddle want to move near to Margaret Cadaver?
5. How do the tourists interpret Mount Rushmore?
6. How do the tourists interpret Old Faithful?
7. What role does Tom Fleet serve?
8. What role does Gloria Serve?
9. What characters have the ability to see what is going on around them?
10. Why does Gramps say "it's not our marriage bed, but it'll do" each night and what does it matter?

Essay Ideas

1. Several characters get renamed or misnamed in this story. What relevance is there to this renaming?
2. Pick one symbol, which you feel is most important: the fireplace, the notes, blackberries, Pandora's box, Old Faithful, or trees.
3. What is the significance of the journals?
4. Several characters have fears. The Winterbottom women are always checking the locks, leaving long lists of phone numbers for contacts, suspecting the neighbors of heinous acts, etc. What are they afraid of and what do they find?
5. Sal is afraid when she wakes from a nap in the Wisconsin Dells and does not immediately find her Gram. She reflects, "Ever since my mother left us that April day, I suspected that everyone was going to leave, one by one" (Creech 59). By the end of the novel, Sal loses Gram, as well as her mom. What does her reaction to Gram's death say about her relationship with her fears?
6. What part of Sal's journey is most important for her to understand her mom?
7. Through the novel, we find a series of quotes provided. Pick any one to discuss how it is important and to whom:
   - "We'll fill up the house with children! We'll fill it right up to the brim!" "Well, this ain't our marriage bed, but it will do."
   - "Don't judge a man until you've walked two moons in his moccasins."
   - "Everyone has his own agenda."
   - "In the course of a lifetime, what does it matter?"
   - "You can't keep the birds of sadness from flying over your head, but you can keep them from nesting in your hair."
   - "We never know the value of water until the well is dry."

White Noise

by Don DeLillo

Content Synopsis

Narrated in the first person by Jack Gladney, the first section of Don DeLillo's (1936-) "White Noise" (1985), "Waves and Radiation," opens with the arrival of students back to the College-on-the-Hill after the summer vacation. Jack enjoys this annual ritual, noting the extraordinary number of possessions the students bring with them, and the "massive insurance coverage" (3) exuded by their parents. "White Noise's" memorable opening establishes both the novel's academic setting, and its concern with mass culture and consumer capitalism.

Jack Gladney is the middle-aged Chair of the Department of Hitler Studies—a discipline he invented in 1968. However, despite founding his own discipline, Jack's sense of his own academic identity is uncertain and insecure, not least because he does not speak German, a skill that has become mandatory in the field of Hitler Studies. In an attempt to bolster his sense of his self, he adopted a fake middle initial early in his career, and is known in Hitler Studies circles as J. A. K. Gladney. Jack also habitually wears dark glasses and an academic gown, which he believes give him more authority and presence. However, these measures sometimes make Jack feel like an impostor, leading him to confess: "I am the false character that follows the name around" (17).

Five times married, Jack's current wife is Babette, a woman who "gathers and tends the children" (5), reads to the elderly and teaches adult education posture classes. Jack's first three wives were all involved in government intelligence work of some kind. Jack presents the ample, motherly Babette in direct contrast to these thin, secretive women. Their household is a rag-tag collection of children from their various marriages, in which no child lives with a full sibling, or with a complete set of parents. Blood ties do not carry much weight for this post-nuclear family. Jack is unsure how many children his wife has, while Steffie has met her half-sister Bee only once-at Disney World, which, as Thomas Ferrarro, writes "is sufficient, in today's America, for them to know each other as kin" (36). Indeed, judging by Wilder's age, the Gladney family unit itself is a relatively recent arrangement, and there is a pervading sense of adult instability disrupting children's lives. Consequently, Jack and Babette tend to perceive their children, especially Steffie, Denise and Bee, as disapproving moral presences in their lives. As Jack comments, "If Denise was a pint-sized commissar, nagging us to higher conscience, then Bee was a silent witness, calling the very meaning of our lives into question" (94).

In spite of their unorthodox family set up, the Gladney unit itself seems relatively stable and happy. Their solidarity is based not on blood relations, but on the communal experiences of life in late twentieth century America, especially shopping.

Shopping is an important means of building and securing the family in "White Noise." When one of Jack's colleagues describes him as a "big, harmless, aging, indistinct sort of guy" (83), he goes shopping with Babette and the children to rebuild his sense of self and his family identity: "I was one of them shopping at last" (83). Indeed, Jack compares his weekly supermarket shop to a religious experience, arguing that he becomes replenished each time he visits its aisles (pun intended). The supermarket is part of the system of modern living that Jack invests with spiritual meaning, like the automatic bank teller which conveys the blessing of "the system" (46) upon him, or the moment when Steffie mouths "Toyota Celica" in her sleep (155). Rather than being disturbed that advertising has infected even his nine-year-old daughter's dreams, Jack interprets this as a moment of sublime beauty.

However, this system of modern living is disturbing for some: an elderly brother and sister, the Treadwells, go missing, and are found a few days later "in an abandoned cookie shack at Mid Village Mall, a vast shopping center" (59). The pair had wandered through the huge mall for two days, "lost, confused and frightened" (59). Similarly, Babette perceives that emblem of modern living, the TV, as a threat to family unity. She hopes watching television together will neutralize what she sees as its brain-numbing power. However, the Gladney children—as well as Jack—find this enforced communal viewing an arduous experience, and the family only really bonds over a TV show on disasters.

Jack's principal guide to this modern (or postmodern) world is a visiting lecturer in the American Environments Department and one-time sports writer, Murray Jay Siskind. Murray is particularly interested in popular culture, especially TV and Elvis, though he does complain "there are full professors in this place [the College-on-the-Hill] who read nothing but cereal boxes" (10). Murray and Jack give a joint lecture on Hitler and Elvis, pointing out similarities between the two men, such as their love of their mothers, and the reliance of each on the crowd. This comparison between fascist leader and a figure from popular culture is extremely important, as it highlights both fascism's use of the techniques of mass culture, and extreme cultic appeal of performers like Elvis.

In a key scene, Jack and Murray visit "the most photographed barn in America" (12). Here Murray acts as an interpreter for Jack, explaining to him that the tourists who have turned up to take pictures cannot really see the barn. Murray argues that once they have seen the signs for the "Most Photographed Barn in America" they cannot see the "real" barn, only its mediated representations. This scene is often cited in discussions of postmodernity, as it neatly encapsulates French philosopher Jean Baudrillard's idea of hyperreality, where the real world is actually replaced or supplanted by its representations. Indeed, the real is not seen to exist unless it has been legitimized by reproduction in the mass media. The attitude of Jack's daughter, Bee, also illustrates this point. When Jack collects her from the airport, they meet passengers from another aircraft who narrowly avoided a fatal crash. Bee believes that because the passengers experience has not been captured by the media, it has no validity. In Bee's words "they went through all that for nothing" (92).

Many characters are unsettled by the idea that the real has been subsumed by its representations. When Babette's yoga class is televised by a local cable channel, both Wilder and Jack respond to Babette's televised image with an anguished cry, fearful that it signals the disappearance or death of the "real" Babette. Characters also find themselves beset by uncertainty over how and whether we know anything about the world around us or ourselves. Sitting in the car with his father in a rainstorm, Heinrich disputes his father's statement that it is raining now, arguing that evidence of our senses is unreliable, and that we can never identify a "now" anyway. This pervasive insecurity persuades Babette to start classes on eating and drinking because, as she explains, "Knowledge changes every day. People like to have their beliefs reinforced" (171).

The Airborne Toxic Event, which dominates the second section of "White Noise," introduces even more uncertainty into the lives of the inhabitants of Blacksmith. Heinrich first spots the chemical leak, while the media is still calling the smoke "a feathery plume" (111). The substance is Nyodene Derivative, a mysterious chemical that, in powder form, "is colorless, odourless and very dangerous" (131). Steffie and Denise soon begin to exhibit the symptoms they have heard on the radio—sweaty palms, vomiting and de ja vu. Jack is confused as to whether these symptoms are real or psychosomatic, that is, caused by the news on the radio, rather than by the chemical itself. He is also reluctant to believe in the magnitude of the disaster, arguing that such things do not happen to college professors. However, the media is soon calling the leak "a black billowing cloud" (115), and then, more ominously an "airborne toxic event," and the Gladney family is evacuated to a Boy Scout camp. En route, Jack notes that the evacuees exhibit a "sense of awe that bordered on the religious" (127). Like the supermarket and automatic bank teller, Jack invests this other aspect of modern living, a chemical spill, with spiritual meaning.

At the scout camp, Heinrich proves to be an authoritative source of information on Nyodene Derivative for many of the evacuated adults. Just as Steffie, Denise and Bee provide a moral center for Jack and Babette, so the teenage Heinrich is able to offer the confused and upset adults some understanding of what has happened. Jack discovers that he may have been contaminated with the substance when he got out of the car to get gas. The SIMUVAC employees at the Boy Scout camp tell Jack that his exposure may or may not

kill him, and they will not be able to tell him what effect his exposure has had for around fifteen years. This information introduces a whole new level of uncertainty into Jack's existence.

By the last section of the novel, "Dylarama," the Gladneys have returned to their everyday routine, though Jack notes that the sunsets have become even more beautiful since the chemical spill. The sunset is a traditional image of natural beauty; that a chemical spill should enhance it, is another indication of the way in which emotions which used to be associated with religious faith or nature are becoming associated with by-products of high-tech modern living.

Denise tells Jack she is worried about Babette's increasing absent-mindedness and the pills that she takes everyday. Jack finds a bottle of Dylar pills taped to the underside of the radiator cover in the bathroom. Babette denies all knowledge of the drug. When his doctor is unable to shed light on the nature of the pills, Jack gives the tablet to the scientist, Winnie Richards. Winnie tells Jack that Dylar is "some kind of psychopharmaceutical"(189): a pill designed to change a patient's psychology. Jack challenges Babette again and she reveals that Dylar is designed to cure the fear of death. She answered an advertisement for a drug trial in one of the supermarket tabloids that she reads old Mr. Treadwell. When she was initially refused the pills, she offered to sleep with the project manager, Mr. Gray, in order to get access to them. An important side effect of the drug is that user becomes unable to distinguish words and things.

Jack is also crippled by a fear of death, and, like Babette, he finds one of the most effective ways to alleviate this is to spend time with Wilder. He becomes increasingly worried about his contamination with Nyodene D. He undergoes several tests, where he routinely lies to his doctors about his diet and alcohol intake, as if misrepresenting his lifestyle will have a material effect on his health. But despite Jack's lies, they tell him he has a "nebulous mass" (280): its uncertain shape and form reflect the uncertain and unpredictable nature of his own death. Jack is "tentatively scheduled to die" (202), though the doctors cannot tell him when or how. The doctors give Jack a printout of his condition in a sealed envelope, and tell him: "Your doctor knows the symbols" (281). The nature and diagnosis of Jack's condition epitomize all that is overwhelming and unnerving about modern living: an overload of information, but none of it intelligible to Jack or absolutely certain, even to experts in the field. Mark Osteen sums the situation up neatly: "there is abundant information around, but nobody seems to know anything" (viii).

Unlike the first section of the novel, in which Jack seemed to find spiritual renewal or replenishment in consumption, in this third section, Jack begins to throw things away. He rakes through the garbage, after Denise told him she put the Dylar pills in the garbage compactor. The sublime beauty Jack heard in the words "Toyota Celica," Jack now finds in the waste and detritus of consumer culture.

Vernon Dickey, Babette's father arrives unexpectedly. Vernon belongs to an older order of men than Jack, men who can fix things with their hands. In contrast to Jack's abstract and esoteric knowledge, everything Vernon knows has a practical application in the physical world. Vernon is at odds with popular mass culture and asks Jack one of the most important questions in the novel, "Were people this dumb before television?" (249). In other words, Vernon asks whether television and the mass culture of the late twentieth century has really changed our relationship to the world around us. This association between Vernon and authentic living is reinforced by the connections between Vernon and death—the one aspect of life that apparently cannot be reduced to its representation by the culture of consumer capitalism. Not only does Jack at first mistake the white–haired old man for death, but Vernon also gives Jack a lethal weapon, a German-made gun.

Jack discusses his fear of death on separate occasions with Winnie Richards and Murray Jay Siskind. Winnie tries to convince Jack that human beings need their fear of death, as it is our consciousness of death that creates our sense of self. Murray also makes this connection between the boundaries of the self and knowledge of death, arguing that because Wilder has no understanding of his mortality, he has a "total ego" (298). Murray also points out that Jack's attraction to Hitler may stem from his unconscious belief that the power of Hitler could protect him from death. Murray tells Jack that there are two kinds of people, killers and diers. He persuades Jack that if he does not want to be a dier, he should instead become a killer, maintaining that "to plot is to live" (291).

Jack discovers that the true identity of Mr. Gray is Willie Mink, and taking Murray's advice, he resolves to kill Mink with the gun that Vernon gave him. Jack goes to Mink's motel, where he discovers Mink is a strange creature—a man who learned to talk from watching television. In a confused and farcical shoot out both Mink and Jack are wounded. Jack takes Mink to a hospital run by nuns in Germantown, who disappoint and disturb Jack by revealing they do not believe in God. A non-believer himself, Jack still desperately wants to believe that others have an unshakeable faith in God.

The final chapter of the novel draws together many of its main themes. Wilder rides across the highway on his tricycle, proving his ability to literally defy death. The sunsets, once an image of sublime, natural beauty, have become even more powerful and awe-inspiring since the Airborne Toxic Event, but the modern world is still a bewildering and frightening place. As the novel closes Jack has not summoned the courage to have the computer printout of his death interpreted, while the supermarket shelves have been rearranged, causing agitation and panic in the aisles.

Historical Context

Don DeLillo's fiction has often been noted for its prescience. Margaret Roberts, for example, claims that his novels have "the evocative power of a soothsayer" (1). Novels like "The Names" (1982) and "Mao II" (1991) seem to foreshadow the rise of Islamic terrorism, while "White Noise's" Airborne Toxic Event eerily echoes the disaster at Bhopal, India, when a chemical leak at the Union Carbide plant caused thousands of deaths. The Bhopal disaster occurred in December of 1984 only a few weeks before the publication of "White Noise," and many reviewers drew connections between it and the Airborne Toxic Event. Of course, the Bhopal chemical leak affected precisely the kind of population Jack Gladney expects to be involved in such disasters, that is, the poor, rather than middle-class academics.

But as well as this specific historic coincidence, "White Noise" also forces us to question our relationship with history itself. In an age of hyperreality, where representations have become more "real" than what they represent, Jack turns to history and Hitler to recover a sense of authenticity. Crucially, commentators have cited the Nazis and, in particular, the holocaust, as one historical event that has not been subsumed by its representations. Murray himself points out that Jack sought power from the Nazis: "On one level you wanted to conceal yourself in Hitler and his works. On another level you wanted to use him to grow in significance and strength" (287). However, Jack's lecture with Murray on the similarities between Hitler and Elvis reveals the way in which the Nazis adopted (and perhaps even invented) many of the strategies later used by popular culture. The Nazis were adept at using film to promote themselves, and manipulated crowds as successfully as any rock star. In other words, retreating to the pre-postmodern age of Hitler and the Nazis may not provide Jack with the authentic existence he craves.

Societal Context

"White Noise" offers us an important analysis of American society and culture in the late twentieth century. Its examination of the impact of supermarkets, television and technology on our relationship with reality and ourselves is often so perceptive (and funny) that commentators occasionally draw on this novel as if it were a piece of cultural criticism, rather than a novel. DeLillo has claimed in interviews that he tried to find "a kind of radiance in dailiness" (DeCurtis 63). In "White Noise," this novel asks crucially—what happens to our spiritual lives in an age of constant television and processed foods? Unlike the Romantic poets who found beauty and spiritual refreshment in nature, DeLillo suggests we have begun to associate such emotions with the products (and by-products) of late capitalism. The contaminated sunsets are the most beautiful Jack has ever seen, and even garbage or a brand name ("Toyota Celica") seems to hold some profound and untouchable beauty for him.

"White Noise" also charts the changing structure of the family, as the old notion of the nuclear family is exploded in an age of divorce and remarriage. Divorce statistics continued to rise through the 1960s and 1970s in the United States, and many voiced fears about the impact of divorce and separation on children and the family. Critics have tended to interpret the Gladneys' convoluted family structure as parody of familial relations in the USA in the 1980s. In particular, critics like Thomas Ferraro note the casualness with which ties of blood and marriage are treated. Denise's father, Bob Pardee, drops by the household without any hint of awkwardness or animosity, while the children in the Gladney household (none of whom live with a complete set of parents or full sibling) seem remarkably unfazed by their situation.

Academia also comes under scrutiny in "White Noise." DeLillo satirizes the growth of "cultural studies" in American universities in the 1970s, where it seems nothing (not even cereal boxes) is exempt from the academic gaze. DeLillo depicts academia as complicit both with consumer capitalism and with cultural relativism. The success of Jack Gladney's Hitler studies is not a result so much of Jack's scholarly activity, but of his recognition of a "gap in the market." Hitler studies represent the commodification of the Nazis for academic consumption. The study of Hitler alongside cereal boxes and Elvis, also indicates a disturbing moral relativism in academia. For the professors of the College-on-the-Hill, there is apparently little difference between the leader of a murderous totalitarian regime and a dead rock'n'roll singer with a penchant for rhinestones.

Religious Context

Religious belief (or the lack of it) is a key theme in "White Noise." DeLillo characterizes late twentieth century America as an age characterized by shifting knowledge and information overload. In this setting, many of the novel's characters crave the old certainties offered by religion. Heinrich's mother, Janet Savory, has abandoned life as a foreign currency analyst for an ashram (a communal spiritual retreat) in Montana, where she is known as Mother Devi. There she takes guidance from a spiritual leader, Swami, whom Jack fears may be able to give his son the certainty he cannot provide: "Would he be able to answer the boy's questions where I had failed, provide assurances where I had incited bickering and debate?" (273).

Jack himself is a nonbeliever, which exacerbates his perpetual fear of death. Jack cannot envision an afterlife and characterises death as "Electrical noise… Uniform, white" (198). In lieu of his own faith, however, Jack relies on the faith of others. As the German nun he meets in the hospital tells him, "The nonbelievers need the believers. They are desperate to have someone believe" (318). Unfortunately, for Jack, however, these nuns have no more religious faith than he does, however, they are dedicated to appearing to believe. As the nun says: "Our lives are no less serious than if we professed real faith, real belief" (319). Just as the most photographed barn in America has been replaced by its representations, so real religious faith seems to have been replaced by the appearance of belief.

Though conventional religious faith no longer exists in "White Noise," Jack Gladney does invest many aspects of modern living with religious significance. A visit to the supermarket is a spiritually replenishing experience, an automatic bank teller machine blesses its users, chemical spills can inspire a religious awe and dread, and the famous and the dead inspire the same cultic followings that used to be solely associated with the divine. Crucially, of course, DeLillo demonstrates that while the kinds of emotions associated with religion still exist, the subject of such religious fervor is no longer any transcendental being, but the transitory detritus of late capitalism.

Given the current strength of organized religion, and in particular Christianity, in the United States, DeLillo's account of the death of traditional religious faith in America may seem premature. However, at the time of "White Noise's" publication these movements (and in particular, the religious right) were just beginning to turn the tide of secularism that had grown in strength in the United States in the 1960s and 70s. Indeed, one could argue that the subsequent success of the evangelical movement in the United States is symptomatic of the same spiritual yearning that DeLillo identifies in "White Noise."

Scientific & Technological Context

Like much of DeLillo's fiction, the impact of science and technology is a major concern of "White Noise." In the first section of the novel, DeLillo is careful to demonstrate the subtle influences of technology on our lives. Denise's address book, for instance, lists only numbers. Jack calls them "a race of people with a seven-bit analog consciousness" (41). The supermarket contains an unfeasible abundance of food, which is impervious to nature's cycles, "Everything seemed to be in season, sprayed, burnished, bright" (36). Technology also introduces an overload of information into the lives of the Gladney family, much of it ambiguous. When the smoke alarm goes off during lunch it is either because the house is on fire, or because the battery has just died. The family finishes lunch without investigating either possibility.

The most pervasive information source in this novel is, of course, the television. Phrases from the television constantly interject themselves into Jack's narrative, as if it is another member of the Gladney family. It is also responsible for much of the misinformation that each member of the Gladney family carries around in their head. Television is also important in "White Noise" because it is part of the system of representation through which reality is validated. After the Airborne Toxic Event, the evacuated residents of Blacksmith seem more angry that their ordeal has barely been covered in the media than that the toxic spill was allowed to happen: "Everything we love and have worked for is under serious threat. But we look around and see no response from the official organs of the media" (162). There is also a suggestion that representation on television or in the mass media actually replaces the real. Part of Wilder, and Jack's, distress at watching Babette on TV stems from their fear that their Babette, the "real" Babette, is now irrecoverable. "I'd seen her just an hour ago, eating eggs, but her appearance on screen made me think of her as some distant figure from the past, some ex-wife and absentee mother, a walker in the mists of the dead" (104).

The Airborne Toxic Event taps into the general public's growing suspicion and incomprehension of science and technology in the 1980s. Episodes like the partial meltdown at Three Mile Island nuclear plant in Pennsylvania in 1979, and the Bhopal disaster in 1984 exacerbated this distrust. DeLillo plays, in particular, on our fear of potentially deadly substances or emissions like radiation (or Nyodene

Derivative), which cannot be detected by our own senses. The imperceptible nature of radiation or Nyodene D. produced a paranoia that the accelerating technological change of the second half of the twentieth century only aggravated, as the general population became increasingly out of touch with scientific developments and discoveries. A great source of anxiety for the adult characters during the Airborne Toxic Event is their ignorance, which forces them to rely on the knowledge of a fourteen-year-old boy, Heinrich, for information about Nyodene D. Heinrich points to the general public's lack of understanding of modern technology explicitly in a conversation with Jack:

> If you came awake tomorrow in the Middle Ages and there was an epidemic raging, what could you do to stop it, knowing what you know about the progress of medicines and diseases? Here it is practically the twenty-first century and you've read hundreds of books and magazines and seen a hundred TV shows about science and medicine. Could you tell those people one little crucial thing that might save a million and a half lives? (148)

In contrast to his son, who has some understanding of modern technology, or his father-in-law, who still possesses the practical knowledge needed to fix things, Jack's copious knowledge, like that of much of the population, seems abstract, esoteric and useless in the postmodern world.

Dylar, the psychopharmaceutical pill that Babette is taking to ward off her fear of death, highlights the fact that, despite scientific and technological advances, man is still beset by a fundamental dread: the fear of death. But Dylar has another important function in "White Noise," as it also undermines our notion of the self and agency. Use of such drugs, like Prozac, has grown exponentially in the West in the past thirty years. However, if our fears and thoughts can be changed by chemistry, we must face the question of what becomes of our "essential self." As Jack says "We're the sum of our chemical impulses. Don't tell me this. It's unbearable to think about" (200). Dylar also erodes the self in other ways. Winnie Richards argues that we need a fear of death to preserve our sense of ourselves. She argues that, faced with death, "You rediscover yourself ... [you] see who you are as if for the first time, outside familiar surroundings, alone, distinct, whole" (229). Without this consciousness of death, she argues, we are unable to delimit the self.

Biographical Context

Until the publication of "Underworld" (1997), DeLillo gave few interviews and made even fewer public appearances. His novels included no biographical information beyond the year and place of his birth (1936, Bronx, New York) and a brief note on his education at Fordham University. DeLillo carried, famously, a business card to interviews that stated simply "I don't want to talk about it" (LeClair 79). He told Tom LeClair, quoting James Joyce, that the lack of personal information available on him was the result of "silence, exile, cunning and so on" (80). As late as 1997, DeLillo was awarded seven out of ten on the reclusiveness scale by "Entertainment Weekly" (Moran 151).

DeLillo's determined and deliberate privateness ensures it is difficult to make many connections between his work and his life. Indeed, "White Noise" baffled some critics who were surprised that DeLillo could write so accurately about children and teenagers, when he himself is childless (Lentricchia 2). DeLillo is certainly around the same age as Jack Gladney, however, the resemblance seems to stop there. Perhaps the only aspect of DeLillo's biography worth noting, with regard to "White Noise" is his Catholic background. Brought up in an Italian-Catholic family, DeLillo also attended the Catholic university, Fordham. "White Noise's" concern with religious faith (or the lack of it) and in particular the German nuns

Jack meets at the close of the novel may stem in part from DeLillo's Catholic sensibilities. His interest in the relationship between representations and the real may also be heightened by his religious background, as an absolute, guaranteed relation between the word and the world is integral to faith based readings of religious texts like the Bible. This theme is more explicitly explored in his later novel "Underworld."

Anne Longmuir

Works Cited

Cantor, Paul A. "Adolf, We Hardly Knew You." *New Essays on White Noise*. Ed. Frank Lentricchia. Cambridge: Cambridge University Press, 1991. 39–62

DeLillo, Don. *White Noise*. London: Picador, 1986

DeCurtis, Anthony. "'An Outsider in This Society': An Interview with Don DeLillo." *Introducing Don DeLillo*. Ed. Frank Lentricchia. Durham: Duke University Press, 1991. 43–66

Ferraro, Thomas J. "Whole Families Shopping at Night." Ed. Frank Lentricchia. Cambridge: Cambridge University Press, 1991. 15–38.

LeClair, Tom. "An Interview with Don DeLillo." *Anything Can Happen: Interview with Contemporary American Novelists*. Ed. Tom LeClair and Larry McCaffery. Urbana: University of Illinois Press, 1983. 79–90

Lentricchia, Frank. "Introduction." *New Essays on White Noise*. Ed. Frank Lentricchia. Cambridge: Cambridge University Press, 1991. 1–14

Moran, Joe. "Don DeLillo and the Myth of the Author-Recluse." *Journal of American Studies*. 34.1 (2000): 137–52

Osteen, Mark. "Introduction." *White Noise: Text and Criticism*. Ed. Frank Lentricchia. New York: Penguin, 1998. vii–xv

Roberts, Margaret. "'D' is for Danger—and for Writer Don DeLillo." *Chicago Tribune* 22 May 1992. Sec. 5: 1+

Discussion Questions

1. Though ostensibly a first-person narrative, "White Noise" is interrupted periodically by brand names. Who is speaking these brand names?

2. Jack's first three wives all worked in intelligence. What's the significance of this? How does Jack contrast his previous wives with Babette?

3. How would you describe the roles and relationships of children and adults in "White Noise?"

4. Murray Jay Siskind says the supermarket is full of "psychic data." What does he mean by this? Do you agree?

5. How does the Airborne Toxic Event embody many of "White Noise's" main themes?

6. Jack and Babette both suffer from an acute fear of death, though both are comforted by the presence of Wilder. Why might Wilder be a comfort? And how does this relate to Wilder's death-defying tricycle ride across the highway?

7. Babette hopes watching TV together as a family will neutralise its brain-numbing power and bring the family together. Does it? Explain.

8. Jack calls the moment when Steffie mouths "Toyota Celica" in her sleep "beautiful and mysterious, gold-shot with looming wonder" (155). How should we read this scene? Is Jack being ironic or sincere? Give reasons.

9. What's the significance of the title, "White Noise?" DeLillo's other working titles were "Panasonic" and "The American Book of the Dead." How do these alternative titles help us understand "White Noise?"

10. Vernon Dickey asks "Were people this dumb before television?" What's Vernon's significance? How important is this question?

Essay Ideas

1. Mark Osteen calls the Gladney family "postnuclear." Discuss the depiction of the family in "White Noise," with reference to this comment.

2. Jack speculates that all plots move deathwards. Discuss plotting in "White Noise."

3. Jack Gladney finds spiritual replenishment in the supermarket and beauty in garbage. Is "White Noise" satiric or is it a genuine celebration of consumer capitalism?

4. Even the German nuns do not believe in heaven in "White Noise." How does the novel depict belief in late-twentieth-century America?

5. After his exposure to Nyodene Derivative, Jack Gladney says he feels like "a stranger to his own dying." Discuss with reference to the themes of death and technology in "White Noise."

A Wrinkle in Time

by Madeline L'Engle

"Story always tells us more than the mere words, and that is why we love to write it, and to read it."

Madeline L'Engle

Content Synopsis

This 1963 Newbery Medal award winner, whose popularity has not diminished from its publication in 1962 to today, opens with the well-worn "it was a dark and stormy night." L'Engle's story then immediately launches into a rich, unique and fantastic narrative. The short novel revolves around protagonist Meg Murray and her five-year-old brother Charles Wallace, who, with friend Calvin O'Keefe, embark on a journey through space and time that will change their lives. These same characters reappear in L'Engle's *A Wind in the Door*, *A Swiftly Tilting Planet*, and *Many Waters*, in a series referred to as "The Time Quartet."

Meg is a typical teenage girl, struggling with typical problems that transcend generations: fitting in at school, dealing with gossip about her family among the people in her town, and living up to expectations stemming from being the daughter of two brilliant scientists. At the age when her adolescent awkwardness has not yet metamorphosed into adult beauty, Meg, socially outcast because of her stubborn refusal to be what her peers and teachers think she should be, views herself as simply "not mother," who is both accomplished and beautiful (2). Unlike Meg and Charles Wallace, their twin ten-year-old brothers, Sandy and Dennys, have no problem fitting in and are extremely popular at school. At the start of the narrative, the children's father has been missing for some time and is presumed by the family to be working on an undercover operation for the government. The rest of the town assumes he is either dead or has left his wife and family for another woman.

While an October storm rages outside the Murray's home, Meg sits in her attic bedroom as long as possible before fear propels her to the more comforting kitchen. Once there, she meets her youngest brother who not only knows she will be coming down, but also knows she wants hot chocolate, which he has ready for her. This is the first evidence provided in the narrative that Charles Wallace is not only extraordinarily intelligent but also possesses gifts that are telepathic in nature.

In the kitchen, Charles Wallace reveals that he has met three women staying in an abandoned house named Mrs. Whatsit, Mrs. Who and Mrs. Which. Mrs. Whatsit arrives at the Murray home shortly thereafter, and, after having a sandwich and saying bewildering things, including something about a "tesseract" to the family, leaves again.

The next day, Meg and Charles Wallace go to visit Mrs. Whatsit and meet Calvin O'Keefe along the way. Fourteen years old, a couple of grades above Meg and the eldest of eleven children, Calvin does not quite understand the gifts he has, which he describes as having "a feeling" that compels him to go somewhere or do something. His adventures with Meg and Charles Wallace allow him to accept and fine-tune his talents. Calvin comes to dinner with Meg and Charles and, warmly welcomed into their home, will continue to be a part of their lives for many books to come.

Later that evening, Charles Wallace announces to Meg and Calvin that "this is it" and that they are going on a journey, probably to find their father. They will be accompanied by the three odd women: Mrs. Whatsit, with her pink stole, the youngest of the three (2,379, 152, 497 years old), Mrs. Who, with her habit of speaking in quotes, and Mrs. Which, who often has difficulty appearing in a corporeal body. The group then "tessers," ("wrinkles") or travels in time, in the fifth dimension, landing on Uriel, a planet in the spiral nebula Messier 101. The feeling of tessering is uncomfortable at best and extremely painful at worst. The three children soon find those The Mrs. trios are not what they appear to be when Mrs. Whatsit transforms into something vaguely resembling a winged centaur. The children climb on "her" back (it's not clear at his point if she is male or female) and fly up into the clouds.

The centaur-like inhabitants of Uriel sing a song below the group as they fly, which inspires joy in any listener, as the "Dark Thing," or "Black Thing" menaces from above. Upon arrival at a summit in the clouds, they are able to see the "Dark Thing" more clearly, and learn that it is a force which threatens to annihilate the universe. The Dark Thing manifests itself as a "dreadful shadow" causing "a fear that was beyond shuddering, beyond crying, or screaming, beyond the possibility of comfort" (65). Meg and Charles

Wallace learn that their father is being held captive behind this darkness.

The children, aided by the Mrs. Trio, begin a journey to their father which must be accomplished in stages. They first accidentally tesser to a two-dimensional planet, where the three ladies enjoy themselves as "it's rather amusing to be flat," but the children almost die, before landing in Orion's belt. Here they visit the Happy Medium who is able to provide, through her crystal ball, a view of Earth which indicates the forces of good and evil struggling to take control. The earth appears to be covered by a smoky haze or fog which represents the presence of the Dark Thing, now defined as "evil…the powers of darkness" (81) against which all the good people in the universe must continuously fight. This battle takes place at the level of the tiniest microbes as much as at the cosmic level. The children are then told that the chief fighter for good is Jesus. Jesus, however, is not the only famous fighter; he is also joined by the likes of Leonardo Da Vinci and Michelangelo, Shakespeare and Bach, Einstein and Madame Curie, Gandhi and Buddha, in short, any people perceived as "lights for us to see by" (82).

The children continue their quest to find and rescue their father as they arrive at the planet Camazotz, which has totally succumbed to the Dark forces. Left alone on the planet, they enter a town "laid out in harsh, angular patterns" (95). Everything is exactly alike, from the houses to the landscaping to the rhythm of the children skipping rope, all completely identical and synchronized. Any activity that threatens to disrupt the regimented order on Camazotz is dealt with swiftly, as is the case with a small boy whose mother spots him erratically bouncing a ball. Barely keeping herself from screaming in alarm, the mother quickly snatches him back into the house. The boy's ball rolls into the street and Meg, Charles and Calvin attempt to return it. The mother refuses it, saying her son would not have dropped a ball in the first place because "the children in our section never drop balls" (98).

The planet's atmosphere and general Darkness has a dampening affect on Charles Wallace's powers, making their trip dangerous and him vulnerable. The epicenter of power on Camazotz lies at CENTRAL Central Intelligence, in the form of "IT." Like the Dark Thing, IT is not clearly described; instead, people talk about their general fear of IT and not wanting to have to see IT at all, ever.

Once inside the CENTRAL Central Intelligence building, Charles Wallace begins to feel as if some force were trying to take control of him: "Hold me tight! He's trying to get at me!" (111). In this instance, the all-powerful IT is described as male. The small group is then met by a man with red eyes who has a red pulsing glow about him like a demonic halo. He attempts to brainwash the children, by hypnotizing them into submission through various means, all of which the children are, together, able to overcome. It is only when Charles Wallace makes the mistake of taking on the man alone that he is overwhelmed and submits his will to the man who, by this time, is identified as being a puppet controlled by IT. Charles Wallace is the first to recognize this, addressing the man: "You aren't you…I'm not sure what you are, but you…aren't what's talking to us" (116).

Once in the grips of IT, endowed with knowledge of the building itself as well as IT's philosophies, Charles Wallace guides Meg and Calvin to Mr. Murray. Although Calvin tries to pull Charles out of his trance, he is unsuccessful. Charles tries, at the same time, to convince the two that Camazotz is a utopian paradise where there are no wars, no pain, no discomfort, and everyone is alike, without the differences that cause problems in societies like Earth's. On Camazotz, there are no individual minds; "Camazotz is ONE mind" Charles tells Calvin and his sister (132).

The children arrive at their father's "cell," where he is imprisoned inside a column of transparent material; he can be seen but cannot see outside. Meg is able to enter her father's cell by putting on Mrs. Who's glasses, a "gift" given to her at the start of their journey. Once inside, Meg is first relieved to be able to give the responsibility she feels to rescue them all over to her father, but quickly becomes angry and disappointed at both his powerlessness on Camazotz and his inability to immediately rescue Charles Wallace. Her father cannot save them. They must save themselves.

Charles Wallace leads the group to IT, which turns out to be a giant, pulsating, disembodied brain. The power of IT begins to take hold of their minds, and in a last ditch effort to save them, Calvin tells Meg's father to tesser the three of them away, leaving Charles Wallace behind. Meg's father, being inept and inexperienced, tessers in such a way that Meg is almost killed by the trip. She awakes on a different planet to intense, numbing cold, totally paralyzed. She is filled with rage and blame, which she directs at her father. It eventually is revealed that she has been affected by moving through the 'Dark Thing' without the protection offered by the Mrs. Trio.

Meg becomes so changed by her close encounter with the 'Dark Thing' during the tessering the she "[is] as much in the power of the Black Thing as Charles Wallace" (161). Soon after arriving on this planet, Ixchel, they are greeted by the inhabitants who have "four arms and far more than five fingers to each hand, and the fingers were not fingers at all but long waving tentacles" and "[have] no eyes. Just soft indentations" (163). One of the creatures comes to Meg and touches her, instantly mitigating her pain. She calls the creature "Aunt Beast." Even though Aunt Beast helps Meg with her physical recovery, Meg is still internally wounded, though not irreparably, by her encounter with the Black Thing. Aunt Beast explains to Meg's Father and Calvin "sometimes we can't know what spiritual damage [IT] leaves even when physical recovery is complete" (178). Shortly thereafter, Mrs. Trio arrive on Ixchel. The group decides that the only way to try and recover Charles Wallace from IT is to tesser with the help of Mrs. Who, Which and Whatsit, the only ones who are able to properly "wrinkle" to a Dark Planet. Meg's anger and resentment at her father's inability to instantly make things better extends to the three women, who remind her that they cannot intervene on Camazotz. Meg finally realizes that she must go alone to help her brother, at which point she seems to have grown up in many ways. Meg now looks at her father with "only love and pride" and smiles at him "asking forgiveness" (183).

Meg is given gifts from each of the Trio: the gift of Mrs. Whatsit's love, a quote that establishes the biblical concept of the weak able to overcome the mighty, and a hint from Mrs. Which about Meg's ability to love others. These gifts are her only arsenal with which to fight IT. She is deposited on Camazotz alone where she proceeds directly to IT for the final confrontation.

After several attempts to defeat IT, Meg suddenly realizes that the way to save Charles Wallace is to simply love him, with all that is in her being. She tells Charles "I love you. Charles Wallace, you are my darling and my dear and the light of my life and the treasure of my heart. I love you. I love you. I love you." (195). Her brother then hurls himself into her arms, and the two are tessered off Camazotz and back to earth. The three Murrays and Calvin land in the vegetable garden behind their house. The book ends as the family unites in the backyard, all members, including the dog, hugging and happy.

Historical Context

One of the marks of great literature is its ability to appeal to readers though history, having as much relevance at the present day as it did when first published. "A Wrinkle in Time" is one of those great works.

In her introduction to the 1997 edition of "A Wrinkle in Time," L'Engle answers the question of how her stories have survived for nearly fifty years, maintaining the same level of popularity as when they were originally published. According to her, they "have a life of their own, and …say different things to different people in different times… and [take] us beyond the facts into something more real." The concept that a reality exists outside the world of facts, which is generally considered the equivalent of reality, is one of the commonly held beliefs that L'Engle explores in her texts.

Societal Context

Questions about our place in the world, the importance of connecting with friends and family, and whether or not we are alone in the universe are a few of many sub-themes threading through L'Engle's fiction. L'Engle often draws connections between the macrocosm of family, society, culture, and the universe, to the world inside us all. In many cases, external reality is deeply affected by the successful navigation of challenges to internal processes of the mind, intuition (in "A Wrinkle In Time"), or the physical body (in "A Wind in the Door"). The interconnectedness of individuals as well as the symbiotic relationship between people and their environments is essential, in many of L'Engle's books, to maintaining a successful self, family and world.

In many ways, the intelligent and sophisticated thinkers in "A Wrinkle in Time," as well as other L'Engle writing, are ostracized from society. Meg and Charles Wallace are social outcasts who only feel comfortable at home. Sandy and Dennys are only able to get along with their peers because they can assimilate well, and successfully hide whatever talents they possess. On Camazotz, the children are told the best way to get along and survive their "reprocessing" is to "just relax and don't fight it" (110). In general, intelligence, especially excessive intelligence, is seen by society at large as a liability.

Calvin takes tremendous comfort in finding the Murrays who are like him, so that he can finally feel part of a group. At their home, shortly after meeting the family, Calvin exclaims "How did this all happen? Isn't it wonderful? I feel as though I were just being born! I'm not alone any more!" (39).

Most of the important and influential characters in this novel are women: Mrs. Whatsit, Mrs. Who, and Mrs. Which, The Happy Medium, Meg's mother and "Aunt" Beast are the characters who offer the trio support, advice and comfort during their journey. The antagonist is simply "IT" and appears to be androgynous (although Charles Wallace does refer to IT as a "he"). "IT's" closest servant, the man with the red eyes, is also male. Meg's father is rendered powerless when he is imprisoned by IT, and can only be saved via the intervention of Meg. While Charles Wallace is, simply put, a prodigy, he is still in need of guidance from his sister and cannot successfully fight IT without Meg's help. Calvin, though brilliant and several grades above Meg, actually gets help from her on his math homework.

The fact that Meg's mother seems to overcome traditional gender stereotyping by being a groundbreaking scientist, traditional social gender role expectations are sill apparent, even in the progressive Murray family. Her at-home lab appears to put her children at some risk: "You didn't leave any nasty smelling chemicals cooking over a Bunsen burner, did you?" asks Charles Wallace. The twins also make the salient comment "We know you have a great mind and all, Mother…but you don't have much sense. And certainly Meg and Charles don't" (20). When Calvin comes for dinner, Mrs. Murray is cooking stew in her lab, and warns "Don't tell Sandy and Dennys I am cooking out here…they're always suspicious that a few chemicals may get into the meat" (34).

The story emphasizes the challenges of connecting with social groups as much as the importance of independence, just as in tessering, in life, "though we travel together, we travel alone" (72). When trying to explain to Meg, her father, and Calvin, why the outcome of Meg's journey to save her brother is unknown even to the Happy Medium, Mrs. Whatsit uses a sonnet as a metaphor. The sonnet, while restricting the poet to a rigid set of rules, also allows freedom: "within this strict form the poet has complete freedom to say whatever he wants, doesn't he?" (186). As is the sonnet, so is life: "You're given the form but you have to write the sonnet yourself" (186). Love is not only the gift Mrs. Whatsit bestows on Meg to fight IT, it is the very thing that allows her to be successful against her powerful antagonist.

Religious Context

L'Engle writes stories that are "Christian" in the broadest sense of the word, representing "her vibrant and changing Christian faith" (Risher). L'Engle's relationship to her faith is flexible and complicated. She believes that she became a Christian "probably when my father inseminated my mother. It's in my genes. It's coded in my DNA" (qtd. in Risher). At the same time, L'Engle's view of what God "is" is very closely related to nature: "If I want to see God, I'll go out on a clear night and look at the stars" (qtd. in Risher). She also sees God as a manifestation or "incarnation" of "pure love," a concept she develops in "A Wrinkle in Time" (Risher). Another one of L'Engle's issues with traditional Christianity is the predominant use of the King James Version of the Bible, in which imagination, something central to her concept of faith, is depicted as evil. To counteract this emphasis, L'Engle chooses to read many different Biblical interpretations as well as reading the Bible in another language in order to "get a fresher feeling" (qtd. in Risher).

One of the first direct references to Christianity occurs on Uriel when the centaur-like creatures sing in order to fight the destructive forces of the Black Thing and IT. Their song is a specifically religious one, beginning: "Sing unto the Lord a new song, and his praise from the end of the earth" (61).

The man with the red eyes who meets the children at CENTRAL Central Intelligence is arguably a representation of evil embodied, who attempts to brainwash them into giving up their individual will to him as well as turning them from God. He states, using particularly Christ-like language that he is "willing to assume all the pain, all the responsibility, all the burdens of thought and decision" (113).

The children's search for a father who seems to have abandoned them, leaving them unprotected in the world, (as the man with red eyes points out), appears to symbolize the conflict people of faith face when God's will is not understood or when God seems to have abandoned them. The man with red eyes capitalizes on this uncertainty and argues that IT will not abandon them in the way their Father has. When Charles Wallace is controlled by IT, he argues to Meg and Calvin "Father? What is a father?...Merely another misconception. If you feel the need of a father, then I would suggest that you turn to IT" (129). While, on the surface IT/the man with the red eyes appears to be offering a Christ-like version of salvation, L'Engle clarifies the differences between what IT offers and what Christ offers when IT explains that the only way to avoid suffering is to have one's will subsumed, thus completely eradicating the individual and allowing IT to continually gain strength and power. In contrast, Christ, in L'Engle's mind, is he who "is continually throwing the worldly power he is being offered away" (qtd. in Risha).

Scientific & Technological Context

L'Engle is acutely aware of scientific backdrop of her novels. She discusses in the introduction to this novel, "When I look up at the night sky I'm looking at time as well as space, looking at a start seventy light years away..." Because she uses a similar description to explain how she feels God's presence, God, nature and science intersect in L'Engle's philosophy; an intersection that is mirrored in her fiction.

The science each Murray parent is engaged in is clearly dangerous both to the health and welfare of their family and indeed to themselves (Mr. Murray is captured and imprisoned when he tries time/space traveling). That said, science itself is not vilified, simply explored and questioned. Mrs. Murray can be seen as a representation of balance between science and faith, she is a woman of absolutes and facts while at the same time being capable of belief based entirely on faith and intuition.

Biographical Context

L'Engle was born on November 29, 1918. Madeline spent most of her childhood and adolescent years at boarding schools, and attended Smith College. After college, she dabbled in the theater world in New York City where she met her husband, Hugh Franklin, who was also an actor. Madeline then gave up acting and focused on her writing. Deciding they wanted to escape city living, the two moved to Connecticut where they operated a general store and lived at Crosswicks, a historic farmhouse where they started a family. Nine years later, however, the family returned to New York City. L'Engle still lives at least part-time in New York City.

The idea for "A Wrinkle in Time" came to L'Engle during an extended cross-country camping trip. Upon its completion, the book was rejected by several publishers, L'Engle asserts at least partially because of the female protagonist (qtd in Blocher). Her husband died of cancer in 1986, and her son, Bion died in 1999. Bion is the generally accepted model for the character of Charles Wallace, a thing Bion "resented" (Blocher).

L'Engle is writer in residence at the Cathedral Church of St. John The Divine in New York City. Though mostly known as a writer of adolescent books, L'Engle has published work in many other forms, including journals, religious essays, poetry, and plays.

Tracy M. Caldwell

Works Cited

Blocher, Karen Funk. "The Tesseract: Madeline L'Engle FAQ page." 12 Oct. 2005.

L'Engle. Madeline. *A Wrinkle in Time*. New York: Bantam Doubleday Dell Publishing Group, 1062.

Risher, Dee Dee. "Listening to the Story: A conversation with Madeline L'Engle". 12 Oct. 2005.

Discussion Questions

1. What is so evil about Camazotz? Do you think that sacrificing free will in order to achieve total freedom from pain is a good thing? Is IT truthful when it states that the people of Camazotz are free of pain?

2. In what ways are Meg's problems similar to problems of modern day girls? Do you think that in general boys or girls have an easier time fitting in?

3. Do you think that in an adolescent social environment, the highly intelligent are often treated as outcasts? Why or why not?

4. Do you think that genius-level intelligence is a gift or a liability? Explain.

5. While this is a "Christian" book written by a "Christian" author, do you feel it is "preachy?" Why or why not?

6. Explain the current relationship between religion and science in this country. Are the two mutually exclusive or do they influence each other, and even blend at some points?

7. How is Meg, as a girl, different from Calvin, Charles and the twins? How is she like them?

8. How does the concept of appearance versus reality come up over and over in the text? In what cases are people exactly what they seem? Where are they the opposite?

9. Why do you think there were many attempts to ban this book?

10. Do you think the Murray family is depicted as "perfect" or is "idealized" to the point that it is not believable? Is Calvin's family more believable?

Essay Ideas

1. Looking carefully at the appearance and dialogue of the Mrs. Whatist, Mrs. Who and Mrs. Which, write an essay exploring what they symbolize.

2. Write an essay that explores and supports an argument about the importance or necessity of religion in this text. How is religion used by L'Engle?

3. Write an essay that analyzes L'Engle's depiction of androgyny or flexible gender in terms of the Mrs. and IT.

4. Write an essay that compares this story with another of L'Engle's "Time Quartet" books.

5. Explore the various settings on the planets visited by the group, analyzing how these descriptions provide important details in developing themes of the story. Alternatively, compare Camazotz's setting with Earth's, in what ways are they different and/or similar?

Zombie

by Joyce Carol Oates

Content Synopsis

"Zombie" is divided into two sections. The first, entitled "Suspended Sentence," introduces us to Quentin, his family, his life, and his past crimes.

Quentin P. (his last name is not revealed in the book) is the white, 31-year-old son of a prominent college professor at the fictional Mount Vernon State University in Mount Vernon, Michigan. He is also a registered sex offender who is serving a two-year suspended sentence after being caught in the act of assaulting a mentally challenged African-American boy in the back of his van.

While Quentin serves his suspended sentence, his father has given him a job as the live-in caretaker of a family-owned rooming house for college students. Quentin's parents, his sister, and his grandmother all live in the surrounding community.

As told by Quentin, his everyday life is filled with mundane experiences. His job responsibilities include taking out the trash, cleaning the house's communal kitchen, spraying for roaches, and pumping out the cistern in the basement. He works by himself, and eats and drinks alone in his room. He attends classes at a local community college, but mostly just wanders the campus like a misfit, jealously observing the easy social interactions of others.

As part of his probation, Quentin is required to attend group-counseling classes and check in with his parole officer on a regular basis.

While describing the circumstances of his everyday life, Quentin also reveals himself to be a determined, ruthless, and calculating serial killer. He is consumed with the idea of abducting and lobotomizing a male specimen to serve as his personal sex slave.

"A true ZOMBIE would be mine forever. He would obey every command & whim. Saying 'Yes, Master" & No, Master.' His eyes would be open & clear but there would be nothing behind them seeing and nothing behind them thinking. Nothing passing judgment" (49).

Using the same clinical, detached language of a scientist, Quentin recounts in excruciating detail how he has abducted, drugged, and attempted to lobotomize four men using the lobotomy techniques outlined in a textbook from the 1940s.

All four attempts have failed, resulting in often painful and often degrading deaths, and yet Quentin's determination to create a zombie has not wavered.

The second section of the book, called "How Things Play Out," describes the circumstances surrounding the abduction of Quentin's fifth specimen.

While cutting the lawn at his grandmother's house one evening, Quentin notices a group of teenage boys swimming in the pool next door. He is immediately taken with one of the boys, whom he nicknames Squirrel, and begins to plan for the boy's abduction.

Quentin knows that capturing someone from the surrounding community is much more risky than his usual practice of finding drifters from out of town, but he is so consumed with the idea of having Squirrel as his zombie that he is willing to take the extra risk.

Quentin begins to methodically stalk the boy to learn his schedule and habits. He starts to hang out at the restaurant where Squirrel works, and follows him home each night. He goes to inspired lengths to plan the abduction, provide himself with an alibi, and plan for ways to cover his tracks.

When the moment of the abduction finally comes, Quentin discovers that the reality of the situation does not match up his fantasies. Unforeseen complications occur, and he is forced to adjust his plans accordingly.

Themes & Motifs

There are numerous themes and motifs throughout "Zombie," including the idea of a subjective viewpoint, how one experiences time, what the true nature of identity is, and the link between sexuality and violence.

Perhaps the strongest motif is that of a subjective, carefully controlled point of view. This book is all about perspective. In fact, it is the perspective that makes this book unique, and in some ways more insidious and more horrifying than a traditional serial killer novel in which the viewpoint is that of an objective narrator or someone trying to stop the killer.

The story is told from Quentin's perspective in a first-person narrative. It is written almost like a personal journal, though Quentin does address the reader directly at one point, indicating that he knows his words are being read.

"Like you who observe me (you think I don't know you are observing Q___ P___? making reports of Q___ P____? conferring with one other about Q___ P____?) & think your secret thoughts—ALWAYS & FOREVER PASSING JUDGMENT" (49).

Because he is the one telling his story to the reader, Quentin filters all information through the lens of his personal agenda. He chooses which information to reveal and what to withhold. He even alters the form of the text to reflect his state of mind. Important ideas are written in all capital letters. Snippets of past conversations with family members, therapists, and others are written in italic text. Sentences are strung together in run-on fashion, connected by a series of ampersands.

"It was dark behind the dorm & the kid was drunk & stooped over vomiting & gagging & when he looked up hearing me the tire iron slammed down over his ear crashing him to the ground before he could register seeing me so it was O.K. I was wearing my hooded canvas jacket & there were no witnesses, still I panicked & ran as I would never do now with more experience" (28).

By carefully controlling the information that we receive, and shaping the circumstances of his life to reflect his own desires, we almost find ourselves identifying with Quentin's quest. Oates tempers this inclination by including enough grim details of his crimes so that we can never separate ourselves from the horrors of his actions. It is an admirable and delicate balancing act.

Since Quentin controls the narrative, he is able to withhold information and obscure the truth about identities and situations when he chooses. He does not reveal his last name in the story, or the first or last name of his father (identified only as R___ P____). His mother's name is not mentioned at all, though his sister (Junie) is identified by her first name.

All of Quentin's zombie victims have impersonalized nicknames: Bunny Gloves, Raisin Eyes, Big Guy, No-Name, and Squirrel.

Quentin is also purposefully vague about his relationship with his former classmate, Barry. It is Barry that Quentin is reminded of when he first sets eyes on Squirrel. In some instances, he recalls Barry as his friend (69), though on another occasion he expresses his anger at Barry for never recognizing him (125). He is also vague about the circumstances of Barry's death, suggesting but never acknowledging that he might have had a part in it.

"Barry who'd drowned in a swimming accident at the school, struck his head on the side of the pool & sank & so many kids yelling & wild tossing volleyballs it wasn't noticed till we were almost all out of the pool" (100).

The fact that Quentin keeps a memento of Barry after his death, as he does with all of his other victims, suggests that he might have had something to do with the drowning accident, though this is never specifically stated.

Quentin's ability to manipulate the truth is not just limited to the information he withholds. He also demonstrates that he is more than willing to create a false narrative to serve his purposes.

When he realizes that he is behind in his studies and class work at community college, he begins to think of excuses he can fabricate "....thinking OK! I'll just visit my profs to explain there's an illness in the family, my Mom in a struggle with cancer, my Dad with a bad heart" (77).

Later, when he is preparing for his abduction of Squirrel, he calls the family attorney to falsely report that he is being harassed by the local police, thus laying the groundwork for obstructing any investigation that might take place after Squirrel goes missing.

Quentin is a hollow person, who is adept at assuming different roles and saying whatever is necessary to further his goals. He knows how to alter his voice and his appearance to prevent people from identifying him. He will often disguise himself as someone else (he refers to one of his aliases as Todd Cuttler) when he goes out trolling for sex or potential victims.

The idea of assuming different personalities first came to Quentin after he was beaten up by a gang of teenagers in Detriot. When he wakes up the next morning, he looks at his swollen, unrecognizable face in the mirror the next day and has a revelation. "& I understood then that I could habit a FACE NOT KNOWN. Not known ANYWHERE IN THE WORLD. I could move in the world LIKE ANOTHER PERSON. I could arouse PITY, TRUST, SYMPATHY, WONDERMENT and AWE with such a face. I could EAT YOUR HEART & asshole you'd never know it" (60).

Quentin's ability to assume different roles is not just limited to his appearance. He can also change how he speaks and what he says in order to assume different roles. Rather than explore his own feelings during therapy sessions, Quentin says what he thinks the therapist wants to hear.

He imitates the other members of the group, breaking down and begging for forgiveness in a completely insincere way. "...& I open my mouth to speak & there's this voice comes out, it's Q___ P____'s but like another guy's too, somebody on TV maybe, or I'm imitating Bim, Perche, Frogsnout [Quentin's nicknames for other group members] stammering saying how ashamed I was to betray the loving trust of my Mom & Dad & that was the worst part of what happened to me..." (46).

Quentin seems to like disguises and deception so much because he does not want anyone to see him for himself. He is afraid of making eye contact with anyone and is consumed with the idea of making a zombie because a zombie will be someone who does not see him for what he truly is.

Another strong motif in "Zombie" is Quentin's difficulty in dealing with the passage of time. Early on in the book, he wonders if the passage of time is something that he has control over, or if it is an uncontrollable external phenomenon. In an attempt to liberate himself from the constraints of time, he breaks the hands off of his clock so it is just the clock face looking at him (6).

Later in the book, Quentin seeks to distance himself from his past crimes. He prefers to live only in the present, as that seems to be his way of avoiding any pain or regret. "I keep memories but no records. How many times I keep memories but no records. My clock face has no hands & Q___ P___ has never been one to have hang-ups over personalities or the past. THE PAST is PAST and you learn to move on" (85).

"Zombie" also contains the themes of intertwining sexuality and violence that many critics have identified as a common element to Oates' work.

While a novel about a sexual serial killer is by nature going to incorporate both of those themes, it is interesting how violence is linked to all of Quentin's thoughts about sexuality. There is an aggression behind all of his sexual actions.

At the age of seven, he wraps the head and neck of a male classmate in the chains of a swing after the boy refuses his sexual advances. When Quentin is in the seventh grade, his father finds a collection of muscle magazines that Quentin has modified in bizarre ways.

As critic Stephen Marcus points out in his *New York Times* review of the book, whenever Quentin talks about creating a zombie, he does so with a mix of tenderness and rage. He wants someone that he can abuse sexually and then cuddle with afterwards.

Marcus' point is supported by the way Quentin feels after abducting Squirrel. "But I was pissed with him. Always you get pissed with them, & want to punish" (150).

But even after Squirrel's abduction goes completely off track, Quentin goes right back to fantasizing about his zombie in romantic terms, echoing the exact thoughts and words that he used earlier in the book.

"We would lie beneath the covers in my bed in the CARETAKER's room listening to the November wind & the bells of the Music Tower Chiming & WE WOULD COUNT THE CHIMES UNTIL WE FELL ASLEEP AT EXACTLY THE SAME MOMENT" (50, 170).

Historical Context

"Zombie" does not have a significant historical context, though Oates does make specific reference to the real-life collision of the Comet Levi-Shoemaker with the planet Jupiter that took place on July 16, 1994. This event serves as the launching off point for the second half of the story ("How Things Play Out").

Later in the book, Quentin puts a series of rocks on top of his air conditioner that he uses to symbolize the fragments that were created when the comet hit the planet. He takes away a rock each day as a way of counting down to the abduction day.

Historical context is also important when it comes to understanding the rise and fall of Quentin's father's mentor, Dr. M___ K___.

All throughout the novel, Quentin's father has benefited from his relationship with the prominent Dr. M___ K___, displaying pictures of the two of them together in three places—in his home, in his mother's home, and in his office at the university.

At the end of the novel, Dr. M___ K___ is discredited posthumously for experiments he conducted during the 1950s that purposely exposed test subjects to dangerous levels of radiation.

These experiments are compared to those that were undertaken by Nazi doctors during the Third Reich, and provide an interesting parallel to the real-life lobotomy procedures that took place in mental asylums during the 1940s and 50s, and Quentin's attempts to create a zombie.

Societal Context

"Zombie" is filled with social tension. Quentin is an outsider, at once yearning to be acknowledged by someone and desperately afraid that someone will see him for who he is. He functions in the novel as a social alter-ego to his father.

While the Professor R____ P_____ occupies a distinguished place in the local community and is recognized and admired by everyone, Quentin talks to no one and skulks about in the background silent and invisible. Instead of teaching science like his professor father, he conducts his own macabre science experiments.

Quentin's position as a caretaker allows him to operate outside of the normal time and space of others. He works alone at odd hours. He does not have to report to work or punch a clock. In fact, he breaks the hands off of his clock so he no longer even has to consider what time it is.

Living completely on his own terms gives Quentin plenty of time to plot and plan and seethe. He eats and drinks by himself. He takes uppers and downers to balance his mood. He rents pornography, masturbates furiously, and frequents adult theatres. He spends endless amounts of time lurking around the campus of the college where his father works.

While Oates does suggest that some of Quentin's alienation might be tied to his sexual orientation, she does not use it as an excuse for his actions, or as a justification.

It is clear, however, that the family does not realize or choose to accept Quentin's homosexuality. His sister tries to set him up with her friends, and his grandmother tells Quentin that she hopes he will get married one day.

Quentin also recalls an incident from his childhood in which his furious father happened upon his collection of men's muscle magazines, and forced Quentin to burn them in the back yard.

Religious Context

Religion does not play a major role in the book, though there are some small elements of religion throughout.

When Quentin starts to break down during his group therapy session, he references God while constructing a completely false sense of remorse and self-loathing.

"I wished I could turn back the clock to infancy I said & start Time again. When I was pure & good. When I was with god. I said I believed in God but

did not think he believed in me because I was not worthy" (46).

Quentin also likens himself to God when describing how easy it was to abduct and dispose of a drifter like Bunnygloves who had no one to care about him or look for him.

"How many hundreds, thousands in a single year, Like sparrows of the air they rise on their wings & soar & falter & disappear & not a trace. & God is himself the DARK MATTER that swallows them up" (30-31).

Later, when disavowing all connections that he has to the past (aside from the small mementoes he takes from each of his victims), he suggests that he might be able to change his ways.

"I could be a REBORN CHRISTIAN is what I sometimes think, & maybe am waiting for that call" (85).

Scientific & Technological Context

Science plays a significant role in the novel. Quentin is the son of a prominent physics and philosophy professor, and has been living under the weight of his father's success for his entire life.

Quentin is his father's scientific alter-ego as well as his social alter-ego. While Professor R____ P____ has used science to advance his professional career and gain the respect of his peers, Quentin uses science to satisfy his base desires.

It is while Quentin is listening in on one of his father's science lectures, sitting anonymously among the students in a darkened lecture hall, that he firsts gets the idea for creating a zombie by lobotomizing a living person.

He then goes upstairs to the university library to learn about the lobotomy procedure from a science textbook, and describes his discovery like a scientist happening upon a miracle solution. "Jesus! At such rare times you can feel the electrically-charged neurons of the prefrontal brain realigning themselves like iron filings drawn by a magnet" (26).

Quentin approaches his quest for a zombie like a scientist, referring to his victims as specimens, and using the same method of trial and error that often leads to scientific discovery. On pages 117–119, for example, he visits the Mount Vernon University Biology Department, where he encounters a female graduate student and asks her to show him where the vocal chords are located, so he will know where to cut them on his zombie.

Biographical Context

Joyce Carol Oates was born on June 16, 1938. She grew up in Lockport, New York, a town 20 miles north of Buffalo and 15 miles south of Lake Ontario.

Oates was a talented student who excelled in English and received her first typewriter as a present at the age of 14. She earned a scholarship to Syracuse University, where she majored in English and was the valedictorian of her graduating class. It was during college that she first achieved literary prominence by winning a *Mademoiselle* magazine short story writing contest.

Oates attended graduate school at the University of Wisconsin, where she met and married her husband, Raymond Smith. Oates and Smith settled in Detroit in 1962, living in the city for six years before moving across the border to Winsdor, Ontario, Canada. In 1978, Oates and Smith moved to Princeton, NJ, where she took a position teaching creative writing at Princeton University. She has taught there continuously for over 30 years.

Throughout her career, Oates has been a very prolific writer who has surprised and challenged critics by her prodigious output and ability to crisscross genres and styles. She has often produced two or three books per year, and has written novels, short stories, essays, and non-fiction pieces.

In 1987, Oates attempted to publish one of her books under the pseudonym of Rosalind Smith. She was surprised and disappointed when her true identity was discovered before the book was published.

"Zombie" was originally published as a short story in the *New Yorker* Magazine. It was published in novel form in 1995.

"Zombie" received a tepid reception from Stephen Marcus in a *New York Times* review published in October of 1995. However, the novel was the winner of the Bram Stoker Award for Superior Achievement in a Novel in 1996 and the winner of the Fisk Fiction Prize from the *Boston Book Review*. It was one of the *New York Times'* Notable Books of the Year for 1995.

Marcus wrote that "Zombie" represents "the continuation of Ms. Oates's longstanding interest in the extreme, the gruesome, the bizarre, and the violent in American Life."

He goes on to criticize Oates for trying to connect Quentin to a number of important tendencies and truths about contemporary American society.

"This dreadful creature is presented to us as not simply living in mainstream America and as not merely being affected by the culture but as in some sense an embodiment of it, as containing and conveying its truth if not its very essence."

Marcus then concludes that the "idea of this narrative—that the uncaught serial killer is somehow peculiarly representative of our current condition—is more interesting than its execution, which, like the writing in which it is embodied, is fluid, fluent, inflated and, finally, neither convincing in itself nor successfully dramatized as fiction."

In a letter to the *New York Times* responding to Marcus' review, Oates criticizes him for inventing a theme for her novel and then criticizing that theme.

She says that she intended Quentin to represent the exact opposite of the proverbial everyman. "It would not have required a brilliant reader, only perhaps an attentive one, to see that, contrary to being an 'allegorical' figure, the serial killer of 'Zombie' is utterly unlike the well-intentioned, kindly, decent people who surround him and in some cases protect him."

Brian Burns

Works Cited

Johnson, Greg. "A Brief Biography." *Celestial Timepiece: A Joyce Carol Oates Home Page,* 1996. 4 August 2008.

"Joyce Carol Oates Biography." *Academy of Achievement,* 2005. 25 July 2008.

Marcus, Steven. "American Psycho." *NYTimes. com,* Oct. 8, 1995. 11 August 2008.

Oates, Joyce Carol. "Psycho Killer." *NYTimes. com,* Oct. 29, 1995. 11 August 2008.

Discussion Questions

1. Why do you think Quentin does not give his last name or reveal the names of his family members?
2. Why does Oates punctuate the novel in such an unusual way? What does this add to the story? What does it say about Quentin?
3. What do you think of the structure of the story? Why is it divided into two sections? What purpose do the short chapters serve?
4. What are some of the different roles that Quentin assumes over the course of the novel?
5. Why does Quentin keep a memento from each victim?
6. Does Oates want us to have sympathy for Quentin's victims? If so, how does she accomplish this?
7. What is Quentin's relationship with his father? What evidence is there that he wants a closer relationship?
8. Do you think Quentin was born to be a killer?
9. What do the drawings add to the book?
10. How are women portrayed in Zombie? How does Quentin's relationship with his father differ from that of his mother?

Essay Ideas

1. What role does science play in this book? What, if anything, is Oates suggesting about the nature of scientific inquiry?
2. Discuss the parallels that exist in the novel between Quentin and his father. How are the two characters alike? How are they dissimilar?
3. What is the motivation for Quentin to create a zombie? Is his goal a realistic one, even by his own twisted reasoning?
4. Does Quentin ever show any genuine guilt or remorse in the book? If so, when?
5. What evidence is there to support Stephen Marcus's claim that the novel acts as a commentary on American society? Does his argument stand up?

BIBLIOGRAPHY

Abel, David. "So it goes for Vonnegut at Smith, 78-Year-Old Author still shaking up the establishment." *Boston Globe*. 5 May 2001: A1.

Allen, David. *Make Love, Not War: The Sexual Revolution: An Unfettered History.* New York: Little, Brown, 2000.

Alsen, Eberhard. *A Reader's Guide to J. D. Salinger.* Westport, CN and London: Greenwood, 2002.

———. "The Role of Vedanta Hinduism in Salinger's Seymour Novel." *Renascence* 33.2 (Winter 1981) 99–116.

Alvarez, A. *The Savage God: A Study of Suicide.* Harmondsworth: Penguin, 1974.

Alvarez, Julia. *"How the García Girls Lost Their Accents."* 1991. New York: Plume, 1992.

———. "An American Childhood in the Dominican Republic." *The American Scholar* (winter 1987): 71–85.

———. *Something to Declare.* Chapel Hill: Algonquin Books, 1998.

Atwood, Margaret. *Alias Grace.* 1996. New York: Anchor Books, 1997.

———. "Author's Afterword." *Alias Grace.* 461–65.

———. "In Search of Alias Grace: On Writing Canadian Historical Fiction." Bronfman Lecture Series. Ottawa. November 1996. *Rpt. in Writing with Intent: Essays, Reviews, Personal Prose, 1983–2005.* New York: Carroll & Graf, 2005.

———. *The Handmaid's Tale,* London: Jonathan Cape Ltd, 1986.

Auster, Paul. *Moon Palace.* New York: Viking, 1989.

Bachrach, Deborah. *The Holocaust Library: The Resistance.* San Diego, CA: Lucent, 1998.

Barak, Julie. "'Turning and turning in the widening Gyre': A Second Coming into Language in Julia Alvarez's 'How the García Girls Lost Their Accents'." *MELUS* 23, no. 1 (spring 1998): 159–177.

Bartkowski, Frances. *Feminist Utopias.* Lincoln, Neb and London: U of Nebraska P, 1989.

Begley, Adam. "The Art of Fiction CXXXV: Don DeLillo." *Paris Review* 35.128 (1993): 274–306.

Behlman, Lee. "The Escapist: Fantasy, Folklore, and the Pleasures of the Comic Book in Recent Jewish American Holocaust Fiction." *SHOFAR* 22.3 (Spr 2004): 56–71.

Belcher, William F. and James E. Lee, eds. *J. D. Salinger and the Critics.* Belmont, CA: Wadsworth, 1962.

Bilton, Alan. *An Introduction to Contemporary American Fiction.* Edinburgh: Edinburgh University Press, 2002.

Blackford, Holly. "Haunted Housekeeping: Fatal Attractions of Servant and Mistress in Twentieth-Century Female Gothic Literature." *Lit: Literature Interpretation Theory* 16. 2 (Apr–June 2005): 233–61.

Blocher, Karen Funk. "The Tesseract: Madeline L'Engle FAQ page." 12 Oct. 2005.

Bloom, Harold, ed. *J. D. Salinger.* New York: Chelsea House, 1987.

———. *Toni Morrison's Beloved: Bloom's Notes.* Contemporary Literary Views Ser. New York: Chelsea, 1999.

Blume, Judy. *Are You There, God? It's Me, Margaret.* New York: Yearling, 1986.

Boswell, Marshall. *John Updike's Rabbit Tetralogy: Mastered Irony in Motion.* Columbia: U of Missouri 2001.

Bradbury, Malcolm. *The Modern American Novel – Second Edition.* Oxford, Oxford University Press, 1992.

Bronfen, Elisabeth. *Sylvia Plath.* Plymouth: Northcote, 1998.

Bryan, James E. "J. D. Salinger: The Fat Lady and the Chicken Sandwich." *College English* 23.3 (December 1961) 226–29.

Buchanan, Bruce G. "A Brief History of Artificial Intelligence." *AI Topics.* 2006. 11 April 2006.

Butler, Judith. *Gender Trouble.* New York and London: Routledge, 1990.

Calcutt, Andrew and Richard Shephard. *Cult Fiction: A Reader's Guide.* London: Prion, 1999.

Cantor, Paul A. "Adolf, We Hardly Knew You." *New Essays on White Noise.* Ed. Frank Lentricchia. Cambridge: Cambridge University Press, 1991. 39–62.

Castells, Ricardo. "The Silence of Exile in 'How the García Girls Lost Their Accents'." *Bilingual Review* 26, no. 1 (Jan–April 2001/2002): 34–43.

Century, Douglas. *Toni Morrison (Black Americans of Achievement).* New York: Chelsea, 1994.

Chabon, Michael. *The Amazing Adventures of Kavalier & Clay.* New York: Picador USA, 2000.

———. "Interview with Scott Tobias." *AV Club.* The Onion. 22 November 2000.

Chalmers, Robert. "Chuck Palahniuk: Stranger than Fiction" *The Independent*, 01 August 2004.

Cisneros, Sandra. "Do You Know Me?: I Wrote The House on Mango Street." *Americas Review* 15 (Spring 1987): 69–73.

_____. "Ghosts and Voices: Writing from Obsession." *Americas Review* 15 (1987): 60–73.

_____. *The House on Mango Street*. 1984. New York: Vintage, 1991.

_____. *The House on Mango Street*. 1984. New York: Knopf, 1999.

_____. "Introduction." *The House on Mango Street*. 1999. xi–xx.

Clarke, Deborah. "Domesticating the Car: Women's Road Trips." *Studies in American Fiction* (2004) 32.1: 101–29.

Cooper, Alan. *Philip Roth and the Jews*. Albany, State University of New York Press, 1996.

Cortiel, Jeanne. *Demand My Writing: Joanna Russ/Feminism/Science Fiction*. Liverpool: Liverpool UP, 1999.

_____. "Joanna Russ." *Significant Contemporary American Feminists: A Biographical Sourcebook*. Ed. Jennifer Scanlon. Westport, Conn. and London: Greenwood, 1999.

Creech, Sharon. *Walk Two Moons*. New York: Harper Trophy, 1994.

Cushman, Karen. Author's Note. *The Midwife's Apprentice*. New York: HarperCollins, 1995. 118–22.

_____. *The Midwife's Apprentice*. New York: HarperCollins, 1995.

_____. "Newbery Medal Acceptance." *Horn Book Magazine* 72.4 (1996): 413–420.

Davis, Tom. "J. D. Salinger: 'The Sound of One Hand Clapping.'" *Wisconsin Studies in Contemporary Fiction* 4.1 (Winter 1963) 41–47.

De Beauvoir, Simone. *The Second Sex*. (1949).

DeCurtis, Anthony. "'An Outsider in This Society': An Interview with Don DeLillo." *Introducing Don DeLillo*. Ed. Frank Lentricchia. Durham: Duke University Press, 1991. 43–66.

De Lange, Nicholas. *An Introduction to Judaism*. Cambridge UP, 2000.

DeLillo Don. *Libra*. 1988. New York: Penguin, 1991.

_____. *Mao II*. London: Vintage, 1992.

_____. *Underworld*. London: Picador, 1998.

_____. *White Noise*. London: Picador, 1986.

DeMarr, Mary Jean. *Barbara Kingsolver: A Critical Companion*. Westport, Connecticut and London: Greenwood Press, 1999.

Dewey, Joseph. "Rick Moody." *Review of Contemporary Fiction*. 23.2 (2003), 7–49.

Dickens, Charles. *David Copperfield*. New York: Signet Classic, 1962.

Dick, Philip K. *Do Androids Dream of Electric Sheep?* 1968. New York: Ballantine, 1982.

Dorloff, Steven. "Vonnegut's Cat's Cradle." *The Explicator* 63.1 (2004): 56–57.

Drabble, Margaret, ed. *The Oxford Companion to English Literature*. 6th ed. Oxford: OUP, 2000.

Drabelle, Dennis. "Weird Fantasies and Amazing Adventures." *Civilization* 4:6 (1997/1998). Academic Search Premier. Grand Valley State University Zumberge Lib. 9 Jan. 2005.

Duffin, Jacalyn. "Margaret Atwood: Alias Grace." *Literature, Arts, and Medicine Database*. 17 November 2003. New York University. 23 November 2005.

Duvall, John. *Don DeLillo's Underworld: A Reader's Guide*. New York and London: Continuum Publishing, 2002.

Enns, Anthony. "Media, Drugs, and Schizophrenia in the Works of Philip K. Dick." *Science Fiction Studies* 33.1 (March 2006): 68–88.

Ferraro, Thomas J. "Whole Families Shopping at Night." Ed. Frank Lentricchia. Cambridge: Cambridge University Press, 1991. 15–38.

Francavilla, Joseph. "The Android as Doppelgänger." *Retrofitting Blade Runner: Issues in Ridley Scott's Blade Runner and Philip K. Dick's Do Androids Dream of Electric Sheep?* Ed. Judith B. Kerman. Bowling Green: Bowling Green State U Popular P, 1997. 4–15.

Freitag, Michael. "The Novelist Out of Control." *New York Times,* 19 March 1989.

French, Warren. *J. D. Salinger*, Revisited. Boston, Twayne, 1988.

Friedan, Betty. *The Feminine Mystique*. New York: Norton, 1963.

Frye, Bob J. "Nuggets of Truth in the Southwest: Artful Humor and Realistic Craft in Barbara Kingsolver's The Bean Trees." *Southwestern American Literature* (spring 2001) 26.2: 73–83.

Gibson, William. "An Interview with William Gibson." By Larry McCaffery. *Storming the Reality Studio:*

A Casebook of Cyberpunk and Postmodern Science Fiction. Ed. Larry McCaffery. Durham: Duke UP, 1991. 263–85.

_____. *Neuromancer.* New York: Ace, 1984.

_____. "Since 1948." *Source Code.* 6 Nov. 2002. 23 Feb. 2006.

Gies, Frances and Joseph Gies. *Life in a Medieval Village.* New York: Harper & Row, 1990.

Gilbert, Sandra M. and Susan Gubar. *The Madwoman in the Attic: The Woman Writer and the Nineteenth-Century Literary Imagination.* New Haven: Yale UP, 1979.

_____ *No Man's Land: The Place of the Woman Writer in the Twentieth Century.* New Haven: Yale UP, 1994.

Gómez-Vega, Ibis. "Hating the Self in the 'Other' or How Yolanda Learns to See Her Own Kind in Julia Alvarez's How the García Girls Lost Their Accents." *Intertexts* 3, no. 1 (1999): 85–96.

Greer, Germaine. *The Female Eunuch* (1970).

Greven, Hélène. *Margaret Atwood. The Handmaid's Tale,* Paris: Didier-Erudition/ CNED, 1999.

Gross, Barry. "Seduction of the Innocent: Portnoy's Complaint and Popular Culture," *MELUS,* Vol. 8, No. 4, "The Ethnic American Dream" (Winter, 1981), pp. 81–92.

Gurganus, Allan. "How do you introduce Paul Auster in three minutes?" *The Review of Contemporary Fiction* 14.1 (Spr 1994): 7–8.

Hacker, Marilyn. "Science Fiction and Feminism" The Work of Joanna Russ. *Chrysalis* 4 (1977): 67–79.

Hall, Alice Petry. "Tyler and Feminism." *Anne Tyler as Novelist.* Ed. Dale Salwak. Iowa City: University of Iowa Press, 1994. 33–42.

Hamilton, Ian. *In Search of J. D. Salinger.* New York: Random, 1988.

Haraway, Donna. "A Cyborg Manifesto: Science, Technology, and Socialist Feminism in the Late Twentieth Century." *Simians, Cyborgs and Women: The Reinvention of Nature.* New York: Routledge, 1991. 149–81.

Hart, Christine. *World War II: 1939–1945.* New York: Franklin Watts, 2000.

Hassan, Ihab. "Almost the Voice of Silence: The Later Novelettes of J. D. Salinger." *Wisconsin Studies in Contemporary Fiction* 4.1 (Winter 1963) 5–20.

Hendershot, Judith and Jackie Peck. "Interview with Newbery Medal Winner Karen Cushman." *The Reading Teacher* 50.3 (1996): 198–200.

Hicks, Heather. "Automating Feminism: The Case of Joanna Russ's 'The Female Man.'" *Postmodern Culture: An Electronic Journal of Interdisciplinary Criticism* 9.3 (1999).

Hill Rigney, Barbara. *Margaret Atwood, Women Writers Series.* New Jersey: Barnes & Noble, 1987.

Hoffman, Joan M. "'She Wants to Be Called Yolanda Now': Identity, Language, and the Third Sister in 'How the García Girls Lost Their Accents'." *Bilingual Review* 23, no 1 (1998): 21–27.

Holt, Marilyn J. "Joanna Russ." *Science Fiction Writers: Critical Studies of the Major Authors from, the early Nineteenth Century to the Present Day.* Ed. E. F. Bleiler. New York: Scribner's, 1982. 483–90.

Huber, Chris. *The Vonnegut Web.* 14 April 2008.

Huf, Linda. *A Portrait of the Artist as a Young Woman: The Writer as Heroine in American Literature.* New York: Ungar, 1983.

Irving, John. "Morrison's Black Fable." *New York Times.* March 29 1981 1.

Iwamoto, Iwao. "A Visit to Mr. Updike." Plath 115–24.

Jameson, Fredric. *Archaeologies of the Future: The Desire Called Utopia and Other Science Fictions,* London: Verso, 2005.

Johnson, Charles S. and Horace M. Bond. "The Investigation of Racial Differences Prior to 1910." *The Journal of Negro Education* 3.3 (1934): 328–339.

Johnson, Greg. "A Brief Biography." *Celestial Timepiece: A Joyce Carol Oates Home Page,* 1996. 4 August 2008.

Kalfus, Ken. "The Golem Knows." *New York Times* 24 Sept 2000.

Kaysen, Susanna. Girl, Interrupted. New York: Vintage Books, 1993.

Kimmel, Michael. New York: Free, 1996.

Kingsolver, Barbara. *The Bean Trees.* New York: Harper & Row, 1988.

King, Stephen. *Different Seasons.* New York: Signet, 1982.

King, Tabitha. "Biography." StephenKing.com. 12 January 2008.

Klinkowitz, Jerome and John Somer (eds.). *The Vonnegut Statement.* St. Albans, Granada Publishing, 1975.

Knelman, Judith. "Can We Believe What the Newspapers Tell Us? Missing Links in Alias Grace." *University of Toronto Quarterly* 68.2 (1999): 677–687.

Konigsburg, E. L. "Educational Paperback Association." 17 Dec. 2005.

———. *The View from Saturday*. New York: Aladdin, 1996.

LeClair, Tom. "An Interview with Don DeLillo." *Anything Can Happen: Interview with Contemporary American Novelists*. Ed. Tom LeClair and Larry McCaffery. Urbana: University of Illinois Press, 1983. 79–90.

———. "An Interview with Toni Morrison." *Anything Can Happen: Interviews with Contemporary American Novelists* Ed. Tom LeClair and Larry McCaffery. Urbana: U of Illinois P, 1983. 252–61.

———. "Rootedness: The Ancestor as Foundation." *Black Women Writers (1950–1980): A Critical Evaluation*. Ed. Mari Evans. New York: Anchor, 1984. 339–45.

Lefanu, Sarah. *In the Chinks of the World Machine: Feminism and Science Fiction*. London: Women's Press, 1988.

L'Engle. Madeline. *A Wrinkle in Time*. New York: Bantam Doubleday Dell Publishing Group, 1062.

Lentricchia, Frank. "Introduction." *New Essays on White Noise*. Ed. Frank Lentricchia. Cambridge: Cambridge University Press, 1991. 1–14.

———. "Libra as Postmodern Critique." *Introducing Don DeLillo*. Ed. Lentricchia. Durham, NC: Duke UP, 1991. 193–215.

Lowry, Lois. *Major Authors and Illustrators for Children and Young Adults*. 2nd ed. 8 vols. Gale Group, 2002. Reproduced in Biography Resource Center. Farmington Hills, MI: Thomson Gale. 2005.

———. "Afterword." *Number the Stars*. Boston: Houghton Mifflin, 1989.

———. *Number the Stars*. Boston: Houghton Mifflin, 1989.

———. "Number the Stars: Lois Lowry's journey to the Newbery Award." *The Reading Teacher* 44.2 (1990): 98–101.

Marouby, Christian. *Utopie et primitivisme. Essai sur l'imaginaire anthropologique à l'âge classique*, Paris: Seuil, 1990.

Marvin, Thomas F. *Kurt Vonnegut: A Critical Companion*. Westport, Conn., Greenwood Press, 2002.

Maycock, Ellen C. "The Bicultural Construction of Self in Cisneros, Alvarez, and Santiago." *Bilingual Review* 23, no.3 (1998): 223–229.

May, John R. 'Vonnegut's Humor and the Limits of Hope,' *Twentieth Century Literature,* Vol. 18, No. 1 (Jan., 1972), pp. 25–36, Hofstra University.

Maynard, Joyce. *At Home in the World: A Memoir*. New York: Picador, 1998.

McKee, Gabriel. *Pink Beams of Light from the God in the Gutter: The Science-Fictional Religion of Philip K. Dick*. Dallas: UP of America, 2004.

McPherson, Pat. *Reflecting on The Bell Jar.* New York: Routledge, 1991.

Medford, Edna Greene. "Imagined Promises, Bitter Realities: African Americans and the Meaning of the Emancipation Proclamation." *The Emancipation Proclamation*. Baton Rouge: Louisiana State UP, 2006. 1–47.

Michael, Magali Cornier. "Rethinking History as Patchwork: The Case of Atwood's Alias Grace." *MFS: Modern Fiction Studies* 47.2 (summer 2001): 421–47.

Millard, Kenneth. *Contemporary American Fiction*. Oxford: Oxford University Press, 2000.

Miller, Ryan. "The Gospel According to Grace: Gnostic Heresy as Narrative Strategy in Margaret Atwood's Alias Grace." *Literature and Theology* 16.2 (June 2002): 172–87.

Milowitz, Steven. *Philip Roth Considered: The Concentrationary Universe of the American Writer*. New York, Garland Publishing Inc, 2000.

Mitchell, David T. "The Accent of 'Loss': Cultural Crossings as Contexts in Julia Alvarez's 'How the García Girls Lost Their Accents.'" *Beyond the Binary: Reconstructing Cultural Identity in a Multicultural Context*. Ed. Timothy B. Powell. New Brunswick: Rutgers University Press, 1999. 165–84.

Moody, Rick. *The Black Veil: A Memoir With Digressions*. Boston: Little, Brown and Company, 2002.

———. "The Creature Lurches from the Lagoon." *The Ice Storm*. Boston: Little, Brown and Company, 2002. 281–292.

Moran, Joe. "Don DeLillo and the Myth of the Author-Recluse." *Journal of American Studies*. 34.1 (2000): 137–52.

Morrison, Toni. *Beloved*. New York: Penguin, 1987.

———. "Rootedness: The Ancestor as Foundation." *Black Women Writers:*

———. *Sula*. 1973. London: Picador, 1991.

———. *Tar Baby*. 1981, London: Virago, 1997.

———. *The Bluest Eye*. London: Picador, 1990.

Murphy, Larry G. "African-American Faith in America." *Faith in America Series*. New York: Facts on File, 2003.

Murrey, Loretta Martin. "The Loner and the Matriarchal Community in Barbara Kingsolver's The Bean Trees and Pigs in Heaven." *Southern Studies* (1994) 5.1-2: 155–64.

Nilsen, Don L. F. "Humorous Contemporary Jewish-American Authors: An Overview of the Criticism," *MELUS*, Vol. 21, No. 4, "Ethnic Humor" (Winter, 1996), pp. 71–101.

Nunley, Jan. "Thoughts of Faith Infuse Updike's Novels." Plath 248–60.

Oakes, James. *Slavery and Freedom: An Interpretation of the Old South.* New York: Alfred A. Knopf, 1990.

Oates, Joyce Carol. "Psycho Killer." *NYTimes.com,* Oct. 29, 1995. 11 August 2008.

Osteen, Mark. *American Magic and Dread: Don DeLillo's Dialogue with Culture.* Penn Studies in Contemporary Amer. Fiction. Philadelphia: U of Pennsylvania P, 2000.

_____. "Introduction." *White Noise: Text and Criticism.* Ed. Frank Lentricchia. New York: Penguin, 1998. vii–xv.

Palahniuk, Chuck. *Fight Club.* London: Vintage, 1997.

Passaro, Vince. "Dangerous Don DeLillo." *New York Times Magazine.* 19 May 1991: 36–8, 76–77.

Perry, Donna. "Joanna Russ." *Backtalk: Women Writers Speak Out.* Ed. Donna Perry. New Brunswick, NJ: Rutgers UP, 1993. 287–311.

Pierce, Hazel. *Philip K. Dick.* Washington: Starmont, 1982.

Pioch, Nicolas. "Munch, Edvard." *Webmuseum,* Paris. 16 July 2002. 28 February 2006.

Plath, James, Ed. "Conversations with John Updike." *Literary Conversations Series.* Jackson: UP of Mississippi, 1994.

Plath, Sylvia. *The Bell Jar.* New York: Bantam, 1981 (1963).

Podhoretz, John. "Escapists." *Commentary* June 2001.

Rapatzikou, Tatiani G. *Gothic Motifs in the Fiction of William Gibson.* Amsterdam: Rodopi, 2004.

Reilly, Charlie. "A Conversation with John Updike." Plath 124–51.

Risher, Dee Dee. "Listening to the Story: A conversation with Madeline L'Engle". 12 Oct. 2005.

Robinson, Beverly J. "Faith Is the Key and Prayer Unlocks the Door: Prayer in African American Life." *The Journal of American Folklore* 110.438 (1997): 408–414.

Robinson, Marilynne. *The Death of Adam: Essays on Modern Thought.* 1998. New York: Picador, 2005.

_____. *Housekeeping.* 1980. London: Faber, 1981.

Rose, Jacqueline. *The Haunting of Sylvia Plath.* London: Virago, 1991.

Roth, Philip. *Portnoy's Complaint.* London, Vintage, 1995.

_____. *The Facts,* London, Jonathan Cape, 1989.

Russ, Joanna. *The Female Man.* New York: Bantam, 1975.

_____. *To Write Like a Woman: Essays in Feminism and Science Fiction.* "Intr. Sarah Lefanu." Bloomington and Indianapolis: Indiana UP, 1995.

Ryan, Maureen. "Barbara Kingsolver's Lowfat Fiction." *Journal of American Culture* (winter 1995) 18.4: 77–83.

Sabbagh, Antoine. "The Human Story." *Europe in the Middle Ages.* Trans. Anthea Riddett. Englewood Cliffs, NJ: Silver Burdett P, 1988.

Salinger, Margaret Ann. *Dream Catcher.* New York: Washington Square P, 2000.

Samuels, Charles Thomas. "The Art of Fiction XLIII: John Updike." Plath 22–45.

Schwartz, Murray M. and Christopher Bollas. "The Absence at the Centre: Sylvia Plath and Suicide." *Sylvia Plath: New Views on the Poetry,* ed. Gary Lane. Baltimore: Johns Hopkins UP, 1979. 179–292.

Shippey, T. S. *Cat's Cradle.* "Masterplots II: American Fiction Series, Revised Edition." MagillOnLiterature Plus. EBSCO. 25 Aug. 2005.

Siddall, Gillian. "'This Is What I Told Dr. Jordan…': Public Constructions and Private Disruptions in Margaret Atwood's Alias Grace." *Essays on Canadian Writing* 81 (winter 2004): 84–102.

Siivonen, Timo. "Cyborgs and Generic Oxymorons: The Body and Technology in William Gibson's Cyberspace Trilogy." *Science-Fiction Studies* 23.2 (July 1996): 227–44.

Singman, Jeffrey L. and Will McLean. *Daily Life in Chaucer's England.* Westport, CN: Greenwood P, 1995.

Sirias, Silvio. *Julia Alvarez: A Critical Companion.* Westport, Connecticut and London: Greenwood Press, 2001.

Snodgrass, Mary Ellen. *Barbara Kingsolver: A Literary Companion.* Jefferson, North Carolina and London: McFarland & Company, 2004.

Sutton, Rosemary. *The Red Shoes: Margaret Atwood Starting Out.* Toronto: HarperCollins, 1998.

Tanner, Tony. "Afterthoughts on Don DeLillo's 'Underworld'." *Raritan* 17.4 (1998): 48–71.

Tate, Claudia. *Black Women Writers at Work.* New York: Continuum, 1984.

Tennant, Colette. *Reading the Gothic in Margaret Atwood's Novels*. Lewiston, New York: 2003.

Teslenko, Tatiana. *Feminist Utopian Novels of the 1970s: Joanna Russ and Dorothy Bryant*. New York and London: Routledge, 2003.

Tiernan, Mary Lee. Karen Cushman, *The Midwife's Apprentice*. "Rev. of 'The Midwife's Apprentice' by Karen Cushman." Book Report 14.2 (1995): 36.

Tyler, Anne. *Breathing Lessons*. 1988. London: Vintage, 1992.

_____. "Marriage and the Ties that Bind." *Washington Post World Book*. 15 Feb. 1987.

United States Holocaust Memorial Museum. *"The Holocaust." Holocaust Encyclopedia*. 25 October 2007.

_____. Washington D. C. 12 January 2008.

Unrue, John C. *J. D. Salinger: A Study of the Short Fiction*. Detroit: Gale, 2002.

Updike, John. "In Response to a request from The Independent on Sunday of London, for a contribution to their weekly feature "A Book That Changed Me." *Odd Jobs: Essays and Criticism*. London: Deutsch, 1991. 843–4.

_____. *Rabbit, Run*. 1960. London: Penguin, 1995.

_____. "Loosened Roots." *Anne Tyler as Novelist*. Ed. Dale Salwak. Iowa: University of Iowa Press, 1994. 120–4.

Uphaus, Robert W. 'Expected Meaning in Vonnegut's Dead-End Fiction,' *NOVEL: A Forum on Fiction*, Vol. 8, No. 2 (Winter, 1975), pp. 164–174, Brown University.

Viorst, Judith. "Nominating Statement for E. L. Konigsburg." 17 Dec. 2005.

Vonnegut Jr., Kurt, *Cat's Cradle*. Harmondsworth, Penguin, 1973.

_____. *Cat's Cradle*. Bantam Doubleday Dell: New York, 1963.

_____. *Jailbird*. London, Vintage, 1992.

Wade, Stephen. *The Imagination in Transit: The Fiction of Philip Roth*. Sheffield, Sheffield Academic Press, 1996.

Wagner-Martin, Linda, ed. *Critical Essays on Sylvia Plath*. Boston: G. K. Hall, 1984.

_____. *The Bell Jar: a Novel of the Fifties*. New York: Twayne, 1992.

Wallace, Molly. "'Venerated Emblems': DeLillo's Underworld and the History-Commodity." *Critique* 42.4 (2001): 367–83.

Warrick, Patricia S. "The Labyrinthine Process of the Artificial: Philip K. Dick's Androids and Mechanical Constructs." Philip K. Dick. Ed. Martin Harry Greenberg and Joseph D. Olander. New York: Taplinger, 1983. 189–214.

Weisenburger, Steven. "Inside Moon Palace." *The Review of Contemporary Fiction* 14.1 (Spr 1994): 70–9.

Weiss, Jerry M. "Selected Stories of Stephen King." *Teacher Vision*. 12 January 2008.

Wenke, John. *J. D. Salinger: A Study of the Short Fiction*. Boston: Twayne, 1991.

Will, George. "Shallow Look at the Mind of an Assassin." *Washington Post*, 22 Sept. 1988: A25.

Williams, Frank J. "'Doing Less' and 'Doing More': The President and the Proclamation—Legally, Militarily, and Politically." *The Emancipation Proclamation*. Baton Rouge: Louisiana State UP, 2006. 48–82.

Wilson, Sharon Rose, ed. *Margaret Atwood's Textual Assassinations: Recent Poetry and Fiction*. Columbus: Ohio State University Press, 2003.

Wyatt, C. S. *The Existential Primer*. 30 October 2005. 28 February 2006.

INDEX